THE DEVEREAUX DILEMMA

THE DEVEREAUX DILEMMA

STEVE MCELLISTREM

AN AUTHORSCOPE ENDORSED BOOK

TWO HARBORS PRESS
MINNEAPOLIS, MN

Two Harbors Press
212 3rd Avenue North, Suite 290
Minneapolis, MN 55401
612.455.2293
www.TwoHarborsPress.com

ISBN-13: 978-1-938690-52-5
LCCN: 2012922347

Distributed by Itasca Books

Cover Design by Jenni Wheeler
Typeset by Mary Kristin Ross

Printed in the United States of America

Acknowledgments

Many thanks are in order for Ian Graham Leask, who helped transform this book into its final shape. I also want to thank those folks who gave me valuable assistance along the way, including Geoff Saign, Jim Roth, Steve Stelzner, Jerry Hanson and my brother Tom, who provided valuable insight and detailed analysis. Their advice aided me in ways too numerous to mention. Any remaining errors in the text are mine. A further thanks to Carrie Rogers for her work getting the manuscript ready for publication. Other friends and family have contributed to this effort as well, lending support and encouragement along the way. I thank them too.

Chapter One

"Exit 29," the computer said in a breathy female voice as the car veered to the right. Jack Marschenko took the wheel, deactivating the autopilot. He swept through the intersection onto Seventy-Third Street, where the abrupt change in the road's conditions tested the vehicle's suspension, evidence of the District's half-assed efforts to maintain the infrastructure in the poorer neighborhoods. Marschenko, having grown up here, knew the area well. At Eighty-third he swerved to avoid a large pothole without slowing.

He turned left on Eighty-Fifth Avenue, slowing as he drove past pawnbrokers, a tattoo parlor, quick-loan services, run-down apartments and hotels. He spotted a guy inside a dumpster, tossing out items he could use, then noticed a gang of hooded teenagers closing in on a solitary civilian. Marschenko shone his spotlight on them, forcing the gang to scatter. Unlocking the door to a housing complex, the man waved his thanks.

Marschenko sped off. Another innocent temporarily saved—the gang was probably stalking the next victim already, he thought. Can't save everyone in this neighborhood. So why keep coming back here? For a strip-club waitress?

Yet as the image of Lily appeared in his mind, he found himself smiling. He'd planned an expensive dinner at Horatio's. Then he'd take her back to her place and delve into her nether regions, bringing her to a shuddering climax. He reveled in her deep and honest laughter. God, her laugh was infectious. For the rest of the evening, she'd devote herself entirely to his needs. Marschenko's body tensed in anticipation.

Up ahead he saw the large pink neon cat above the doorway of Kitty Kat's Korner. The Korner shared a parking lot with Romy's Bar. From the outside the two buildings looked much the same; inside they couldn't be more different. The Korner boasted a high-class clientele and décor to match. Romy's—a dark, dirty place—catered to alcoholics. His mom used to drink there.

Marschenko pulled into the lot and swung into an open spot next to a sleek sports car. He shut off the engine and stepped out of the car, leaving his Elite Ops helmet and Las-pistol on the passenger seat. He'd only be inside a few minutes, and the Korner barred weapons. He locked the car and set the alarm with a voice command, then visually swept the lot as his car windows became opaque. Eight rusted junkers belonging to patrons of Romy's sat on the other side of the lot. Half a dozen luxury vehicles were parked near the Korner's door. A slow night.

As Marschenko strolled through the lot, a shape lunged at him from between two cars, hitting him hard just above the knees. Marschenko fell to the ground, the man landing on top of his chest, straddling him, a knife pressed against Marschenko's throat.

"Give me your cash card," the man rasped. He wore dark camouflage clothing, his face blackened.

Marschenko reached for his wallet but the man's weight on his chest made it difficult to move.

"I can't get at it," Marschenko said. "You're too heavy." He tried to sound terrified, hoping to put the mugger at ease. As the mugger shifted position slightly, his knife blade left Marschenko's throat for an instant.

Marschenko swung his legs up, forcing the man off. Leaping to his feet, Marschenko barked out the emergency command that opened his car door. He reached in for his Las-pistol but the mugger scrambled up and darted across the lot before Marschenko could retrieve it, so Marschenko grabbed his helmet too.

Two of the Korner's security guards ran out of the building but Marschenko waved them away. "I'll take care of it," he said.

Donning the spacious helmet, filled with communications and sensory software, Marschenko linked to Elite Ops HQ via satcom—allowing the night watch coordinator to see what he saw. He locked the Las-pistol into the port embedded into his left palm, enabling him to fire as quickly as he could think to do it, faster and more accurately than a man firing the same weapon conventionally.

The two security guards retreated into the safety of the building. Using the infrared feed on the helmet's visor, Marschenko tracked the mugger's heat signature. Sprinting across the parking lot, he followed the infrared trail. When he reached the street, he spotted the mugger up ahead. He suppressed the urge to kill the man. The poor bastard was probably just trying to feed his family. Adjusting the setting on his Las-pistol from medium to low, Marschenko fired a blue pulse as the man dodged around a corner. An agile mugger—Marschenko had to give him that. Adrenaline coursed through Marschenko's body as he sprang forward.

The night watch coordinator spoke softly in his ear: "Do you require assistance, Jack?"

"Adrian, that you?" Marschenko replied.

"Yeah, you lucky dog. You got me tonight."

"What the hell did you do to pull night watch duty?"

"Long story. Your friend looks like he's been enhanced."

"That's what I was thinking. He moves too quickly to be a Natural."

Marschenko reached the corner where the mugger dodged his first shot, noting the black mark on the building's face left by the chem-laser. Still a half-block ahead, the mugger approached an open alleyway. Marschenko took aim and fired. Once more the mugger dodged around a corner. Marschenko sprinted after him, reached a dark alley and noticed with satisfaction that it ended with no outlet. Gotcha, he thought.

"Alley's dark," Marschenko said. "A code violation."

"Got it," Adrian replied. "Sending a citation now."

For a second, Marschenko regretted verbalizing the infraction, knowing some struggling business owner was going to be fined. But the problem had to be fixed.

His helmet amplified the ambient light, illuminating the alley as if it were daytime. Despite the mugger's camouflage clothing, Marschenko could see him clearly. The man moved left, then right, searching for a way out, then ducked behind a dumpster. Marschenko eased forward slowly and spotted the mugger cowering in a ball behind the dumpster. Maybe he wasn't enhanced. Marschenko contemplated the best way to teach him a lesson, then took aim at the man's buttocks.

Before he could get off his shot, an explosion knocked Marschenko off his feet. The smell of cherries infused the air. It had been a trap. He'd been lured here. As he sent a distress call, the knockout gas dragging him under, he heard Adrian's voice slowly fading: "Jack, Jack, stay with me, Jack."

* * *

Marschenko awoke to a sharp pain behind his eyes, the lingering odor of burnt cherries nauseating him. He shook his head to try to clear it. Big mistake.

He squinted against the glare of the single bulb hanging from the ceiling. Where the hell was he? A concrete room with no windows: maybe twenty feet square. A bank of electronic equipment stood against the far wall.

Looking down, Marschenko saw that he was seated on a toilet. He was bound at the wrists and ankles, and tethered to rings embedded in the floor and the overhead beams by a plastic webbing—a virtually indestructible stretch polymer that allowed movement and prevented him from hurting himself. With no lock to pick, the only way to free himself was with a Las-knife or power saw. He still wore his T-shirt and shorts. His pants were folded neatly on a shelf opposite him, and his helmet lay on the floor in the center of the room, next to his Las-pistol. A small green light on the Las-pistol blinked slowly, indicating the weapon was still charged.

A faint scratching sounded behind him. Marschenko turned, saw nothing. Probably a mouse. Mice didn't bother him. Rats did. He stood awkwardly, his legs straddling the toilet, and moved toward the helmet and Las-pistol. He came up four feet short. Damn!

He sat back down and looked around. The electronic equipment on the far wall was sophisticated stuff. Apart from that and a large TV, the room contained only a desk and chair. Directly across from him, stairs vanished into darkness above. Marschenko activated his subdural transmitter and broadcast an SOS. He got no response, sent the message again. Nothing but silence. Not even static. Whoever had taken him must have put a dampening field over the room. It might take a while for the Elite Ops to find him.

A door opened and shut at the top of the stairs, then someone purposefully descended. Marschenko counted fourteen steps. Dark shoes came into view, followed by tailored blue trousers and a form-fitting black shirt. The man was of average height, his tightly knit frame muscular in his expensive clothes. He wore no rings, had no visible tattoos. His dark hair was closely cropped, his nose bent in the middle where it had been broken. Crow's-feet surrounded the eyes, while the forehead was lined with the beginnings of middle age. Creases of sorrow made his face oddly compassionate. Yet when he stopped a few feet in front of Marschenko, his intense hazel eyes looked fierce. And he moved with a feline grace that reminded Marschenko of a panther.

"This light too bright for you?" The man spoke softly.

"Yeah," Marschenko croaked, then coughed to clear his throat. "Who are you?"

The man stepped back toward the wall and dimmed the bulb. "My name is Jeremiah Jones. You met my son Joshua a few years ago."

Marschenko's stomach clenched. "Thanks," he said, keeping the fear out of his voice. "What did you use to…?"

"Stun grenade," Jones said.

"Stun grenade! You could have taken yourself out with that."

"That's why I was curled up in a ball, Jack. Yeah, I know your name. I've read your file. I've been tracking you for the past month. I'm surprised at how easy it was to take you. I'd have thought you'd be on alert after I broke into Carlton Security's archives and retrieved the vid-footage. Or didn't they tell you about that?"

"I have friends. They'll be coming to look for me."

"They won't find you, Jack."

"What do you want?"

"You kidnapped my son," Jones said, his voice cracking slightly. "Where is he?"

Marschenko stared at him. "I don't know what you're talking about."

"You were just doing your job." Now the voice was strong, back in control.

Marschenko said nothing.

"Classified, top secret and all that."

"That's right," Marschenko agreed.

Jones moved back to the stairs. He sat on the third step, relaxed, in no hurry at all.

"Who are you? You've been enhanced."

Jones didn't respond.

"You move like an animal. Are you a pseudo? That's illegal."

Jones got up from the stairs. "I want you to tell me where Joshua is."

"I assume you're going to torture me," Marschenko said. "You won't get anything from me."

Jones leaned back and crossed his arms. "I don't need to torture you, Jack. You're going to talk eventually. I know you—how you hate being alone. Your mother used to lock you in the cellar, didn't she? All by yourself. No one to talk to. And I know what they've been pumping into you. You're due for another dose of time-release capsules tomorrow. That's going to be a painful withdrawal, especially cold turkey. You really think you could hold out?"

Jones looked resolute, hard, feral. The brown-green eyes seemed to glow with an inner light. How could Marschenko ever have thought he was compassionate?

Marschenko looked away. "Long enough for my friends to find me," he said, bolstering himself.

Jones uncrossed his arms and pointed at the ceiling. "This isn't just a dampening field. I'm using a scatterer too."

Fear tightened Marschenko's belly as he looked up at the ceiling. How the hell was he going to get out of this?

"If you're going to torture me, get on with it. Let's see what you've got."

Jones shook his head slowly. "I told you, I'm not going to torture you. Torture's not very effective at getting the truth. I need the truth. And I'm not giving you any drugs to loosen your tongue. I know that the nanobots circulating through your bloodstream communicate with the cerebral monitor implanted behind your forehead to prevent truth drugs from taking effect. We both know that too high a dosage could kill you. I don't want you dead, Jack. I want information. Besides, you're not to blame. You're confused by all the meds and propaganda your superiors feed you."

Marschenko eyed Jones warily. Jones appeared to know a lot about the Elite Ops troopers, stuff he couldn't have learned from Marschenko's file.

"Where's Joshua?"

"You're not going to get any answers from me."

"Why keep going back to that strip club, Jack? You got a thing for Lily?"

"You stay away from her."

"Or what, Jack? What are you going to do to me?"

"You touch one hair on her head and I'll kill you."

"Relax, Jack," Jones said. "I don't want to hurt Lily. And I've got nothing against you personally. You were just following orders. You're a professional. Like me."

"Look, Jones, if you believe in God and country, you'll let me go. I'll see if I can get you any info on the kid. That's the truth. But if you keep me here, there's gonna be hell to pay. Believe it."

"You want the truth, Jack? I can do anything I want. You're in my world now. I make the rules. You want to talk about God? I'm God. You can do as I ask or not. It's all up to you. There's only one way you're getting out of here and that's to tell me everything you know. You may not believe that yet. But you will. It might take a week, or a month. But sooner or later you'll understand that I'm the only one who can help you."

Jones stood, walked to the wall, patted it, then faced Marschenko and leaned against it. "This place is well hidden. No one knows about it but me. No one will find you unless I tell them you're here."

Jones returned to the center of the floor, where he picked up the Las-pistol, pointed it at Marschenko and slowly pressed the trigger.

Marschenko knew the weapon couldn't fire but he flinched anyway, closing his eyes as he prepared for the pain.

"Set to your brainwaves and fingerprints," Jones said. "Useless to anybody else unless it's reprogrammed." He reached for the helmet, put it on. It looked absurdly large on him. He shook his head from side to side, the helmet wobbling on his shoulders. In a muffled voice he said, "Roomy."

He pulled the helmet off, chuckling lightly, then said, "I'd better take this pistol, just in case. But I'll leave the helmet as a reminder of the life you used to have—the life you can have again if you cooperate. It's up to you."

"You got any water?" Marschenko said.

Jones pointed to a small tube hanging from the ceiling. Marschenko had missed seeing it earlier. "There's nutri-water in there. Just suck on it. Don't struggle or you could break the tube. Then you'll be without water. I'll be back in a few days. By then you'll be in pain, a lot of pain. Until then the television will let you see what's happening out there in the world you used to inhabit."

Jones turned on the television, set it to the 24-Hour Real News Network, where a commentator was explaining how the rise in tensions between the nonreligious Devereauxnians and the Christians, Muslims, Jews and other religious groups was leading to increased civil unrest. Adjusting the volume to a comfortable level, Jones headed for the stairs. He placed a foot on the first tread and looked back.

"Like I said, I figure you were just following orders. If you didn't kill him, I won't kill you—unless you don't talk. Then you die."

"You won't kill me," Marschenko said.

Jones shrugged, then turned away. "So long, Jack."

Marschenko nearly called out for Jones to wait but he held back and Jones disappeared up the stairs.

Marschenko's breaths came more quickly. He wanted to scream. Jones was right about the withdrawal. Marschenko could already feel the tingling: a prelude to the pain. Elite Ops troopers who retired were weaned off their medication over a period of months, not days. They never quit cold turkey. Would he even survive the process? Would he want to? He'd heard about a trooper who was captured and held for over a week before being rescued. Poor devil went mad. Would that be his fate?

Even worse, Marschenko was alone. No reassuring voices in his head. No one to talk to. Trapped in a basement just like when his mom got mad at him. The dim light reminded him of the hours he'd spent alone with the rats. He could still hear them scrabbling at the walls, their claws scraping the cement. Just a hallucination. He peered into the corners. Too dark to see. He had to find a way out. Couldn't wait for the Elite Ops to rescue him. He worked on the bonds, rubbing them back and forth against the rings in the ceiling beams.

Chapter Two

Jeremiah Jones stared at the sentinel camera until he heard the slight click of the door unlocking itself. Then he opened the door and stepped into Elias Leach's office, where multicolored lights imparted a sunset glow to the room.

Eli stood up from behind his desk, turned to his elderly cleaning lady, Mrs. Harris, and said, "That will be all, Manyara."

Mrs. Harris muttered something about nonsense and secrets as she shuffled over to her cart. "Leave you two bigshots to ruin the world," she said as she wheeled the cart out the door, shaking her head.

Eli chuckled as he gestured for Jeremiah to take a seat. "Couldn't get along without her. Her incessant insults keep me grounded." Then he moved across the office to a small divan opposite the chair Jeremiah took.

Jeremiah studied him. Forty years older than Jeremiah's forty-two, Eli stood five-feet, two-inches tall. The hair atop his head had long vanished, leaving only a white fringe around the edges. He'd mentioned once that he chose not to re-grow his hair or his body, though he could have done so quite easily, because he wanted people to know that appearance was unimportant. Yet Jeremiah knew he was sensitive about his height too, rarely standing in the presence of others. Sitting on the sofa he looked almost childlike—certainly not threatening. He loved to cultivate an avuncular air. In conversation, his eyelids often drooped, as if he were half asleep, but Jeremiah knew better than to assume that Eli was ever anything but fully alert. Today he wore a red cardigan and dark brown pants, and sat with his legs crossed, one finger tapping lightly on the arm of the sofa.

He was the most dangerous man Jeremiah had ever met.

He was also the brightest. He ran CINTEP—the Center for International Economic Policy—an independent organization ostensibly working to open free markets worldwide. In reality that was a secondary aim. Under the direction of Elias Leach, CINTEP eliminated dictatorial regimes, fought terrorism, engaged in espionage and developed strategies to ensure the political and economic dominance of America around the globe. Jeremiah had been a field agent—a ghost—then Head of Operations. But after Joshua was kidnapped he worked only haphazardly, as a consultant, while he devoted the bulk of his time to searching for his son. He'd been in and out of uncounted government buildings and databases in the past four years; he'd searched orphanages, shelters and schools; so far he'd found nothing.

"How've you been?"

"I'm fine," Jeremiah answered.

"Have you got Jack Marschenko?"

Jeremiah furrowed his brow. "Marschenko?"

"Come now, Jeremiah. Richard Carlton's been calling me constantly. Somebody broke into his computer system last month, downloaded archival vid footage and exited the system without leaving a trace as to his whereabouts. He thinks it was you."

"Why?"

"Carlton claims he finally recovered the footage you were seeking, the feed that was supposedly damaged beyond repair. It puts Marschenko at the park where your son disappeared. He says you're the only one who was seeking access to it, so you must have been the hacker. He's furious, wants you arrested."

Jeremiah shrugged. "He can't prove anything."

"I'm worried about you, Jeremiah. Carlton Security runs the Elite Ops. If Richard Carlton decides you had something to do with Marschenko's disappearance, he'll sic his troopers on you like the wrath of God. I don't want to lose my Head of Operations."

"Former Head of Operations," Jeremiah corrected him. "I'm still on leave. And the Elite Ops are soldiers. They'll comply with the rule of law."

"Marschenko didn't...if he took Joshua. Listen, Jeremiah, although the Elite Ops are technically government employees, Carlton Security owns all their equipment, all the software. More of the privatization of the military. And with all that hardware in their bodies," Eli shivered, "all the hormones and proteins and programmed nanobots, who knows how they'll react to somebody snatching one of their own?"

"What did you tell Carlton?"

"I told that asshole nothing. He stonewalled us for a long time on the vid feed from the park, saying it was damaged beyond repair."

"I still can't figure why the Elite Ops took Joshua."

"I don't know, Jeremiah. For the last four years I've kept my ears open. I've checked every source I have for anything that might help locate your son. There's been no hint of his whereabouts."

"I appreciate your help," Jeremiah said. He fought to keep his voice under control. Privately he wondered just how much Eli had done. If Eli cared about Joshua's disappearance, it was only because of the impact that event had on Jeremiah's ability to run Operations. All Eli ever concerned himself with was making sure the job got done. Jeremiah shook his head. "It doesn't make any sense. No ransom, no demands. Nothing."

Eli's hands spread apart. "Maybe Marschenko acted alone."

Jeremiah got to his feet and began pacing. He took measured breaths. Calming breaths. "Marschenko's no perv. This wasn't some random event. Whoever sent Marschenko knew I was a ghost. Somebody with high sources in the government."

Eli shook his head. "It wasn't that."

"How can you be sure?"

"If Joshua's kidnapping was ordered by someone highly placed, I would know. Jeremiah, please. Stop making yourself crazy. You can't blame yourself for Joshua's kidnapping. Sooner or later Marschenko will tell you what he knows. Meanwhile, I have a job for you."

"What kind of job?"

"A field assignment of vital importance."

"Aren't they all?"

"Yes." Eli smiled briefly and gestured for Jeremiah to sit. Jeremiah remained standing. "The President herself will be joining us any moment now."

"The President's coming here?"

"She'll be on projection," Eli said.

***

Jay-Edgar, Eli's thin, pasty technology expert, opened a channel to the White House. A holo-projection appeared in the semi-darkness, a three-dimensional image of the President of the United States, Angelica Hope. The former actress and professional tennis player wore her famous blond hair up in a bun and what appeared to be silk pajamas under a richly decorated robe. Although she'd only been in office eighteen months, Jeremiah noticed a few more lines on her face. At her right hand sat General Ralph Horowitz, Chairman of the Joint Chiefs of Staff, still in uniform despite the late hour. Eli shifted on the divan so as to be able to view the projection without turning his neck. Jeremiah settled his chair a few feet away so that he and Eli could be captured by 3-D cameras for the President too. He'd never cared for 3-D projections. They gave him a headache.

The President said, "Elias, it's good to see you again. I hope you're doing well."

"Very well, Madam President," Eli replied. "This is Jeremiah Jones, my former Head of Operations…and one of the ghosts."

Jeremiah said, "Madam President."

"Have we met before, Jeremiah?" the President asked. "You look familiar."

"No, ma'am," Jeremiah said. "But I was at your inauguration, providing supplemental security. If you saw me there, you have a most impressive memory."

The President waved away the compliment. "On to business. Gentlemen, we're facing a crisis. Our nation's security—indeed, its very survival—is at stake. I'm not talking strictly about the resurgence of terrorist activity, though that is one aspect of the problem. Nor am I solely concerned with the demand by several states to be allowed to secede: Texas, Minnesota, Vermont. It's more than that. Not since the Civil War have we as a nation been so divided. Many factors are to blame, and everyone recognizes the need to take action. Since Congress is as fragmented as the rest of the country, I've asked Elias to handle the most immediate threat to our nation's stability and one that could have the most severe long-term consequences."

"Let me get right to the point, Jeremiah," Eli said. "We want you to go after Devereaux."

"Walt Devereaux? Secretary General of the United Nations?"

"The former Secretary General, yes," Eli said.

Jeremiah glanced at the President, who remained seated, calmly regarding him. At her side, General Horowitz raised one eyebrow as he stared at Jeremiah.

"You want me to kill Walt Devereaux?"

"No, no," Eli said, holding up his hands to emphasize his point. "We need him alive and unharmed. We believe he's created a bio-weapon, perhaps a super-virus that could wipe out humanity."

"That's crazy," Jeremiah said. "Devereaux's always been a man of peace."

President Hope said, "Devereaux reported to my predecessor, President Davis, that he had formulated weapons of mass destruction. We don't know whether he actually built them or just put together a blueprint as an intellectual exercise but we want to talk to him before Gray Weiss gets a hold of him." She used the correct Germanic pronunciation, so Weiss' last name sounded like vice.

"The Attorney General?" Jeremiah shook his head. It still irked him that Weiss, a close friend of Richard Carlton, had prevented Jeremiah from obtaining a warrant to search Carlton Security's vid-files. "Why is he involved?"

"Mr. Weiss is a deeply religious man," the President said. "He's also extremely ambitious. And he's been obsessed with Devereaux for a long time—ever since Devereaux published *The Ladder*, in which he insisted there is no God. Weiss believes that Devereaux is the anti-Christ, and that capturing Devereaux will catapult him to the Presidency."

"But why is he after Devereaux *now*?"

"Well, lately Devereaux's begun discussing the ladder of enlightenment again, as well as the necessary evolution of humanity, which has brought the conservative religious movement to the forefront again. People are angry—on both sides. The level of violence has risen dramatically in the past few months. Some of our analysts are suggesting that Devereaux intends to use his bio-weapon to force the evolution of humanity. And Weiss is attempting to take advantage of that."

Jeremiah had a sudden insight. "You're really after Weiss, aren't you."

"Yes and no," the President said. "With the Justice Department largely independent of the White House's reach, I can't recall Weiss. However, it's imperative that Weiss not succeed in arresting Devereaux. You must find Devereaux first."

"If Devereaux is arrested," Eli said, "those bio-weapons, should they exist, might be used against the country. He may have given them to the Escala."

"Ess KOL la?" Jeremiah said. "Who are they?"

"E-s-c-a-l-a," Eli said. "Spanish for ladder. That's what they call themselves, though many call them pseudos. They're actually the Mars Project astronauts—brilliant scientists—and they've been enhanced with animal DNA to enable them to survive on Mars. They're followers of Devereaux, who is their biggest supporter. He wants the Mars Project, dropped by President Davis, to move forward."

"You'll be filled in on the Escala later," the President said. "The point is—up until now we've had no reason to believe Devereaux was a threat. But recent electronic intercepts indicate that Devereaux may be plotting to release a deadly bio-weapon soon. And with Weiss planning to arrest him, Devereaux may disperse the virus. Or the Escala might do so. Devereaux is dangerous, and some of his followers are fanatics."

Jeremiah said, "Just like Weiss and his followers."

"True," the President said.

"Our biggest fear," Eli said, "is that Devereaux manufactured one or more of the bioweapons he designed. He may even have unleashed the virus that wiped out Rochester, Minnesota."

"The Susquehanna Virus? I thought Susquehanna Sally created that?"

"She claimed responsibility. We have yet to verify that." Eli closed his eyes for a moment, then opened them and said, "Or find her, for that matter. And Devereaux predicted we would face something like the Susquehanna Virus a couple of years before it was released. So we can't be certain he wasn't involved in that tragedy."

"That simply doesn't sound like Devereaux."

"I agree," President Hope said, "but until we speak with him, we won't know the truth."

"Jeremiah?" Eli said.

Jeremiah shrugged. He knew there was no alternative but to accept the assignment. He began to miss his old partner, Julianna, who had terminated their partnership with a knife to his belly. Together they'd been the best team CINTEP had ever assembled.

The President spoke again: "If Weiss publicly arrests Devereaux, we'll get mass riots. And if Devereaux built the bioweapons he designed and gave them to the Escala, they could destroy humanity. Even if he never produced the weapons, he has the blueprints in his head. And if he gave the designs to the Escala, they might create the weapons and unleash them. We plan to negotiate with the Escala quietly, behind the scenes, but we need Devereaux as the intermediary. Diplomacy is the key. And Weiss is no diplomat."

"I still don't understand why the Escala would want to attack us."

Eli said, "Something went wrong during the genetic surgery. They developed a kind of rage, which is why the Mars Project was canceled, and why they might strike back if Devereaux, their only real advocate, is imprisoned."

General Horowitz interjected: "Devereaux and the Escala are the immediate threat—especially in light of Weiss' cowboy tactics. Also, they're the key to solving the present crisis. Strategically, however, Weiss may be the biggest threat that faces our country. Weiss has stated publicly that our democracy is ineffectual in facing the present challenges. He's advocating for a strong leader, and he's hinted that this strong leader—himself—need not necessarily be elected. What if he captures Devereaux? The weapons would be his. What if he decides to hold the country or the world hostage?"

"Why not assassinate Weiss?"

President Hope replied, "Because our nation was founded on the rule of law. I will not assassinate the Attorney General—or Devereaux, for that matter."

Jeremiah shifted in his chair. The President seemed sincere. Yet sincerity was a politician's greatest asset. And she had once been an actress.

"This is end of the world stuff, Jeremiah," Eli said. "If these weapons are out there, if Devereaux gave them to the Escala, if Weiss gets a hold of them, all humanity could be at risk."

Jeremiah closed his eyes. He didn't want this job. It wasn't going to get him any closer to finding Joshua. But how does one say no to the President? And how could he turn his back on the world?

He opened his eyes. "Where is he?"

"In Minnesota," Eli said.

Jeremiah put his elbows on the armrests and steepled his fingers. "Very well," he said. "I'll try."

The President smiled broadly. "That's all we can ask, Jeremiah. Elias will provide you with the Identi-card necessary to grant you access to the area. He'll give you all the details. Gentlemen, I'm grateful for your assistance."

As the President signed off, the projection instantly darkened, the spotlights over Jeremiah fading, leaving indirect lighting to bathe the room in the familiar sunset glow Eli seemed to favor. Jeremiah sat quietly, already regretting his decision. On the other hand, he really didn't have much choice. The President asked you to do something and you either agreed to do it or you found yourself in very deep trouble, despite the sincerity of her smile. And with Eli on her side, Jeremiah might find himself imprisoned or dead if he refused. Although he believed Eli liked him, he wasn't naïve enough to assume that Eli would let friendship get in the way of the job. Eli's enemies had a way of disappearing.

"That'll be all, Jay-Edgar," Eli said.

"Yes, sir," Jay-Edgar answered, disappearing on quiet feet.

"Well," Jeremiah said, "what about those details?"

Eli reached for his PlusPhone, angled in such a way that Jeremiah couldn't see the party on the other end, and said, "We're ready for you now."

The door opened and a young woman entered wearing a black silk dress that exposed only a hint of cleavage and ended just below the knee. She walked confidently: a brunette of mixed heritage, wide eyes, full lips, high cheekbones. Her thick hair swept down well past her shoulders and partially covered the computer interface she wore at her left temple. Such interfaces were not uncommon now, but they were still rare enough to draw attention. Not that this woman needed to draw more attention to herself. She was nearly six feet tall, her lean build accentuating her height. Except for her interface, she reminded Jeremiah of his late wife Catherine—something similar in the way she carried herself, as if unconcerned with how the world saw her. Jeremiah's breath caught in his throat. This woman was taller than Catherine and thinner. Perhaps a little more athletic. Like Julianna but softer. Hell, everyone was softer than Julianna. Jeremiah was softer than Julianna.

The woman kept her eyes on Jeremiah as she crossed the room. He thought he detected a message there but had no idea whether it was hostile or friendly. When she reached the divan, she sat next to the old man, crossing her legs, the silk dress moving up to expose a hint of her lean thigh muscles.

Turning to pat the woman on the hand, Eli gestured toward Jeremiah and said, "Lendra, meet Jeremiah Jones. Jeremiah, this is Lendra Riley. She will be accompanying you on your journey."

Lendra nodded to Jeremiah, then turned to Eli. "Please, my dear," the old man said, "tell Jeremiah what we know of the current situation with respect to Walt Devereaux and Gray Weiss."

Lendra looked through Jeremiah and began speaking:

"As you probably know, Walt Devereaux went underground three years ago, at the time his mansion was breached by a team of assassins from Israel, which was angered by his harsh condemnation of Israeli policies. He's not been seen in public since, though he makes many appearances over the web. Rumors placed him in Europe, China and South America. Several months ago Weiss began arresting Devereaux-nians, questioning them." She glanced at Eli. "He used harsh measures against them in his quest to learn Devereaux's whereabouts."

Eli said, "He plans to charge Devereaux with treason."

"Due to the bio-weapons he created?"

"Actually, no," Eli said. "That's being kept from the public to prevent panic."

Eli turned to Lendra, who said, "Weiss intends to use the newly enacted Harris-Bock Patriotism Amendment, under which treason is defined as conspiring with one or more persons for the purpose of advocating publicly any course of action that materially harms the interests or welfare of the people of the United States."

"That law's a joke," Jeremiah said.

Lendra said, "Weiss' plan, as I understand it, is to apply the law only to Devereaux. And with the current state of the high courts, there is virtually no chance Devereaux's conviction would be overturned."

"But what about the rioting, the civil unrest?" Jeremiah said.

Eli said, "I personally believe Weiss wants the anarchy. He wants an excuse to create scapegoats of the Devereauxnians. And when Devereaux's trial and the mass demonstrations begin, he'll make sure they turn into riots. Then he'll swoop in and clean up the streets, making himself look all the better. Now that the Posse Comitatus Act has been repealed, permitting the Army to operate inside this country, and now that he has soldiers under his authority, he'll be able to use the violence as a springboard to the presidency."

Jeremiah fought down the frustration and anger. He could sense the truth behind Eli's argument. Weiss made no secret of his ambition to be President. Nor had Weiss made a secret of his dislike of Eli, a fact that Jeremiah believed influenced Weiss when he refused Jeremiah the opportunity to examine Carlton Security's vid-files. It was then that Catherine had given up, escaping the darkness of loss with a bottle of pills.

"So where in Minnesota is Devereaux?"

"The same place Weiss is now. Crescent Township."

"Crescent Township. Why does that sound familiar?"

"It's where that famous statue is—'Emerging Man.' Southeastern Minnesota."

"That's right," Jeremiah got to his feet and began pacing. "I passed through there once about twenty years ago. Beautiful place back then—rather quiet."

"I know you dislike flying," Eli said, nodding in understanding. "So you'll be driving. When can you leave?"

Taking a deep breath, Jeremiah ran his fingers through his hair. "In a few hours."

"Fine. Lendra, dear, pack a bag."

Lendra stepped from the room with a backward glance at Eli.

"Okay," Jeremiah said, "who is she really?"

"What are you talking about?"

"She's no field agent."

Eli shrugged, conceding the point. "I have high hopes for her. She's very bright."

"Things can get messy and dangerous out there."

Eli issued a grim smile. "Since you get migraines when you try to wear an interface, she'll go along to provide you with information and keep in contact with me. Don't expect her to be of any assistance if you find yourself in a tight spot."

"Are you sleeping with her?"

Eli laughed, shook his head. "I keep falling in love with them. Remember Sadie? She was the last one. I'm too old for that kind of nonsense now."

Jeremiah nodded. "Me too."

"You?" Eli snorted. "Don't be ridiculous. You need to rebuild your life."

Jeremiah pointed toward the door. "I don't know what you told her, but this trip will be strictly business. I don't want things any more complicated than they are."

Eli held up his hands. "I didn't tell her anything. But I think she romanticizes you. How could she not? You're one of the most accomplished ghosts. You're a legend."

Jeremiah shook his head. "She deserves better than me."

"Come now, Jeremiah, you're not so bad."

"Yes, I am," Jeremiah answered. "And you know it. After all, you're the one who made me."

Chapter Three

Jeremiah drove his van through the crowded city. Even at this late hour, traffic was too heavy to spot a tail, so he had to rely on his scanners. Lendra, frowning, sat in the passenger seat. The relaxing sound of the Beijing Symphony Orchestra playing a Chinese waltz drifted softly from the speakers but the music apparently had no effect on Lendra. She said, "Why isn't my interface working?"

"I've activated a dampening field and a multi-phase scatterer to keep prying eyes away. You won't be able to communicate with the outside world for a while yet."

Lendra shook her head. "You're paranoid, you know."

"Maybe—but I'm alive."

She stared at him for a second, then turned away, staring out the front window.

Jeremiah turned his thoughts to Marschenko. He hoped the threat of several more days of solitude would unlock Marschenko's lips. But in case Jeremiah failed to return, he'd have to make provisions for Eli to eventually locate the big Elite Ops trooper. Opening the communication database of his onboard computer, Jeremiah plugged in a series of instructions to be delivered to Eli in a week unless he canceled them.

After that, he re-checked the instruments on his dash, made sure he wasn't being followed and turned into the warehouse district. Lendra kept quiet and for that he was grateful. As he approached a building, he pressed a remote, timing it so that the garage door swung open just before he reached the entrance.

After they exited the van, Lendra said, "My interface still isn't working."

Jeremiah waved at the walls. "The whole facility is protected. I'm afraid you'll have to be incommunicado until we leave."

"What is this place?" Lendra asked.

"Home away from home." Jeremiah pointed to a sofa and kitchenette in the corner. "Make yourself comfortable. I'll be back in an hour or two."

"Where are you going?"

"I have some unfinished business. Don't leave the building. There's a restroom in the back if you need it."

Lendra offered a tentative smile. "Why don't I come with you? I could help you pack."

Jeremiah saw the warmth in her eyes, heard the conciliatory tone in her voice. If Catherine hadn't died so recently, he might find himself falling for this woman. He said, "I don't think so."

"Why not?" She grinned. "Is your place a mess?"

Jeremiah almost smiled. "No, it's not a mess. I'm just not ready to invite a woman over yet. Okay?"

Lendra nodded. "I understand."

* * *

Back at his apartment Jeremiah grabbed the moldy pizza box off his coffee table and threw it in the recycler before moving into the bedroom. Opening his closet, he removed two pairs of Camo-Fit coveralls—one well used, the other new: Ultimate Camos. Rather than showering he sprayed himself with Insta-Clean and wiped himself dry, then tried on the Ultimate Camos. He activated the camos' sensors with the press of a button and everything but his head disappeared. Then he reached back and pulled the hood over the top, adjusting the face-piece. He stared into the mirror. Even with his enhanced eyesight and at a distance of only a few feet, he could detect no more than a swirl of movement, a faint blurring of the wall behind him as he moved his arms. Good. They were working perfectly. He deactivated and doffed them, then carefully packed them in the bottom of a small bag with a few other clothes.

Next he tried on the older generation camos and activated them. They also worked. Not as effective as the newer model, the sensors no longer functioning perfectly, they allowed him to follow his movements at least a little. He preferred these—liked to be able to see faint shadows as he moved his arms and legs. They were less disorienting. This older generation of camos had served as the model for the new line of Camo-Fit clothing now fashionable among the social elite—comfortable and slimming, with a hint of danger. He deactivated these as well, but kept them on. Finally he put together a few weapons, including his newest—an exceedingly rare particle beam cannon. He selected a Las-rifle and two Las-pistols, stun grenades, then added a handheld scanner, a scatterer and his night vision scope.

Grabbing his bags, he left the apartment and locked the door behind him. He knocked softly on his landlady's door. She opened it inside a minute, a small elderly woman with ruddy cheeks, her tablet computer in her hands.

"Mrs. Ivanovich."

"Mr. Jones. I knew it would be you. Do you know what time it is?"

"I'm afraid I need to ask you a favor again. I have to leave for a while. Can you…"

"Of course. Don't worry. I'll keep an eye out for your son." Mrs. Ivanovich's eyes teared up. "But…you know, dear, it's been four years."

Jeremiah's shoulders slumped. "I can't stop hoping, Mrs. Ivanovich. In my mind, I know he's gone. But in my heart," Jeremiah tapped his chest, "I can't give up."

Mrs. Ivanovich crossed herself and smiled sadly.

"I'll say a prayer for him tonight."

"Thank you."

"You know, Mr. Jones, I've been thinking. A nice young man like you—now that you're single again—you need to start living."

"Ah, Mrs. Ivanovich, the only way I could ever make a woman happy is by leaving her."

"Now, Mr. Jones, don't say that."

"How about you, Mrs. Ivanovich, are you happy?"

"Why, yes, Dear, I am."

"See, it works."

Jeremiah flashed her a smile as she slowly shook her head.

* * *

Jeremiah stopped his van behind the warehouse. He wanted to check on Marschenko in the basement before picking up Lendra. He'd thoroughly tested the soundproofing and knew that Lendra wouldn't be able to hear Marschenko's screams no matter how loud. Locking the vehicle, he checked his scanner to ensure no one was tracking him, then opened a metal door and entered a heavily insulated room, where a neuro-stimulator hung on the wall. He looked at it and thought of Weiss using the same device on Devereaux's followers to get their mouths moving. No. He left it hanging there and took the stairway to the basement, sealing the door behind him.

Jack Marschenko stood before the toilet, his arms above his head, thrashing around as much as his bonds allowed. He'd obviously heard Jeremiah's footsteps, for he was already on his feet, pushing toward the stairway when Jeremiah reached the bottom tread. Two days' growth covered Marschenko's drawn face but his T-shirt, made from shrink-fabric designed to hug the body, was still too tight around his chest. His muscles bulged with effort. His pale eyes, close set and unblinking, stared at Jeremiah as he roared, "I'm gonna kill you, you son of a bitch! Where the hell've you been?"

Jeremiah muted the sound of the television and said, "Calm down, Jack."

"I'll kill you, I'll kill you, I'll kill you."

Jeremiah held up his hands, waited for Marschenko's raving to cease. The man spat, his eyes rolling, yelling unrecognizable words. He seemed to have forgotten Jeremiah for the moment as he fought his bonds. After two days with nothing but nutri-water, he looked a little less bulky. His upper body leaned forward, the webbing holding him up. The muscles in his neck stood out, spittle hung from the corner of his mouth, and a vein in his forehead throbbed as he tried to leap at Jeremiah. Jeremiah sat on the stairs and let Marschenko's wrath abate. When he determined that Marschenko was capable of listening to reason, he spoke quietly.

"Where is my son?"

"How could you do this to me?" Marschenko asked. "How could you just leave me here? Haven't you got any compassion? For God's sake, let me go."

Jeremiah kept his voice hard: "Quit whining. You'll feel better in a couple days. Your body's used to the drugs and hormones, and it's fighting you right now."

He wondered why the big man's suffering bothered him. In the past, he wouldn't have thought twice about it. Was he getting soft? Had Catherine's death made him too sympathetic? Or was it just the realization that Marschenko had been so doped up, so controlled by his handlers that he didn't know right from wrong?

"For God's sake, Jones," Marschenko said, "I can't take it anymore. I'll be dead in a couple days. I need those hormones to survive. You gotta let me out."

"Sure, Jack." Jeremiah leaned forward, elbows on his knees. He softened his voice: "Just tell me about my son."

"I can't, Jones, I can't. You're dead. You hear me? When I get outta here, you are so dead. I'm gonna kill everyone in your family too. Understand? I'm comin' after all of 'em. Any other kids you got—dead. Your wife—dead. Your parents—dead. There's gonna be nothin' left when I get through with you."

Jeremiah smiled grimly. He didn't tell Marschenko there was no one left to kill, no one left to care about. He said: "You still don't get it, Jack. You don't leave until you tell me what you know."

Marschenko's legs gave way as he began blubbering. Hanging by his arms, he cried and snuffled. "Okay…I left him, yeah…Disney World…Okay? Last I saw him…Mickey Mouse roller coaster…Okay? Now…let me go."

Jeremiah shook his head at the obvious lie. "Why'd you take him?"

Marschenko took in a great gulp of air. "Don't know…orders."

"Who ordered it?"

Marschenko began shaking his head. "No, no…idea. Let me out, Jones…Let me out…you goddamn son of a bitch!"

Marschenko found his legs again, continuing to thrash and lunge, twisting, pulling, screaming, his voice hoarse with effort. As he moved, his right leg hit the toilet hard. Jeremiah winced in sympathy, but Marschenko ignored it in his fury. The big Elite Ops trooper already had a bad bruise on his left leg, where he must have slammed it against the toilet earlier, either in the throes of withdrawal or a fit of rage.

After a few moments Marschenko calmed down again. His head drooped and he began murmuring to himself quietly.

"Listen to me, Jack," Jeremiah said. "Listen to me."

Slowly Marschenko lifted his head, his eyes gradually focusing on Jeremiah.

"I'm leaving town for a while. I'll be gone at least a few days, maybe longer. There's a possibility I won't be back. You understand, Jack?"

"What?"

"This might be the last time you see me, Jack. This might be your only opportunity to tell me the truth. I don't want to hurt you, Jack. I don't want to hurt anybody. I just want my son back. If you had a son, you'd know how I feel. So just tell me what you know."

Marschenko's lips trembled; his mouth opened. For a second it looked like he might say something. Then he slammed his jaws together and dropped his head.

"If I don't come back," Jeremiah said, "you die."

"I don't know squat, Jones. I don't know anything."

"Goodbye, Jack. Keep drinking that nutri-water if you want to live."

Marschenko shook his head, his eyes tightly closed, tears leaking out as a low rumble built inside his gut. "Nooooo…"

* * *

Jeremiah drove onto the tollway, the scanner at the entrance reading his vehicle's designation and automatically billing CINTEP for the mileage. Lendra watched him from the passenger seat, waiting to brief him as he eyed the surrounding traffic, running scans on each vehicle. After he ensured they were not being followed and set the autopilot to a steady cruising speed, Lendra said, "Do you want me to tell you what little we know about Devereaux's bio-weapons?"

"No. Tell me about Devereaux."

Lendra looked straight ahead, her gaze unfocused as she pulled details from her interface. She said, "Walt Devereaux is brilliant. He was a child prodigy. His parents were quite religious, but after his book *The Ladder* came out, his mother committed suicide. Seven years ago."

Jeremiah thought of Catherine and suppressed a shudder. Why did you give up, he wondered silently. There's still a chance I'll find Joshua. And as long as there's a chance, I'll never give up.

"His father," Lendra continued as she fingered her necklace: a glass bulb at the end of a delicate chain, "died in a car accident when he was fourteen—malfunctioning auto-pilot. As for Devereaux, he understood complex mathematical formulas at age five, tested out of college physics at nine. Had more trouble with the social sciences but still managed to graduate from Oxford at age thirteen."

Lendra stared ahead as she searched her database again. "Oh, and here's something interesting. His maternal grandfather was one of two sculptors who worked on the 'Emerging Man' statue."

"Really? That certainly lends credence to the theory that Devereaux is in Crescent Township."

Jeremiah spotted a strange energy dispersal configuration on his scanner. "Hold on a second," he said. He recalibrated the scanner, noting that the configuration was well behind him.

"Are we being followed?" Lendra asked.

"Yes."

Lendra grabbed the bulb of her necklace and turned to stare through the rear window, as if she might somehow be able to detect their pursuer among the many vehicles in sight. "How can you tell? Which car is it?"

"You won't be able to see him." Jeremiah tapped a display on the dashboard, where a series of dashes and dots indicated tractor-trailers and smaller vehicles. He put his finger on a group of hazy-looking dots that had melded into a large blot. "The guy's using a scatterer, diffusing energy and bio readings, but he's about three miles back."

A frown wrinkled Lendra's forehead. "So what should we do?"

"For the moment, nothing. It's possible Eli put him on our trail."

"Why would he do that?"

Jeremiah said, "He might have sent a backup, but doesn't want me to know he doesn't trust me to get the job done. It's been four years, after all, since I was in the field. Or maybe he's testing me to see if I can spot the tail. Or possibly it's someone else. This is supposed to be a top-secret mission, so I imagine there are lots of people who know of it. That's just the way Washington works."

"Well, shouldn't we lose him? I mean, after all, you're a ghost."

"So?"

"I thought you could disappear in a puff of smoke or something?"

"I don't know what kind of stories you've heard. But I was just a field agent. Nothing special."

"Oh, come on." Lendra's mouth widened in a smirk. "I've heard you and the other ghosts pulled off some amazing jobs."

"I wouldn't trust Eli's stories. He's prone to exaggeration."

"Trogan Brosk told me a few too."

"Trogan Brosk has a big mouth. That's one of the reasons he was downgraded to an office job."

"He said you were the best."

Jeremiah shook his head. "Julianna was the best."

He adjusted the scanners, hoping to find a frequency or an energy signature that would allow him to identify his pursuer, but after a few minutes of fruitless effort, he gave up.

"What more can you tell me about Devereaux? I know he received a special exemption to become Secretary General of the U.N. And he won the Nobel Peace Prize."

"He earned several PhDs, including one in epigenetics."

As Lendra recited Devereaux's history, Jeremiah snuck occasional glances her way. She really did look a lot like Catherine. Her eyes. Her cheekbones. Her nose. Not her lips: they were fuller and redder. She gazed into the distance, scanning the data in her interface, a small frown creating a line between her eyebrows. The interface—a small, flesh-colored device attached to her left temple—made her appear almost inhuman. If he concentrated on that, Jeremiah could convince himself she looked nothing like Catherine. But even as he watched her, she caught him staring. Jeremiah turned back to the windshield.

Without looking at her, he sensed Lendra studying him. He wondered what her game was. He felt drawn to her and wondered how much of that was simple loneliness.

Lendra continued: "Devereaux won the Nobel for his stint as Secretary General of the U.N., where he stopped twelve escalating conflicts over economic or geographic issues. Twelve of them. However, he considered himself a failure because the religious wars continued."

Jeremiah spotted the exit for I-70 up ahead. He disengaged the autopilot and took the steering wheel, maneuvering the van under the scanner that would log him off the tollway. Now the road would start to get bumpy. He slowed down, engaged the van's heavy-duty suspension, keeping an eye on their pursuer via the scanner, but he knew the guy wasn't likely to lose him at this point.

"He was asked to run for President of the United States after leaving the U.N., but he refused. Said he was a citizen of the world—not a Democrat or Republican—though it was the Greens and the Doves who really kept after him, pushing him to accept. After turning them all down, he turned from genetics to philosophy, and eventually he concluded there was no God. That's when he conceived of the ladder of enlightenment, which focuses on self-actualization without reference to a higher being. Some schools even teach his ladder now."

"That must drive the religious types crazy."

"He claimed his purpose was to push humankind to evolve. After publication of *The Ladder*, he became almost a god to some, a devil to others. He's probably the most loved and most hated man in the world. Have you read his book?"

Jeremiah nodded.

"It's brilliant," Lendra said. "It's too bad so many religious people close their minds to his ideas. Why can't they accept that morality needn't be based on a deity? Why shouldn't people find their own meaning in life? Why do they have to follow rules prescribed by some ancient *prophet* who claims to know God's will?"

"Most people need something greater than themselves," Jeremiah replied.

For a while he concentrated on the road. Although I-70 wasn't in terrible shape, it received only patchwork repairs year in and year out. There never seemed to be enough money in the budget for an overhaul of the transportation system. And given the price of fuel, most people didn't travel that far anyway.

Jeremiah surveyed the surrounding countryside. There were still quite a few people dwelling here, eking out a living away from the protection of the city. The brave. The foolish. The poor. He knew the number of houses would drop significantly in a few miles. People tended to cluster into big cities these days, leaving the rural areas for the corporate farms, the radicals and those who had nowhere else to go.

The traffic lightened until only a few dozen dots and dashes remained on his scanner. But the fuzzy group three miles back stayed constant. An airship passed over the van on its way west, its massive size seemingly far too heavy to stay aloft. How could anyone be comfortable traveling that way? Or even in a plane? Or a jet-copter?

Jeremiah said, "Tell me about the Escala."

Lendra nodded. "Also sometimes called pseudos, usually as a disparagement. They were enhanced with animal DNA to enable them to survive on Mars. But they also have increased speed and strength, endurance and healing ability. Unfortunately, there was a problem with the genetic surgery. The Escala became easily enraged and irrationally violent."

"And yet they follow Devereaux's teachings. Peace and cooperation."

"Apparently the rage only shows itself at times. Also, the Escala are essentially Devereaux's children. Their very existence is a result of his research, but we don't really know much about them post-surgery. They had an altercation with the Elite Ops that resulted in a draw."

Jeremiah whistled softly.

"Anyway, since then the Escala have been hiding out in Rochester, where the Mayo Clinic used to be."

"Where the Susquehanna Virus escaped from?"

Lendra nodded. "About twelve years ago. Susquehanna Sally claimed she'd released it as a warning to change our unsustainable ways, but she's made only a few appearances since then and we've never been able to confirm that she was behind the virus. Its release might have been accidental. At any rate, it wiped out a large portion of the population. The city was largely abandoned. That's why Rochester was chosen for the Mars Project surgeries, which were top secret. A lot of that information is still classified."

"And the virus?" Jeremiah said. "Still active?"

"Yes. And the virus is the main reason the Elite Ops weren't sent in to Rochester to wipe out the Escala—"

"I would have guessed that the Elite Ops weren't sent in because the government feared the Escala would unleash Devereaux's bioweapons on humanity."

"That position may have some merit," Lendra conceded, "but there's no proof the bioweapons exist. The Susquehanna Virus, however, does. It's suspected that the Escala are immune to it. The Elite Ops are not. And the fear is that the Escala would use the virus as a nuclear option against the Elite Ops. Richard Carlton claims they threatened to do so. Anyway, as long as the Escala haven't tried to fight their way out, they've been allowed to stay confined to that area."

"Are Devereaux's bioweapons something like the Susquehanna Virus?"

"We don't know," Lendra said. "He only had one brief conversation with President Davis. He hasn't spoken to President Hope about them at all. He told Davis that the ideas just popped into his head in the middle of the night."

"You believe that?"

"With somebody as bright as Devereaux, it's certainly possible. At any rate, all we really know is that Devereaux's conceived of these weapons and that he's had time to build them."

"Well, let's stop for a short break. After we're back on the road, you can research Devereaux's followers and his organization. I want to know everything. The tiniest detail might lead us to him."

"There's a lot of information out there. And ninety-nine-point-nine percent of it is worthless."

"We've got time. We won't be in Minnesota until tomorrow."

"What about our tail?"

"He won't bother us yet," Jeremiah said, hoping he was right. "He'll know we're aware of him. And he can't get close without giving himself away. So he'll keep his distance."

"How can you be so sure?"

"It's what I'd do. And from his equipment, he's no amateur. Stopping will be good. He won't expect that."

* * *

While Lendra researched Devereaux's followers and his large, loosely affiliated organization, Jeremiah fiddled with his scanner. Their pursuer closed to a mile behind. But no matter how Jeremiah modified his scanner he couldn't get a complete lock on the guy. His only consolation was that, with his random variable shielding, the guy couldn't get a good lock on him, either. As Jeremiah was adjusting the biometric component of his scanner, he noticed a sharp spike in their pursuer's electrical output.

The van lurched under a power surge. The electrical systems flickered. Jeremiah, his heart suddenly pounding, reached down and flipped the auxiliary battery control. He also shut down all non-essential systems, including his shielding. It had been too long since he'd been under attack. This shouldn't have bothered him as much as it did.

"What was that?" Lendra asked. "I just got disconnected."

"Our friend." Jeremiah pointed his thumb to the back. Up ahead a car slowly pulled to the side of the road. In the rearview mirror a truck did the same. Jeremiah wondered how many vehicles had just been disabled by that pulse.

"Are we under attack?"

"A small test."

"What kind of test?" Lendra asked.

"To see if he could strand us. Take us down at his leisure. He knows I'm on to him, so he decided to take an easy shot."

Lendra's voice shot up half an octave, her eyes wide with fear. Once again she grabbed the glass bulb of her necklace, gripped it fiercely. "Well, shouldn't we go after him? Stop him somehow? Are we going to let him come after us all the way to Minnesota?"

Jeremiah kept his voice even—reassuring: "I shut down all our advanced systems. I modified our electrical output to make us look like every other vehicle on the road. That eliminates our defenses but makes us essentially invisible to his scanner."

Lendra's voice dropped back into something approaching her normal range. "How can you be so calm?"

"Panicking won't help."

Lendra's lower lip quivered. She nodded. "I guess I should call Eli back."

"You can try, but I think you'll need to reboot your system after that power surge."

Lendra's attempts to restart her interface failed. She reached up and pulled it away from her head, then held it out for Jeremiah to see, and said, "I need to fix this, but I can't do it in a moving vehicle."

Jeremiah stared at her left temple. He knew there was a port connector there just under the surface of her skin, but he couldn't see any sign of it. He said, "We'll stop for the night in a little while. I'll give you a hand. Should have you back up and running in no time."

Lendra looked back, frowning.

"Don't worry," Jeremiah said. "He'll have to check out everybody who stopped—make sure he didn't disable us. By the time he realizes we're not back there, we'll be fifty miles away."

"But he could get us in our sleep."

"Trust me, Lendra. He's not foolish or desperate enough to make a frontal assault. Besides, it'll take him hours just to find us again."

Chapter Four

When the front door of the Tessamae Shelter crashed open and soldiers burst into the lobby, shattering the calm Minnesota night, Sister Ezekiel hurried from her office. Why, she wondered, did they always break down the door, and why did they always come in the night?

As the soldiers pushed their way inside the shelter, the homeless men who came here for sanctuary tried to push their way out, but they were no match for the heavily armed troops. Sister Ezekiel was jostled along with her unfortunate guests helpless to restore order. She looked through the door, which dangled from twisted hinges, and saw more soldiers in their ponchos, glistening in the rain. Thunder lent fear to the tension. There was no escape.

Then a troubled guest called Redbird tried to push past a soldier, who brought her stun club up to stop him. Redbird dodged to the side and the soldier's lunge carried her into Cookie Monster—huge, hairy, gentle Cookie Monster.

Sister Ezekiel heard the stun club sizzle as it made contact with Cookie Monster's chest. He roared in pain, drawing the attention of the other soldiers, who must have thought he initiated an attack. Several jabbed Cookie Monster with their stun clubs. Yet he didn't fall. He flailed away at the clubs, knocking one out of a soldier's hand. That's when the other soldiers jumped him.

They beat him, poking him with their clubs, driving him to the floor as he tried to protect himself. Meanwhile most of the men in the lobby ran for the door. Sister Ezekiel searched for Cookie Monster's near-constant companion, Rock Man, expecting the poor deaf-mute to be caught in the crush of bodies, but didn't spot him. The men who reached the doorway ran into a wall of soldiers, who herded them back inside.

Even after Cookie Monster lay unmoving on the floor, one of the soldiers continued to prod him with his stun club. Sister Ezekiel ran forward, flanked by Henry and Doug.

"Stop it!" Sister Ezekiel ordered. "Can't you see he's unconscious?"

The soldier looked up, his hostile eyes slowly focusing on her face. Then he blinked, shrugged apologetically and backed away, staring down at the gigantic form of Cookie Monster. The rest of the soldiers formed a semi-circle around the entrance, stun clubs and Las-rifles in their hands.

Dr. Mary McCaffery emerged from her room at the back of the shelter and joined them. "What's going on here?" she asked.

"Good question," Sister Ezekiel said. She turned to the soldiers. "What are you doing here?"

"We got orders to secure this shelter," a sergeant replied.

"Whose orders?"

"Colonel Truman, Sister."

"And where is Colonel Truman?"

"He'll be here shortly."

Sister Ezekiel glared at the sergeant until he looked away. Together with Doug and Henry, she helped Dr. Mary lift Cookie Monster onto a gurney. Henry nearly dropped him, but the sergeant stepped forward and grabbed Cookie Monster's shoulders, preventing Cookie Monster's head from hitting the floor. The big man almost didn't fit on the gurney. His feet came right up to the edge; his massive arms hung over the sides; his long black hair, containing the merest touch of blue, dangled from the end opposite his feet, seven feet away. His normally cheerful demeanor was hidden behind closed eyes and the cuts on his face and the bushy beard that disappeared into his hairy chest.

After they got Cookie Monster settled on the gurney, Dr. Mary tapped the shiny interface she wore on her left temple, patted her graying hair in place with a blotched pudgy hand and began treating his wounds. She slapped a QuikHeal bandage on a deep gash over his left eye, then wheeled Cookie Monster to the infirmary, adjacent to

Sister Ezekiel's office and visible through wall-windows that could be darkened for privacy.

Sister Ezekiel looked into the infirmary, where Doug and Henry were assisting the doctor. Doug, tall and thin, with a perpetual slouch and a flat face, his black curly hair cut almost to the scalp, held a saline bag in a large mahogany hand. Poor Doug. For some reason, he saw little to like about himself. On the other side of the gurney, the short plump albino, Henry—who saw the world in simple terms, good versus evil—cut the big man's clothes away. Dr. Mary placed a thin sheet over Cookie Monster's tree-trunk legs and waist, though he was not awake to be discomfited by his nakedness.

Glancing around the lobby, Sister Ezekiel assessed the damage to her shelter. Apart from the door, there was a broken window. Not only rain but insatiable mosquitoes entered the shelter through the openings. Strange how all the poisons and pollutants in the air didn't kill off the mosquitoes. For some reason the Dear Lord found fit to let them survive. But now they were a problem—carrying all manner of diseases. Not only the deadly Susquehanna Virus but mutations of older maladies like malaria, Rift Valley and West Nile, which came now in greater potency than when she was a child. And the men who frequented the shelter were ill equipped to fight any illness at all, let alone the Susquehanna Virus.

How she longed to slip off to the chapel, where she could pray, meditate and even sleep. She knew the Dear Lord would forgive her naughtiness, for He understood fatigue. It seemed ages since Sister Ezekiel had experienced a good night's sleep. Every day brought a different problem. But these soldiers, they were likely to be a much bigger problem than usual. The last time soldiers had busted in, looking for a political dissident, they'd stayed three days, disrupting the shelter's routine and scaring off a good many unfortunates. She hoped that wouldn't be the case this time.

She closed her eyes, imagined herself drifting off for a few precious minutes, then returned to the infirmary. Adjusting her glasses—the Church frowned on genetic surgery—she saw Dr. Mary dip her sponge in a salve and apply it to burns on Cookie Monster's chest and shoulders.

"Are those from the stun clubs?" Sister Ezekiel asked.

Dr. Mary nodded as she applied more salve to a bruise on Cookie Monster's arm. She then turned to a cut on the back of Cookie Monster's right hand where a club had caught him, ripping the skin badly. Henry, acting as her assistant, handed her a QuikHeal bandage, which she applied to the cut.

"Wonderful things," Dr. Mary said. "An anesthetic numbs the pain, an antibiotic deep-cleans the wound and a coagulant stops the bleeding. You don't even need me. Just pop one of these on every patient who walks through the door."

"Don't even joke about that, Doctor," Sister Ezekiel said. "I don't know how we got along without you these past two months."

"Oh, I'm sure you did fine. You just needed a better supply of these."

"We were desperate for medical help before you came. You are a true miracle—an angel sent by God."

Dr. Mary waved off the compliment. For some reason she seemed uncomfortable with gratitude. Every time Sister Ezekiel tried to thank her, she fidgeted or shrugged and changed the subject, as if undeserving of praise. That didn't mean Sister Ezekiel was going to stop honoring her. Dr. Mary was a saint. She could have earned a lot more at a clinic or hospital.

Sister Ezekiel asked, "Is he going to be all right?"

"Hard to say. What we really need is a neuropsychologist to determine the level of damage. It looks like he took a dozen hits with a stun club. I don't know how he managed to stay conscious long enough to absorb that many blows."

"One of the soldiers struck him several times after he was down," Sister Ezekiel said.

"What?"

Sister Ezekiel caught the fierce look in Dr. Mary's eyes and felt a sudden fear. Henry must have seen something in the doctor's face too, for he took a step backward. Dr. Mary often displayed a gruff exterior, using caustic comments to voice her displeasure with everything from the government's incompetence and untrustworthiness to the senseless violence she witnessed weekly. On rare occasions, especially during the quiet moments after the men had gone to bed, Dr. Mary let her softer side show. But right now she looked as angry as Sister Ezekiel had ever seen her. Sister Ezekiel nodded and said, "I don't understand why anyone would do such a thing."

"Soldiers are stupid and brutal," Dr. Mary said. "And when they get scared, they attack."

"He didn't even do anything. He simply got in the way." Sister Ezekiel touched Cookie Monster's warm hand. "Such a gentle creature."

Dr. Mary sighed and her anger seemed to melt away. Sister Ezekiel marveled at how she could go from intense anger to casual acceptance to optimistic happiness almost instantaneously and without effort. It took a great deal of willpower for Sister Ezekiel to maintain her iron control throughout the day. She feared giving in to too much emotion.

Ruffling Cookie Monster's hair, Dr. Mary said, "We really should be treating him like a victim of a lightning strike. That's probably how much electricity he absorbed. I expect he'll experience short-term memory loss, personality change and have difficulty concentrating on more than one thing at a time—not to mention headaches, nausea, tinnitus and irritability."

"I'd hate to see him angry," Doug said.

Dr. Mary grinned, the wrinkled skin around her brown eyes tightening. Her perfectly aligned white teeth glinted in the overhead lights, an incongruous contrast to her leathery cheeks. "That would be quite a sight."

Sister Ezekiel said, "Henry, can you and Douglas put some plastic up over the door and window? We're getting bugs and water in the lobby. I assume you don't need any more help at the moment, Doctor?"

"He'll be asleep for a while," Dr. Mary said. She took the saline bag from Doug and hung it from the post at the side of the gurney.

The buzz of conversation from the lobby quieted down. When Sister Ezekiel glanced out through the wall-window, she saw the soldiers standing at attention before a tall, black, rather young-looking soldier at the entryway, who was addressing the sergeant. Sister Ezekiel darkened the wall-window leading to the lobby, then followed Henry and Doug out the door.

"Colonel Truman, I presume," she said as she approached him. She noticed now that he wasn't a young man. A few white hairs scattered through his short curly hair gave him a distinguished look. His bearing was ramrod straight, his eyes a piercing brown.

"That's right, Sister. Forgive me for not shaking hands but you've got blood on yours. Are you all right?"

Looking down, she noticed that she not only had blood on her hands but on her habit as well.

"It's not mine," she said. But she immediately retreated to the infirmary and wiped her hands on a disinfectant towel. When she returned to the lobby she said to the colonel, "Do you mind telling me the meaning of all this?"

"I'm sorry, Sister. The sergeant got a little carried away."

"A little carried away? They ripped down my front door, broke a window, attacked my guests."

"We'll get someone to fix the door and window," Colonel Truman said.

"What's so almighty important that you have to break in here in the middle of the night?"

"We're looking for someone, Sister."

"Of course. You're always looking for someone. Who is it this time?"

"You should appreciate this, Sister. We're looking for Devereaux."

"Walt Devereaux?"

"The one and only."

"And you think he's here?"

"Anything's possible. We have orders to check every man in the shelter."

"That's ridiculous," Sister Ezekiel said. "Walt Devereaux is a very wealthy man. This is a sanctuary for the homeless."

"We know all about this place," Colonel Truman said. "Just like we know Morgan Tessamae was an anarchist."

The hair on the back of Sister Ezekiel's neck rose. "Morgan Tessamae was a saint. She escaped an alcoholic, abusive father and a husband who was an addict. Her Tessamae Foundation deeded us four hundred acres, bought this old store for our use and gave us the means to maintain it for at least twenty years. Because of her we've been able to help men addicted to drugs and alcohol, as well as those who suffer from mental and emotional impairments."

"She wanted a haven for addicts and political dissidents. She hated the government, criticized it constantly."

Sister Ezekiel's face suffused with anger. She folded her arms. "Are you one of those people who believes it's treasonous to criticize the government, Colonel?"

Colonel Truman put his hands up and smiled. "No, Sister. I'm no fanatic. And I'm not here to discuss anarchy or politics. I'm just looking for Devereaux. I've been instructed to install a DS-9000 at your shelter. And I have the documents confirming said installation. Major?" He turned to his left, where a thin, black female soldier a head shorter than Colonel Truman stepped forward, opened her briefcase and handed the colonel a tablet. Colonel Truman glanced at it before holding it out to Sister Ezekiel. The screen held a picture of the colonel with some text below it.

Sister Ezekiel took the proffered tablet. "I don't understand. What is a DS-9000 anyway?"

"A DNA scanner."

"And you think it's going to help you find Devereaux," Sister Ezekiel said. Pushing up her glasses, she began scrolling through the documents on the tablet. Filled with legalese, they looked impossible to decipher. Even her attorney would be hard pressed to digest all this information in less than a day.

"If you look at the top document, Sister," Colonel Truman said, "right under my picture you'll see that this installation has been ordered by a United States federal district judge. If you have any questions, you may contact the Attorney General's office during regular business hours."

"And this is regular business hours?" Sister Ezekiel asked. "The middle of the night?"

"I understand your concerns," the colonel said. "Do you have a lawyer? You probably ought to call him or her now. My orders are to begin installation immediately. I can give you five minutes if you'd like to make the call first."

Sister Ezekiel scrolled through the screens again without really seeing anything, just buying time. She wondered if her lawyer, Ahmad Rashidi, could help. In the past, when soldiers or the police came to the shelter looking for someone, they never gave her the opportunity to call him. By the time she was able to do so they'd already found who they wanted or realized that the person they were seeking wasn't at the shelter. But Ahmad had told her she had the right not to allow entry without a warrant.

"Is this a warrant to search the premises?" she asked.

"It's a writ of mandate," Colonel Truman said. "And before you protest that a writ of mandate does not serve as a warrant, you should know that national security issues establish exigent circumstances to support the writ."

"Very well, Colonel," Sister Ezekiel said. "You may set up your DS-9000. I still plan to call my lawyer at a decent hour."

"A wise move, Sister. I'm sure your lawyer will verify that everything we're doing is perfectly legal. And I apologize again for the zeal of my people." Colonel Truman lowered his voice. "It's so difficult to get good personnel in the Army these days. May we talk in private, Sister?"

"Certainly. This way." Sister Ezekiel pointed to her office.

Colonel Truman led the way. After she followed him inside, he closed the glass door, then pointed through the wall-window to the infirmary, where Dr. Mary continued to monitor Cookie Monster.

"Who are they?" he asked.

"Dr. Mary McCaffery," Sister Ezekiel replied, "and Cookie Monster. We don't know his real name. Everybody here uses nicknames."

"We're aware of that," Colonel Truman said. "That's one of the problems. We have no way to identify these men—determine who they really are. They've fallen through the cracks in more ways than one. Not only that, do you have any idea how easy it is to hide these days? How easy it is to acquire a disguise? Facial transplants, black market genetic surgery, fictitious e-histories, false identities—it's becoming a real problem. So we'll be scanning all your people, building a database and…wait a minute!"

He moved over to the wall-window and stared through it at Cookie Monster, whose head was now the only part of him not covered by a sheet. Pointing at Cookie Monster, Colonel Truman said, "Is that a pseudo?"

"A pseudo?"

"A genetic mutant—a person who has altered his DNA with animal coding."

"You mean, like the Mars astronauts?"

"Yes." Colonel Truman strode to the door. "Come with me, Sister." He opened the door to the infirmary and led the way to Cookie Monster's gurney. Dr. Mary looked up when they approached, her eyebrows raised in a question. Sister Ezekiel shrugged.

Bending to peer at Cookie Monster's face, Colonel Truman inhaled slowly, then nodded. "The texture of his hair, his size and obvious muscular development, his slight animalistic odor. I think he's a pseudo. What do you think, Doctor?"

"I think you're in my infirmary without my permission. Why are you here?"

"We're looking for Walt Devereaux."

Dr. Mary waddled forward and inserted herself between Cookie Monster and the colonel. "I can assure you that this man is not him."

Colonel Truman backed up a step. "He is a pseudo, though. Is he not?"

"I don't know. What's more, I don't care."

"They're very dangerous. Killers."

"The Mars Project gone awry?" Dr. Mary laughed. "More government propaganda. There's nothing in animal DNA that can turn people into killers."

"Are you an expert on DNA manipulation, Doctor?"

"I dare say I know more about it than you, Major." Dr. Mary winked at Sister Ezekiel.

"It's Colonel. Colonel Truman. What can you tell me about this man's background, Sister?"

Sister Ezekiel fought to control her anger. "He's a regular at the shelter, though I couldn't tell you how long he's been coming here. I imagine he got his name from his appearance, as well as the blue fur coat he often wears. With his shaggy beard and unkempt hair he bears a decent resemblance to the character on the Sesame Street vids. Don't you think so?"

Colonel Truman nodded. "My wife loves those shows. They remind her of a more innocent age."

"A lot of people love them for that reason," Dr. Mary said. "Everybody's nostalgic for the old days, even though those old days weren't really all that sweet or innocent."

"He also loves cookies," Sister Ezekiel continued, "especially chocolate chip cookies. When someone offers him a cookie, his mouth breaks into a huge smile. His head bobs up and down in this—I don't know, frenzy—and everyone who sees him has to laugh. He's the gentlest creature you'd ever want to meet."

"Yes, well, he may appear that way to you, Sister. But if he's a pseudo like I think he is, he's very dangerous."

Sister Ezekiel studied Cookie Monster, asleep on the gurney. She'd heard, of course, that some people chose to tinker with their genes to make themselves different: usually more athletic or prettier. Cookie Monster, though not ugly, had an almost animal quality about him, rather like a bear or a gorilla. And the Mars Project astronauts were supposedly hiding in the area.

Colonel Truman stepped to the doorway of the infirmary and looked out over the lobby for a moment. Then he turned back to Sister Ezekiel and said, "So you don't remember when he first started coming here?"

Sister Ezekiel shook her head. "Since April, maybe March."

"Does he live here at the shelter?"

"No. He lives somewhere out there," Sister Ezekiel waved her hand to indicate the area to the east, "off in the woods with most of the other men who come here."

"And he's never caused you any trouble?"

"Cookie Monster?" Sister Ezekiel said. "I don't think you could find a more likable man. He looks after a lot of men here, especially poor Rock Man."

"Who's Rock Man?"

"Just a deaf-mute who likes to collect unusual rocks. He's harmless too."

"Is he here now?"

"I haven't seen him."

"And what about you, Doctor?" Colonel Truman turned to Dr. Mary. "How long have you been here?"

"About eight weeks."

"Where were you before that?"

"Los Angeles."

Colonel Truman pointed to his temple. "I see you're wearing one of those fancy computer interfaces."

Dr. Mary reached up and touched the device. She'd explained to Sister Ezekiel that it allowed her instantaneous access to vast medical databases, which was essential when treating people who came from all over, with a wide variety of ailments. It connected to a port in her temple that transmitted signals to and from the brain—a wireless hands-free computer.

"That seems like an expensive piece of equipment for someone working in a setting like this."

Dr. Mary took a half step forward. "Is there a question in that statement, Colonel?"

"I'm wondering why you would choose to work in these circumstances. Surely you could earn a great deal more working elsewhere?"

"No question about it, Colonel. Just as a man of your intellect and discipline and—dare I say—good looks could earn a great deal more in the private sector. Why would you choose to stay in the Army all these years?"

"Touché, Doctor." Colonel Truman bowed his head and Dr. Mary returned the gesture.

Surveying the infirmary, Colonel Truman said, "I'll post a guard here at the door. Just to be on the safe side."

"A guard will only make Cookie Monster nervous," Dr. Mary said.

"I'm afraid I must insist."

Dr. Mary looked at Sister Ezekiel.

Sister Ezekiel said, "Very well. I'll call Ahmad. I was hoping to wait until morning but it looks like we'll need him here sooner. Colonel?" Sister Ezekiel held out her arm toward the door. "Shall we return to my office and let the good doctor work in peace?"

"Fine," Colonel Truman answered. After assigning a guard to the infirmary, he instructed Major Sims to bring in the scanner. And as the soldiers began moving large metal parts into the lobby, their boots leaving muddy streaks on the floor, he said, "We need everybody's profile in the DS-9000's database so we can run a comparison check. Anybody coming in or out of the shelter will have to step through the arch of the machine."

"And how long will this machine be in place?"

"Hopefully not long, Sister." He glanced out at the lobby and yelled, "Hey, watch that!"

A large metal object crashed to the tile floor, causing everyone in the room to jump. Tic, a nervous skinny man, ran for the door, and two soldiers simultaneously hit him in the chest with their stun clubs. As Tic fell to the floor, Sister Ezekiel hurried toward him. The poor man groaned softly, then pulled himself into a fetal position, writhing in agony.

"Hold it," the colonel shouted. "Back off, people. Medic!" He stepped forward and bent to take a long look at Tic, who was twitching, holding onto his stomach and moaning. As the medic approached, the colonel straightened.

"Henry," Sister Ezekiel said, "fetch the doctor. Hurry!"

While the medic opened her kit, Sister Ezekiel knelt before Tic, took his hand and began to pray. Henry started for the infirmary but was stopped short by a long, drawn-out yell. Everyone in the lobby turned toward the sound.

Through the doorway of the infirmary Cookie Monster charged—a great naked beast—carrying the guard's Las-rifle by the barrel and dragging the guard, who clung to one of Cookie Monster's tree-trunk legs. The soldiers in the lobby aimed their weapons at the gentle giant.

"Don't…hurt him." Dr. Mary panted as she huffed out of the infirmary behind them, moving surprisingly quickly for a woman of her bulk.

"No!" Cookie Monster yelled, his booming voice echoing throughout the shelter. He stopped in the center of the room, hands held high, blood trickling from his left arm where the saline bag had been attached.

"Hold your fire," Colonel Truman commanded.

Dr. Mary caught up with Cookie Monster and managed to grab hold of his arm, dragging it down to her level so she could retrieve the Las-rifle. He let her grab the weapon and she then helped the guard to his feet, handing him back his Las-rifle as the other soldiers began to close in on them.

Dr. Mary stepped in front of Cookie Monster, arms held wide, facing the soldiers. "Just woke up a bit confused," she said calmly.

"Step away from him, Doctor," Colonel Truman ordered as he unholstered his Las-pistol.

Sister Ezekiel rose to her feet, heart pounding in her chest, her mouth suddenly dry. Every instinct told her to run. Instead, she made her way toward Cookie Monster and Dr. Mary, cleared her throat and said, "He's not going to harm anyone."

"Stay back, Sister," Colonel Truman said. "He's dangerous."

"Oh, for God's sake," Dr. Mary said. As Sister Ezekiel reached her side, Dr. Mary stepped over to Colonel Truman, her hand extended toward the colonel's weapon. "Put that down."

Sister Ezekiel held her breath. The colonel stared at Dr. Mary, his pistol now aimed squarely at her ample chest. Dear Lord, Sister Ezekiel prayed, don't let him shoot that brave woman.

"He's gentle as a lamb," Dr. Mary said.

After a moment's hesitation, Colonel Truman re-holstered his pistol, though his soldiers kept their weapons trained on Cookie Monster.

Dr. Mary turned back to Cookie Monster. She grabbed his hand and spoke calmly: "Cookie Monster. You need to get back into bed."

"Bed?"

"You need to finish your medical treatment."

Cookie Monster looked around the room, studying every face, as if checking for a friend. A few soldiers smirked at his nakedness but most seemed tense, their faces pinched, their eyes narrow.

Sister Ezekiel said, "Are you looking for Rock Man?"

Cookie Monster's massive head swung in her direction. "Rock Man?"

"He's not here," she replied. "Please. Get back into bed."

Doug said, "I'll get you some cookies."

Dr. Mary pulled Cookie Monster by the hand. "Come on."

Cookie Monster meekly followed her back into the infirmary. For several seconds nobody moved. Then Dr. Mary poked her head out the infirmary door and asked, "What happened to Tic?"

Sister Ezekiel said, "He got nervous and tried to run. Two soldiers hit him with their stun clubs."

Dr. Mary addressed the medic. "What are you doing for him?"

"There's not much you can do for a stun club hit, ma'am," the medic said.

"What about balancing his electrolytes?"

"Yes, ma'am, I was just about to hook up a saline bag."

"Good." Dr. Mary retreated to her infirmary.

Colonel Truman looked at Sister Ezekiel. "I'm going to have to arrest Cookie Monster, you know."

"He's like a child. He didn't mean to hurt your soldier."

"It doesn't matter. He can't go around attacking my men. He's a menace." Colonel Truman turned to his remaining soldiers. "I want the DS-9000 set up by the entrance. Once we have it ready, Sister, every man here is going to have to be run through it."

"I ain't goin' through no scanner," Doug said.

The colonel turned to Doug. "You hiding something?"

Sister Ezekiel answered. "Half the men here are hiding something. That's why they're here. We ask no questions."

"We won't be arresting people for minor offenses, Sister. We're not looking for drugs or other illegal items. We just want Devereaux."

"And you'll trample on society's outcasts to find him."

"I'm just doing my job, Sister." Colonel Truman pressed a button on his lapel and spoke into his headset: "Everything's secure at the shelter, sir." He listened for a few seconds, then said, "We're setting it up now. We should have a good idea in a few hours." More listening, then, "We'll see you shortly."

Turning to Sister Ezekiel, the colonel said, "The Attorney General is on his way."

Chapter Five

The windmills of Wisconsin lined the freeway, their long white blades spinning lazily in the night, their energy supplementing the solar and nuclear power that kept the City of Madison and its suburbs running. Up ahead, looming out of the darkness, Jeremiah saw the city's orange lights. Madison's suburbs mostly looked dark, their residents hunkered in their fortresses, Bibles open, guns loaded, fearful of the criminals and mad liberals infesting the city. Driving into the city center past the well-lit perimeter road that served as a barrier between the Godless and the saved, Jeremiah took only a few minutes to reach the Four-Key Security Hotel overlooking Lake Mendota. After his vehicle was scanned, he drove into the secure underground parking lot.

"Is it safe to do this with someone behind us?" Lendra asked.

"Relax," he answered. "This is the safest hotel chain in the country. And I'll be right next door. Plus, I'll put extra alarms on your entry points—door and windows—that will sound in my room. You'll be fine."

"Couldn't we stay in the same room?" Lendra whined.

Jeremiah sighed as he entered the lobby. Two heavily armed security guards scanned them for weapons. The desk clerk, a short brunette with a tight shimmer cloth shirt that emphasized her muscular shoulders, wore a stun club at her side. She smiled at them politely and said, "Welcome to Four-Key Security."

Lendra put a hand on Jeremiah's arm, then stepped in front of him and said to the clerk, "A double room, please." To Jeremiah she said, "I'll handle this. Look, they have a restaurant on the roof. Why don't you get us a table? I want to clean up a little. Order me a vodka stinger, okay?"

Jeremiah smiled. Just like Julianna—a take-charge woman. He waited for Lendra to complete the check-in process, then rode up in the elevator with her to their floor, where he handed his bag to the security guard taking Lendra to their room. He continued up to the restaurant and examined the dozen or so diners eating at this late hour even though he knew none could be his pursuer. No way the man—Jeremiah assumed it was a man—could have caught up to them yet. And even if the man had lucked onto them somehow, he wouldn't dare try anything here. The wait staff all moved with the fluidity of fighters, stun clubs hanging from their belts.

Jeremiah sat and ordered a water. Marschenko, he realized, might be drinking nutri-water at this very moment. A good man. Eventually he'd tell Jeremiah what he knew. Jeremiah tried not to think about holding Marschenko captive, concentrating on his surroundings instead. But after twenty minutes, he wondered what was keeping Lendra. She should have been here by now.

A familiar tune he couldn't quite identify played softly in the background. He closed his eyes for a moment and decided to give Lendra a few more minutes before ordering. Finally she breezed into the restaurant wearing a deeply cut red silk dress. She flashed Jeremiah a grin as she crossed to him, ignoring the stares of the diners at the other tables. Why wasn't he surprised at her outfit?

Jeremiah stood and said, "They told me we can sit out on the deck if you like, under the stars."

"Please." She followed him outside, looked down at Lake Mendota below them, then turned to take in the Capitol, bathed in soft orange lighting that Jeremiah knew came from biochemical elements requiring less energy than LED lights. The waiter, a crewcut blond about Lendra's age with bright blue eyes and a skintight shirt that showed off his developed torso, brought her drink as well as a fresh glass of water for Jeremiah, then stood to the side, eyeing Lendra while she studied the scrolling menu on the pop-up screen, pictures of each dish appearing every few seconds. Jeremiah had seen them all before. While he waited, he listened to the soft strings and pleasant riffs on the familiar tune. What was that song? And then he had it: "On Wisconsin." A fight song turned into a symphonic waltz, slowed down and performed on cello and violin.

"Artichoke-Mint Delight, please," Lendra said to the waiter. "And a Winnipeg Chablis."

"Hawaiian Chicken," Jeremiah added, pointing to his water.

The waiter nodded, withdrawing only after another glance at Lendra.

"No wine?" Lendra asked, taking a long drink and licking her lips.

"I like to stay alert," Jeremiah answered.

"Poor man. All dressed up and no one to fight. Nothing happened on the way here. Maybe the roads aren't as dangerous as you said."

"We were on tollways through all the big cities," Jeremiah answered. "But I disabled a couple trucks about a hundred miles outside Cleveland. Still you're right. It's been pretty quiet."

"You disabled two trucks?"

"Waiting off the highway with charged weapons, looking for vulnerable targets. I zapped their electrical systems with a photon pulse as we passed. No big deal."

"Why didn't you say something?"

"You were nervous enough. And they weren't a threat."

"So are we safe here?"

Jeremiah nodded. "Did you notice that perimeter road around the city center?"

"That really bright one?"

Jeremiah nodded. "That's the city's version of a security fence. Every vehicle crossing the road is scanned—every person too. If I'd left our scatterer on, we'd have been stopped within a block."

"What about your weapons?"

"I locked them in a separate unit in the back of the van. Combination scatterer and dampening field. Reflects an echo of solid metal. No weapons inside this hotel. We'll be fine here."

Lendra raised an eyebrow, then turned to look out at the Capitol. "Did you know that this city is actually eco-positive, removing more pollutants than it produces?"

Jeremiah shrugged. "I doubt that's true. Our governments have an annoying tendency to lie to us."

"I take it you're not political," Lendra said.

Jeremiah shook his head. "There are things I worry about, like this trend to segregate along religious beliefs. A terrible idea. Makes people less tolerant. But mostly I stay away from it. Politicians drive me crazy."

"Even President Hope?" Lendra asked. She took a long swallow as she stared into Jeremiah's eyes. He noticed that her pupils were dilated, her expression a little too slack.

He said, "What did you take?"

"Take?" Lendra frowned, then nodded. "Oh. Neo-dopamine. I have a prescription for it."

"That's a relaxant, isn't it?"

Lendra ran her finger around the rim of her glass. "Sort of. More complex than Aquitine. Does a lot more than just relax muscles."

"Should you be drinking?"

"I feel fine." She giggled. "Although I have the strangest feeling that we're being watched."

"We are," Jeremiah said. "That's the price you pay for staying in a Four-Key Security Hotel."

"Even in our room?"

"Yes."

The waiter returned with their meals and for a time they ate quietly. The food, as Jeremiah expected, was only adequate. Lendra's meal looked nothing like the picture. But then one didn't stay at a Four-Key Security Hotel for the food. Lendra took only a dozen bites, instead filling up on the rolls and the Winnipeg Chablis. Finally she pushed her plate away.

"So," Lendra said after swallowing the last of her wine and holding up her empty glass for the waiter, who stood in the shadow of the doorway, "tell me about Catherine."

As the waiter departed, Jeremiah, his appetite now gone, set his napkin atop the uneaten portion of his meal. Lendra stared at him, her chin in her hands, elbows on the table. All patience. Jeremiah waited for the waiter to return. The man approached quietly, his movements controlled, slipping around chairs and tables to hand

Lendra a new wineglass, then picked up their plates and cast another lingering glance at Lendra.

"What's to tell?" Jeremiah finally said after the waiter disappeared. "She killed herself."

"Because your son was kidnapped?"

Jeremiah nodded. "Partly, anyway."

Lendra tilted her head and spoke softly: "How did the abduction happen?"

"Catherine got sick—food poisoning, maybe—went into the restroom and left him by the door." Jeremiah glanced at Lendra, felt the unspoken judgment that Catherine should have taken the little boy inside the women's bathroom with her—Catherine's deadly burden. "She claimed she was inside for less than a minute, throwing up. When she stepped outside he was gone. She yelled for him, called security immediately. They locked the water park down no more than four minutes after it happened. But by then Joshua was already gone."

Sorrow rose inside Jeremiah—a great tidal wave. It threatened to drown him. He blinked rapidly three times. A self-hypnotic trick. He visualized himself in a stone dungeon, free of all feeling, all pain. Centered. Insulated. It was a way of re-creating himself as nothing more than a machine. Cold steel. He sat on the metal cot and looked down at the brick floor, faintly illuminated by a torch on the wall. He knew every inch of this dungeon.

"Sounds almost like an inside job," Lendra said.

"I thought of that. But I cleared all the employees."

"I can imagine how you did that."

"I didn't torture them. I didn't even have to question most of them."

Lendra pursed her lips. "And they cut out his ID chip so you couldn't track him." Lendra leaned forward, exposing the rounded tops of her breasts. Her glass bulb necklace dangled between them, sparkling in the low light.

Jeremiah lifted his eyes to hers and nodded. She focused on him, her gaze penetrating.

Emotions hammered the dungeon. Anger. Sorrow. Lust. The walls shook; the door vibrated. Jeremiah stared at the dungeon's door, wondering if it could sustain the assault.

"So after they took your son, Catherine killed herself?"

"Not right away," Jeremiah said. "We kept hoping to hear from the kidnappers, but we never did. So I began to work later and later into the evenings, looking for any clue that might help me find him. And slowly Catherine withdrew from me. Or maybe I withdrew from her. A few months ago," Jeremiah paused, "four months and sixteen days ago, I came home from work after midnight, as usual—saw her body on the bed, the clumsiness of the arms and legs. No one would choose to lie that way. I knew she was gone. She left a note on my nightstand asking me to forgive her, telling me she just couldn't live with the pain anymore."

"I'm sorry," Lendra said. "I didn't realize it was that recent."

A stone fell from the dungeon wall. Guilt and anger trickled in. Jeremiah again blinked three times, but another stone fell. It was an old dungeon, falling apart.

"And now you torture yourself over her loss," Lendra added. "And over Joshua's loss too."

"Shouldn't I?"

Lendra sat back and slowly swirled the wine around inside her glass. She studied the liquid for a moment, then met his eyes and said, "It's a common reaction, as I'm sure you know. But you did nothing wrong. In time you'll see that."

"I should have been there when they took Joshua. But I was recuperating. I'd been on a mission with Julianna—our last mission together."

"When she tried to kill you."

Jeremiah nodded.

"You and she were lovers."

"Before I met my wife, yes."

"But not after?"

Jeremiah shook his head. "Julianna had all the tools. Cold,

calculating, never shied away from violence. An almost ideal assassin. Better than me. Killing came easy to her."

"Why do you think she tried to kill you?"

"I never got the chance to ask her. Money, power, who knows? It's not important."

Lendra tilted her head to the side. "Tell me about your last mission."

"Our assignment was to eliminate the former dictator of a small African nation, who was living in exile in South America. He claimed to be a Devereauxnian, used that as an excuse to murder several thousand countrymen."

"I remember reading about that. Mubarno, wasn't it?" When Jeremiah nodded, she continued, "He said that Islam was a fraud that had to be wiped out."

Jeremiah said, "When the international community began to converge on Mubarno, he slipped away one night, taking several billion dollars from the country's treasury. Our job was to kidnap him, learn the whereabouts of the money, get it and then dispose of him."

Lendra held Jeremiah's gaze, one eyebrow arching slightly. Her dark hair framed her face. In the soft light her eyes appeared almost liquid.

"It didn't take long to find him," Jeremiah continued. "I turned Julianna loose on him. I could have taken his bodyguards out, but Julianna wanted to use a finesse approach. She talked with Mubarno for three days, quizzing him on Devereauxnianism."

"Why do you think she took so long?"

"I don't know. She'd already gained his confidence by the end of the first day. He invited her back to his room. She waited a couple more days before accepting. At that point I took care of his bodyguards. Everything was proceeding smoothly, but what I didn't know was that Julianna had sold Mubarno to his successor."

"El-Awhari?" Lendra asked.

"Yes. A strict Muslim. He got to execute Mubarno publicly. That solidified his position as the new dictator, which was all he cared about. What he really wanted was the opportunity to rob his people just as

Mubarno had. So in the end, not much changed. We weren't the saviors I'd hoped we'd be. Except that El-Awhari knows we're out there, so he's much more careful about killing his subjects. In that sense, I suppose, we did all right. Fewer people have died under his regime than under Mubarno's.

"Anyway, when I went up to Mubarno's room, she had him on the bed—drugged. As I turned to congratulate her, she pulled a knife and planted it in my gut. Never saw it coming. Never expected her to betray me. Made no attempt to stop her. Just stood there. Lucky she didn't hit a vital organ. But the knife was coated with a neural tranquilizer. Instant paralysis. I couldn't move. She bent down and put a QuikHeal bandage on me. Don't know why. All she said was: 'Sorry, darling.'"

Jeremiah managed a laugh that came out as a snort. "Then she brought in a couple of men, loaded Mubarno into a trunk and walked away. God, I wanted to kill her." Jeremiah noticed tension building in his hands. Before they could clench into fists, he straightened the fingers and placed his palms flat on the table.

Lendra reached across the table and settled her hand on his. "So Julianna didn't really want you dead. Why did you leave her?"

Jeremiah glanced down, surprised at the warmth of her hand. Was the heat generated by the neo-dopamine? He searched Lendra's face. She seemed fascinated by his story. Again he wondered if Eli had something to do with her attentions. Jeremiah slid his hand free, allowed the cooling night air to wash over it.

"A few years before the Mubarno job, we had one in Columbia. Terminate a druglord who'd bought off a judge. Simple. The only catch was that we had to do it in front of the judge. To warn him. So we snatched the druglord and took him to the judge's home. Julianna rounded up the judge's wife and three little girls, forced them to watch her kill the druglord. Then she turned and blew the kids away."

"My God!"

More stones fell, the dungeon collapsing on itself.

"I was out back," Jeremiah spoke mechanically, as if he could detach himself from the horror of the memory, "preparing our getaway. Didn't realize what she was doing until too late. Killing the girls triggered an alarm set to their brainwaves. So Julianna killed the judge and his wife too. We barely got out alive."

"Did she say why she did it?"

"She said it was a more effective warning. Wasn't the first time she altered a plan mid-operation. Anyway, that's when I left her. And I never worked with her again until the Mubarno job."

"You think she might have been involved in taking your son?"

"No," Jeremiah said. "If Julianna was involved, she'd have left me a message."

"You still have feelings for her."

"That doesn't mean I don't want to kill her."

Looking out from the shambles of a dungeon around him, the stones strewn about his feet, the torch flickering, Jeremiah took a deep breath, then exhaled slowly.

"Where is she now?" Lendra asked.

"I don't know. Eli says she became a freelancer, selling her services to the highest bidder. I suppose if I really wanted to know, I could ask Eli. He probably knows. Hell, you might too."

Lendra smiled briefly. "Is Julianna the reason you're not interested in me?"

Jeremiah took a sip of water. It somehow tasted cleaner than the water back east. He concentrated on its purity and said, "So what about you? Tell me a little about yourself."

"Not even going to acknowledge my question?"

Jeremiah just stared at her.

Lendra opened her hands. "Okay, if you want to play it that way…I studied neuro-psychology and computer science, did a little hacking on the side. I was doing a post-graduate fellowship when Eli offered me the job. Sounded more interesting than academia. And I've enjoyed it. I learn all manner of interesting things, and I get to meet unusual and powerful people."

"Like the President?"

Lendra smiled. "And you."

Jeremiah rubbed his face. "I'm not worth knowing."

Lendra frowned. "The things you've done for our country. The sacrifices you've made. Eli showed me some of your file. And I think you deserve happiness. Except you believe that would be a betrayal of your son. Am I right?"

"We should probably head back to the room. You'll want to get your interface up and working again."

"You're not a robot," she said, climbing to her feet. "Sooner or later, you'll have to face your emotions." As he stood, she came unsteadily around the table and wrapped her arm around his, the liquor and the medication apparently catching up with her. Jeremiah met the waiter's eye until the man looked away, then walked Lendra out, her head on his shoulder.

The warmth of Lendra's body infused him with desire as they rode the elevator to their floor. Jeremiah steeled himself. He refused to get involved with this girl, no matter how much he wanted to, no matter how much she threw herself at him.

When they entered the room, Jeremiah activated the alarms. He turned and found Lendra blocking his way to the beds. She walked into him, wrapped her arms around him. And for a moment he simply stood there, allowing her to hug him, enjoying the feel of her supple body, the scent of her perfume. Then he gently disengaged himself, held her at arm's length and said, "Did Eli put you up to this?"

Lendra stiffened. "What do you think I am? A whore?" She reached for her interface and the small repair kit she'd placed on the desk, then entered the bathroom and slammed the door behind her. The click of the lock sounded loud in the sudden quiet.

Jeremiah lay on the bed nearest the door and closed his eyes. He'd thought the person he longed for was Catherine—kind and thoughtful Catherine, sensitive Catherine, who could no longer take the pain of this world. But after his conversation with Lendra he realized that wasn't completely true. He mourned Julianna too. Julianna, who had somehow evolved from a gifted assassin into a psychopathic killer. Catherine and Joshua and now Julianna. What was Julianna doing tonight? Almost against his will he found his finger tracing the faint scar she'd left behind. The visible wound.

Then, as happened every night, he wondered about Joshua. Was the boy lost, scared, alone? Was he still alive? Did Marschenko know the answer?

Jeremiah rolled over to his side and pulled the pillow over his head. Stone by stone he began to rebuild his dungeon, even though the mental exercise no longer seemed reliable. With every nightmare the stones weakened, eroded by fear and sorrow—by imagination. He'd seen so many horrors in this life, so many things that could go wrong. His mind tormented him with those possibilities now. It used to be so easy to separate himself from pain and fear.

Now pain and fear were all he knew. All because he'd decided to work one last mission with Julianna. One stupid final mission. He'd known Julianna was on edge. Why had he agreed to work with her? Why hadn't he seen her betrayal coming?

And then the kidnapping changed everything.

Jeremiah was not one to harbor false hopes. After four years, the likeliest scenario was that his boy was dead. He told himself he could accept Joshua's death. But his emotional core hungered for his son to be alive.

Chapter Six

Sister Ezekiel kept her face centered on the PlusPhone's camera so that her lawyer, Ahmad Rashidi, would be able to see her clearly. She had changed her habit—not that the bloodstains bothered her, but she knew they upset others. Ahmad, visible from the waist up, wore one of the fashionable shimmer coats that changed color whenever the light shifted. His coat, however, looked more gray than silver—too dirty to work properly now. A bushy beard covered the shirt underneath his jacket. Bloodshot eyes stared back at her and his dark hair, with its graying sideburns, stood out in all directions. "I'm sorry to call you at such a late hour," she said, "but we have soldiers here."

Ahmad frowned. "Is that a TopDog 2000? They make the best PlusPhones."

"Focus, Ahmad. They want to arrest Cookie Monster and install a DNA scanner. They think we're harboring Walt Devereaux."

Ahmad chewed a couple times, his cheek bulging with khat, then shook his head. "Devereaux? When did you get a TopDog 2000?"

"It came last week," Sister Ezekiel said. "An anonymous gift. Concentrate, please. They want to set up this scanner to locate Walt Devereaux."

"Walt Devereaux," Ahmad said. Then his eyes opened wider and he said, "*The Walt Devereaux? Evil incarnate?*"

"I thought you weren't religious."

"This ain't about religion, Sister. It's a cultural thing. Religion helps define culture, and the absence of religion can destroy it."

"And is culture why you chew khat?"

Ahmad chuckled. "It's not illegal when used for medicinal purposes."

Sister Ezekiel frowned. "I didn't know you had a medical condition."

"I'm a lawyer," Ahmad said, struggling to hold back the laughter, "so I haven't got a heart." Now the dam burst and he erupted in great guffaws. Sister Ezekiel offered him a patient smile and waited for the laughter to subside. When Ahmad chewed khat, he laughed easily.

Finally he pulled himself together and said, "How do you feel about Devereaux?"

"Very sad. For every person who leaves the Church, Jesus weeps. And I feel the same way."

That seemed to sober Ahmad up a bit. He raised a thick eyebrow, his jaw working slowly. Then he said, "And what's this about soldiers wantin' to arrest Cookie Monster?"

"He attacked one of them."

"What did the soldier do, steal his cookies?"

"It's complicated," Sister Ezekiel said. "I realize it's a long drive from Minneapolis. But can you come down here?"

"Of course," Ahmad replied, rubbing his eyes.

"In the meantime, is there anything we can do?"

Ahmad lifted his hands. "You could make me a decent breakfast. I'll be there in a while. I wish I could study the documents on the way down—too bad they're locked to that tablet. I guess it doesn't matter. I can't wake Judge Moline this early or she'll lock me up and throw away the key."

"What about this DNA scanner?" Sister Ezekiel asked. "What do we do about that?"

"They probably got the writ by claiming a national security issue."

"And that means?"

"It means you're probably gonna hafta wait 'til I get there to look over the paperwork. And more than likely, there's nothin' we can do about it."

"And Gray Weiss is coming here too."

"The Attorney General? Holy cow, Sister! When you make enemies, you don't go halfway, do you?"

"Please, Ahmad. I'm not in the mood for your jokes right now."

"Sorry, Sister. Just trying to lighten the mood. Isn't there a price on Devereaux's head? Didn't your pope put a bounty on him?"

Sister Ezekiel cringed. "He did no such thing."

"Well," Ahmad shrugged, "not officially. But didn't he offer a great reward to anyone who could deliver Devereaux to justice? And I believe there were quite a few cardinals or bishops who offered monetary rewards."

"The Pope was talking about spiritual rewards. As for the cardinals and bishops, well, there are always a few radicals in every religion. As I recall, there are a few ayatollahs or imams out there who put a fatwa on Devereaux."

"All right, Sister." Ahmad chuckled. "My radicals probably outnumber your radicals. But my radicals are right."

Sister Ezekiel shook her head. "Everything always has to be a joke with you. When can you be here?"

"A few hours," Ahmad said. "Remember, I want a good breakfast."

"And if Walt Devereaux is here, will you help me protect him, perhaps grant him asylum?"

"Why the heck would you wanna do that, Sister?"

"It's what Jesus would do, Ahmad. It's the right thing."

"You're amazing, Sister. You're somethin' else. So kind, so caring. Okey dokey." He pointed at her. "You find him, we'll save him."

"I knew I could count on you," Sister Ezekiel said.

* * *

Gray Weiss, the Attorney General of the United States, carefully closed his umbrella as he entered the Tessamae Shelter. Outside, the lights atop his famous mobile command center flashed through blue, green, yellow and red. Sister Ezekiel had seen the large truck featured on numerous broadcasts—home of the roving Attorney General, the man who wandered the country keeping in touch with the people. Weiss wore a staid blue suit and moved imperiously, like he owned the place and everyone in it. He noticed everyone in the room, made eye contact with them all, shook hands with a half-dozen soldiers and nodded to the homeless men. He had charisma, Sister Ezekiel conceded. He probably wasn't acting, either. Sister Ezekiel had seen many phony people in her day. Weiss seemed genuine.

"This is Sister Ezekiel," Colonel Truman said. "Gray Weiss, Attorney General."

Gray Weiss stepped forward and gave her a warm, two-handed shake.

"Mr. Weiss," Sister Ezekiel said, "I hope you'll sort out this mess for us."

Weiss held onto her hand for a long moment, smiling, his bright teeth perhaps even whiter than Dr. Mary's. He seemed totally focused on her. "Of course I will. It's a pleasure to meet you, Sister. I've heard wonderful things about your shelter. You do fantastic work here—most impressive. I wish we could have met under better circumstances. Please accept my apology for the lateness of the hour and the regrettable violence."

Sister Ezekiel asked, "Was it necessary to barge in in the middle of the night?"

"We felt that surprise was essential. We hoped to catch Devereaux within the confines of the shelter. If he's not here, it'll just be a little longer process. We've cordoned off the entire area—the town and the woods off to the east, all the way to Rochester. No one's getting out without going through our identification checkpoints."

"Well," Sister Ezekiel looked around at the men lining the lobby—the men who had been mistreated and forgotten for years, the men who had, for the most part given up, and whom society had certainly given up on—and shook her head, "I haven't seen him here. And there are less than a hundred men here at the moment."

Colonel Truman added, "Several tried to escape in the confusion when my men hit the shelter. We got them all, though there are definitely more living in the woods. I can send out a few patrols to round them up."

"Good idea, Colonel. Bring back as many as you can find."

As the colonel spoke into his headset, Sister Ezekiel said to Weiss, "You're rounding up homeless men?"

"I would think," he answered, "of all people, you'd be happy to see Devereaux caught."

"Because he preaches that there's no God? I'm sorry to disappoint you, Mr. Weiss, but I bear Mr. Devereaux no ill will."

"I find that hard to believe, Sister."

"Faith, Mr. Weiss, is about believing even when the facts tell you otherwise. The Good Lord exists, despite Mr. Devereaux's opinion. I talk to Him every day. He gives me guidance and support. He shows me miracles, small and large. I carry on His work. And part of my ministry is to convince others that He exists and that He loves them. Some day, I hope, Devereaux will come to believe in Him again."

"I wouldn't bet on that, Sister."

"I don't gamble, Mr. Weiss. I pray—for Devereaux and for you. I pray for the whole world. By the way, I already told Colonel Truman that we haven't seen anyone who looks like Devereaux. You can, of course, check with the doctor. She's seen many of the men rather more intimately than I have. But I don't think she'll be able to help you, either."

"Thank you, Sister. And I thank you for your prayers too. I can certainly use them. Where is this doctor?"

"In the infirmary," Sister Ezekiel pointed to the doorway, "treating several wounded men."

"I think one of them is a pseudo," Colonel Truman interjected.

"A Mars Project astronaut?" Weiss said.

"I don't know, sir. I don't recognize him, and the DS-9000 isn't up yet."

"Did you scan his fingerprints or irises?"

Colonel Truman glanced over at Major Sims, who looked down at her PlusPhone and shook her head, then glared at one of the sergeants. Colonel Truman said, "I'll do that right now, sir."

"Let's all go," Weiss said. He stepped into the infirmary, acknowledging the soldiers on guard duty with a nod, then stopped and stared at Cookie Monster, who was zipping up a pair of coveralls far too short for him. The cuffs ended halfway down his forearms and calves. The seams around his shoulders strained against his massive bulk. He looked like he might burst out of the fabric if he sneezed. Sister Ezekiel nearly laughed. Slowly, tentatively, Cookie Monster lowered himself to a sitting position on the gurney.

Tic lay on a bed sleeping, and several other men who had suffered cuts and bruises in the original melee stood off to the side whispering. When Weiss entered the room, they hushed, lowered their heads and quickly moved past him out the door. As the last one exited, Weiss stepped toward Dr. Mary with his hand outstretched and a disarming smile. Sister Ezekiel watched Dr. Mary's expression, wondering if she would succumb to the famous Gray Weiss charm.

She needn't have worried. Dr. Mary merely glanced down at his hand and said, "I take it you're the one responsible for all this?"

"I'm sorry, Doctor," Weiss said, lowering his hand. "This violence is most regrettable. But we're after a very dangerous man and that sometimes means using a higher level of force than is comfortable."

Dr. Mary turned to Colonel Truman. "What setting are those stun clubs on? And are they the Lockheed Martin Two-Point-Nines?"

"Yes, they are," Colonel Truman answered. Gently, the colonel reached for Cookie Monster's hand, as if afraid of startling the big man. But Cookie Monster allowed him to press each finger to the PlusPhone. "They're set at four."

"Four!" Dr. Mary exclaimed. "You're not dealing with fit young men. It's one thing to hit a big man like Cookie Monster with a four, but a little guy like Tic, it's a wonder you didn't kill him."

"Dr. McCaffery, is it?" Weiss interjected.

"Dr. Mary."

"Yes, well, how is it that you know so much about stun clubs?"

"I did a year at a clinic in Los Angeles. They tested the Two-Point-Nines there in a couple of riots. I saw my share of cases."

Weiss nodded. He looked at Dr. Mary with concern, though he

spoke in a mellifluous voice: "There have been far too many riots lately, far too many preventable acts of violence. I know you're upset by what the soldiers did. Understandably so. I wish there were an easier way to achieve our objective. But if there is, I can't think of it. We need to find Devereaux. We need him off the airwaves. Surely you can appreciate that?"

Dr. Mary ignored the question and turned to Sister Ezekiel, who said, "What do you wish us to do? Apart from allowing you to set up your scanner?"

"I want you to trust that what I'm doing is right. I don't want to be seen as a jackbooted thug, bringing law and order at the point of a gun. I know too well how force can be misused."

Dr. Mary said, "So you want us to be happy about your invasion of our shelter?"

"I want you to cooperate with us. Help us do our job. Get us out of your hair as quickly as possible. Surely you don't object to that?" Dr. Mary folded her arms under her breasts and stared at him. After a moment he said, "Yes, well...I don't know much about you, Doctor. And that worries me."

"You think I'm a criminal?"

"In this day and age you could be hiding a lot."

Dr. Mary looked down at her plump belly. "It's kind of hard to hide this. Every year God makes my hair a little thinner and my body a little thicker."

Weiss laughed, then turned to Sister Ezekiel. "However, I know a good deal about you, Sister. And I certainly understand the pain you've endured." He stepped past her to the wall-window that led to her office, looked through it, his back to the room, allowing her at least a shred of privacy, and continued, "No wonder you decided to devote your life to God. Most impressive, the way you turned a truly awful nightmare into a catalyst for good."

The blood rushed to Sister Ezekiel's face. She said, "I was already a servant of God when that happened, Mr. Weiss. And I forgave those men a long time ago."

Across the room, Cookie Monster sat on the gurney looking at her with his usual emptiness, as if the conversation had drifted by above his head. The guards at the door stood still, ignoring her. But Colonel Truman looked up from his PlusPhone. He watched her, not slyly or out of the corner of his eye but steadily—a hesitant smile that might have contained sympathy. His eyelids drooped fractionally. Dr. Mary seemed to sag in sorrow.

Colonel Truman cleared his throat and said, "No record of the fingerprints on file, sir." He held up his PlusPhone.

"Nothing?" Weiss said. He turned from the wall-window and strode over to the colonel. He grabbed the PlusPhone, ran his eyes across it. "So he's not with the Mars Project?" He turned toward Cookie Monster and stared at the giant's face. Cookie Monster watched him unconcernedly.

In the quiet that followed, images flashed through Sister Ezekiel's brain: two men punching and kicking her, breaking her bones and stealing her virginity, leaving her shattered and sickeningly numb. She saw Dr. Mary watching her closely, felt the humiliation all over again. It had been a long time since anyone had brought up that horrible nightmare. She'd thought she'd buried it long ago.

Why was she still embarrassed by the assault? Her body was just a vessel that held her soul, and her soul had not been damaged. Noticing a drop of blood on her left shoe, she conquered an urge to wipe it off on the back of her leg. Another flashback: to paramedics and police—everyone acting so solicitous, succoring her when what she wanted was vengeance despite her vows. She pulled herself back to the present. Somehow Weiss had deflated her, diminished her by complimenting her. Was it because she still hadn't overcome her shame and anger from an ancient wrong? Or was it simply pride? Did she rankle at having her hidden past exposed to Dr. Mary?

Weiss handed the PlusPhone back to Colonel Truman and turned to face Sister Ezekiel again. He must have seen something in her face because he said, "I'm sorry if I upset you, Sister. I didn't mean to. I just meant to say that what you've done is most admirable. I don't know how you manage to spend your life around men. Some of them must be violent criminals, rapists. I don't think I'd have the courage to do what you do if I were in your shoes."

Sister Ezekiel, her anger fading, couldn't help but admire his gifted tongue. Realizing that he'd cut her off at the legs, Weiss now propped her up effortlessly, brilliantly.

Dr. Mary spoke up: "You needn't pretend to be ignorant of courage, Mr. Weiss. You're quite a brave man. So say the media. And who am I to argue? A career with the CIA, then law school and a judgeship. Your willingness to travel into areas ravaged by crime, your efforts to fight for law and order, your work with blighted communities to bring about peaceful streets."

Weiss dropped his head, as if embarrassed by the praise.

"But," Dr. Mary continued, "Sister Ezekiel is a different kind of brave. She confronts her fear every day. She does what she does without publicity, without ambition, without an agenda of any sort except to provide for men who can no longer provide for themselves. Regardless of her reasons for being here, she's a hero in my book. The bravest of the brave. You are a seeker after power. And that taints you. Although you are a brave man, never forget that she's a better person than you or I will ever be."

Sister Ezekiel gave Dr. Mary a grateful smile. She felt an immense rush of love for this kind woman, and proud that someone as selfless as the doctor should rise to her defense. How could she ask for a better staff?

"I would never suggest otherwise," Weiss said. "I was merely trying, in my own clumsy way, to pay the good sister a compliment. Please forgive me for touching on such a sensitive subject. Perhaps I should stick to business. Now this man," Weiss pointed to Cookie Monster, "definitely concerns me."

Weiss took several steps toward Cookie Monster, who scrunched up his face in a ferocious scowl, bared his teeth and growled. Weiss jumped back as Cookie Monster slapped himself on the thigh and laughed heartily. Dr. Mary grinned. And Sister Ezekiel found herself smiling.

"Don't mind him," Sister Ezekiel said. "He does that to everyone."

Weiss put a hand to his chest. "He nearly gave me a heart attack."

Dr. Mary said, "I take it as a good sign. It means he's probably feeling a lot better."

Weiss rubbed his chin, eyeing Cookie Monster warily. "I still think he's a pseudo. Perhaps his mind is starting to go. At any rate, his presence confirms that Devereaux is in the area."

"Why do you say that?" Sister Ezekiel asked.

"Devereaux has been known to associate with pseudos. And recently, a reliable source confirmed that Devereaux was in this area."

"So you've only got hearsay evidence that he's here?" Dr. Mary said.

"Are you a lawyer too?" Weiss looked at Dr. Mary with arched eyebrows. "You certainly have a wide range of knowledge." Weiss paused for a second. "From a cosmopolitan city to rural Minnesota. An odd move, wouldn't you say?"

Dr. Mary returned his stare without flinching. "I'm trying to give a little something back. You should think about doing the same one of these days."

Weiss nodded. "Very commendable. That's a pretty nice interface you're wearing, Doctor."

"It's also pretty necessary. I run into a wide variety of ailments in this place. Having ready access to current medical thinking is critical when the facilities I work in are so far behind the times."

Weiss finally broke eye contact with Dr. Mary, as if conceding her right to be there. "Devereaux is definitely not behind the times. He's undoubtedly been altered or enhanced physically. He's probably no longer recognizable. But I would guess he's still tall and lean and well spoken."

"Well spoken doesn't fit very many," Dr. Mary said. "Some of these men are quite intelligent. But most have mental illnesses or brain damage caused by drugs. As for Devereaux, I don't know that I would have recognized him before he altered his appearance. People rarely look like they do on the cover of Newsweek. Even you don't look as good in person as you do on TV."

Major Sims stuck her head through the doorway and said, "Excuse me, sir. The DS-9000 is ready to go."

"Let's get started," Colonel Truman replied. "We'll need your male employees to go through first, Sister."

Sister Ezekiel laughed. "You think any of them could be Devereaux?"

"We can't rule anyone out," Weiss said. He pointed at Cookie Monster. "We'll do him too. Right after we get the comparators."

"Very well," Sister Ezekiel said. "But Jackson and Tremaine—my cooks—are still in the kitchen. Can you scan them later?"

"Of course," Weiss said. He pointed to Cookie Monster and said to the guards, "Bring him out."

Out in the lobby, Doug and Henry stood in a corner, the tall black man and the short plump albino, chatting with the homeless men, as far away from the DS-9000 as they could get. Huddled together like so many sheep while a handful of soldiers surrounded them, the men kept glancing at the machine that blocked the entryway. The DS-9000 was large and charcoal gray, with a metal arch that was clearly the mechanism by which it analyzed one's DNA. It contained monitors on one side, a series of touchpads on the other, and a light band that traveled the length of the arch.

Sister Ezekiel walked over to the group of men in the corner, Colonel Truman at her heels. She said, "Doug. Henry. The colonel here wishes you to go through the scanner."

"Me?" Doug asked.

"Routine," the colonel said. "We need a couple people to go through for comparison's sake. Plus it might help put the men at ease seeing you two go through first. It's painless. Only takes about a minute each. Who's first?"

"I'll go," Henry volunteered, his eyes narrowing until the pinks nearly disappeared behind his pale eyelids. "I hope you find the son of a bitch. He deserves whatever you do to him."

"Henry," Sister Ezekiel admonished. "That's hardly a charitable attitude. God commands us to love our fellow man."

"Sorry, Sister, but he's evil."

Major Sims stepped forward. "If you'll step over here, sir," she said. "Just stand under the arch until the machine beeps."

Henry moved to the designated area and stood with his hands at his sides, while a technician started the machine. A low hum emanated from it, then a series of clicks. Across the top of the arch, a blue light spread from left to right, painting Henry's pale skin a sickly hue. When it finally reached the other side, the machine beeped.

"You may step out," the technician said.

"See," Weiss said, "there's nothing to it."

"All right," the colonel said to Doug. "You're next."

Doug hesitated, looked at Sister Ezekiel as if hoping for a reprieve. But she could only shrug her shoulders. One of the soldiers jerked his stun club toward the machine and Doug trudged over, stopping under the arch. As the scanner hummed and clicked, Doug shut his eyes, moving his lips in what seemed a silent prayer. The blue light progressed across the archway. Finally the scanner beeped. Doug opened his eyes and relaxed his face.

"You may step out," the technician repeated.

Doug exited the arch. As he began walking away, a chime sounded from the machine. Doug froze. Major Sims stepped over next to the technician and checked a screen as the nearest soldier moved next to Doug, hefting her stun club. Sister Ezekiel watched Doug's face. His eyes widened in fear. A sheen covered his forehead.

"You'd better take a look at this, sir," Major Sims said.

Colonel Truman and the Attorney General strode to the scanner.

Oh, Dear Lord, Sister Ezekiel thought. Doug is Devereaux! He doesn't look anything like the man—black rather than Devereaux's white, and far too young. Still, he is tall and lean.

While everyone in the room waited, a buzz of whispers emanating from the homeless men as well as the soldiers, Weiss and the colonel examined the screen. Touching the display, Weiss read for a moment before turning to Sister Ezekiel. "I'm afraid, Sister, that your man is a fugitive."

Sister Ezekiel's stomach grew queasy as she looked at Doug, who looked nauseated himself. When she spoke, her voice had a slight tremor. "Douglas is Walt Devereaux?"

Weiss shook his head. "No, but he is a fugitive. Escaped from a minimum-security facility while serving time on a possession charge. Had just over a month remaining in his sentence."

"You must be mistaken," Sister Ezekiel said. But when she turned to Doug, he dropped his head and refused to meet her eyes. "Douglas."

"Sorry, Sister."

"Why, Douglas?"

"I couldn't take bein' penned up like that. I had to get out."

"So little time left to serve." Sister Ezekiel shook her head slowly.

"Take him outside," Weiss said to a pair of soldiers. "Put him in the Porta-cell. Keep a guard on him."

The homeless men muttered among themselves, shifting their feet and staring at Doug as he looked back at them sadly. No doubt many of them had known of his status. Sister Ezekiel knew the men opened up to each other more than they did to her. She found it difficult to relax around them. But everybody liked Doug. He treated them all fairly and with respect.

"What's going to happen to him now?" Sister Ezekiel asked as the soldiers led Doug away.

Weiss shrugged. "That's really not up to me to say, Sister. It's a matter for the local authorities."

"But you're the Attorney General. I need Douglas here. He's a great help."

"I'm sorry, Sister. The law is clear."

"Well, can't you put a detention collar on him? Restrict him to the shelter? I'll vouch for him, make sure he doesn't leave."

"I'll think about it," Weiss said. "In the meantime, Colonel, let's get the rest of these men through the scanner, starting with—what did you call him, the chocolate beast?"

"Cookie Monster, Sir." Colonel Truman stepped over to Cookie

Monster, who stared at the machine, a faint tremor running through him. "It's okay," the colonel said. "I promise it won't hurt. You won't feel a thing. In fact, the doctor can come with you."

Dr. Mary smiled gratefully at the colonel. She patted Cookie Monster's hand, then led him to the DS-9000. After she got him settled under the arch, she took one step back and held her arm straight out so Cookie Monster could continue to hold her hand.

"That's fine," Colonel Truman said. "Very good. We'll still be able to get a reading, right?"

"Yes, sir," the technician answered.

For a third time the scanner ran through its program, the blue light over the arch moving across from left to right. Sister Ezekiel caught the sudden tension in the room. The only sound came from the DS-9000 itself—a high whining hum and a series of clicks. The homeless men, the soldiers, Dr. Mary and Weiss: everybody waited quietly for the scanner to complete its task.

Cookie Monster shook as the scanner worked. When the machine finally beeped, men resumed conversations with each other and the familiar buzz of low talking returned.

"You may step out," the technician said.

Dr. Mary tugged on Cookie Monster's hand and he practically leapt out from under the archway. He hugged Dr. Mary, his eyes squeezed shut, a grimace on his face.

Major Sims, Colonel Truman and Weiss all huddled around the screen.

"What do you make of this, Hayes?" Colonel Truman asked.

The technician edged into the pile and stared at the monitor. "I don't know, sir. I've never seen anything like this before. Looks like a B-F-S-T of point-eight-nine. And there are strange double helixes here and here and here." He indicated three spots on the monitor.

"And that means?" the colonel asked.

"I'm not sure," Hayes answered, "but I think it means he might not be human. Well, he's human, obviously, but his genetic code is different."

Dr. Mary said, "What does that mean exactly? Can you dumb it down for us?"

Sister Ezekiel looked at her, wondering why she would ask such a question. Dr. Mary obviously knew about such things. She was the brightest woman Sister Ezekiel had ever met.

"I'll try, ma'am," Hayes said. "I'm not an expert on this. But the Brin-Wright F statistic—or BFST—quantifies the amount of genetic difference between two groups of people. It runs from zero to one. The higher the number, the more likely you're dealing with a new species. Anything over one and you're talking a different species. We're using Devereaux's DNA profile as our base. So if we find him, we'll come up with a zero reading. And the helix graph will come up with an identical curve, here." He pointed to a spot on the monitor.

"Okay," the colonel said.

"A BFST of point-eight-nine is unheard of," Major Sims interjected.

"That's right," Hayes agreed. "The greatest variation ever found between two human groups is point-seven-three. He blows that away."

"And look at this," Major Sims said. "His brainwave activity is extremely high. He's very intelligent."

"Cookie Monster?" Henry said, his eyes wide.

"No question about it," Major Sims said.

Dr. Mary led Cookie Monster to Sister Ezekiel and handed him over. Then she made her way to the scanner and wedged herself between the colonel and Weiss, who stepped aside to admit her to their circle.

"So," Weiss said. "This proves Cookie Monster is a pseudo."

"Not necessarily," Hayes said. "The aberration in the readings could suggest some other kind of DNA manipulation, or possibly just heavy drug use with some serious chemicals."

"What about the brainwave activity?" Weiss asked.

Major Sims pointed to another screen. "It only proves he's extremely intelligent. But there are no aberrations in the graph to imply genetic enhancement."

"What do you think, Doctor?" Colonel Truman asked.

Dr. Mary shrugged. "As I recall, the pseudos from the Mars Project came in at point-nine-four. A point-eight-nine clearly puts Cookie Monster outside that group. It means he might not be a pseudo at all. As Mr. Hayes here said, it might just be high drug usage with designer chemicals. God only knows how many men here are going to pull a high number because of that factor. As for the brainwave pattern, I've seen scans higher than this, but you're right. He's smart."

"Perhaps he's a Gaian," Sister Ezekiel interjected.

"A Gaian?" Colonel Truman asked.

Sister Ezekiel smiled. "Mother Earth worshipers. People who believe we should become one with nature. It's been rumored that some of them have attempted scientific procedures to make themselves one with the plants and animals."

"Yes, I'm familiar with them," Colonel Truman said. "Are there many in the area?"

"I don't know," Sister Ezekiel replied. "But we get many different kinds of worshippers here. We don't ask for religious affiliation."

Weiss said, "Any Gaians attempting to alter their DNA would be acting illegally unless they're registered. Unregulated DNA manipulation is very dangerous. That's why we passed the DNA Integrity Act. You'd better lock up Cookie Monster too, Colonel, while we check the rest of the men."

Sister Ezekiel pointed at the men standing around the lobby. "A lot of these men were heavy drug users at one point. Many were sentenced to prison. But with the jails so full, they've been released on parole. Are you now planning to re-arrest them?"

"No, Sister," Weiss replied. "Fugitives like Doug, pseudos like Cookie Monster, and Devereaux. That's all."

"You haven't proven that Cookie Monster's a pseudo," Dr. Mary said in a loud voice, "yet you're calling him one. You think you can do anything you want, don't you."

"Certainly not," Weiss answered. "I'm bound by the law, as we all are."

"Then perhaps you should arrest Sister Ezekiel," Dr. Mary said. "She's been harboring a fugitive. Maybe, just to be on the safe side, you should lock us all up. We're obviously a threat."

"All right, Doctor," Weiss said. "That will be enough."

"Are we breaking the law if we don't agree with the government's position on absolutely every issue? Is that why you harass and intimidate us?"

"Doctor," Sister Ezekiel said, "I think we should give Mr. Weiss the benefit of the doubt. He's just doing his job."

Weiss laughed, but his cheeks burned with anger. "Thank you, Sister. You know, some people trust me completely."

"Not me," Dr. Mary muttered.

"Look, people," Weiss spoke up so everyone in the room could hear him: "I don't like doing this, believe me. I know you resent me. You think I'm against you. And if I were in your shoes I might feel the same way. But I'm not. I've been charged with looking at the big picture, with making the hard decisions. I don't want to be a tough guy. I don't get joy from locking people up. But to keep our society moving forward, to keep some semblance of order, a certain amount of dirty work has to get done."

Weiss paused, looking his audience over. "You have a president," he continued, "who can't get along with Congress and who refuses to acknowledge the mess this country is in. And I will not allow it to remain a mess. My mission is to restore civil order, reduce crime, make the streets safe for every American. And I'll do whatever I must to see that those goals are achieved. I will not allow this country to become a lawless wasteland."

Dr. Mary leaned over to Sister Ezekiel and whispered, "There aren't even any cameras around. He must really believe this crap."

Chapter Seven

After breakfasting in pointed silence, Lendra stowed her bag in the back of the van, then slumped into the front passenger seat and stared straight ahead as Jeremiah exited the hotel's secure ramp and returned to the freeway. He passed three tractor-trailers caravanning west over the bumpy road and reflexively checked his scanner. But he knew the trucks were legitimate.

"Did you get your interface working?" Jeremiah asked.

Long seconds passed before Lendra said, "Finally. Took most of the night."

"I'm sorry if I offended you, but I can't afford any distractions. Any messages from Eli?"

Lendra yawned as she shook her head. "Nothing new."

"If you want to sleep for a while," Jeremiah pointed to the bench seat with his thumb, "it's pretty comfortable back there."

"I'm fine." Lendra turned away, stared out the side window, showing him the back of her head. After a time she said, "Maybe I'll close my eyes for a bit." She reclined the seat and shifted restlessly a few times before finally turning to face him. Bringing her legs up off the floor, she tucked her hands beneath her cheek and closed her eyes like a storybook angel. In minutes, she appeared to be asleep.

For the next hour Jeremiah drove in near-silence. He knew he ought to focus on the mission, but his mind kept drifting to Joshua. Was he in a shallow grave somewhere? Sold into slavery?

A low tone emanated from the dashboard. The scanner. Jeremiah's neck hairs rose. He checked the energy signature and saw that it was the same one he'd detected the day before, now behind them nearly a mile. Their pursuer must have driven past them during the night, then re-locked onto Jeremiah's signal this morning.

Instinctively Jeremiah blinked three times, centering himself in his dungeon, preparing himself for battle. He increased power to the shield. Should he wait for the enemy to make the first move? If Lendra weren't here he'd attack. Up ahead another van moved slowly in the right lane. He checked his scanner as he passed it; seven people stared out the windows at him. Their own little group. Jeremiah accelerated past them. As far ahead as he could see, the road was clear.

Crossing the Mississippi River into Minnesota, Jeremiah noted the river bluffs covered with trees. The Minnesota side looked wild: no buildings visible from the freeway. The Wisconsin border boasted extensive commercial development. And the river itself contained hundreds of boats—tugs and barges mostly, with a few large passenger vessels sprinkled among them.

An electric pulse hit the van.

The vehicle stuttered, then jumped forward, the alarm sounding. In less than two seconds Jeremiah activated the auxiliary battery, deactivated the alarm and sent full power to the variable shield. Another pulse hit the van; this time the shield dispersed it.

"Looks like we fight," Jeremiah said.

Lendra sat up quickly. "Huh? What's happening?" she asked. "Where are we?"

"Ah, you're awake. Good. We're in Minnesota."

"Are we under attack?"

"I'm afraid so."

Lendra's hands clenched the armrest tightly and her body tensed.

"Hold on." Jeremiah stomped on the accelerator, bringing the van up to ninety. When he reached the next exit he sped up the ramp. Lendra grabbed the handle on the door and clung to it, her jaw rigid, as Jeremiah approached the stop sign. He slowed just enough to make the turn, then jerked the wheel, careening the van around the corner onto a county road. Speeding through the countryside, he looked for a good place to wait. When he spotted a side road, he took it, stopping the van near a small stand of trees.

"I'll call Eli," Lendra said.

"Fine," Jeremiah said. "Wait here." He slipped his hands into the gloves of his camos, then dropped the hood over his head and activated the sensors. Lendra gasped as he essentially disappeared—his old camos giving off only faint swirls of movement to betray his position. Jeremiah ducked into the back of the van, grabbed an ear bud/microphone, checked the frequency, and inserted it into his left ear. "Channel 8.76," he said.

"Wait!" Lendra said.

Jeremiah grabbed a small bag from behind the bench seat, deactivated the shield and threw the bag out of the van. Then he reactivated the shield and stepped outside himself. As he passed through the barrier of the shield, an electric tingle made his hair stand on end. He picked up the bag and ran for the trees, dropping to his knees and assembling the Las-rifle he'd packed. Snapping the power cartridge in place, he set the power level to medium. The thirty-inch weapon felt good in his hands, its eight-pound weight comforting. That meant he had a full cartridge. He double-checked the indicator to make certain the chemicals inside had activated completely. Slowly he swept in a circle, checking for anything that moved. Back along the road a motorcycle came into view and veered into a field several hundred yards away, its rider low in the saddle.

Jeremiah glanced at his hand-held scanner to verify that he had the right target before firing. It showed the recognizable electronic signature of their pursuer. As the motorcyclist disappeared behind a small grove of trees, Jeremiah fired a purple pulse. Too late. The shot missed, striking an oak. Fortunately the area must have seen a lot of rain recently, for the tree did not burst into flame. Jeremiah checked his scanner, saw the target stop somewhere beyond the trees. He altered it to scan for a bio-signature and located a human reading several hundred yards away.

He figured the enemy would wait, hoping to make him nervous, jumpy. A good plan normally. But Jeremiah had long ago learned to block out such emotions.

The ear bud crackled, then Lendra's voice came through clearly: "What do you want me to do?"

"Stay there," he ordered. "I'll be back shortly. Keep the doors locked, the shield up. You'll be fine."

Jeremiah checked his scanner again. Now it read only Lendra's bio-signature. The guy must have activated a scatterer. Jeremiah grabbed four stun grenades from the bag and placed them inside his pockets, then ran to the drainage ditch and turned in the direction the motorcycle had gone. He experienced a strange exhilaration, a joy in movement that he hadn't felt in a long time, as if his body was finally freed to do what it had been meant for. If he hadn't seen his Brin-Wright F Statistic after his genetic enhancement surgery, he'd believe he was like the Escala: part human, part animal. When he reached the county road he stopped, listened for a few seconds, then took off again, across the road and into the drainage ditch on the other side. The grove hiding their pursuer lay up ahead.

Jeremiah followed the ditch, parallel to the county road. As he neared the grove, he slowed, placing his feet carefully, looking and listening for anything that sounded out of place. A single crow cawed off in the distance, and about a hundred yards away down a dirt road, an old shed stood. A fresh tire track ran down the center of the road.

His finger on the trigger, Jeremiah ran for the shed. Its door stood ajar, the inside hidden in darkness. He reached the corner of the building, then sidled to the doorway. Hesitating only a second, he kicked the door open and tossed a stun grenade inside. A second after it exploded, he rushed inside. Empty.

Around back he found the man's motorcycle: hydrogen-cell powered, whisper quiet. The modifications made to it were extensive, including an array of communications equipment, scanners and a brand new scatterer.

As he turned away, he heard the sizzle of a Las-weapon, echoed almost immediately by a hiss as it struck a shield. The van. Another sizzle and hiss followed. Then another.

Lendra spoke in his ear, her voice high and strained: "Someone's shooting at the van. I think he's hiding behind a tree. Can't see him. What should I do?"

"Don't do anything," Jeremiah said as he left at a run. "I'll be right there." He reached the grove in seconds, loping effortlessly over the terrain, working his way back toward the van between tree trunks, checking for booby traps, though the guy couldn't have had time to put down anything very sophisticated. More sizzles told him their pursuer was still shooting at the van—obviously trying to destroy the shield. Movies often showed shields exploding when a Las-weapon fired at them continuously. But those were usually low-quality shields. Jeremiah had the best that money could buy.

"I think he's behind a tree off to the right," Lendra said, her voice marginally calmer. "Still can't see him."

Jeremiah reached the edge of the grove and peered through the silky hood that kept him invisible. The shield surrounding the van glowed orange, so it was still safe. Only when it reached a reddish hue would it be on the verge of collapse. Jeremiah studied the trees, searching for their pursuer. Then he spotted a Las-rifle's red pulse—the highest power setting. It came from behind a tree several meters in front of him.

"The shield's glowing," Lendra said, her voice quavering slightly.

"It'll be fine," Jeremiah whispered. "Stay put." He worked his way along the treeline to the left, hoping to get a view of the shooter, and finally spotted a swirl of movement; the man was wearing camos. A small rectangular box hung in the air at waist-high level: the man's scatterer. Jeremiah changed the setting on his Las-rifle to low power, then fired a short blue pulse at the center of the swirl of movement, just above the scatterer. As the man dropped, his Las-rifle clattered to the ground. Jeremiah ran forward, picked up the man's Las-rifle and tossed it toward his van, then felt along the bulky clothing until he found the camos' hood and pulled it off.

"I've got him," Jeremiah said to Lendra as he reached inside the man's camos, found the activation unit, switched it off and then broke it. He tore the man's jacket along the left arm as he ripped off the scatterer and caught sight of a *Semper Fi* tattoo.

The van door opened, a click audible over the hum of the van's shield. When Jeremiah glanced toward the van, he saw the orange color of its shield fading as the energy from the man's Las-rifle dispersed.

"Who is he?" Lendra asked as she approached, her eyes on Jeremiah's Las-rifle.

"He'll come to in a moment." Jeremiah said. He pulled his scanner out of a pocket and checked carefully for biosigns. Apart from his, Lendra's and the man's, there were no signatures even close to human-sized. Jeremiah deactivated his camos and removed his hood.

The man groaned, his eyes blinking slowly as he rolled onto his back. He squinted up at Jeremiah.

"What's your name," Jeremiah asked him.

The man's eyes widened. He said, "I know you're a killer. And you aren't getting Devereaux."

A quiet hum sounded in the distance; a slight vibration tickled Jeremiah's feet. "Get back in the van," he said to Lendra. He shoved her in that direction as a red laser pulse sizzled by, narrowly missing him, striking a tree and sending up a plume of fire. Jeremiah threw himself at Lendra, pushing her to the ground as another red pulse sailed past. He said, "Stay down."

Then he sprinted back into the trees, cursing himself for his carelessness. He shouldn't have assumed the guy was alone. He'd been too long out of the field.

Another laser pulse sizzled, striking the tree he was using for shelter. A branch above him burst into flames with a roar. Over the din, he heard a rustling sound, turned to see the big ex-Marine lunging at him with a knife. Jeremiah tried to parry the blow with his Las-rifle but he was a fraction of a second too slow. The knife sliced into his forearm. He dropped his Las-rifle and grabbed the ex-Marine's wrist tightly, saw the big man's eyes suddenly narrow, and knew what was coming. As the ex-Marine drove the knife forward, Jeremiah resisted. But even as Jeremiah pushed back, the ex-Marine turned his wrist, applying all his strength to the weak point of Jeremiah's thumb, pulling the knife back toward himself. It was an unbeatable move, the kind of move that works against even a prepared opponent, against even an enhanced human like Jeremiah, but it assumes the opponent will try to hang on. Jeremiah didn't. In the instant he felt the pressure on his thumb, he pushed away hard, helping the ex-Marine pull the knife backward. At the same time, he reached over and grabbed the big man's hair, yanking his whole body forward. The knife, razor sharp and traveling backward with all the force the attacker could muster, sliced through the ex-Marine's abdomen.

The man gasped in shock, then toppled, all the fight gone out of him.

Jeremiah collected his Las-rifle again, rage building inside him at his own stupidity. He reactivated his camos and slid deeper into the trees, sprinting to his right. From a parked vehicle up the road, someone fired in his general direction. Red pulses hit the trees around him, setting more branches aflame. The guy was shooting at him over the hood of his car, activating a personal shield between pulses. Jeremiah kept moving to his right. He switched the power setting on his Las-rifle to high, waiting for the right opportunity. He needed to time his shot perfectly. He'd only have a split second to make the kill, while the enemy dropped his shield to fire at Jeremiah.

Stepping from behind a tree, his Las-rifle aimed toward the car, Jeremiah serpentined forward, hoping to draw the man's fire. Again Jeremiah experienced a kind of predatory joy, every muscle quivering with excitement, every sense hyperaware. He felt absolute confidence in his ability to take the man out. And when the man poked his head up above the hood, opening his shield to fire, Jeremiah squeezed the trigger.

His red pulse hit the man in the head, instantly killing him. Jeremiah sprinted forward. He reached the car in seconds, saw no one inside, then ran back toward the ex-Marine, who lay on the ground, his hands clutched to his stomach, cursing softly as bits of burning ash floated from the flaming branch above him.

Lendra still crouched on the ground next to the van, safe.

Jeremiah breathed a sigh of relief as he removed his hood and deactivated his camos. Grabbing the ex-Marine's knife, Jeremiah flicked it aside. Then he pulled back his sleeve and checked his arm. It bled freely.

"You okay?" Jeremiah asked Lendra.

She looked up at him. "I think so," she said.

Jeremiah glanced up at the tree. The branch seemed to be burning itself out. Reaching into a pocket, Jeremiah pulled out a large QuikHeal bandage, then knelt in front of the wounded ex-Marine.

"Who are you?" he asked.

The man glared at him for a second, then said, "Raddock Boyd."

"Well, Raddock Boyd," Jeremiah said, "that's a nasty wound. I was stabbed like that once." He waved the QuikHeal bandage in front of Boyd's face. Boyd followed it with his eyes, then looked past it at Jeremiah.

"You won't get Devereaux," Boyd said. "We'll stop you."

"Who sent you?"

"Friends of Devereaux."

"Why me? How did you know to follow me?"

Boyd looked at the bandage again. "That for me?"

"Answer my questions," Jeremiah said.

"I'm not afraid to die," Boyd said. He removed his hands from his stomach, as if to prove his point. "As long as Devereaux is saved."

"You don't have to die today," Jeremiah said. "Now tell me, how did you know to follow me?"

"Orders."

"Whose orders?"

"We know who you are," Boyd said. He clutched his stomach again. "We know you work for Elias Leach and that you've been sent to kill Devereaux."

"How do you know this?"

Boyd didn't answer. His face paled. The mole under his left eye lightened in color. Jeremiah decided he could wait no longer. He ripped open Boyd's shirt, then removed the bandage from its package and placed it firmly over the deep cut in Boyd's abdomen. He pressed the strip on the bandage that adjusted the flow of painkillers and antibiotics, set the dispersal to maximum.

Almost immediately Boyd's eyes lost focus as the anesthetic worked its way into the wound.

"Who sent you?" Jeremiah asked again, but Boyd simply smiled, a dreamy expression on his face. Jeremiah would get no information from the ex-Marine now. He spoke quietly, "You got the wrong intel, Raddock, I'm one of the good guys. I don't want to kill you, but if you get in my way again I will."

He left Boyd lying on the ground and made his way over to Lendra. "Let's go," he said, grabbing her elbow. "There might be more of them headed this way."

Inside a minute they were back on the road, but Jeremiah couldn't relax; Boyd knew too much about his mission. It struck Jeremiah that Boyd might know even more than he himself did, a thought that raised the hair on the back of his neck. Had Eli sent him? That seemed doubtful. Was Lendra here to assassinate Devereaux? No, whatever she was, Lendra was no Julianna.

Chapter Eight

Lendra had seen footage of Jeremiah during training sessions, yet she found herself amazed at how quickly he could move, how deadly he could be. Raddock Boyd, the tough ex-Marine, had stood no chance against him. Nor had his partner. She remembered Eli's prediction that Jeremiah would be a little rusty and suddenly wondered if Eli had arranged for Boyd to find them, just to give Jeremiah a last-minute practice session. Eli specialized in that kind of obsessive preparation. He thought of everything. If she hoped to take Eli's place some day, she would have to learn to do the same.

When Jeremiah took his eye off the road to check his scanner, Lendra said, "You're bleeding."

"Med kit's in the back," Jeremiah said. "QuikHeal bandages inside."

Lendra rummaged through the kit until she found a bandage, then said, "Give me your hand."

Pulling back his shirtsleeve, she examined his arm. Although the cut was six inches long and nearly half an inch at its deepest, the bleeding had almost stopped. She knew more about his enhancements than he did, but still—this kind of healing was remarkable. She held his hand a few seconds longer than necessary, breathing in the intoxicating, almost animal muskiness of his sweat. Then she tenderly applied the QuikHeal bandage and pressed the low dispersal setting.

"Thanks," he said.

"You probably don't even need it." She released his hand. "Why didn't you kill him?"

She studied his face. He could have killed Boyd easily, justifiably. Why hadn't he? She recalled a notation from his file—a psychologist's concern that his innate morality might inhibit his performance in the field. Yet he had acted swiftly and decisively back there, taking out the shooter without mercy, even though he'd spared Boyd's life.

"I don't kill out of convenience," Jeremiah said. "Keep an eye out for Highway 52. That's our exit."

"Boyd could still be a threat," Lendra persisted. "He could contact others."

"Boyd is part of a much larger organization," Jeremiah said. "That equipment he and his partner had, and their intel—they've got some high backing. Whoever sent them knows who I am, knew our route and where we were likely to stay. Boyd's just one tiny piece of it. And he was a Marine. I didn't need to kill him."

He pointed out the window. "Look." Glancing that way, Lendra caught a brief glimpse of a large animal with black and yellow striping disappearing into the woods. Jeremiah said, "Did you see that?"

"A tiger?"

Jeremiah nodded. "What would a tiger be doing loose in Minnesota?"

Lendra accessed the CINTEP database via her interface and said, "There are over a hundred tigers in Minnesota. Ecoterrorists have been breaking them out of zoos for years, bringing them here and setting them free."

"Look at me," Jeremiah said.

Lendra turned to face him.

Jeremiah studied her for a long moment. "You took neo-dopamine again, didn't you?"

Lendra shrugged. "I got nervous waiting in the van. As you pointed out, I'm no field agent."

"You got some kind of psychological problem?"

Lendra stared out the window. Jeremiah's profile suggested that he found weakness endearing in otherwise strong women. And Eli had told her that Jeremiah would discover her claustrophobia during the trip. "It's what he was trained to do," Eli had said. "Find other people's weaknesses."

Lendra considered how best to draw him in. She couldn't lie; he'd catch that. "I have claustrophobia—a mild case."

"You should have told me. You got any other issues I should know about?"

Lendra shook her head. "Just the one." She reached for her necklace, caressed the glass bulb filled with her medication. "And the neodopamine worked."

Jeremiah stared into her eyes and she returned his gaze, aware that her pupils were slightly dilated. Her cheeks flushed with anger and embarrassment, but she hoped they didn't show it. Jeremiah nodded. "Don't withhold relevant information from me again."

"I won't." Lendra pointed to a sign. "There's Highway 52. Weiss' soldiers have checkpoints set up around Rochester. They've cordoned off the entire area."

Jeremiah took the exit and headed north. As they neared Rochester, Jeremiah braked for the first checkpoint, showed the soldier his Identi-card, and was waved through. The town bustled with soldiers, all wearing gas masks, conducting searches. Jeremiah drove through town at little more than a walking pace. The Mayo Clinic, rising up beside the highway in a series of tall white buildings, looked like it had been at the center of fierce fighting. Several buildings appeared to have been bombed. Piles of rubble sat before the gaping holes in the exterior walls, and most of the windows were broken.

"There was a battle here," Jeremiah said. "Las-weapons and particle beam cannons. Heavy-duty ordnance. I wonder when it happened. You got any information on it?"

"I'll call Eli. See what he knows."

Jeremiah eased the van past the Mayo Clinic, toward the north side of the city. Soldiers kept an eye on them as they rolled past. Lendra didn't see a single civilian anywhere. A glance down a side road showed vegetation sprouting up through the asphalt. The road looked impassable.

When Eli didn't answer, Lendra connected to his PlusPhone and left a message explaining the signs of battle. "That's odd," she said to Jeremiah. "No answer."

Jeremiah snorted. "Typical."

"Typical? He's always in the office. I wonder where he could be."

"Oh, he's there. He just doesn't want to talk to you."

"Why would you say that?"

"He's always testing, playing games. He's probably stringing you along too, hinting at his imminent retirement, telling you that if this mission goes well, you'll prove your worth as a potential successor." Jeremiah must have seen something in Lendra's face, for he laughed. "He'll leave when they carry him out on a stretcher. You think you're the first one he's promised to consider as his replacement?"

"But his health... He's thinking of buying that retirement place."

"In Albuquerque?" Jeremiah said. "He's been talking about that for years."

"So he's not going to retire?"

"Not a chance."

Lendra tugged on her earlobe. She knew Catherine used to do that when she was thinking. Eli had recommended she copy the gesture. And as much as she despised herself for obeying him, she knew it was necessary. If she were truly to rise to the top of CINTEP, take Eli's place some day—and she still intended to do that even if Eli wasn't ready to retire just yet—she had to be able to handle men like Jeremiah. Plus she found him fascinating.

"Now, let's get back to Devereaux and this Tessamae Shelter where he's supposed to be hiding."

"The psychological profile on Devereaux," she said, "is that he carries a tremendous amount of guilt. His strict Catholic upbringing, his desire for his parents' approval—especially his mother's—and his guilt over his father's death and his mother's suicide all weigh heavily on him."

At the mention of suicide, Lendra glanced at Jeremiah. Was he remembering Catherine, sprawled ungainly on the bed? Was he feeling again the guilt that came from knowing he'd arrived too late?

"That's one of the reasons he's at or near the shelter," Lendra continued. "He visits it because he admires the nun who runs it."

"Perhaps," Jeremiah conceded. "What's so special about the nun?"

"She's a strong Catholic with an independent mind—something

of a renegade. The shelter she runs is a haven for the disaffected—all men, almost all hiding something. Apparently, she refuses to allow the Church any say in the day-to-day operations of the shelter. If Devereaux approached her seeking sanctuary, she'd offer it."

"But now that Weiss is there, why doesn't Devereaux just run?"

"First, the Army has the place surrounded. No one gets in or out except through them."

Jeremiah shook his head. "Devereaux's got a big enough organization that he could figure out a way if he wanted to. Hell, he might be gone already. If it was me, I'd have taken off at the first sign that Weiss was on his way."

"That's a possibility," Lendra acknowledged. "But there's another reason Weiss and Eli believe he'll stay. Devereaux's psychological profile shows a man who's deeply conflicted. We think he's got a martyr complex. Plus, for the past few months he's been advocating for the Mars Project to go forward as planned, so it seems likely he's with the Escala."

"Okay. It's all we've got. So we'll just have to run with it. You say the Escala are hiding in the area, which means they've escaped from Rochester and are probably in the woods somewhere between here and Crescent Township. Of course, Weiss knows that too. We need to find a way in through the Escala. What about the Elite Ops? Any of them in the area?"

"Not that I know of," Lendra answered. "Though I wouldn't be surprised if the President orders them in."

Jeremiah nodded slowly as he drove, obviously planning his next move. Lendra, studying his face, decided that Eli was right. Jeremiah could be her greatest asset. With him, she could run CINTEP. Without him, she might not be able to hold the agency together, especially if Jeremiah actively worked against her. Eli believed Jeremiah would find her irresistible if she played him correctly. But he was sharp enough to spot any false approach, so she had to make herself actually want him. She had to convince herself that she was infatuated with him. Not a difficult thing to do.

Lendra contemplated Jeremiah's comment that Eli was just stringing her along. Could that be true? For a while, the only sound in the van was the hush-quiet purr of the engine and the humming of the tires on the rough road, punctuated by the occasional rush of a vehicle bumping along in the opposite direction.

"There's the exit for Crescent Township," Jeremiah said as he slowed to a stop. The road stretched northeast off Highway 52. Another group of soldiers had set up a checkpoint there. Once again Jeremiah handed over his Identi-card. When they saw the presidential authorization, they quickly waved the van through.

Jeremiah turned right. Up ahead potholes and fallen brush left the road barely passable.

"So what's our plan?" Lendra asked. "Go straight to the shelter?"

"Let's visit the famous statue—Emerging Man. I need to think."

"Eli won't be happy at the delay."

"That's the spirit." Jeremiah winked at her. "Always a silver lining if you look hard enough."

Lendra nearly opened her mouth to comment, then thought better of it. She needed to prove to Jeremiah that, in her own way, she was as tough as he was, and she deserved to be Eli's successor. If Eli was playing her, he'd regret it. She'd promised herself she'd run CINTEP one day and no matter what it took she intended to reach her goal.

Chapter Nine

While Major Sims directed the last few homeless men through the DS-9000, Colonel Truman monitored Captain Baynes' progress searching the town and Captain Lopez's progress through the woods east of the shelter. So far, there was no sign of Devereaux. Truman rubbed his eyes, trying to keep the fatigue at bay. He fingered his wedding ring, wondering yet again why he continued to wear it. He and Emily had been strangers for years now. Though they still shared the same house, they lived separate lives—she with her protester, vegan friends; he with the Army. The only thing holding them together was their daughter, McKenna, who lived in Portland. They saw her twice a year.

The scanner beeped and Major Sims said, "That's all of them so far, sir."

Truman stopped twirling his wedding ring. "No matches, obviously."

"None, sir. No major anomalies, either."

"That'll be all, Major. Detail a squad to man the DS-9000, then move the Porta-cell behind the shelter. I don't want it out front where every passerby can gawk at our prisoners. Also, let's get soldiers posted at the nearest intersections—north and south. Make our presence known but not too intrusive. You know the drill."

After Major Sims began her assigned tasks, Truman poked his head into Sister Ezekiel's office, where she and Dr. Mary sat chatting quietly. "We're finished for the time being, Sister."

Sister Ezekiel said, "For the time being? What does that mean?"

"I'll have to check with the Attorney General, Sister, but I'm sure we'll be here for a while yet."

Dr. Mary said, "And in the meantime we just ignore that monstrosity in the lobby? I don't think you appreciate the delicate nature of these men's psyches. They've already been scarred by society. They don't trust authority. And now you do this to them?"

"Do your best, Doctor," Truman said. "I can only apologize so many times."

He backed out of the office and made for Weiss' mobile command center—a reinforced panel truck crammed with communications equipment. The Attorney General remained a mystery, staying largely in his mobile command center, seldom interacting with the troops. He was supposed to be charismatic but, except for the speech he'd given inside the shelter today, Truman had seen nothing of that side of the man.

Weiss sat before a bank of monitors, checking various world events. He waved Truman inside the truck. "I assume you had no luck?"

Truman shrugged. "We can't find him if he isn't here. Have you considered that our information was wrong?"

Weiss sighed melodramatically. "Of course I've considered it."

"I'm sorry, sir. I didn't mean to question…"

"Quite all right, Colonel. I'd much rather have you question authority in the pursuit of truth than blindly follow some fool."

The colonel straightened himself another millimeter. "Thank you, sir."

"I tell you, Colonel, I have a feeling about this place. Devereaux's grandfather was one of the sculptors who created that statue. His ancestors are buried in that cemetery to the southeast. What about known associates, or pseudos? Any of them show up on the scanner?"

"No, sir."

Weiss nodded. "We'll give it a few days. Track down as many of these homeless men as we can. Were you ever briefed on the Battle of Rochester?"

"No, sir. I've heard rumors, of course. And I couldn't help but notice as we came through the town that there had been some sort of firefight there. But no hard facts."

Weiss rubbed his eyes with his hands. "Rochester is where the pseudos were engineered. It was the perfect place for a top-secret project. After the Susquehanna Virus decimated the city, only a few die-hard civilians remained behind."

"And the pseudos were engineered for Mars?"

"Exactly. But something went wrong. They went crazy. We had to send in the Elite Ops. I don't have all the details of the battle, but the pseudos were driven back into the Mayo Clinic. Then the Elite Ops suffered some kind of malfunction to their systems. And President Davis elected not to send them in after the pseudos. He was afraid they might contract the virus. And he figured if the pseudos came down with it, well…we'd already written them off."

"So Cookie Monster is definitely a pseudo."

Weiss nodded. "And there are more of them out there."

The sound of Bach filled the air: *Jesu, Joy of Man's Desiring*. Weiss' PlusPhone. Weiss held up a hand to indicate that the colonel should remain where he was before answering his PlusPhone out of Truman's view.

"RC," he said with a smile. "How are you?"

Who was RC? Truman wondered.

"Gray Velvet. Smooth as ever. A couple things. First, did you know Jeremiah Jones is on his way there under orders from the President?"

"He's already passed through the last checkpoint," Weiss answered.

"Really? You haven't arrested him?"

"On what charge?"

"Kidnapping, assault, conspiracy to commit terrorism. I don't care."

"I have to follow the rule of law, RC. Find me some proof and I'll arrest him."

"Very well. Second, I've sent four Elite Ops troopers your way."

Elite Ops? That meant Carlton Security. Richard Carlton. Truman stared at Weiss, but the Attorney General kept his attention focused on the PlusPhone.

"I don't need your Elite Ops, RC. I've got Colonel Truman here with his troops."

"Sorry, Gray. Again, orders from the President. You know why.

Don't worry. They'll be keeping a low profile. You won't even feel their presence. Are you alone?"

"I have Colonel Truman here," Weiss said. "You can speak freely."

A slight pause.

"I have concerns about Jones. We both know he abducted Jack Marschenko. If you can't arrest him, you should at least put him in custody."

"I'll consider that, RC," Weiss said. "Later."

Weiss disconnected the PlusPhone, then looked up with a tight smile. "Colonel, I realize I've been somewhat distant these past few weeks. I've been wrapped up in this whole Devereaux thing. I've also been observing the way you handle your soldiers. You're doing a damn fine job."

"Thank you, sir."

"I know you think this might be a waste of time, Colonel. I might feel the same way in your shoes."

"It's not that, sir. It's just that if he's built these terrible bioweapons, why aren't we sending the entire Army after him? Why aren't we calling in the FBI, the CIA, the NSA?"

"Remember Al Capone?"

"The gangster?"

Weiss nodded. "We—the government—couldn't convict him of racketeering, so we took him down for tax evasion. Devereaux is going to be the same way. We might never prove he's developed these bioweapons. They're probably prototypes, so small they'd fit in a container the size of a fingernail. They could be hidden away or disposed of very easily. No," Weiss shook his head, "the only way we're going to stop Devereaux is by arresting him for treason for the vile things he's said."

"But if the weapons are out there—"

"I'm betting Devereaux's still got them. If he'd handed them over to the pseudos, they would have used them already. That's why we need to get to Devereaux quickly, so he won't have a chance to begin large-scale production. We're going to go down as heroes, Colonel—like Eliot Ness."

"I just want to stop him, sir, before innocents die."

Weiss put his hand on Truman's shoulder. "You're a good man, Colonel. Now, remember, we don't want to start a panic. We're here to arrest Devereaux for treason. Let's keep the bioweapons thing on the Q.T. Oh, and one more thing." Weiss turned to his computers and called up a picture of a man on one of the monitors. "Have you ever seen this man before?"

Truman stepped forward and eyed the man in the picture. A youngish man with an ordinary looking face—except for the eyes—brown, with a hint of green. They looked at the camera intensely: the eyes of a predator.

"No, sir," Truman said.

"That's Jones. He's a CINTEP ghost. I'm sure you've heard of the ghost program."

"Yes, sir. Assassins and spies."

"And he's one of the best."

"Is he here to assist us, sir?"

"I doubt that. The President already informed me that she doesn't want me to pursue Devereaux any longer. My guess is that he's here looking for Devereaux, just as we are. He and I also have a bit of a history. He blames me for some bad things that happened to him in the past."

"I can distribute photos to the troops. We can keep an eye on him."

"Yes, do that," Weiss said, sending the image to Truman's PlusPhone. "I can't arrest him. But I want to know where he is, what he's doing."

"Yes, sir." Truman forwarded the image to his troops with a note to keep an eye out for Jones.

"How are the searches going?"

"Captain Baynes is nearly done checking the townspeople but Captain Lopez has found it slow going through the forest, sir. It's going to take days to get through all those woods. More troops would speed up the process. Too many of my soldiers are tied up securing the perimeter. I was thinking of leading another detail into the area."

"You think that's a good idea? You're running the whole show here."

Truman shrugged. "Assuming I still have your permission to speak freely, sir, it burns me up when top brass stay home and let other people do the dirty work. I need to know the lay of the land myself."

Weiss nodded once, crisply. "Of course. You're absolutely correct. I can see why General Horowitz is so high on you."

Truman's face warmed with the praise. He said, "I'll leave Major Sims to man the DS-9000. She's better at that technical stuff than I am anyway. The sooner we get all these men profiled, the sooner we can get out of Sister Ezekiel's hair."

"Very well. Is the good sister causing problems?"

"No, sir. I'm sure she'd like us to leave, but she's been very cooperative. Still, she might know more than she's telling us."

"I agree. She's a wonderful woman. A real saint. And I adore her. But I think Devereaux's here and he may have already contacted her. If he has and she's hiding him, she will have to be punished, nun or not."

"The doctor's a bit feisty too."

"Yes." Weiss pursed his lips, tapped them with a forefinger. "What do you make of her?"

"Intelligent. Assertive. No-nonsense. I rather like her, sir."

"Something about her bothers me. I can't put my finger on it. I've just finished running a search on her and come up with damn little. A clinic in Los Angeles. Before that, a hospital in Phoenix and a stint at a low-income facility in San Diego. Medical School at the University of Iowa. Never married. No credit problems. Almost no credit history at all. Very unusual."

Truman stood with his hands locked behind his back, unsure how to respond to that.

"All right, Colonel," Weiss said, "off to the woods with you. Let's round up these homeless men."

* * *

Truman led a detail of soldiers east, toward Rochester and the Susquehanna Virus. From aerial reconnaissance, he knew that the original woods petered out several thousand feet away. Beyond that lay a development of high-end homes, a suburb of Rochester, abandoned along with most of the city twelve years ago when the virus escaped.

Afterwards, a group of fundamentalist Muslims proclaimed that the Susquehanna Virus was a punishment sent by God to destroy the Christian infidels. The previous year, Truman remembered, a group of fundamentalist Christians issued a proclamation that God had triggered a massive earthquake in Iran as vengeance for that nation's largely Islamic population.

Truman reached the end of the woods, where the ground sloped away to the abandoned development below. He stopped and stared. Beside him, Lieutenant Adams said, "Whoa," as she came to a halt. She was the youngest officer in Truman's command, almost the same age as his daughter McKenna.

The neighborhood looked like something out of a horror movie: the remnants of beautiful mansions barely recognizable, as if someone had attacked the development with mutant vegetation. Every house had been at least partially destroyed. Foliage grew up inside homes, breaking through windows and roofs—every wall still standing bent and twisted under the pressure of the heavy growth. Piles of rubble mounded up where half a dozen homes had once existed; their owners must have bulldozed them to prevent them from becoming havens for undesirables—vandals, addicts, gangs and terrorists.

The side roads looked impassable, trees sprouting up through cracks in the asphalt, wild grasses and shrubs invading from the yards on either side, leaving only narrow trails that wound snakelike off to the north and south. The main street east had fared a little better. Rocks and cement blocks filled potholes, and the foliage that grew up through the cracks had been trampled by foot traffic. But as he watched, not a soul moved. The place looked completely deserted.

To the north, Truman could just make out the imprint of a golf course, which mostly held the encroaching weeds at bay. Genetically modified grasses, no doubt—designed to grow slowly and inhibit common pests like dandelions and creeping charlie. Yet the grass was gradually losing the battle: now waist high and going to seed. A row of cherry-pear trees bordered the course, their sweet fruit nearly ripe. Truman had a fondness for cherry-pears not shared by his wife. Emily refused to buy anything not organically grown. And she only purchased pre-genetically modified foods. So Truman often took his meals at the officers' club, where he could order cholesterol-friendly steak and cherry-pear pie without a lecture from his wife.

A crow cawed three times, then lifted itself into the air and flew off to the southeast. A gray squirrel scampered up a tree. Underneath the musty odor of decaying vegetation, Truman detected the smell of burnt wood.

He signaled his team and they moved down the hill, then east along the main road, where everything felt crowded: branches snaking toward the center of the street, occasionally plucking at their uniforms as they passed. The lurking presence of the houses, half hidden in dark shadows behind trees and out-of-control shrubs, gave the neighborhood an eerie feel.

"I don't like this," Adams said as she shook her head. "I'd rather be fighting terrorists. This place is spooky." She pointed to a house overtaken by a large maple growing up through its center. It had a shattered glass roof, twisted metal framing embedded in a host of branches. The structure's golden walls pushed outward in the middle as if in the process of being blown apart by an explosion. The house looked like it might fall at any second. Adams shook her head. "Have you ever seen anything like that before?"

"I have, actually," Truman replied. "There was a time when the rich built homes around trees." He once visited a wealthy classmate whose home contained a greenhouse over sixty feet tall, which surrounded a magnolia tree genetically altered to bloom five times a year. A growth-stunting agent prevented the tree from outgrowing the greenhouse. A long spiral path led up from the ground floor. Guests, encouraged to walk the path, searched for bluebirds the classmate imprisoned inside.

Truman had almost become physically ill at the blatant excess flaunted.

This golden maple house looked like a lesser version of the one Truman remembered. And now, with the owners long gone, the maple had resumed its normal growth pattern, bulging beyond the confines of the greenhouse, taking the roof and walls with it.

Truman motioned for Adams to continue forward. She took a dozen steps, then halted again and pointed to another house, mostly fallen in on itself. One dirty gray stucco wall leaned at an impossible angle, its base four feet off the ground. The branches of several trees stuck through its broken windows, tilting the wall so that it formed a canted roof. It looked as if it might plummet earthward at any moment but it was no doubt stronger than it looked. Someone had obviously camped under its cover recently, for smoke drifted up from a fire pit and garbage lay strewn about.

Truman nodded, then continued on.

A number of trails led through the development off the main road—some more utilized than others. Truman realized that hundreds of people could be living here in the basements of houses or the partial structures still standing. What seemed a wasteland from the air was really a well-traveled forest. And although most of the houses had been pretty well destroyed, people had come to the area afterwards and gathered what was salvageable, putting together lean-tos and other rickety shelters.

Truman checked in with Captain Lopez, who had gone north along the largest path away from the main street. He decided to move south. Adjusting his PlusPhone scanner, he reminded his troops to keep an open comm link. "Remember," he said, "there are wolves and bears in this area—even a few lions and tigers freed from zoos by ecoterrorists—so keep a sharp eye out. And you all saw that Cookie Monster fellow."

"You think there are more pseudos out here, sir?" Adams said.

"Count on it," Truman replied.

Adams' face paled slightly.

Truman's PlusPhone flickered for a second. He tapped it with his fingers until it stayed on. As he moved south along the path, Truman's PlusPhone scanner came alive with multiple hits, farther to the east. Seven. No, eight people.

"Are you reading this activity, Lieutenant?" he asked.

"Yes, sir," Adams replied. "Moving too quickly to be human. Pseudos?"

Truman nodded. "Likely."

Adams cleared her throat but said nothing. She had proven before that she had an active imagination. She moved stiffly, gripping her Las-rifle tightly. Truman hoped to God she wouldn't shoot anyone by mistake. "You have something to say, Lieutenant?"

"Some of the homeless men have seen creatures, sir. Big and fast. Violent."

"We have Las-rifles, Lieutenant."

"Yes, sir," Adams replied. But her voice sounded shaky. Truman recalled that she'd never seen combat operations before.

"Relax, Lieutenant. Remember your training."

Adams nodded. She checked her Las-rifle's power setting as she paralleled Truman along the path. "What if they're not pseudos?"

"What else could they be?"

Adams glanced behind her at her fellow soldiers, then blushed. She pulled her Las-rifle in tight to her flak jacket and pursed her lips. "We heard there are mutants in these woods. Humans damaged by the Susquehanna Virus."

Truman shook his head. "That's mythical crap, Lieutenant. Like Bigfoot, or the Loch Ness monster. The kind of story that often crops up in remote areas, especially where people aren't well educated. There might be a bear loose, or even a tiger. But most likely it's Cookie Monster's friends. They won't be any match for us."

"Yes, sir," Adams replied.

Why did so many of his troops believe in the supernatural? Even the "educated" ones like Adams? Letting their religious leaders tell them how to answer the hard scientific questions seemed crazy.

"Just breathe deep," he said calmly. He rapped her knuckles lightly.

"Ease up your grip. Focus on the job. You'll get through it fine."

"Thank you, sir."

The images on Truman's PlusPhone scanner moved even more quickly now. He ordered Captain Lopez to an intercept point and brought his detail up to double time. If he was right, the two forces would converge in approximately half a mile, with the "enemy" caught between them. Adrenaline surged through him as he hustled over the rough terrain.

Though he knew Adams couldn't be correct, that there were no nightmarish creatures in the forest, he found the hair on the back of his neck rising as his own imagination kicked in. These people they were after—these pseudos—were moving faster than he would have thought possible. He'd never seen them in action, but if they'd fought the Elite Ops to a draw, they were dangerous. Truman's squad stood little chance against them. Yet he couldn't back down. This was his job. He tried to swallow, managing to moisten his throat slightly.

And then the blips were gone.

His PlusPhone scanner showed only his fellow soldiers as targets. The eight people they'd been tracking simply vanished. He said, "Lieutenant, what does your scanner show?"

Adams checked her PlusPhone, then looked at him with wide eyes. "They're gone, sir."

Captain Lopez's voice sounded in his ear: "We've lost contact, sir."

"Keep moving," Truman replied. "Target the coordinates where they disappeared." But he had a bad feeling that they were chasing air.

"How could they just vanish?" Adams asked.

"They might have dropped into a hole in the ground," Truman said.

"What if they didn't, sir?"

"Mutants, Lieutenant? Demons? Is that what you're thinking?"

"I don't know, sir," Adams said, her voice quavering.

"They're not demons, Lieutenant. Worst-case scenario is that they've got scatterers—new tech stuff that's better than our scanners. If so, they've got some serious hardware. But we're not dealing with demons. You can bank on that."

Truman hoped he was right. If the pseudos had particle beam cannons, he and his squad were finished. Even if they only had Las-rifles, they could pick Truman and his people off one by one.

Truman increased to double-time, his detail keeping pace. They ran along the path until they encountered Captain Lopez's squad, but they found no trace of the enemy, no holes in the ground, just a small clearing. Trails led off in three directions, but the people they were chasing could have taken any of them.

Truman studied the fifteen homeless men Lopez had rounded up. They looked old, frail, mentally ill. The captain had bound them all together and they stood in a cluster, breathing heavily. They obviously posed no threat to the soldiers. Shame and anger filled Truman's mind, even though he recognized that he might have done the same as a younger man.

"Take them back to the shelter," he said. "And, Captain, untie them. They're not prisoners."

As Lopez and his squad took the homeless men back to the shelter, Truman replayed the data from his PlusPhone scanner, plotting direction and speed, extrapolating where their prey had likely gone. Every indication led him to believe they'd come out on the highway south of the shelter. He turned his detail in that direction and they resumed their search.

Chapter Ten

From her office, Sister Ezekiel heard Ahmad Rashidi's distinctive voice out in the lobby. In his middle-eastern accent he said, "Don't shoot. I surrender." She glanced out through the wall-window, saw him standing in the doorway, two stun clubs pointed at him. He raised his hands, a briefcase in one, his PlusPhone in the other.

"He's my lawyer," Sister Ezekiel said to the soldiers as she exited her office. "Good morning, Ahmad."

"He's going to have to be scanned," Major Sims said. She got up from her chair, followed by the technician, Hayes, who had been going over the results from the earlier scans with the major.

Ahmad said, "Mornin', Sister. Nice day for a splash of radioactivity, no?"

"If you'll step over to the arch, sir," Major Sims said. She pointed to the DS-9000. Hayes stood at the controls and when the pudgy Ahmad stepped over to the machine, the technician started the scanner. As it ran through its course, Ahmad groaned and grimaced, feigning pain.

"Ow! Ouchie! Hey, watch it!" he yelled. "That smarts! Agh! My God, does this torture never end? Oh, the agony! The awful, unbearable agony!"

Dr. Mary appeared at the door to the infirmary. "What's going on here?" She saw Ahmad under the arch and said, "Oh, it's...*you.*" She turned to Major Sims. "He's a menace, Major. You'd better double-check your results."

The machine beeped and Ahmad stepped out without being told. He said, "Thanks a lot, Doc. Nice to see you too."

"You're too late for breakfast," Dr. Mary said, flashing her bright teeth in a wicked grin. "No food for you."

"Now that hurts. I brave the dangers of the highways, come all the way down here from Minneapolis through an untamed wilderness where I saw a tiger. Can you believe it? Standing by the side of the road, staring at me as I drove past, like he was about to clamp his jaws onto one of my tires. A huge beast! And after all that you can't find it in yer heart to spare a dried-up egg? A piece of cold toast? A half-eaten bowl of oatmeal with a maggot floating on top?"

"How about some pork sausage?" Henry asked, a smirk on his pale face.

Ahmad shook his head. "Allah forgives your sacrilege, my boy. As an infidel, you don't know any better."

"I'm sure we can find something for you in the kitchen, Ahmad," Sister Ezekiel said.

"Hold the bacon too," Ahmad said to Henry. He turned to the major. "We done here? You sure you don't need to insert a testicular electroshock emitter? Or a rectal probe?"

Henry snorted with laughter. Major Sims glared at Ahmad as Dr. Mary chortled. Hayes' shoulders bobbed up and down while the guards at the door sniggered quietly. Sister Ezekiel sometimes wished she could join in the fun. But someone had to be the adult.

"Come into the office, Ahmad," Sister Ezekiel said. "Henry, bring him a tray."

Ahmad stepped into her office and Sister Ezekiel gestured toward her chair.

"So," Ahmad said, "they must not have found him yet."

When Sister Ezekiel shook her head, he said, "What about you? You run across him?"

"Haven't seen him. He might not even be here."

"If Weiss says he's here, he's here. Plus, I was thinkin' about it on the way down. You're the kinda person Devereaux would take advantage of. The coward must be hiding."

"We're not here to criticize, Ahmad. We're here to help—him and anyone else who needs our assistance."

Ahmad held up his hands in surrender, then picked up the piece of quartz that Sister Ezekiel displayed on her desk. Rock Man had given it to her a few weeks ago when she'd told him how beautiful it was. He'd ignored her protests that it was much too valuable to give away and proudly handed it to her. White and gray, with a thin striation of black through the center and polished to a high sheen, it looked like a rare jewel and she treated it as such. If Rock Man considered it a treasure, she would too.

Ahmad set the rock aside and took up the tablet Colonel Truman had provided. As he scrolled through the various documents, Sister Ezekiel stood by the open doorway watching. She smiled at the way all his humor disappeared when he pored through the legalese, like nothing else existed.

He stroked his beard with his left hand, holding the tablet with his right, his dark fingers caressing the bushy salt and pepper hairs. Sister Ezekiel knew he did this when he didn't have khat to chew. Probably, despite his contrarian nature, he was afraid to chew the leaves with the Army and the Attorney General here.

"Where's Gray Weiss, out in his mobile command center?" Ahmad asked.

"I believe so," Sister Ezekiel answered.

"Okay. Lemme check a few things before we go visit him."

While she waited for Ahmad to complete what he was doing, Sister Ezekiel looked through the wall-window into the lobby. Major Sims and the technician, Hayes, had returned to the table next to the DS-9000, where they continued to sort through the scanning results. The two guards monitoring the entryway faced each other, talking and smiling, but Sister Ezekiel couldn't hear them. The lobby was quiet. Most of the homeless men had left the shelter after they'd been scanned. As she leaned against the wall, Sister Ezekiel noticed a beautiful young woman enter the shelter—an innocent creature of breathtaking beauty. Like Dr. Mary, the newcomer wore an interface. The two guards stopped her, and Major Sims rose from her chair.

Major Sims held out her hand and the young woman produced her ID card. The major examined the young woman's ID, her eyes bouncing between the card and the woman's face while the two guards did their best not to stare at her. Ignoring them all, the young woman looked around the room confidently until she caught Sister Ezekiel's eye through the wall-window. She smiled. As Sister Ezekiel smiled back, Henry appeared from the kitchen with a tray. Walking toward the office, he caught sight of the woman and nearly dropped the tray, his mouth open, eyes wide.

"Come along, Henry," Sister Ezekiel called from the doorway as the major directed the woman to the scanner.

"They scanning gorgeous young women now?" Ahmad said.

Sister Ezekiel turned, saw her lawyer eyeing the woman—a cat following the movements of a goldfish.

"The major must be a lesbian," Ahmad said. "If she's Devereaux, that's one helluva disguise."

Henry chuckled as he placed the tray on the desk. "You crack me up, Ahmad. You're the funniest lawyer I ever met."

"Ahmad, please," Sister Ezekiel cautioned him. "Let's focus on helping Douglas and Cookie Monster, and on getting that monstrosity out of here. I'll go see what she wants."

She stepped out to the lobby as the DS-9000 completed its scan. "May I help you?" she asked.

"My name is Lendra Riley," the woman said. She looked briefly at Major Sims before turning back to Sister Ezekiel. "I have a personal matter I'd like to discuss with you."

"My," Major Sims said, pointing to the machine, "aren't you the bright one. Never seen a reading that high."

"My enhancements are legal." Lendra pointed to her ID card. "Sister, may we talk?"

"Very well," Sister Ezekiel replied. "However, someone's using my office at the moment."

Major Sims held up her hand. "What's the nature of your business, honey?"

Lendra said, "As I indicated, it's personal. Can we take a walk outside, Sister?"

"I don't know if I should allow that," Major Sims said.

"Come now," Sister Ezekiel said as she gestured for Lendra to precede her out the door. "You can't detain her just because she's intelligent."

Sister Ezekiel stepped outside and said, "It's not often the shelter receives female visitors. And, except for Dr. Mary, I've never seen one come here alone. What can I do for you?"

Lendra stared at the Attorney General's command center, then the Army transport trucks parked at the edges of the parking lot. "Actually, Sister, I need you to come with me."

"You do, do you?" Sister Ezekiel stopped. "Why?"

Lendra turned to look at her. "It has to do with Devereaux and the soldiers you have here. I have a colleague who would like to meet you."

"A colleague?"

"We're here on orders from the President."

"President Hope?" Sister Ezekiel backed up a step, stunned. She searched Lendra's face for any sign that the young woman was joking and realized that Lendra was serious. "Very well," she said. "Lead on."

Lendra led her north toward the statue. Across the street, three two-story office buildings, recently abandoned, faced the shelter. Ahead, Sister Ezekiel could just make out Ernie Olsen's Market, which served the town's dwindling population. Just beyond that, "Emerging Man" towered over the road. Once a tourist attraction, now an almost forgotten jewel buried alongside a rarely traveled highway. Everyone chose to meet at "Emerging Man." And why not? It was beautiful. She wandered up this way at least once a week. She loved the flowing curves, the suggestion of straining muscles as the granite man attempted to rise above the earth. Most of all, she delighted in the conflicted face—the subject's struggle to balance happiness with sorrow. How could certain religious "leaders" call it atheistic rubbish? It didn't make any kind of statement about religion or God. It was simply art. And like all great art, it left the interpretation of its significance and meaning to the observer. The statue certainly didn't offend her. Yet many in the religious community called it "abomination" and "sacrilege." What narrow-minded fools.

Sister Ezekiel took off her glasses and cleaned them on her handkerchief as they walked. "Tell me something, child. Do you believe in God?"

"I keep an open mind," Lendra said, "although I think Devereaux's ladder provides compelling evidence of the necessity to move beyond religion if we wish to survive."

"Who is your colleague?"

"I'd rather let him tell you, Sister."

"I don't know anything about Devereaux."

"Then it will likely be a very short conversation."

As Sister Ezekiel expected, Lendra turned when they reached the parking lots for the statue. The north lot, once filled with tour buses, now sat empty, grown over with weeds. Farther up the street at the north edge of town, Sister Ezekiel could just make out an Army checkpoint. Strangely, the Army had let a tour bus of schoolchildren through to visit the famous statue.

At one end of the south lot, a line of children, each hoisting a large stick of cotton candy purchased from Bert's souvenir stand, marched toward an armored bus under the watchful eyes of a pair of security guards, their rainbow-colored treats bright against the drab green and brown of the bus. Good old Bert. Whenever schoolchildren visited the statue, he outdid himself with the cotton candy.

A heavyset woman with curly red hair and a tan uniform stood by the door of the bus counting the children as they slowly made their way up the stairs. Three teachers kept the children in line and tried to move them along. Off to the side, ignoring the statue, an athletic-looking man watched the children boarding their bus. He stood with shoulders slumped, his face fallen as he followed the children's progress. Sister Ezekiel, having seen deep suffering in her life, knew this man was in pain.

When a little boy with dark hair near the back of the line spotted Sister Ezekiel, he did a doubletake and ran into the child ahead of him, his cotton candy flying out of his fingers and landing at the sad man's feet. The man picked up the candy, brushed off the dirt and handed the treat to the boy as one of the security guards sauntered over.

Holding up his hands, the sad man backed away and the security guard nodded.

Although half a dozen people stood before "Emerging Man," Sister Ezekiel instinctively knew they were meeting the sad man. She was proven right when he spotted Lendra. The sorrow in his expression disappeared as he straightened his shoulders. A little taller than average and slim, but with a hard wiry look, he carried himself effortlessly, sauntering across the pavement toward them, smiling with what seemed to be genuine affection as he neared.

He said, "It's not often I see a nun wearing a habit."

"They're not required," she answered. "I wear it because I like to be reminded of why I'm here."

The man extended his hand. "I'm Jeremiah Jones. Thanks for meeting me."

He gave her a firm grip, his hand warm, and a brief electric tingle shot through her. She ignored it, studied his face instead. The frown lines surrounding his hazel eyes advertised again, as if she needed the confirmation, that he had spent a lot of time in sadness. And yet his eyes were bright, shiny, well nourished and alert. Sister Ezekiel had met thousands of men over the years but none with the kind of intensity this man displayed in just a look. There was something magnetic about him. Immediately she liked him. And she generally trusted her first impressions of men, though on rare occasions she found herself fooled.

"I'm here, Sister, because of Gray Weiss and Walt Devereaux, as I'm sure Lendra mentioned." He pointed to a bench at the edge of the parking lot. "Would you care for a seat?"

Sister Ezekiel preceded him to the bench and sat down heavily. "Dear Lord," she said, "I am tired. I could use a nap."

"Would you like something to drink, Sister?"

"Some water would be wonderful."

"I'll get it," Lendra offered. "Jeremiah?"

"The same, please."

Jeremiah sat beside her and stared up at the statue, saying nothing, as if just enjoying the day. She felt comfortable next to him, relaxed enough to close her eyes for a moment and enjoy the warm breeze on her face, the smell of cotton candy wafting from the souvenir shack, the trill of a wren coming from a tree to her right. As the stresses of the morning began to melt away, she found herself staring into Jeremiah's eyes. He reached for her wimple and removed it, allowing her long blond hair to cascade about her shoulders. With the back of his hand he caressed her cheek and this time when he smiled all the pain vanished from his eyes.

She jerked her head up, suddenly awake, as his hand brushed across her cheek, the pleasant aroma of soap filling her nostrils.

"You had an ant on your cheek," Lendra said as Jeremiah opened his hand to reveal the ant. He nudged it onto the bench and the insect scurried away.

"I'm afraid I fell asleep," Sister Ezekiel said, blushing, "I didn't get any last night." She reached up and tucked a loose strand of gray hair into her wimple, then adjusted her glasses. Lendra offered her a bottle of water. Thanking the young woman, Sister Ezekiel opened the bottle and took a long drink. She hadn't realized how thirsty she was.

How she wished she could control her dreams. Awake she would never allow herself to contemplate images like that. She was happy doing God's work. Being a nun was her best, highest purpose. She hadn't desired a man in years. And despite her dream, she didn't desire this one, either. She was just tired.

Jeremiah leaned in close and said, "What can you tell me about Walt Devereaux?"

She shrugged. "I'm sure you know more about him than I do."

"You haven't seen him at the shelter?"

"No. And I don't know why he would come here. Why are you all so sure he's here?"

Jeremiah pointed to the statue. "It's beautiful, don't you think?"

She nodded. "I've always thought so."

Jeremiah stared at her, his dark eyes intense in the sunlight. "You don't believe it's a symbol of atheistic thought, glorifying evolution at the expense of God?"

She smiled. "I see you've been reading the plaques installed by various religious groups. No," she answered his question. "I see the statue as representational. It could equally well serve as a metaphor for humanity's struggle to reach the heavens—to become closer to God."

Lendra said, "Did you know that one of the sculptors—Ryan Connelly—was Walt Devereaux's maternal grandfather?"

Sister Ezekiel sat up straight. "What?"

"Oh, yes," Lendra replied.

"The plaques don't mention that. How could…"

Jeremiah said, "This is an old statue, Sister. Most of these plaques were installed years ago, before Walt Devereaux became famous. And I suspect not much money has been spent on upkeep over the past two decades. The governments—state and federal—have their hands full trying to finance much more urgent concerns."

Lendra said, "I doubt many people even know of the connection."

"But Gray Weiss," Jeremiah said, "undoubtedly does. And he wouldn't be in Crescent Township if he wasn't sure Devereaux is here."

"Well," Sister Ezekiel said. "You certainly have surprised me. But I'm afraid I can't help you because I haven't seen Devereaux. And if I had, I still wouldn't help you. You seem very sincere but I don't know who you are or what you're capable of."

The schoolbus pulled out of the lot, the two security guards now mounted in glass-domed turrets at the front and back of the vehicle. The dark-haired boy waved at Jeremiah from a side window. Jeremiah held up his hand in return, though his smile seemed sad. The bus turned south on the highway, probably heading to the house where Ryan Connelly once lived or the cemetery where he was buried. Jeremiah leaned forward and lowered his voice. "We're here because the President believes Devereaux has created bioweapons that he's given to the Escala—Mars Project Astronauts sometimes called pseudos, and suspected terrorists. I see by your reaction that you know something about these Escala."

Sister Ezekiel shook her head. "Mr. Weiss didn't say anything about bioweapons or terrorists. He only talked about the harm Devereaux's Ladder has done to the country."

"Weiss has his own agenda," Jeremiah said. "And if he captures Devereaux, the resulting trial will bring out the fanatics on both sides. Rioting, looting, mayhem. Weiss wants that. He wants the anarchy so he can step in as the righteous savior."

"And you want to save Devereaux?"

"Devereaux's bioweapons could wipe out humanity. Whether he's built them or not, he's got the blueprints in his head, which makes him extremely dangerous. The President just wants to talk to him, negotiate a quiet settlement with him and the Escala. She has no intention of putting him on trial."

"No. She'll just lock him away somewhere, make him disappear like so many of her predecessors have done to others."

Jeremiah said, "I have no desire to hurt Devereaux, Sister."

She stared at him for long seconds. "But you'd do it if you had to, wouldn't you?"

She waited for him to look away but he maintained eye contact, his expression determined, yet still sad. Finally he said, "My job is to protect this country."

"That's what Mr. Weiss says too. And you both sound very sure of yourselves. But this country is in pretty bad shape. So neither one of you seems to be doing a very good job. I'll say it again. I don't know where Devereaux is, so I can't help you."

"What about these Escala?"

"Mr. Weiss has one locked up behind the shelter right now. I don't know if he's one of these Escala, but Mr. Weiss seems to think he is."

"Very well, Sister." Jeremiah reached over and shook her hand. Again his warm grasp caused a brief electric tingle to shoot through her. She hoped she wasn't blushing. "Thank you for your time."

Lendra took Sister Ezekiel's elbow and helped her to her feet. She said, "Mr. Weiss is not the caring leader the conservative press would have you believe."

Sister Ezekiel nodded. "Don't worry, child. Mr. Weiss' charms don't work on me. But understand this—I will do what I must, what God has chosen me to do. I hope you can accept that."

"Lendra will walk you back, Sister," Jeremiah said. "Please be careful."

As they strolled along the sidewalk toward the shelter Lendra said, "I sense that you're suppressing a lot of anger, Sister."

Did she know about the rape? Probably. Sister Ezekiel sighed. No need to get upset over it. She said, "I've learned not to judge too harshly anymore. The world isn't as black and white as you might believe."

"I admire your ability to control your emotions."

"And I admire your self-confidence, your belief that things will work out for the best in the end."

"I know that good doesn't always triumph," Lendra said. "But is Devereaux good?"

"Just because he insists that we need to live without God, doesn't mean he's evil. In fact, I rather admire him. He's a man of integrity. He's simply wrong. I've told you what I know. I haven't seen him. And you aren't going to change my mind about him. If he makes his presence known to me, I'll warn him away. I won't be a party to his capture."

"I think you've already encountered him, Sister. He just hasn't identified himself to you yet. But he will, because you're a good person and he'll know he can trust you."

"And what about your colleague, Jeremiah, is he a good person?"

"Like you, Sister, he has a troubled past."

Sister Ezekiel stopped, grabbed Lendra's arm. "Does Jeremiah know what happened to me too?"

"No," Lendra said. "I didn't tell him."

Sister Ezekiel felt relief, then annoyance. Why should it matter whether he knew about the rape? "I've moved beyond that," she said. "It was a long time ago."

"That's my point, Sister. Jeremiah hasn't. His son was kidnapped four years ago and is still missing. His wife killed herself not long ago. He blames himself for both those tragedies."

"Ah, that's why he looks at children so sadly."

From the direction of the shelter the sound of weapons fire intruded: the hiss and sizzle of lasers; the quick bangs of grenades; then the roar of an explosion. Screams followed. Two more explosions occurred nearly simultaneously. The ground trembled. "Oh, dear Lord," Sister Ezekiel said.

They stood still and watched as black clouds billowed skyward.

She began to run forward.

"Wait," Lendra yelled.

"I should have known something like this would happen. Where soldiers go, war follows. That's always the way."

"Hold on, Sister," Lendra said as she grabbed Sister Ezekiel by the arm. "It's too dangerous there."

Sister Ezekiel nearly fell as Lendra tugged at her habit. She stopped and glared at the young woman. "Let me go," she ordered. "My place is at the shelter."

Lendra released her arm. "We can't. It's too dangerous. Let's just move ahead a little until we can see what's happening."

Sister Ezekiel ran towards the weapons fire, stopping a few hundred yards up the sidewalk.

Near the road, in the shelter's parking lot, a flatbed truck was parked. Atop the bed three large men crouched, firing away at the shelter and the Army troops, who crouched behind their transport vehicles. Another attack came from the vacant buildings across the street. Caught in the middle, stopped in the center of the street, was the schoolbus.

"The children," she yelled. But as she tried to move forward, Lendra pulled her back.

"They're okay for the moment, Sister," Lendra spoke calmly despite the laser blasts filling the air. "No one's firing at them." She took out a PlusPhone and directed its camera at the action, focusing on the combatants, the schoolbus and the flaming vehicles. "Jeremiah," she said, "where the hell are you? I could use a little help here."

Out of the corner of her eye Sister Ezekiel saw a movement in one of the buildings across from the shelter. She reached for Lendra and pulled her down as a blue laser pulse flashed past. Lendra dropped the PlusPhone. The next pulse hit the small object, instantly melting it.

The laser moved off, returning sporadically to keep them pinned to the ground. She had to get to the children. But how? As she and Lendra crouched together, exposed to the man in the window, she began to pray. The noise from the fighting diminished until all she could hear was the sizzle of lasers and the occasional scream. Then another explosion hammered her eardrums, temporarily dazing her.

"Sonic grenades," Lendra shouted into her ear.

She nodded. Her muscles tense, her stomach roiling, Sister Ezekiel watched the battle progress, always keeping her eye on the schoolbus. Lendra had been right. The fighters on both sides were being careful to avoid hitting it. Laser pulses flashed past it like fireworks—blue, red and purple—crackling as they sizzled through the smoke and flames. Yet for the moment, at least, the bus remained unscathed.

Chapter Eleven

Colonel Truman, leading his squad along the projected path of the bio-signs they had detected, heard an explosion in the distance, followed shortly thereafter by two more in quick succession. They appeared to be coming from the shelter.

"We're under attack," Major Sims spoke into his earpiece.

"Keep that perimeter established," Weiss' voice cut in to Truman's earpiece. "This could be a diversion to allow Devereaux to escape."

Truman repeated Weiss' order and led his squad toward the shelter. Scrambling west through undergrowth that clawed at his uniform, he felt the familiar battle hollowness come over him—the calm that came from rigorous training. He began receiving reports through his comm link, but learned little more than that hostiles were attacking the shelter. When he reached the road, he turned north. Twice more, explosions thundered up ahead, nearly knocking him off his feet. Through a thick cloud of black smoke, he could barely make out the shelter. Weiss' mobile command center sat in the small parking lot out front, glowing red, its multi-colored lights blinking on and off. Smoke billowed from the two transport vehicles nearest the command center.

Atop a flatbed truck, three large men fired blue laser pulses at the shelter. Blue pulses, thank God, meaning their weapons were set on low power, although that was no guarantee of safety. Even low-power laser pulses could be lethal if they struck a person in the heart or head. Another attack came from the buildings across the street—also blue pulses. Were they just conserving their power charges or did they not want to kill?

Just north of the flatbed, caught in the middle of the street, was an armored bus painted brown and green—a military castoff with manned turrets at front and rear. Truman saw children's faces through the windows and realized it was a schoolbus.

Although no one was shooting at the bus, the guards in its turrets fired sporadically: medium-power purple bursts aimed at the flatbed. Keep firing on the attackers and they'll start to fire back, Truman thought as he shook his head. Idiots. Red and purple laser fire spewed from both the shelter and a group of soldiers in the parking ramp just to the north of it. Captain Lopez. Via his comm link, Truman directed the shelter's defense, speaking to his squad leaders clearly and calmly.

Through the increasing smoke he saw that the men shooting from the flatbed truck were gigantic. A slight glow surrounded them—a variable energy shield powered by a field generator. Very high tech.

"Concentrate fire on the flatbed," Truman said. "We've got to get through that shield. And whatever you do, don't hit that bus."

In his ear Major Sims' voice sounded brittle: "The DS-9000 is taking heavy fire. Shield is engaged. Repeat, shield is engaged."

"We're moving to your southern flank, Major," Truman said.

Keeping low, he led his squad closer to the shelter, his troops firing as they moved. "We need to get that bus out of there," he said even as he spotted the driver slumped over the wheel.

The fighters on the truck looked like Cookie Monster. Pseudos. They wore military style coveralls but with shaggy beards and long hair, they looked distinctly non-military. One of them wore no beard. A woman. Her long golden hair cascaded down her back, sparkling under the iridescent glow of the shield.

Truman couldn't help but stare at her. With the shield flicking on and off at rapid intervals, she timed her shots perfectly, firing as the shield flickered off, then as the shield resumed its protection, she repositioned herself for the next shot. Only enhanced humans could so precisely time their shots to the fleeting openings presented by the variable shield. His soldiers' return fire bounced harmlessly away.

The pseudos on the truck ignored Truman's squad. Humiliation and rage swept through him as he rushed forward through the haze.

Lopez spoke into his earpiece: "We'll charge the flatbed."

"Negative," Truman shouted. "Circle around to the north, Captain. No shooting until you can come at the flatbed from the back. Less chance of a missed shot or a ricochet hitting the bus."

Truman ordered Captain Baynes to circle around from the west and join up with Captain Lopez. Meanwhile, Truman's squad edged closer to the enemy, coordinating a barrage of laser fire against the flatbed truck. But the shield held. Truman ordered half his squad to redirect their fire on the building across the highway. His troops fired multiple shots, every laser burst opening a hole the size of a tennis ball in the brick wall. The pseudos in the building finally directed their fire at Truman's detail. At least I got their attention, Truman thought as he dropped behind a shrub. What he needed and lacked was a particle beam cannon—so expensive and rare the Army had none. Only the Elite Ops carried such weapons.

A blue laser pulse flashed past Truman's ear, sizzling loudly and searing him as it passed. For a few seconds he heard nothing but a roar. Then Captain Lopez's voice came through his earpiece: "They've got us pinned down. We'll have to go farther north to cross the road. It's gonna be a few minutes before we can get into position. Also, my squad is running low on energy charges. Cutting back to half-power."

Truman had to get that damn bus away from the fighting. The front of the shelter already looked scorched. Its recently repaired front door had been blown off and the DS-9000 stood fully exposed. The pseudos atop the flatbed now fired red pulses at it. Full power. For the moment the shield around the scanner held, though it glowed an ominous red.

A purple pulse hit Truman's helmet a glancing blow. He fell to the ground, his head burning. Ripping the superheated helmet off, he caught the bitter stench of burnt plastic and metal. He noted the crease through the side of his helmet and realized he'd just cheated death. Had that pulse come from the bus?

"You okay, sir?" Adams asked.

He nodded. "Follow me, Lieutenant."

Moving forward in a crouching run, Truman reached the side of the shelter, where Gray Weiss hunkered down with half a dozen soldiers a few feet behind his mobile command center. Across the street the pseudos in the office buildings now put purple suppression fire into the command center until the vehicle was little more than molten metal. Weiss and the soldiers with him backed away as the heat from the command center intensified. Incredibly Weiss carried an old fashioned handgun.

"Sonic grenades," Truman yelled, the sound of his voice carrying clearly over the sizzle of the lasers. Truman ducked down, his hands over his ears, as several troops lobbed grenades toward the flatbed truck. The resulting explosion caused every soldier to hesitate for a moment. It should have stunned the pseudos behind the shield for at least a few seconds but they seemed oblivious to it, something Truman would have insisted was impossible had he not seen it for himself.

The sizzle of the enemy's laser fire grew louder as the pulses intensified. It seemed like a hundred pseudos were firing on his troops, though it was only five or six. My God, Truman thought, what an enormous amount of firepower they have.

The pseudos on the truck continued to pour red laser fire into the shelter, targeting the DS-9000. Major Sims and her soldiers returned fire steadily, poking their heads around the ruined doorway every few seconds and firing quick bursts at the truck.

"The shield is overloading," Major Sims said over the comm.

"Prepare to disengage," Truman said.

He hurried over to Weiss' side. The heat here was intense. He could barely breathe through the thick, acrid smoke. Coughing, he asked, "You okay?"

"We've got to get that bus out of here," Weiss spoke hoarsely. "We can't do anything until those kids are safe. And those pseudos on the truck know it."

"The DS-9000's shield is about to go. We have to disengage it."

Weiss shook his head. "We need that scanner. Keep the shield up as long as you can. And keep that perimeter in place. I don't want Devereaux sneaking out during the attack. I'm going to make a run for the bus."

"It would be suicide, sir."

"If you can put enough lasers on their shield, I might have time to get to the bus and drive it out of here."

The sound of a siren grew louder as a police vehicle neared. Colonel Truman hoped they'd have the good sense to keep back. They'd be no match for the pseudos.

"It's too dangerous," Truman argued. "To keep their shield on, we'd need at least half a dozen troops to concentrate full power on the shield from a distance of…" he calculated quickly, "no more than twenty feet."

"God will protect me. Besides, we've got no other options."

Truman turned to his squad. "I need eight volunteers to make a run for the truck." Lieutenant Adams raised her hand. So did Sergeant Mecklenberg—a big kid from Montana who'd been offered a chance to train for the Elite Ops but had turned it down. No one else moved. Truman nodded, then pointed to his troops. "Adams, you and Mecklenberg take Nguyen, Faruzah, Honsi, Esparza, Yu and Orgento. You need to get to within twenty feet. Power settings to maximum. Hit that shield with everything you've got for as long as you can. Mr. Weiss and I will try to reach the bus."

Before they could move, the DS-9000's shield exploded and bricks flew out from the shelter's front wall into the parking lot.

Adams, face pale and teeth clenched, checked her Las-rifle. Then she nodded to Truman and sprinted toward the truck, her troops forming a line behind her, firing as they ran. Weiss jumped up and sprinted in a serpentine weave toward the bus, Truman following. His squad put everything they had into the shield and the buildings opposite but Truman doubted it was enough to protect them; there was no cover in the parking lot at all.

Seventy yards from the bus, Weiss stopped behind a burning troop transport. Truman ran up next to him, breathing shallowly in the intense heat, and fired a long burst at the pseudos in the buildings opposite, who withdrew momentarily. As Weiss took off again, Truman glanced at the flatbed. The pseudos atop the truck fired quick laser pulses—blue—as their shield phased off, hitting Private Honsi and Specialist Faruzah. Honsi fell, clutching his stomach, but Sergeant Mecklenberg grabbed Faruzah and dragged him forward with one arm while firing with the other. Good boy. Truman took off after Weiss.

Forty yards from the bus, Weiss dove into some low shrubs on the boulevard, breathing heavily. Truman threw himself down beside the Attorney General, took a deep breath and looked toward the bus. A window behind the driver's door shattered. Children screamed. A laser pulse must have ricocheted off the shield.

Now Weiss got to his feet and sprinted for the bus. Truman bolted after him, firing his Las-rifle at the flatbed as he ran, but he stopped almost immediately when he realized he couldn't keep his aim steady. Better not to fire than to hit one of his own people.

Dashing across the pavement, Truman and Weiss drew to within meters of the bus when the female pseudo on the flatbed suddenly turned and fired a blue laser pulse that hit Weiss in the right shoulder. Weiss fell heavily, crying out as he hit the ground. His pistol slipped from his hand and skittered toward the bus, striking the front driver's-side wheel.

Truman grabbed Weiss by his armpits and dragged him toward the bus, bracing himself for the shock of a laser pulse. Weiss moaned, half-conscious. Mingled with the stench of flaming fuel and molten metal pouring from the destroyed transport vehicles and the mobile command center, Truman caught a whiff of burnt flesh. Finally he reached the bus, set Weiss against the front wheel and began pounding on the driver's door. His back itched even though he knew the fighters from both sides were trying not to hit the bus.

He glanced over to where Lieutenant Adams fired at the shield. Her Las-rifle's charge went dead at the same moment as Mecklenberg's. As they tried to reload, the shield on the flatbed phased off, just for an instant, and the pseudos fired again. Lieutenant Adams cried out and fell. She hit the ground heavily. Mecklenberg grabbed her and dragged her behind Private Honsi, then set her down carefully. Truman would have to remember to recommend him for a medal.

"Open the door," Truman ordered as he hammered on the bus.

Finally the door swung open. The driver, a heavyset red-haired woman, still slumped over the wheel, alternately grunting and whimpering as she clutched her stomach. Blood oozed from between her fingers. A pretty teacher bent over her with a damp cloth. She stared at Truman, her eyes wide and her face pale. A man and a woman stood in the aisle beyond her, talking to the children in firm but gentle voices, telling them to keep their heads down and to stay calm. "We've got to get this bus out of here," Truman said.

"We can't move her," the pretty teacher said. "She's been shot. The steering wheel's fused into her stomach."

"We'll take care of her," Weiss said to the teacher. He'd somehow recovered enough to get to his feet behind Truman, his gun back in his hand. "We've got medics outside." Weiss then pointed to his injured shoulder with his gun and said to Truman, "I'm afraid I can't help you much."

Truman stood on the step-plate, then reached up and grabbed the bus driver under the shoulders. As he pulled her clear of the seat, he heard a ripping sound. The bus driver screamed and thrashed about, hitting Truman's head with her fist. Some of the children screamed along with her. Others cried.

"Medic," Weiss shouted over the noise.

Truman lowered the bus driver to the street. She clung to his arms fiercely, writhing in agony, sobbing. Truman held onto her as Weiss shut the door and slowly backed up the bus, the loud beeping from the vehicle adding another layer to the assault on Truman's ears.

"I've got you," Truman yelled above the noise.

He felt vulnerable in the road, no longer protected by the bulk of the bus. But logic told him that the pseudos weren't out to kill anyone. They'd had multiple opportunities to take him out and had already demonstrated that their aim was phenomenal. So the only rational conclusion was that they didn't want to kill him.

He tried to call for a medic on his comm unit, only then discovering that the bus driver had knocked his headset off when she'd hit him. Just then he caught a flash of movement in the center of the street. A man ran past him toward the shelter and the flatbed truck. The man glowed with the sparkling incandescence of an energy shield and carried something that looked like a narrow bucket—a black cylindrical tube two feet long and nine inches in diameter.

A particle beam cannon?

Truman shivered. If the man directed that weapon at the shelter on a wide beam, he might bring down the whole building.

The man slowed to a jog, drawing fire now from the men in the building and the flatbed, as well as from a dozen soldiers. Every time a laser shot hit him, his shield glowed brighter. He stopped in front of the shelter, knelt down and aimed the particle beam cannon at the truck. He waited for what seemed a long time, absorbing scores of shots. Then the glow around him flickered for a fraction of a second and he fired his weapon. A roar of immense power filled the air and the energy field surrounding the fighters on the flatbed died.

Truman pulled himself free of the bus driver and sprinted toward the truck as a sonic grenade exploded. He fell to the ground, his body frozen by the shock of the detonation. The three fighters atop the flatbed, somehow unaffected, sprang to their feet, leapt to the ground and ran across the street.

More sonic grenades exploded as two fighters in the buildings across the street slipped through the windows and jumped to the ground. Together the five sprinted away, moving with a superhuman speed and grace.

Truman managed to lift his Las-rifle and fire at the retreating figures.

A pseudo stumbled as a purple laser strike hit him. Another purple pulse came from the shelter, hitting another pseudo, who nearly fell over. But the blond female propped him up and pulled him along. In seconds they were gone—down the street and into the woods.

Truman knew he couldn't go after them. His troops stood no chance against their firepower, especially not on their home territory. Any pursuit was liable to run into an ambush.

"Stand down," he yelled as he got to his feet. "I need a medic over here." He pointed to the bus driver, who now lay curled up in the fetal position.

Then Truman turned his attention to the man with the particle beam cannon. And as a precaution, he aimed his Las-rifle at the man's chest. Not that it would do any good against the man's shield. Dozens of his troops converged on the man, who seemed unconcerned with their presence. Truman grabbed the nearest soldier's comm unit and spoke into it: "Stay calm. Stay alert. I want reports, people—status, casualties, readiness. Captain Lopez, Captain Baynes, return to base."

The bus glided quietly down the street, returning from where Weiss had driven it to safety. Weiss parked it at the side of the road, opened the door and yelled, "Medic! Two kids have been hit."

Truman reached the man with the particle beam cannon, noted the hazel eyes glittering behind the shield, the older but still recognizable face from the photo Weiss had given him only a short time ago. This was Jeremiah Jones. The killer. And for some reason he'd saved them.

Chapter Twelve

Soldiers emerged from cover and approached Jeremiah through the drifting smoke. A black Army colonel with the nametag Truman reached him first, Las-rifle pointed at Jeremiah's chest. But he lowered his weapon almost immediately.

"Thanks," Jeremiah said.

"Thank *you*," Truman replied.

Jeremiah nodded. As he deactivated his shield, several of the soldiers who had gathered around him reached over and patted him on the shoulders and back, murmuring their thanks.

Then Jeremiah remembered Gray Weiss' distinctive voice yelling for a medic.

He turned and jogged toward the bus, Colonel Truman keeping pace, continually talking into his comm unit. Jeremiah hoped he wasn't going to see dead children, though it would have to be a pretty unlucky shot to kill one of those kids. The attackers had only used full power when firing into the shelter.

Before Jeremiah reached the bus he saw Lendra descending the stairs. She must have gotten inside after the bus backed up the street. A sergeant wearing a medic's insignia ran past her into the bus. People yelled and screamed, hurling questions through the smoke and chaos.

"What's the damage in there?" Colonel Truman shouted.

Two security guards now emerged, carrying a little boy with a bloody shoulder. Behind them, the sergeant carried another boy out the door, a gash above his left eye. It was the boy Jeremiah had seen drop his cotton candy earlier—the one who looked a little like Joshua. Jeremiah fought a sudden bout of nausea. The sergeant yelled, "These kids got lucky. Minor wounds."

Relief washed over Jeremiah.

As the crowd parted to let the men carry the children through,

Jeremiah made his way toward Lendra, Colonel Truman continuing to shadow him. When he reached Lendra, she told him she was all right, but her face looked pinched and gray.

Then Weiss emerged from the bus, carrying an old fashioned automatic pistol in his left hand; his right dangled limp. He had a burn mark on his right shoulder, the laser strike marring the cut of his suit, but only a small amount of blood advertised the wound. Weiss wore a tight smile.

Stopping in front of Jeremiah, Weiss said, "Jeremiah Jones."

"Gray Weiss," Jeremiah answered.

"That's a particle beam cannon," Colonel Truman said, pointing to the weapon in Jeremiah's hands.

Jeremiah ignored him, keeping his eyes on Weiss.

An old police officer pushed forward through the crowd, asking, "What's going on here?" He also carried an ancient gun—one that looked even older than he was—and it shook in his hand so badly that Jeremiah hoped he could holster it before it accidentally discharged. He was probably the only law in town. Only the big and wealthy cities could afford true police protection. Everyone else relied on the National Guard or private security forces.

"Nice gun," Jeremiah said to Weiss. "Looks heavy. You the one who got the bus out of the way?"

Weiss nodded.

"Good job," Jeremiah said. "But I'd expect no less from you."

Weiss looked at Jeremiah as if unsure whether the comment was sarcastic. "I'm serious," Jeremiah added. "That was a brave thing to do, especially with only a pistol."

"We got lucky," Weiss said bitterly. "We were completely overmatched. Fortunately, God sent you just in time." Turning toward the old police officer, Weiss asked, "Who are you?"

"I'm Chief McKinney."

"Gray Weiss."

"I heard you were in town," Chief McKinney said. He tried to holster his clunky gun and dropped it to the pavement. When he bent to pick it up, his pant legs rode up and Jeremiah noticed a small Las-pistol strapped to his ankle.

"I'm looking for Walt Devereaux," Weiss said. After a glance at Jeremiah, Weiss gingerly put his gun into an inside pocket on the right side of his suit. Then he turned to Colonel Truman and said, "We need to medevac that bus driver and probably those kids. Anyone else hurt?"

Colonel Truman nodded. "Major Sims is in pretty bad shape. Dr. Mary's working on her right now. And we got ten others with Las-rifle burns, including you."

Weiss looked down at his shoulder. "I've had worse. Get a couple jet-copters in here right away."

Colonel Truman turned away and began speaking into his comm unit.

"Chief," Weiss said to McKinney. "I want you and your men to help get that schoolbus on its way. We're going to close this whole block. Nobody gets in unless they've got a legitimate reason for being here—at least for the next few hours. And nobody says anything to any media outlets."

Jeremiah couldn't help but admire Weiss' savvy order. Lendra, still looking a bit dazed, smiled briefly too, obviously aware, just as the Attorney General was, that the press would arrive soon. Word of events here would travel quickly but, by asking for restraint, Weiss could claim he did not intend to use the situation for personal gain.

The old police chief shook his head. "Well, sir, I don't have any men 'cept myself. Once in a while, Ernie Olsen over at the grocery store helps me out. But if anything serious crops up, why, I either call the BCA—that's the Bureau of Criminal Apprehension—'course you probably already knew that—or the state highway patrol and they usually call the National Guard. You want me to call 'em?"

"No," Weiss said. "You go see if you can help the people on the bus."

The old chief saluted crisply, then turned and shuffled away. Jeremiah suspected the salute was not done without a certain amount of irony. As he followed the chief's progress, he saw Sister Ezekiel emerge from the bus, looking tired and pale, as if she'd aged five years since he'd seen her last. She must have climbed onto the bus with Lendra. Now she slowly made her way over to them.

"This is terrible," Sister Ezekiel said. "Two little boys wounded. And what about the shelter? How many inside are hurt or dead? What about Dr. Mary and Ahmad?"

Colonel Truman answered her: "Only Major Sims took serious injuries. Dr. Mary is with her. My medics are treating the kids and the minor burn victims now."

Jeremiah glanced toward the shelter, saw that the front door and a good chunk of the front wall were gone. The windows were all broken. Black smoke drifted up from the gaping hole in the center. The pungent odor of burning plastic overrode every other smell. He said, "I'm afraid your shelter's in need of some major repairs as well, Sister."

Sister Ezekiel sighed. "As long as no one was killed. Things can be replaced. People can't."

Weiss nodded, then said, "Now, Jeremiah, I suppose I should be thanking you for helping us out. I appreciate what you did for us."

"Just happy to be doing God's work," Jeremiah replied.

"But that cannon you're carrying is illegal," Weiss said. "So is that shield. I'm going to have to confiscate them. Colonel?"

Colonel Truman stepped forward, his hand outstretched.

Jeremiah said, "I've got valid permits for them."

"That's impossible."

"They're up to date. You got a problem with the permits, take it up with the courts. But I'm not handing the cannon or the shield over."

"I don't believe this." Sister Ezekiel threw out her arms, her steel-gray eyes gleaming intensely. "Two little boys have been shot. Only by the grace of God are they still alive. Major Sims is badly injured. And you two are arguing over who gets to carry the biggest gun?"

"I'm sorry, Sister," Weiss said, "but we need to secure the safety of this place."

"With more weapons?" Sister Ezekiel yelled, her face flushing with anger. "The innocent always suffer for the ambitions of men. That's the way the world has always worked. Well, I'm tired of it. I'm tired of all you *men* with your guns and your political agendas and your indifference to human suffering."

Jeremiah stared at the ground, feeling chastened. He noticed that all conversation had stopped in the face of the nun's outburst. With his peripheral vision he saw Colonel Truman glance at Weiss, who shook his head briefly. The colonel stepped back.

"I know the President sent you here, Jeremiah," Weiss said. "But while you're within the confines of our perimeter, you'll follow my orders."

"I don't think so, Gray," Jeremiah answered. "She never said anything about that to me."

"Look, Jeremiah, I don't want to have you arrested, especially after you saved our bacon. But I'll do it if I have to. I can always charge you with kidnapping Jack Marschenko. Now, are you going to give me the cannon?"

Jeremiah looked at Lendra, who shrugged and said, "I'll put a call in to Eli—see what he says."

Sister Ezekiel interrupted, "We have to take care of the wounded, not to mention the men who need food and a place to sleep, men who haven't got anywhere else to go. Who were those people who attacked my shelter? And are they going to come back?"

Weiss turned to the nun. "They're Devereauxnians, Sister. And pseudos—fugitives from the Mars Project."

Jeremiah said, "Those are the Escala? Impressive. First time I've seen them in action. They move like soldiers, not astronauts."

Weiss said, "They're dangerous criminals. They just wounded thirteen people. Not to mention destroying the DS-9000. That whole Mars Project was a terrible mistake. Altering their DNA to increase their survivability on Mars was a crime against nature. Their sterility was God's way of punishing them for trying to become something other than human. And their uncontrollable aggression makes them a threat to humanity. They need to be stopped. At least we've passed the DNA Integrity Act to make transgenic alteration illegal, so these monstrosities will eventually die out."

Colonel Truman touched his hand to his earpiece for a moment, then interrupted, "Excuse me, sir, but that Cookie Monster fellow was sprung. So was the escaped prisoner who was working at the shelter."

"Cookie Monster?" Jeremiah said.

"A pseudo," Weiss replied.

"So maybe they were just trying to break him out, as well as destroy your scanner."

Weiss turned to Colonel Truman. "How did they free the prisoners?"

"Multi-phase chem-lasers," Colonel Truman answered. "Probably Las-knives. The Porta-cell was sliced open. The prisoners' ID chips were cut out of their necks and left on the cell floor, so we have no chance to track them down. They did it quickly and expertly." Truman paused for a moment, listened to his earpiece again and added, "Jet-copters will be here in three minutes."

Jeremiah heard them approaching. He turned to the north and as they came into view he suppressed a shiver. The two jet-copters looked awkward in the air: large bulbous vessels, rather like bumblebees, but with rigid wings. Jet engines at the sides and back of each copter worked in tandem, making the copters as maneuverable as helicopters but much faster. Intellectually Jeremiah knew they were safe. He'd flown on jet-copters before. But each experience had been terrifying, not to mention nausea inducing. He'd sworn never again to go up in one.

Sister Ezekiel touched Jeremiah's wrist briefly. "Thank you for saving my shelter. But I want both you and Mr. Weiss to leave as soon as possible." She glared at the two men, her voice clipped, her anger obvious. "You're destroying much more than just property." Compressing her lips tightly together, she headed across the parking lot, weaving her way around burning transport vehicles toward the damaged front door.

Weiss looked at Jeremiah and grimaced, then shrugged. After a moment he headed for the shelter. Jeremiah and Lendra fell in behind, Lendra gripping Jeremiah's arm tightly. Still talking into his comm unit, Colonel Truman trailed them.

Just inside the doorway, a twisted hunk of metal and plastic—the DS-9000—beeped sporadically. It looked beyond saving. Sister Ezekiel stood in the center of the lobby, hands on her hips, looking down at a heavyset woman who was crouched over a black soldier in a neck brace: Major Sims, Jeremiah realized.

The heavyset woman—Dr. Mary, no doubt—looked up at Jeremiah briefly before turning her back on him and bending over Major Sims to carefully inflate a pair of leg casts. She stuck her hefty rump up in the air and wiggled her bottom as she reached across the major. Jeremiah found his eyes drawn to her ample rear.

"Sister!" An albino rushed forward from a hallway where a group of men were gathered and threw his arms around the nun.

"It's okay, Henry," Sister Ezekiel said, her body tense. She pushed him away to arm's length, then leveled her gaze at him and said firmly, "We're fine. How are things here?"

"Several men were injured when that thing blew up," Henry said. "They're in the infirmary with the medics. Dr. Mary's so brave. She made us stay low, kept Redbird and Iggy from running out into the street. We're lucky most of the men cleared out after the scans."

"All right," Sister Ezekiel said. "Here's what I need you to do. Go back to the kitchen and see how bad it is. I need to know if we can get it cleaned up in time for the evening meal. Find Jackson and Tremaine. Our cooks," she explained to Jeremiah and Lendra as Henry departed.

Colonel Truman knelt before Major Sims. "How you doing, Bettany?"

Sims opened her mouth in a wide grin, her eyelids fluttering as if she could barely stay awake. "Dez," she said. "How you doin', Dez?"

"I'm fine, Major. You're obviously feeling no pain."

"No pain," Sims agreed. Then she glanced over at the ruined scanner. "Couldn't save it, though. The shield just...boom!"

"That's okay," Truman said. "You did a fine job. How do you feel?"

"I could use a kiss," Sims said. "Hey, how 'bout you, pretty girl?" She looked up at Lendra. "You want to give me a kiss?"

Jeremiah smiled as Lendra clasped his arm a little tighter.

"Love the drugs," Sims continued. "Feels like...lemon." She closed her eyes and began to hum softly.

"Are you going to stay open, Sister?" Weiss said.

She turned on him, her eyes narrow with fury. "Have you ever gone to bed hungry, Mr. Weiss? Do you know what it's like to have no one care whether you live or die? I wonder if you even see these men as people."

"I didn't mean to offend you, Sister," Weiss said. "And yes, I've gone to bed hungry."

For a moment, the two stared at each other, challenge in their faces. Then Sister Ezekiel sighed and said, "I'm sorry. I'm tired. I have nothing against you personally, Mr. Weiss. You have the guns and the law, so do what you must. Find Walt Devereaux. Then leave. I have a shelter to run. And if all we can provide is soup, then that's what we'll serve. But we're not going to let these men go to sleep with nothing in their stomachs." She nodded toward Weiss' shoulder. "Dr. Mary can have a look at that when she finishes with Major Sims."

"Treat the soldiers first," Weiss said. "I can wait." He stepped over to the scanner.

Jeremiah looked at it more closely. The light on its power cell flickered weakly.

Weiss said, "I suppose it's ruined."

"It might make an interesting sculpture," Jeremiah said.

"You don't have to sound so happy about it."

"No," Jeremiah said. "It looks good. You could put it on display along with your mobile command center over by 'Emerging Man.' Even charge admission. I admit they don't have the same depth or artistic importance as the statue, but still—three pieces for the price of one. You could probably recoup your costs in a hundred years."

Weiss laughed, a harsh bark, then glanced around the lobby. Finally he directed his attention to the weapon in Jeremiah's hand. He said, "All right, Jeremiah. Pursuant to the Patriot Amendment, I'm co-opting you for the remainder of your stay in this area. You're now under my authority."

"Shouldn't you check with the President first?" Jeremiah said, handing over his Identi-card.

Weiss grabbed the card. "I will," he said. "Oh, and I want that particle beam cannon."

"I told you, I've got a valid permit—"

"Your permit is discretionary. And I'm revoking it. As the Attorney General of the United States, I am hereby ordering the seizure of that weapon. Colonel?"

The soldiers in the room turned to Jeremiah. As the colonel stepped forward, his hand outstretched, Jeremiah glanced at Lendra. She tapped her interface and shook her head. "Eli says he has no authority to prevent Mr. Weiss from taking the weapon."

Weiss said, "Don't force me to arrest you, Jones."

Jeremiah stood still for a few seconds, delaying, hoping a solution might show itself. He finally said, "Let me just make sure it's locked in the safe position. You people have probably never seen one of these before. Don't want anybody getting hurt." He swung the cannon up, pressed the eject button and removed the converter. Then he handed the useless weapon to the colonel.

"Hey!" Colonel Truman said.

Weiss said, "Jeremiah, hand over that piece."

"This is a dangerous weapon as you just admitted. I've been certified to fire it. The Army doesn't even own one. Only the Elite Ops carry them. You guys might accidentally blow up this town if I gave you a working particle beam cannon. No, I'll let you take the outer shell but not the converter."

Dr. Mary now got to her feet. She brushed up against Jeremiah, the beginnings of a grin forming on her lips. "Love your cannon," she whispered as she passed.

Jeremiah froze. No, it couldn't be Julianna. He stared at the doctor, studying her puffy face, looking for anything familiar, finding nothing reminiscent of his old partner.

Dr. Mary quickly turned to Colonel Truman. "Major Sims is stable for the moment. I want to keep an eye on her for a little longer.

Then you can medevac her out." The doctor's voice, rich and vibrant, contained some indefinable familiarity to the cadence or tone. But how could Julianna be here?

"Dr. Mary McCaffery," Sister Ezekiel said, formally introducing Lendra and Jeremiah.

The doctor offered Jeremiah her hand. As he grasped it, he felt a tingling in his stomach. Her dark brown eyes offered no sign of recognition. And she wore a perfume he'd never smelled before but his nose twitched anyway, as if on some subconscious level he remembered her aroma. She gave his hand a firm shake.

"Nice to meet you," she said. "Call me Dr. Mary." Then she turned to Weiss and said, "The medics seem to be handling your soldiers. Let me take a look at that shoulder."

Jeremiah moved halfway across the room and caught Lendra's eye. He beckoned her over.

"What do you think of Dr. Mary?" he asked quietly.

Lendra studied the doctor, who was helping the Attorney General remove his coat and shirt. "Strange," she replied, "I was just thinking there's something off there. The way she carries herself—very confidently, very strongly."

"I think that's Julianna."

"What? How do you know?"

"I don't—not for sure." Jeremiah put his arm on Lendra's shoulder and turned her toward the ruined doorway. "But I want you to check out Dr. Mary McCaffery. Quietly."

"How can that be Julianna? Even if she had genetic surgery, she's way too heavy and too old."

"Let me know as soon as you get an answer."

"Right. I'll call Eli again too. Update him on our progress."

"By the way," Jeremiah said. "You kept calm out there very well when the shooting went down. Good work. Tell Eli you deserve a raise."

"I was scared to death."

"Yes, but you didn't panic. And you didn't take neo-dopamine, either."

As she walked outside, Jeremiah turned toward Weiss and the doctor. Weiss sat in the middle of the lobby on a charred but functional chair while Dr. Mary cleaned his shoulder wound. Due to the cauterizing effect of the laser, the skin around the wound bubbled, looking red and raw. Jeremiah had felt the sting of a laser before, so he knew that this was about the time the pain kicked in—right after the shock wore off. Weiss took the pain with only a grimace. He was tough: no question about that. When Dr. Mary finished cleaning the area, she applied a QuikHeal bandage and adjusted the flow of anesthetics and antibiotics. Immediately, Weiss' face lost its pinched look. Then she manipulated Weiss' arm, lifting it to various positions while examining a monitor that displayed the damage to muscle and nerve.

Once, while stretching Weiss' arm, she glanced at Jeremiah briefly. She looked nothing like the woman he'd known. Her smell, her voice, the way she moved: all different. Especially her eyes. He was so used to the arctic blue of her eyes. And this plump, middle-aged woman looked nothing like the athlete he remembered. But he somehow knew that Dr. Mary was Julianna.

Chapter Thirteen

Doug awoke.

One moment, oblivion; the next, woozy consciousness. He opened his eyes and lifted his throbbing head—discovered that he was on a huge, firm bed in a cave. Light emanated from a small globe hovering above his head. He reached toward it and the globe moved farther away. Amazing. This had to be a glow globe, filled with helium and powered by bacteria that produced light-emitting chemical reactions. He'd seen vids of them but had always suspected trick photography. When he pulled his hand back the globe repositioned itself over his head. He couldn't help but laugh. That lasted only a second as a sharp jolt pierced his head. Slowly, carefully, trying to keep the pain to a minimum, Doug moved to the end of the bed. How did he get here?

He remembered—

—Cookie Monster reaching out with a spray can, saying, "Sorry," and squirting him in the face. This had to be Cookie Monster's room, hidden underground. Doug recalled running through the woods surrounded by giants, Cookie Monster at his side. No one told him where they were going. In fact, no one spoke to him at all as they made their escape.

He eased himself to a sitting position, smelled the dampness of the rock mingling with a musty animal odor and traces of some unidentifiable food. Off in the distance through the open doorway, from a direction he could not place, he heard what he thought were voices. Closer in he picked up a humming from the glow globe.

Despite a foggy grayness to his thoughts, he recognized the drug-induced oblivion he had emerged from as a sort of death: the kind of death he'd visited often in his hazy and violent youth. Nothingness. That's what Devereaux said death was. Just nothingness. It wasn't so bad: not something to be afraid of. And if Devereaux was right, if death was oblivion, then the fear of it made no sense, for in death we would never feel or know anything again. We would simply cease to be. If we could just stop hoping for it to be something other than what it was, we could accept it and move beyond it.

Why was death so scary? Was life so great that to lose it would be tragic?

Devereaux preached that enlightened people could find comfort in the nothingness of death as long as they accepted the truth of it—that once you were finished with this life, once you had accomplished all you could, and were tired and infirm and feeling yourself fading from the world, then you could let go, relax, close your eyes and let your consciousness ebb out. That didn't mean you shouldn't fight for life, just that you shouldn't see death as evil. Death is the inevitable end of life.

And what about the sudden, accidental death of the young? Devereaux said that was no different whether God exists or not. Life is arbitrary. Always has been.

Doug looked at the sole picture on the wall—a 3D photograph of "Emerging Man." He wouldn't have guessed Cookie Monster to be an art lover. While he stared at the picture, Doug recalled the escape. After the attack at the Tessamae Shelter began, the guards by the cell door dropped to their knees, their weapons facing outward. Two more settled themselves behind trees: all four intense, alert, waiting. That was when Cookie Monster ran into the bars of the cell, grunting and yelling. Alarmed, Doug backed into a corner out of the way, wary of Cookie Monster's size and unpredictability.

The soldiers ordered Cookie Monster to shut up, but the big man ignored them, carrying on like some mad animal, running back and forth across the cage, slamming himself into the bars with a force that shook the entire cell. One of the guards swung his stun club over to Cookie Monster, prodding him with it. At that moment, the moment of greatest distraction, their rescuers moved. Doug didn't see it. It happened so fast, and he was watching Cookie Monster take the hit from the stun club. Incredibly, Cookie Monster didn't fall. He hesitated for a second, absorbing the blow, then backed away. Doug would have been knocked unconscious. Possibly his heart would have stopped. Cookie Monster just shook it off as the guard with the club went down.

Doug looked out then and saw the other guards already on the ground. A big man, almost as big as Cookie Monster, brought some sort of laser up and sliced right through several of the cell bars. The purple light of the laser extended only a few inches past the device—a Las-knife.

Two other attackers emerged from behind trees—one of them female…and huge. Not as big as the men—maybe only six-foot-four to their six-foot-nine or seven-foot height. But she was broad in the shoulders, like them. She wore the same camouflage coveralls as they. Only the lack of a beard made her immediately identifiable as a woman. Like Doug she was black. Under her big Afro, her face was ugly. But she moved beautifully, with controlled power, her muscles rippling beneath the coverall. The men, although slightly smaller than Cookie Monster, had heavily muscled torsos, narrow waists, massive thighs.

Like Cookie Monster, these people had to be pseudos. Were they Mars Project Astronauts too? As Doug stood in the center of the cell, Cookie Monster moved toward the opening and turned his back to the pseudo who had sliced through the bars. The pseudo administered a painkiller and neatly cut the ID chip out of Cookie Monster's neck.

"Come on," Cookie Monster said, his eyes locked on Doug's, a flicker of intelligence there that Doug had never seen before. Despite his bushy beard and the multi-colored bruising from the beating he had taken, Cookie Monster looked almost genteel. He gestured for Doug to approach and turn around. When Doug complied, the pseudo numbed his neck and cut out his ID chip also.

Then they took off through the woods, heading away from the shelter, off to the east, where almost two thousand acres of wild land lay before them. They skirted fallen houses and open basements, for the most part avoiding the deteriorated roads that ran through the abandoned neighborhood; instead, following paths that meandered often but always headed east. They skirted to the north of the old cemetery, turning before they reached the one ramshackle home Doug had visited in the recent past—a house just off the old main road. He'd been nervous when he went there and had stayed only a short time. He couldn't imagine anyone straying too far off the highway that ran through town. Only the very brave or the very crazy lived in the woods. Recently, rumors had spread of wild creatures out here, more dangerous than wolves and bears and even tigers.

Laughter bubbled up inside him. He fought it down.

These were the creatures of rumor—these pseudos.

Doug had struggled to keep up with the pseudos surrounding him. After a couple of minutes, he breathed heavily; then his legs began to feel like lead; finally he labored to suck in oxygen, taking huge gulps as he stumbled along. When he almost fell, Cookie Monster put a hand around his right arm and the black woman on the other side grabbed his left. They pulled him along between them, his feet seldom touching the ground.

After maybe fifteen minutes of running, they let go of Doug's arms and stopped. Doug had no idea where they were. All he knew was that they were in the middle of a forested area, among oaks and cottonwoods and any number of other trees he couldn't identify. The undergrowth here was lighter, which made this a good spot to rest.

Cookie Monster ignored him, as did the others. In fact, after nodding to each other, the four pseudos took positions surrounding Doug but facing away, as if keeping a lookout. They still had not spoken to each other and this lack of conversation began to wear on Doug's nerves.

"You're pseudos, ain't you?" he asked.

They swung to face him, eyes narrowing in anger, nostrils flaring, muscles tensing. Cookie Monster put his finger to his lips and returned to his position facing outward. The others did the same.

"There," one of the pseudos said, as he pointed back in the direction they'd come. He issued a low, piercing whistle that was almost immediately answered. A few seconds later, five more pseudos appeared out of the woods. Three males, two females. They too wore lightweight coveralls in camouflage green. Two of them appeared to be injured.

One of the females stood out in his mind—a blond Amazon with long flowing hair—just as well muscled as the other two females but with a statuesque beauty the other two lacked. The third female pseudo had dark hair and a severe look about her, but she stood with a confidence that made Doug think she was in command.

The nine huddled together for a moment speaking too softly for Doug to hear, then broke apart.

"What about him?" the commanding female asked, pointing at Doug. They all looked at him, anger or suspicion in their eyes.

"I'll bring him later," Cookie Monster said.

The pseudos huddled again, this time without Cookie Monster, and when they separated, the commanding female placed something into Cookie Monster's hand while the others slipped away, quietly disappearing into the trees. Then she too vanished almost soundlessly.

"You're Devereauxnians, ain't you?" Doug asked.

"As are you," Cookie Monster said.

"How did you know that?"

"I watch," Cookie Monster pointed to his ear, "and listen."

"I wanna help," Doug said. "That's why I came. Devereaux told me he was gonna be here—in Crescent Township. That's why I broke outta jail."

"How do you know it was Devereaux? Many people claim to be him."

Doug reached into his pocket and pulled out a small disk that looked like a coin, except for its blue-green color. On one side a ladder was engraved; on the other, an image of Emerging Man. He showed the coin to Cookie Monster. "Devereaux sent me this. Said it was his calling card."

"Devereaux told you he'd be here?" Cookie Monster said as he took the disk and studied it. Apparently satisfied, he handed it back. "Did he ask you to break out of prison and meet him here?"

Doug shook his head. "He told me not to come."

Cookie Monster nodded emphatically. "Damn right. You're an escaped convict. You'll bring attention just by being here."

"And you won't?" Doug said. "Nine pseudos runnin' around with sophisticated weapons?"

"We don't like to be called pseudos. As a black man, you should understand how cruel it is to dehumanize someone."

Doug nodded. "Sorry."

"Apology accepted."

"What do you wanna be called?"

"We're just people. We call ourselves Escala."

"Escala? What's that mean?"

Cookie Monster smiled. "It means we're evolving. We're on the ladder of enlightenment, trying to better ourselves."

"I like that," Doug said. "Escala, I'll remember that. So, you seen Devereaux? He mentioned he'd be here for a short time. And I just had to see him for myself. Until he came along, I had nothin'. He saved me, let me know I could become somethin' greater than I was. I had to tell him how much he meant to me."

That was when Cookie Monster reached out with the spray can and squirted it in Doug's face. Now Doug's head throbbed. For just a moment he wished he had a Blue Angel to take the pain away. No, that life was over. He was no addict. Closing his eyes, Doug rested his head on his hands, elbows on his knees, and took a couple deep breaths.

"Hello," Cookie Monster said.

Doug jumped to his feet and immediately regretted it as the space behind his eyes pounded.

"I didn't mean to scare you," Cookie Monster said.

"Just a headache," Doug said. "Where are we?"

"Safe. Had to knock you out for security reasons. Here, inhale." Cookie Monster sprayed a small vial into Doug's face. Almost involuntarily, Doug inhaled a chocolate aroma and his head cleared, the fog and pain dissipating. At the same time, he felt a growing annoyance at the way he was being handled.

"I can't be trusted because I ain't like you? You think you're better than me because you altered your body?"

"I didn't say that."

"You know, a bigger body don't make you a better person."

"We have an obligation to evolve."

"Devereaux was talkin' about our minds."

"That's part of it," Cookie Monster conceded.

"You can't achieve enlightenment through testosterone."

"That sounds like Devereaux," Cookie Monster said.

Doug laughed. "I guess I stole it from him. You know where he is?"

Cookie Monster shook his head.

"But he's been here?"

A nod.

"Will he be back soon?"

Cookie Monster shrugged.

"I guess I'll wait here then." Doug reached out and touched the cave wall. It felt slightly damp, cool to the touch, though his fingers came away dry.

"Have you spoken to Devereaux recently?" Cookie Monster said.

"No. I hoped he'd contact me but I ain't heard from him since I got here. I don't even know what he looks like now."

"Now?"

"I assume he's changed his appearance," Doug said, "but every time I talked to him on the vid, he looked like he used to in the past."

"The fewer people who know what he looks like, the safer he'll be."

"And only you can be trusted with that knowledge?"

"Let me show you around," Cookie Monster said. He gestured toward the doorway and waited for Doug to precede him. When Doug reached the hallway—a nine-foot-high tunnel carved through rock—the post-lightning smell of recently ionized air greeted him. Glow globes floated near the ceiling to his left, down the curving hallway, and voices came from that direction. To his right, the hallway disappeared into darkness. Doug walked past several open archways, all of which led into bedrooms similar to the room he'd just vacated. In one room, an Escala lay sleeping, a bandage on his massive thigh, but otherwise naked. Doug was surprised that there were no doors on any of the rooms.

As he advanced along the hallway, the sound grew until he was able to detect the laughter of children mingling with adult voices. The hallway opened to a large room that was actually a huge cave. The domed ceiling rose maybe a hundred feet in the air. Sparkling rocks decorated the dirt walls, highlighted by a trio of spotlights in the center of the room that moved in a circle and changed color, passing through red, yellow, green and blue. Several smaller glow globes hovered in the corners. At the far end, a stairway led up into darkness—the way out.

On one side of the cave, about thirty yards away, several young Escala children played a game with sticks and hoops. On the other side, maybe twenty yards from Doug, six giant men and women sat at a large table, engaged in conversation.

In the moment Doug took this in, the adults turned his way. Their eyes locked on him, trapping him with their intensity. Behind him, he heard Cookie Monster emit a low chuffing sound, almost a growl, and the children stopped their laughter, glancing over at him before returning to their game in a more subdued fashion. The adults continued to stare at Doug. Cookie Monster led him by the arm, gently, to the table. As he approached, Doug recognized the three women who had helped rescue him. The homely black woman sat next to a large man with red hair and a great many freckles. He was the only man not wearing a beard. Across the table from them, between two dark-haired Escala males with short beards, sat the blond Amazon. The dark female who had spoken for the group in the woods sat at the head of the table.

Cookie Monster stopped, pulling Doug next to him, placing his large arm around Doug's shoulders.

"Why?" the dark female asked.

"He's a Devereauxnian too," Cookie Monster replied.

"You have a plan?"

"Always." Cookie Monster grinned. "I have to patrol." He swung around to face Doug. "You'll be safe here." Then he strode to the stairs and took them two at a time, leaving Doug alone with the adults.

"This may work out nicely," the dark female said, nodding. She gestured to the only chair not in use. As Doug sat, she said, "I'm Quekri." Then she pointed to the homely black woman and said, "Temala."

Temala smiled, showing widely spaced teeth. Doug thought she looked hungry, like a cannibal eyeing a missionary—probably stupid too.

"Dunadan," Quekri said, indicating the red-haired man. Then she nodded to the other side of the table where the two dark-haired men sat on either side of the blond Amazon. "Shull, Zeriphi, Warrow." Finally Quekri looked at Doug and said, "You hungry?"

Doug nodded.

"Zeriphi." Quekri looked at the blond Amazon. "You're in estrus. Food?"

Zeriphi, the blond Amazon, stared at Quekri with a puzzled expression. Then her eyes widened and she turned to look at Doug. After a few seconds Zeriphi nodded. She bowed slightly, pushed back her chair and left the room. What was that about? And the word, estrus—that sounded vaguely familiar.

"What's estrus?" Doug asked.

Quekri raised her eyebrows. Temala grinned. Dunadan placed his freckled hand over Temala's and rubbed it gently, while Shull and Warrow exchanged glances before they all turned their attention back to Doug. Confused by their refusal to answer him, Doug watched them watching him, whatever they'd been talking about before he entered the room forgotten.

He thought about saying something to break the tension. Then he realized that the tension was coming from him. Their faces bespoke curiosity, nothing more. Still, their silence bothered him. He liked to talk, enjoyed the sound of voices. He felt less lonely when he was around people who talked. These people made him feel lonelier.

"I came here 'cuz I knew he was here," Doug finally spoke. "I'm a Devereauxnian just like you." When he got no response, he continued, "We're all in this together. We all wanna help him." Still, they said nothing. "Were you involved in the old Mars Project?" he asked. "I know they experimented with modifying human DNA to increase the chances for survival on Mars. But the mutations didn't work very well, from what I heard."

Nothing. He might as well have been talking to the rocks.

"When I was in jail," Doug spoke just to hear a voice, "I began to follow Devereaux's teachings. But maybe I should start at the beginning. I got into drugs because that's what kids in my hood did. We didn't go to school much. Couldn't get no education there anyway. Momma didn't care if I learned nothin' or not. She was too busy tryin' to survive, workin' three jobs just to bring home enough for food and a lousy apartment. My old man split before I was born. My friends and I hung out on corners. Waitin'. Like maybe things would get better if we just waited long enough. Occasionally we got high. Pretty soon, I needed to get high all the time. At first the drugs made me feel more alive. Then they started suckin' my soul, my essence, away. I got arrested several times. Finally picked up my third strike—you know? Third felony?"

No response.

"And that's when I began to study Devereaux's teachings. I even recruited others to join me on the ladder. The ladder of enlightenment." The adults around the table finally reacted. They leaned forward, focusing on him. "You know about that, right?"

They nodded. Shull twisted his neck to the side and Warrow reached over to scratch his back. Shull chuffed softly.

"I studied other subjects too," Doug continued. "I discovered the thrill of knowledge. That was powerful stuff. It wasn't long before I created a vidblog, began talkin' about my experiences. That put me into contact with others, most outside of prison, all ready to devote their lives to Devereaux's message. That's when Devereaux first contacted me. I asked him, 'Why me?' and he said I was one of many. We're like an army of ordinary people searching for meaning. We're not alone. He's there with us all the time. That's reassuring. Have you been out in the real world lately? Do you know what it's like out there now?"

"We see the news," Dunadan said. Temala and the others nodded.

"You almost got to be out there to understand it," Doug said. "Whole country's gone mad. The rich keep buildin' walls around their communities, increasin' their security, consolidatin' in places where they can defend themselves against terror attacks or revolt by the masses. But the masses don't revolt. They're beaten. The rich hold out the promise of success. They say that stimulatin' economic growth for the rich benefits everybody but the only jobs they provide are low payin', demeaning and unstable. And we got no choice but to accept the bones they throw our way. We got no power. Any attempt to organize brings out the anarchists and that brings out the private security forces or the National Guard."

"What about the police?" Warrow asked.

"Police are a joke in most parts of the country," Doug said. "They work for the wealthy. They got to. It's a game of survival for them too. Mostly they look the other way while the rich do what they please. No, the police only got one real job anymore. Keep the druggies and the poor away from the rich. That's how I ended up in prison."

"Sounds like you had it pretty good there," Quekri said.

"True," Doug agreed. "Prison was the best thing that coulda happened to me. Since I was a nonviolent offender, they put me in a class-two prison instead of a maximum-security place. It was there that I found the ladder—and others who wanted more from life too. With less than a year left in my sentence, Devereaux contacted me. I don't know if any of you've met him—I ain't—but just talking with him over the vid, or hearin' his voice in a comm letter, gave me such a lift that I knew I could accomplish anything."

Doug looked around at his audience. They were really listening now. Shull and Warrow had gone still. Dunadan kept his hand over Temala's but his eyes on Doug's face. And Temala continued to look at Doug with an intensity that made him nervous.

"When he told me he was gonna be here," Doug said, talking mostly to Quekri, "I had to join him. Couldn't even finish out my sentence. I just came runnin'. He told me not to but I couldn't wait no longer. I had to help him. And I been waitin' to see him ever since. He's contacted me on the vid or by comm letter but he ain't never shown himself in person. Not yet, but soon. He will."

Doug nodded to emphasize the point and his audience nodded too, acknowledging his faith that Devereaux would someday appear.

Zeriphi returned with a platter containing bread, cheese and some gray substance in a large bowl. Gelatinous and lumpy at the same time, it looked like oatmeal covered in mud. A small bowl of grapes and a glass of water rounded out the offering. Zeriphi placed the platter before him. Doug reached for the bread and cheese, ignoring the gray muck.

Angling her eye at the lumpy concoction, Zeriphi said, "It's good."

Doug shuddered, shook his head violently.

"Don't be a baby," Zeriphi said.

Doug blushed as he sniffed at the bowl tentatively. He detected a pleasant musky aroma. Still, he wrinkled his nose and began making a sandwich of cheese. Zeriphi grabbed his hand and stopped him. She then took a knife from the platter and spread a thick layer of the gray gunk on a slab of bread, covering it with cheese. She proffered the sandwich to Doug. "Try it," she commanded.

Doug grimaced as he looked at the sandwich. "I don't think so."

"You'll like it." Zeriphi shoved the sandwich into Doug's hand. When he looked at her, she pushed his hand toward his face, nodded in reassurance.

He bit tentatively into the bread, hoping not to gag. But it was delicious, almost melting in his mouth. "Wow, this is fantastic." Taking a huge bite, he chewed slowly, savoring the rich mushroom and bean flavor, commingled with onion, garlic and some spices he could not identify. He realized he was famished. As he ate the sandwich, a warmth slowly spread through him.

"Thanks for makin' me try it," he said to Zeriphi. "I've never tasted anything like it. You're a marvelous cook." The Escala exchanged glances and smiles. Doug felt the need to explain his hesitation. "It just looked awful. Can I have another one?"

Zeriphi moved her chair closer to Doug's and prepared another sandwich for him. While he ate, she continued to stare at him and he found it increasingly difficult to turn his attention away from her: her blond hair, high cheekbones, rounded face and dark brown eyes, large and luminous. They pulled at him, drew him in until he saw nothing else. As they gazed at each other, he felt like he was under a spell, finally broken by Quekri's voice:

"Zeriphi will keep you company tonight."

Zeriphi nodded. "Eat," she said as she lifted the remainder of the sandwich to his mouth.

Chapter Fourteen

After the jet-copters took off with the wounded, Jeremiah stood in the lobby, his back to the gaping hole that led to the outside. Through the wall-window of the infirmary, he watched Dr. Mary treat the soldiers with minor injuries. Lendra approached him quietly.

"I found practically nothing on Dr. Mary McCaffery," she whispered. "It's like she just appeared out of nowhere a few years ago."

"That's because she did," Jeremiah answered.

"I still don't see how that can be Julianna."

Jeremiah shrugged. "It is. What about Cookie Monster? You got any more information about him or these Escala?"

"Not specifically. I'm still working on that. They're probably underground somewhere. I'll keep looking for any records or historical documents that might show where they could be."

Jeremiah stared at Dr. Mary through the wall-window again, his body tensing.

Lendra grabbed his arm. "I told Eli you believe the doctor is actually Julianna. He recommended that you kill her or stay away from her."

Jeremiah removed Lendra's hand. "I've got to talk to her, find out what she's doing here. You get your bag from the van before dark. I think we should spend the night. Have Sister Ezekiel show you to a room—one that locks. I have a feeling things are going to get ugly out there."

"Should I get your bag too?"

"Don't bother. I'm going out later. Just make sure you set the van's security system."

Sister Ezekiel emerged from the dining area, Colonel Truman and Gray Weiss beside her. Together, they moved toward the infirmary, heads bent in discussion. Weiss said with a frown: "Devereaux's deadly creations—these pseudos—seek to make humans obsolete. Consider the hubris of the man, creating a new species." As Sister Ezekiel took off her glasses and began cleaning them on a handkerchief, Weiss pointed to them and added: "Your church recognizes the importance of staying true to your humanity and properly bans genetic manipulation."

"I sometimes wonder," Sister Ezekiel replied. She put the glasses back on.

Jeremiah shook his head. How did forcing someone to wear glasses or a hearing aid further the teachings of Christ?

"And as for Devereaux," Sister Ezekiel said, "Jesus commands us to love all God's creatures." She entered the infirmary ahead of Weiss. Truman halted for a moment at the door before following them inside.

Lendra glanced around the room to make certain it was clear, then said, "What do you have in mind?"

"A little reconnaissance."

Lendra frowned, pursed her lips together. "She's capable of anything. She stabbed you, for God's sake. You can't possibly be considering—"

"I need to find out what she knows."

"Wouldn't it make more sense to look for Cookie Monster?"

"That's what I'll be doing. Julianna's very good at what she does. She might know something that's not in the computer records."

"And you think she'll just tell you?"

"Perhaps. Besides, she's a threat."

"Are you going to kill her?"

"Not yet."

Lendra glared through the wall-window at Dr. Mary. "I think you want to see her because you have unfinished business with her."

"That too," Jeremiah said. His eyes kept returning to Dr. Mary, who was now talking with Weiss and Colonel Truman.

"Eli told me to remind you that she's been charged with treason. The safest option may be to take her out."

"Eli always thought he'd make a good ghost," Jeremiah answered.

Lendra sighed. "I'll be in the van, studying the Escala. I'll be back before dark."

* * *

"Excuse me, Doctor," Jeremiah said as he stepped into the infirmary. "Could I trouble you to look at this arm?" He pulled back his sleeve to display the QuikHeal bandage. Dr. Mary, who had been talking in low tones to Sister Ezekiel, Weiss and Colonel Truman, looked at him in surprise.

"How did you get that?" Weiss asked.

"I cut myself shaving."

"Let me see that," Dr. Mary said. She stepped closer and peeled the bandage back. "Not too bad, although it could use some cleaning. I've got some salve in my room. Why don't we look at it there? This way, Jeremiah, is it?" Dr. Mary led him down a hallway to a small room at the back of the shelter, which had escaped damage during the fight. Gesturing for Jeremiah to precede her, she followed him inside and closed the door after herself. He noticed a small bed and nightstand on one wall, a desk on the other. Behind the desk, several shelves contained old hardcover books and various medical supplies. He moved toward a chair in front of the desk as she darkened the window to the outside and pressed a button next to the door three times in rapid succession. The light went on, then off, then on, an almost imperceptible hum emanating from speakers in the corners.

Leaning back against the door, she said, "Privacy field. If you scream, no one will hear you."

"I wasn't planning to make a lot of noise."

"It may become necessary. Why don't you take off your shirt, Jeremiah?"

"Why don't you take off your disguise, Julianna?"

She laughed. "I know you're angry with me, darling. But I saved your life."

"Saved my life? You stabbed me. With a poisoned knife."

"Oh, please. It was only a paralyzing agent. I put it on the blade to keep you from killing me, which you'd have done if I hadn't incapacitated you. Besides, I didn't hit any vital organs. And I put a QuikHeal bandage on before I left. So you're welcome."

"If you think I'm going to thank you for betraying me…"

"Oh, grow up." Julianna pushed herself away from the door and took a couple steps forward. Jeremiah backed up until his legs bumped the chair. He nearly fell into it. "Relax," Julianna said. "If I'd wanted to kill you, you'd be dead."

Jeremiah opened his mouth to protest, but closed it almost immediately. Even though he couldn't dispute the truth of her statement, he had no intention of relaxing. He'd often wondered why she hadn't finished him off. Why would a proven killer like Julianna leave an enemy alive when she didn't have to?

She took another two steps, stopped directly in front of him and wrapped her arms around him. Then she kissed him.

He kept his eyes open, untrusting, though hers were closed. An electric surge went through him, a tingle that shot from head to toe. He tasted her again. It had been a long time.

"I should kill you," he said when she released him.

"Later," she replied with a lecherous smile, leaning forward to kiss him again.

Jeremiah shook his head, holding her away. Although he couldn't discern anything out of the ordinary from the feel of her shoulders, he knew that Julianna was wearing a body suit as well as a mask. He touched her face with his fingers, pushed against the neo-skin.

Pointing to the computer interface above her ear, he said, "When did you get this?"

Julianna pulled the interface from her temple and held it up for him to see. "I had it installed last year." Then she lifted her head slightly.

Without saying a word, Jeremiah reached out for the mask. He slid his fingers under the neck of her sweater, found where the mask touched the body suit and peeled it away slowly, carefully lifting it over Julianna's head, removing the attached wig at the same time, revealing at last the face he knew so well: the small thin nose, the clear bronze skin, the high cheekbones and full lips, the dancing eyes—brown now instead of the arctic blue he remembered. He studied them. He'd always found her eyes disconcerting. Lasers. Piercing him to the heart.

Yet they themselves were impenetrable. Diamonds. Dazzling in their brightness, harder than stone. Now that they were no longer blue they seemed to have a liquid quality. Of all the weapons he'd encountered in his life, none had been as deadly as those eyes. Still, when she looked at him now, he wanted to touch her, hold her. How many times had he told himself never to trust those eyes?

She took the mask from him and walked over to her nightstand. Setting the mask and interface down, she loosened her blond hair, letting it fall to her shoulders. When she turned back to him, he looked down at her pudgy body and grinned, recalling her slim and athletic figure. "You always did like body suits," he said.

"And you always loved your magic camos."

"What are you doing here?"

"Same as you. Looking for Devereaux."

"For the bounty?"

Julianna shook her head. "I've got other reasons. Who's the little honey you brought with you?"

"Lendra? Eli's assistant. Thinks she's going to be running CINTEP one day."

"She's a cutie."

"She's very smart. Probably dangerous."

Julianna lifted an eyebrow. "Homicidal?"

"If she comes after you, it won't be a direct attack."

"I've always had good peripheral vision." Julianna looked away from Jeremiah, then reached out to the side and touched his chin. "That's your nose, right?"

Jeremiah laughed as he shook his head. "Just be careful around her."

"She's definitely infatuated with you."

"Lendra? She's just following Eli's orders."

"Maybe at first," Julianna said. "But I noticed the way she looks at you. Intense. Who can blame her?"

"I'm not interested in Lendra."

Julianna smiled. "Or me, apparently."

"My wife died four months ago."

Julianna nodded. "I heard about that. Catherine was never right for you—she was weak."

"She was sane."

Julianna chuckled softly.

"Tell me something," Jeremiah said, "for old time's sake. Do you know anything about what happened to my son? He was taken shortly after you stabbed me."

Julianna shook her head. "I heard about that too. Sorry, Jeremiah. It wasn't me. If it had been, I'd have made sure you knew it."

Jeremiah sighed. "That's what I figured."

"Believe it or not, Jeremiah, I wasn't out to get you. You were simply in the way."

"That makes me feel much better. Now, you want to tell me why I shouldn't have Weiss arrest you?"

"Because if we work together, we can find Devereaux before Weiss does."

"Who hired you to find him?"

"Nobody," Julianna said. "I'm here for personal reasons—for atonement."

Jeremiah snorted. "What, you're a Devereauxnian?"

"Actually, I am."

Jeremiah studied her brown eyes, as if he might find truth there. He said, "Nice try. You almost had me there."

"I'm serious, Jeremiah."

"Suddenly you've found enlightenment? I don't think so. You're just like me. A professional killer. Dress it up any way you want but that's what we are. Killers. We're the monsters Devereaux preaches against. We represent humanity's violent past. We don't find redemption in some feel-good credo."

"You don't think we can be saved?"

"I don't want to be saved. I am who I am."

"You haven't been the same since your son was taken."

"How would you know?"

"Devereaux can bring you peace."

Jeremiah shook his head. He couldn't talk about this now: not with her, not with anyone. He needed to think.

Julianna reached behind her, grabbed a small glass jar from a shelf, and gestured toward the bed. "I've got some salve that'll take care of your arm."

"When did you become a doctor?"

"I didn't. I had the basic medical course at CINTEP and that interface tells me everything I need to know."

"You always were a quick study. That damned eidetic memory."

"Did you know Eli tried to keep that a secret from you?"

"Why would he do that?"

Julianna shrugged. "There are lots of things he doesn't want you to know."

Jeremiah sat. He couldn't argue the point. Eli's mania for secrecy had plagued Jeremiah for years. While Julianna took a seat next to him, reached for his hand and gently applied a cool salve to his wound, Jeremiah studied her. He wondered what was really going on in her mind. She always seemed to be playing psychological games with him. Was she really a Devereauxnian? And did she really think she could drive a wedge between he and Eli?

"Why did you do it?" he asked suddenly.

"Betray you?" she asked.

He nodded.

"Very simple, darling. Money. Power. Freedom. It's not as if there are good guys and bad guys in our world. We're all the same. You choose to play for one side. But you could earn far more as a freelancer."

"How does that reconcile with Devereauxnianism?"

Julianna released his hand. "It doesn't. I'm out of that business now."

"What happened to your eyes?" Jeremiah asked. "I miss the blue."

"Couldn't be helped. Surgically implanted contacts."

"Where's Devereaux?"

Julianna laughed. "The quick change of subject? Trying to catch me off-guard? Sorry, but I don't know where he is."

"What's your next step?"

"I'm here to protect Devcreaux," Julianna said. "Plain and simple."

"What about the bioweapons he's designed? How do they tie in to the whole peace and cooperation and betterment of the species thing?"

Julianna shook her head. "Government propaganda. They're afraid of Devereaux. His movement has grown enormously. They're terrified of losing power. You of all people should know how often they twist the truth to serve their ends. How many missions did Eli tell us were absolutely vital? Mubarno, for instance. Look at his successor. He's no better. The world's exactly the same. Only Devereaux offers hope."

"So you're saying Devereaux never designed bioweapons?"

Julianna shrugged. "He may have thought them up. He might even have designed them. But he never would have built them." Julianna shook her head. "The government, the military, they want the weapons. That's why they've sent you after Devereaux."

Of course, Jeremiah realized. Why hadn't he thought of that before? "And what about the Escala?"

"Clearly Devereaux's with them," Julianna said. "I haven't found their hideout yet. I've befriended one of them—a man named Cookie Monster—but he hasn't told me anything yet. The two of us, though, working together again…"

"And what happens when we find Devereaux? You try to stab me again?"

"We'll work that out. I think if you spoke to Devereaux for even a short time, you'd realize how ridiculous these accusations against him are."

"You know that Weiss is going to bring the media into this very soon. And that's going to mean more trouble. We're going to have a war on our hands."

"Sounds like fun," Julianna said.

Jeremiah shook his head. Despite Julianna's craziness, he realized he still cared for her. A part of him would always love her, he supposed. He didn't trust her; he knew she was selfish and dangerous and possibly insane. The smart play was to take her off the field. Yet he couldn't kill her. How had he gotten so screwed up?

Julianna stood. "We'd better rejoin the group. Don't want them to get the wrong impression."

Chapter Fifteen

Sister Ezekiel stepped into her office and found Ahmad Rashidi sitting behind her desk, Colonel Truman's tablet of legal documents in front of him, chewing a wad of khat, his eyes wide open and alert. Coming from the speakers in the corners, she heard a zither playing some Middle Eastern tune, its strings lightly dancing over the melody.

"Ahmad? Good Lord, I completely forgot about you in all this frenzy."

"No problemo, Sister. I just finished looking through all these writs and such. Hope you don't mind me puttin' a little muzak on."

"Not at all. Were you working this whole time?"

"Well, no. There was a brief period where I was crouched under your desk cursin' Devereaux and soiling my pants. Good thing I wore brown, huh?"

"How could I have forgotten to check on you?"

Ahmad grinned. "That's okay. I know where you keep the spare underwear." He shifted in his seat. "But did you have to starch it?"

"Please, Ahmad. Your jokes aren't funny." But she smiled.

"I'm not joking. I'm trying to understand your culture. Is putting starch in your underwear a Catholic thing? Because we Muslims like our underwear comfortable."

Sister Ezekiel shook her head but her smile grew broader.

"Just tryin' to lighten the mood, Sister. Anyway, Dr. Mary popped her head in after the shootin' stopped and made sure I was okey-dokey. Frankly, just between you and me," Ahmad looked both ways, as if concerned that someone might be spying on them, "I think Dr. Mary has the hots for me. And who can blame her?" He spread his arms wide. "Where's she gonna find a catch as big and beautiful as me?"

"You're unbelievable," Sister Ezekiel said.

"And I have good news for you, Sister. Even though these documents are in good order, you got nothin' to worry about with the scanner 'cuz I don't believe they'll be able to get another one here for at least two days, and by that time I can file for a TRO—a temporary restraining order—and Judge Moline is pretty good about keepin' the status quo copacetic, so she probably won't let 'em install the new one without presentin' evidence to support their need for it. What they got now ain't exactly smokin' gun material. I can't even tell from these why they think Devereaux is here."

"Thank you, Ahmad. As always, you've done a marvelous job. But we have more important things to worry about right now."

"Yeah, I heard about the kids. They'll be okay. Inshallah."

"God certainly had a hand in keeping them alive. And the bus is now on its way back to Minneapolis. Colonel Truman provided a squad to escort it."

"Allah will protect them. Besides, the real danger is down here—where the evil lies."

"You're not going to try to blame Devereaux for all this, are you?"

"Who else is there to blame? I'm not sayin' he pulled the trigger. And I'm not even sayin' he intended for all this to happen but you gotta admit that bad things keep happenin' because of him."

"Not because of him," Sister Ezekiel said. "Because of people reacting to him."

"But we must react to him, Sister." Ahmad's eyes grew narrow as he frowned. "We must defend ourselves against his attack on our faith. The Koran states: 'Strive hard against the unbelievers and the hypocrites, and be firm against them. Their abode is hell, an evil refuge indeed.' And Devereaux, by denying Allah, is attacking Him. Do we not have a duty to defend Islam, even to the death?"

"Nonsense. Devereaux never attacked any organized religion. His misguided ladder attempts to show that we must live as if there were no God. But it's not as if he proved there's no God."

"He insults us, Sister. Allah commands us to fight his blasphemy."

"So all this violence is God's will?"

"Everything that happens on Earth is Allah's will."

"Perhaps you should return to Minneapolis."

"No." Ahmad held up his hands. "I'm sorry, Sister. I said I'd help you and I will. If Devereaux's here, I'd like to see him. Besides, I already started draftin' the TRO. I'll have it in Judge Moline's office first thing tomorrow mornin'."

"I'm glad you can stay, Ahmad. Actually, we could use some help in the kitchen."

Ahmad's eyes opened wide. "What, peelin' potatoes? I'm a lawyer, not a cook."

"If we all pitch in, you'll be able to eat that much sooner."

"You want me in an apron? When did I turn into a woman?" Ahmad waved his arms furiously in front of himself. "Get me a burka. Don't look at my body!"

* * *

Sister Ezekiel took comfort in the small act of preparing the evening meal. To her surprise, most of the dining area remained usable. "We got lucky," Colonel Truman explained. "The pseudos fired only on the scanner and adjusted their power settings to minimize the damage. It could have been much worse." A few laser strikes had hit the ceiling, dropping debris on the tables and creating tennis ball-size holes to the outside. And a few pulses had gone through sidewalls into the dormitory area. But only one table had been demolished by laser fire. All the benches survived. While the soup simmered, Sister Ezekiel brought Henry through the dining room's double doors to the lobby, where the Attorney General now stood in close conversation with Colonel Truman.

"Excuse me," she said. "Were you planning to eat with us this evening?"

"I believe I will," Weiss said.

"And your people, Colonel?"

"I will, Sister. And I'll ask my troops but I believe most of them prefer Army rations. Do you have enough for those of us who wish to join you?"

"We'll make do."

"We could supplement the meal with our rations," Truman said.

"Yes," Weiss agreed, "by all means. If we can be of any assistance, let us know."

"We'll be fine tonight. But I'd be happy to take any food you can spare for future use. Plus I have a request."

"Please," Weiss said.

"Could you keep the troop presence out front to a minimum? I don't want my guests to feel uncomfortable."

"I'm afraid I can't take soldiers away from the entrance. This place is a target. You need the security we're providing."

"Can I have Henry stationed outside the—" she gestured to the ruined doorway— "to reassure the men that a meal will be served tonight?"

"Good idea." Weiss waved his hand. "Colonel Truman can make that happen."

Henry exited through the opening. Within minutes, a dozen men made their way inside. Mostly long-time guests, old and frail, dirty and unwashed, their gaunt faces never ceased to clutch at Sister Ezekiel's heart. They stopped at the entry and looked around cautiously. Fortunately, the damaged scanner had been removed, so the lobby no longer looked like a war zone. Sister Ezekiel inhaled deeply. She could still smell burnt plastic.

"Come in," she said. "Welcome. Pardon the mess." She stepped toward them, touched Flyer gently on the arm. "Hello, Redbird, Iggy," she said to two other favorite guests. "Straight on through to the dining room. Watch your step."

"Were these men scanned?" Weiss asked the colonel.

"God knows, sir. Can you tell them apart?"

"Good point." As Weiss looked them over, Sister Ezekiel turned to examine them as well. To a man, they wore beards, ranging from wispy to full, and shabby clothes. Their long-sleeved shirts and thin trousers had holes at the elbows and knees. She supposed they looked dreadful to someone like Weiss. The thought prompted her to say:

"What do you think of these men, Mr. Weiss? Do you see them as shiftless and lazy? Do you understand why they're really here?"

"I've already apologized for any offense I might have caused, Sister. I understand that society has abandoned many—promising jobs that never existed. Dangling hope before them with programs and initiatives that were never properly run. Challenging them to pull themselves up with hard work and education while high-paying jobs have gone to other countries, and automation has further dragged down wages." Jeremiah and Dr. Mary entered the lobby. "Ah, there you are, Jeremiah. All patched up?"

"Yes." Jeremiah issued a tiny smile, barely noticeable. "What are you rambling on about now?"

"I'm talking about problems in this country that need to be addressed, that aren't being addressed now—schools and hospitals falling into disrepair, the overtaxed middle class refusing to pay for more social services, the rich circling their wagons. I'm talking about children who don't get an education, then don't get good jobs, then give up on life and find themselves on the streets, or in prison, or in shelters like this.

"I'm talking about anarchy in the streets. Hatred and despair and intolerance. And I'm talking about trying to find a way to put all that behind us, to move beyond the self-centered thinking of individuals that weakens this country. I have reached the unavoidable conclusion that we need a strong central government to keep us atop the world. That's what I'm talking about."

Several soldiers standing by the doorway applauded.

"Does that help answer your question, Sister?" Weiss asked.

"Those are marvelous words," Sister Ezekiel said.

"You sound like a man who wants to be President," Jeremiah said.

Weiss grimaced. "I don't care about the office itself. I care about fixing this country. I care about undoing the injurious acts of the past and putting America back on top for good. Is that wrong?"

"One man's right," Dr. Mary said as she looked from Weiss to Jeremiah, "is another man's wrong."

True, Sister Ezekiel thought. But why did Dr. Mary look at Jeremiah when she said it?

"Dinner is served, Sister." Ahmad grinned broadly from the doorway. "I always wanted to say that."

"Ahmad," Dr. Mary said, "you've found your true calling, I see. I love the apron."

"It's more than that, Doc. I think you're infatuated by the man inside the apron."

Dr. Mary laughed.

"Mr. Weiss, Colonel Truman, Jeremiah," Sister Ezekiel said, "this is my lawyer, Ahmad Rashidi."

"Call me Ahmad," the lawyer said as he shook hands.

Sister Ezekiel gestured toward the dining room. "Why don't we all sit down to dinner? Please join us for a prayer."

"Of course," Weiss said, holding out his hand to indicate that Sister Ezekiel should precede him. "Coming, Jeremiah?"

"Go ahead and start. I want to check on Lendra," Jeremiah said.

* * *

As Colonel Truman followed Weiss into what was left of the dining area, he said, "I've been wanting to tell you that the troops were most impressed with your actions today, sir. So was I."

Weiss shrugged. "I just did what needed to be done, Colonel. And I couldn't have done it without your help."

"Still," Truman said. "Where you lead, we'll follow."

"That's most kind, Colonel."

"It's too bad about those boys getting hit."

"Yes. I called their parents, gave them the news."

"You did?" Truman nearly stumbled in his surprise. "That was good of you."

"They're furious with Devereaux for causing such unrest. But they're thankful the kids are still alive."

Truman sat facing the lobby, his back to the wall, his opinion of Weiss ticked up a notch at Weiss' unnecessary act of kindness. Weiss also sat against the wall, next to him rather than across the table. Sister Ezekiel directed traffic, telling men where to sit for the meal. A dozen soldiers had followed them into the dining area—nine men and three women. They took two tables at the far end of the room.

Beside him, Weiss reached inside his suit and pulled out a small, dented flask.

He smiled. "It's been a long day. Care for an aperitif?"

Truman raised his eyebrows. "Haven't heard that word in a long time. I have one as well." Truman removed a thin flask from his jacket.

"What's yours," Weiss asked.

"Blackberry brandy. Yours?"

"Schnapps," Weiss said. "Why don't we start with mine and save yours for dessert?"

"Good idea," Truman said. He held out his cup as Weiss struggled to twist the top off the damaged flask. The stubborn cap finally removed, Weiss measured out half the flask. While Weiss poured the rest into his own cup, Truman said, "I wonder why Jeremiah saved us."

"He's an unusual man, Colonel," Weiss said. "Very dangerous. He's killed many times for CINTEP."

"Why do you think the President sent him here?"

"She believes that arresting Devereaux is the wrong thing to do."

"But what about the weapons he's designed?"

"She wants to negotiate with him and the pseudos." Weiss shook his head. "One thing I learned in the CIA was that you don't negotiate with terrorists, no matter how they disguise themselves." Weiss held up his cup in a toast, favoring his injured arm only slightly. "Cheers," he said. Truman clinked metal with him, then took a sip, the liquid warming his throat from top to bottom.

Sister Ezekiel approached the table.

"Ready for the prayer, Sister?" Weiss asked.

"Is that alcohol?"

"I didn't know Catholics had a problem with drinking," Weiss said.

"It's just that many of the men here are recovering addicts or alcoholics—like Flyer over there." She pointed to an old man sitting in the corner, sneaking peeks toward their table while having an animated conversation with an invisible friend. "Could you at least keep your flasks out of sight?"

"Consider it done," Weiss said. He and Truman put them away

as Lendra entered the dining room, Jeremiah trailing her. They made their way toward the bench across from he and Weiss.

"Ah, Miss Riley," Weiss said. "I see Jeremiah found you."

"Yes," Lendra said. "Have you seen your most recent picture on the web?"

Weiss frowned and shook his head.

"Here." Lendra handed over a PlusPhone. On its face Truman saw a video of Weiss climbing into the bus, while Truman crouched over the red-haired bus driver. The caption above it read: Attorney General Saves Busload of Children.

"How did this get out there?" Weiss asked.

"I suspect one of your soldiers took the picture," Jeremiah said. "That means the media will be here very soon."

"Shocking," Jeremiah said. "Once again you become the hero."

"I didn't plan this, Jeremiah," Weiss said, handing back the PlusPhone. "Why don't you have a seat and we'll talk about it?" Weiss gestured to the empty bench on the other side of the table.

"Thanks," Jeremiah said, "but the doctor is saving a place for us."

"We're just about to say 'grace,'" Sister Ezekiel said. "Please sit down. Perhaps you would do us the honor, Mr. Weiss?"

"Certainly," Weiss answered. He stood, then bowed his head and spoke in a loud clear voice: "Dear Lord, it has been a trying day for all of us, soldiers and civilians. We thank You for saving the children today…" Truman tuned Weiss out.

As much as he admired Weiss, he found himself a little uncomfortable with the religious aspect of the man. Not that Truman didn't believe in God. But he didn't understand the need to display one's faith so openly. And he hated the way religion had permeated the schools.

Instead, he watched Jeremiah and Lendra take their places. Jeremiah sat beside the doctor, his back to the wall, and surveyed the room. Truman followed his lead and noticed that most of the people waited respectfully for Weiss to finish. A few shifted in their seats, however—eager to eat. The dozen soldiers sitting together kept their heads bowed but Truman heard them whispering to each other. He would have to talk to them after the meal. They weren't as well behaved as many of the homeless men. "...help us to accept Your purpose, oh Lord. We humbly thank You for this meal. Amen."

Murmured Amens sounded throughout the room, immediately followed by the chatter of voices and the clinking of silverware on metal bowls. Weiss again took his seat next to Truman.

Truman cleared his throat as he reached for a sandwich.

"Yes?" Weiss asked.

"Well...it's about Jeremiah...you said earlier that you and he had a history?"

Weiss nodded. "A few years ago someone kidnapped his son."

Truman tasted his soup—a watery broth with reconstituted vegetables that provided little in the way of flavor—while Weiss continued:

"There was very little evidence at the scene. A bloody towel with the boy's ID chip inside. But the towel was a common brand. No prints. No DNA apart from the boy's. It didn't lead the police anywhere."

Truman bit into the bread, a heavy wheat variety—no doubt healthy but lacking the buttery flavor of the bread in the officers' mess. It tasted like the homemade bread Emily kept trying to get him to eat—no flavor enhancements. Sister Ezekiel, wandering between tables, putting a hand on the occasional homeless man, making comments too soft for him to hear, caught his eye and he held up the sandwich, smiling at her.

"Jeremiah," Weiss continued, "insisted on obtaining video feed from the security company that had the contract with the amusement park—Carlton Security."

Truman lifted his head. "The same Carlton Security that outfits the Elite Ops?"

"Exactly. At least the President kept the funding for that program in place. That's about the only thing she's done well since she got into office."

"You don't think the Elite Ops are a bit much?" Truman asked, feeling a slight chill.

"They're a necessary part of the modernization of the military. We have to keep getting more efficient. Overwhelming force with minimal numbers. You should appreciate that, Colonel, in light of the difficulties we've had recruiting good people the past few years." Weiss took another sip. "And considering the problems we had fighting the pseudos off today."

Truman winced. "You think they'll be back, sir?"

Weiss pursed his lips for a moment, then said, "If we find Devereaux, yes. But I won't call in more troopers unless it's necessary. I'm sure the four troopers Richard Carlton has sent will arrive shortly. He's done a tremendous job with the Elite Ops program so far. He developed all their hardware."

"I thought Devereaux created the Elite Ops."

"His work was mostly theoretical but you're right—his research became the foundation upon which Richard's scientists built."

"And didn't Carlton work with you in the CIA?"

"You've done your homework on me, Colonel."

Truman smiled. "It pays to learn as much as possible about your boss." He studied the homeless men. Most of them ate deliberately, keeping an eye on Sister Ezekiel, but a few crammed their food into their mouths without looking up. Truman took a larger bite, getting processed meat and cheese with the bread. Not awful but not as tasty as Army rations. After swallowing he said, "So what happened with the video feed?"

"Carlton Security claimed that the feed was damaged, that it couldn't be accessed. Jeremiah sought an injunction allowing him to examine Carlton Security's database and files, and for national security reasons I refused to grant that request." Weiss paused for a moment. "Then, earlier this year, Jeremiah's wife killed herself."

"Wow," Truman said as he studied Jeremiah, sitting between Dr. Mary and Lendra. All three ate quietly, barely looking at each other. "What happened to the boy?"

"As far as I know, he's never been found. Anyway, Jeremiah blamed me for refusing him access to Carlton Security's system. He claimed that a Carlton Security employee must have been involved in the kidnapping, but of course there was never any proof of that."

"So he then kidnapped a member of the Elite Ops?" Truman said, whistling softly. "That's pretty impressive. Shouldn't you arrest him?"

"I've only got Richard Carlton's word for that. No physical evidence whatsoever. I need probable cause." Weiss finished off his schnapps and slid the cup over to the colonel. Cautiously looking around, Truman downed his too, then unscrewed the top of his flask and emptied half into each cup. Weiss pulled his cup back and took a sip. "Ahh," he said, "at least part of this dinner is satisfactory."

Truman remembered something he'd heard a while back and said, "Didn't Richard Carlton push to have you appointed Attorney General?"

"Yes. He's a good friend." Weiss looked at Truman and nodded slowly. "You probably heard the rumors that he and I exerted illegal or undue influence, or that we somehow blackmailed the President into appointing me to this position. Let me assure you that those rumors are completely false."

Truman took a long sip of brandy and said, "I didn't mean to imply there was any impropriety in your appointment. I have nothing but respect for you."

"Thank you, Colonel," Weiss said.

A noise at the doorway drew Truman's attention. Four homeless men stood there for a moment, then stepped hesitantly into the dining room. They looked around nervously. Behind them, encouraging them along, Henry wore a strained smile. "It's okay, guys. The soldiers are just here for our protection. Ain't that right?"

"Come in and have a seat," Weiss said, gesturing to the open bench across the table. The men cautiously made their way across the floor. All four looked old and thin, worn down. Three had dirty beards. One wore a long overcoat, frayed at the sleeves. As they moved toward the table, Sister Ezekiel stepped forward to direct them.

"Sit here, Rock Man." Sister Ezekiel said, signing to the old man in the overcoat as she indicated the bench directly across the table from Weiss. "I'll bring you a tray." Rock Man settled himself on the bench but the other three men looked warily at Truman and headed for the next table, where they sat by Flyer. "Rock Man is a deaf-mute," Sister Ezekiel said softly. "He reads lips a little." As she turned away, Rock Man stared at Weiss. Something about the directness of his gaze made Truman feel uncomfortable even though the man wasn't looking at him. He finally realized it was the fact that Rock Man hadn't blinked for long seconds—as if he were engaged in a staring contest with Weiss. Truman glanced over at Weiss, who smiled at Rock Man, nodding gently. Finally Sister Ezekiel returned, placing a bowl of soup and a sandwich in front of Rock Man. He signed his thanks, then began eating slowly, using his napkin between bites.

As Truman watched Rock Man eat, he noticed that Rock Man didn't smell as bad as the other homeless men. His face looked cleaner. And his hands, though the fingernails were somewhat ragged, were not the hands of someone who'd been doing hard labor all his life. While Truman studied Rock Man, the room became very quiet in one of those coincidental moments where all conversation momentarily stopped. As Truman looked up to see what caused the silence, voices rose again. Sister Ezekiel moved to Rock Man's side, touching his shoulder.

"These men are here looking for Walt Devereaux," she said to Rock Man, signing as she did so.

Rock Man signed something to Sister Ezekiel.

"I'll ask," Sister Ezekiel answered. Turning to Weiss, she said, "Did you ever meet Devereaux?"

Truman looked out at the room and noticed people beginning to look their way, conversations quickly ending.

Weiss spoke in a calm, measured voice that carried throughout the room:

"I never had the pleasure. And it would have been a pleasure. I don't despise him as a person, just his philosophy. He's done some amazing things. And no one is arguing that all society's ills are Devereaux's fault. There were obviously problems even before he came out with his ladder. But those problems could have been fixed with a little old-fashioned faith. He tried to take our faith away from us."

As Sister Ezekiel translated, Rock Man twisted on the bench to get a good look at her hands. Then Ahmad Rashidi interjected, "He's an infidel. And he'll burn in eternal Hellfire. But he didn't do anything illegal."

Dr. Mary added, "Surely it wasn't a crime to say what he believed?"

"His words encourage terrorism," Weiss answered, "even if he doesn't intend those consequences. Look at those attacks today. A lot of people could have been killed. Indirectly, all that carnage can be traced to Devereaux. Sometimes acts can be legal in the strictest technical sense and yet cause harm far worse than more heinous and proscribed actions. Not to mention that under the Harris-Bock Patriotism Amendment—"

Ahmad Rashidi jumped to his feet, his face red with anger. "That is an *ex post facto* law and it's unconstitutional. Not only that, it implies that Christianity is the official religion of the United States."

"Let's leave the interpretation of the law to the courts," Weiss answered calmly.

No one replied to that. Instead, quiet conversations broke out, men leaning over to whisper in their neighbors' ears, all the while staring at Weiss. Truman grew uneasy and for a second contemplated calling in a squad to calm things down. But Sister Ezekiel, having finished translating for Rock Man, remained standing next to their table—a pure white figure of authority, running her gaze over the room—and now the men grudgingly returned to their meals. Rock Man, who had followed Sister Ezekiel's movements intently, took up his sandwich again. Weiss slowly pushed the rest of his bread over to the mute, who signed his thanks.

"That was very nice of you, Mr. Weiss," Sister Ezekiel said.

As Weiss waved the compliment off, Henry's voice came from the lobby, "Hey, Doc, we need your help out here."

A note of panic in the voice made Truman spring to his feet and run for the door. He heard Weiss moving behind him. From the other side of the room, Jeremiah was already almost to the lobby. The doctor, Lendra and the lawyer followed more slowly. Half the room seemed ready to join the rush while the other half—the shelter regulars—reached out for abandoned sandwiches.

In the center of the lobby, framed by two sentries with their Las-rifles pointed at the floor, Henry supported a big man with short gray hair. The man had one arm wrapped around Henry's small shoulders. A *Semper Fi* tattoo decorated his other arm, which was now pressed against his stomach. Dried blood painted the front of the man's clothes. When he saw Jeremiah, he tensed.

"You still following me?" Jeremiah asked.

"I wasn't following you," the man said.

"You know him?" Weiss asked Jeremiah.

"Hey, you're the Attorney General," Boyd said as he glared at Weiss. "You aren't getting Devereaux."

"I'm not?" Weiss asked.

"We'll stop you. We'll do whatever it takes. You can't persecute an innocent man."

Dr. Mary waved him to silence. "What happened?" she asked.

"I cut myself shaving," the man replied.

Dr. Mary laughed. "There's a lot of that going around," she said. "We'd better get you back to the infirmary."

"I'm fine," the man said. "I just need another QuikHeal bandage."

"You've lost a lot of blood. It looks like you've been stabbed."

The man said nothing, simply glowering at Weiss.

"You'll have internal bleeding," Dr. Mary said. "Maybe some serious cuts to your intestines, spleen and liver. You really should let me take a look at that."

"So you're a Devereauxnian," Weiss said.

"That's not a crime," Sister Ezekiel said. "And as long as he needs our help, we'll provide it." She touched the man's elbow. "There's no charge for our services."

"You really should let me take a gander at that for you," Dr. Mary said.

The man jerked his head up. "A gander?" he said softly. He stared at the doctor for a second, then looked away. "Okay...thanks."

Something about the way he reacted made Truman uneasy. As if the word gander had been some kind of code. There was nothing in

Dr. Mary's demeanor to suggest she had delivered a secret signal and she betrayed no sign of nervousness but Truman decided to keep a careful eye on her just the same.

Dr. Mary assisted the man to the infirmary. Truman followed. Behind him, Jeremiah and Lendra, Sister Ezekiel, Ahmad Rashidi and Weiss all crowded in too, taking up positions inside the door. Dr. Mary lowered the man to a seat.

"How do you two know each other?" Weiss asked Jeremiah.

"He tried to kill us," Lendra said.

"A misunderstanding," the man said.

"An unfortunate accident," Jeremiah agreed.

Dr. Mary peeled the bandage off the man's stomach and pressed a scanner against his skin. Truman edged a little closer but she did nothing suspicious, merely checked the scanner, adjusted the readings, then set it aside and said, "You've got some internal bleeding. I'm going to have to put in a few sutures. Help me get him up on the gurney."

"Hold on a second," Weiss said to her. He stepped up close to the man. Truman moved forward to be in position in case the man tried something. "Who are you?" Weiss asked.

"Raddock Boyd. I'm here to protect Devereaux."

"Well, Raddock Boyd," Weiss said, "you'll be staying here tonight."

"You can't arrest me."

"You want to be careful," Weiss said with a smile, "when telling me what I can and can't do. But for the record, I'm not arresting you. I'm detaining you while we check your identification, make certain there are no warrants out on you. We'll decide what to do with you in the morning. If Miss Riley here wants to press assault charges against you, we'll turn you over to the local police. Colonel, after the doctor finishes with him, see that he gets an ID chip implanted—one that can't be cut out without poisoning him."

Boyd struggled to his feet and said, "Those are illegal."

"I'm afraid he's right, Mr. Weiss," Ahmad Rashidi said. "After the disaster of '32, when a hundred and fifty-seven people died—"

"I have the power to order them," Weiss interrupted, "in times of civil emergency. And what happened today looks like a civil emergency to me. I've already lost two prisoners today. I don't intend to lose any more. Don't worry," he said to Boyd as he poked the big man in the chest. Boyd sat back down heavily. "They're perfectly safe as long as they're not tampered with." Weiss nodded to Truman, who hesitated only a moment before calling a medic to insert the chip.

Chapter Sixteen

Jeremiah walked to his van under a setting sun that decorated the clouds with pinks and golds, bronzes and purples, courtesy of the vast quantity of particulate matter in the air—an amount that was being added to by the smoke emanating from the Army's vehicles. He tried not to look at the sky. Sunsets reminded him of Catherine. Amid the melted, twisted wreckage, several dozen recently arrived reporters filmed footage of the shelter and Weiss' famous mobile command center. Unbelievable. Here Weiss was trying to establish a secure perimeter and he was letting reporters in. A few took pictures of the soldiers patrolling the street. One young man with a huge orange Afro and a scruffy beard stood off to the side pretending not to be a reporter. Jeremiah figured he had a hidden camera in his fake hair—a multi-lens digital unit with 3D capability.

So far the Army had kept the press from entering the shelter, but Jeremiah knew Weiss would issue a statement shortly. He'd been honing his delivery at dinner, rehearsing his lines before a live audience.

In the lingering light, townspeople mingled, reminiscing about the fight to reporters and each other. The media invasion, Jeremiah realized, further complicated matters. The chances of getting Devereaux out of the area quietly were becoming more and more unlikely.

The challenge sent a tingle through Jeremiah. He felt himself coiling in anticipation as he bounced along on the balls of his feet, watching everyone who passed, everyone who looked at him, everyone who dared peek out a window. He yearned for a fight.

Unlocking the van's security system, he slipped inside and stuffed the particle beam cannon's converter into his overnight bag. His fingers lingered over his Ultimate Camos. But Jeremiah decided against taking them. He doubted he'd need them tonight. Instead, he sprayed Insta-Clean on the bloody arm of the camos he'd worn earlier. He let the chemicals work for a few minutes to remove the dried blood from the sensors.

While waiting, he contemplated his options. Lendra had so far found no useful Intel on where the Escala might be hiding. Nevertheless, Jeremiah felt confident he could turn something up by morning. Nighttime was ideal for hunting. He'd concentrate his efforts on locating the Escala who had attacked the shelter earlier. They would have left some trace of their passage. He knew they'd be formidable because of their animal DNA, but he felt like his enhancements could compete with theirs. Could he actually be like them? Could Eli have lied to him, given him animal DNA, then faked the test results so Jeremiah would believe he was still completely human? Just asking the question told Jeremiah the likely answer. He wanted to test himself against the Escala, discover the truth. Downloading a satellite image of the area, he studied it, looking for good hiding spots in the ruins of the overgrown housing development.

He also examined the summary file on the Susquehanna Virus. CINTEP's analysts suspected that Susquehanna Sally had in fact released the virus as an act of terrorism, though she'd disappeared after claiming responsibility and had seldom been heard from since—only a few posts ranting about environmental issues. The virus itself hid in the immune system, mutating in each new host, then launching an attack on the heart and brain, often shutting the body down in a matter of hours. Only 33 of the 427 people infected in that first wave had survived. Now the greatest risk of infection came from mosquitoes and fleas.

Returning to the image of the area, Jeremiah saw that there were literally hundreds of spots where the Escala could be hiding. He would need a scanner to try to locate them electronically. Might they hide in the ruins of the development? No way to know. Jeremiah grabbed his best scanner and activated it briefly, checking for unusual bio-sign readings. Nothing yet.

When he got back to the shelter, Weiss was holding forth before a dozen reporters, a large contingent of Colonel Truman's soldiers, Sister

Ezekiel, Lendra, Ahmad Rashidi and a handful of homeless men. The one called Rock Man stood near the front, apparently reading Weiss' lips. And Julianna, trapped within her Dr. Mary disguise, stood at the door to the infirmary. He could have sworn she winked at him as he made his way across the lobby. He nearly smiled, finding it reassuring in a way to have Julianna covering his back again, even if he couldn't fully trust her.

Weiss looked smug as he bathed in the glow of the reporters' questions, aiming his comments at their digital vids. Jeremiah wondered if Weiss had pegged the kid with the orange Afro as a reporter. The kid stood off to the side, looking like a homeless man, asking no questions.

"This country is falling apart," Weiss said. "We have a big problem and it's only getting worse. Civil disorder is at an all-time high. Terrorists have stolen our country from us. We're locked into battles of their choosing and we can't win if we engage them on their terms. We must all work together to fight for freedom. And we must be willing to sacrifice a little—just a little—for the sake of our great country."

Jeremiah saw Lendra eyeing him as he circled the crowd but he continued to move toward Julianna.

"Our government," Weiss threw his arms out wide, "refuses to do what needs to be done. It has decided that there will be no money for anything but essentials. And the list of essentials keeps shrinking. Health care? On life support. Education? Failing. Environment? A wasteland. Transportation? It's reached a dead end. Defense is the only essential left."

Jeremiah stopped making his way around the room and looked at Weiss, who was reveling in his wordplay. Shaking his head, Jeremiah continued on, edging around the albino Henry.

"What we need is a change. We need a government that doesn't have to answer to every special interest group. We need a leadership that is no longer hostage to the demands of the few. The politics of elitism must be eliminated, and the current electoral process cannot accomplish that task. Uninformed voters cannot be allowed to determine the fate of our nation. And as long as special interest groups rule the electoral process, they will create uninformed voters by fabricating *reality* for voters to latch on to as truth."

A reporter asked, "What are you proposing?"

"We have to change the way we think about government," Weiss answered. "To preserve our way of life, we need to change democracy fundamentally. To crush the terroristic forces of anarchy that threaten the very foundations of what we are, we need to adapt the institutions that keep the darkness at bay.

"There's a beautiful statue just a few blocks away called, 'Emerging Man.' It used to draw thousands of visitors a year. Now? Well, now it's probably a few hundred. And those who dare visit put their lives at risk. Like the children today who were caught in the crossfire—two of them badly injured. Only by the grace of God did they survive. How do we create a better future for our children and grandchildren? By making our streets safer. And that means—contrary to what Devereaux would have us believe—that individual rights must sometimes be sublimated to the greater good. Hope cannot be allowed to vanish from the face of the earth."

When Jeremiah reached Julianna, she turned her head and blew into his ear. Jeremiah stepped back a few feet as Julianna laughed softly. Lendra, her eyes narrowing, watched them intently.

"The President," Weiss said, "for all her good intentions, for all her valiant efforts to stave off economic collapse and civil unrest, has been ineffective. Our enemies have grown stronger during her tenure. The solution, the only solution, is sweeping change. A change not of degree but of kind. A government of strength—unassailable, yet flexible and benevolent.

"Are you advocating the elimination of free elections?" another reporter asked.

"I'm proposing," Weiss said with a smile, "a strong central government with the means and flexibility to respond with force against those who seek to make us live in fear."

Many in the room applauded, including two conservative commentators masquerading as reporters. Not Sister Ezekiel though, nor Ahmad Rashidi. Rock Man stared at Weiss, his mouth open.

"Can you believe this guy?" Julianna said. "What a clown."

"He has the gift," Jeremiah said. "He's very charismatic."

"Don't tell me you agree with him?"

"No, I'm merely stating a truth."

As Weiss moved past Rock Man and began shaking hands, Lendra approached Jeremiah, her eyes darting to Julianna every few seconds. When she reached them, she said, "What was that all about?"

"I don't know," Jeremiah answered. "I missed the beginning. What did he say before I got here?"

"The reporters wanted to know if the rumors about Walt Devereaux being here were true. Weiss refused to answer their questions. Said he couldn't talk about it. But he said if Devereaux *is* here, then anyone with knowledge of his whereabouts has an obligation to turn him in. He reminded us that Devereaux continues to incite his followers to evolve, to move beyond the old definition of what it means to be human. Then he launched into his tirade about changing the government. That's when you walked in."

"So in political-speak," Jeremiah said, "he's acknowledging that Devereaux is here by refusing to deny it. But why?"

"It creates chaos," Lendra said.

"Exactly," Julianna said. "By implying that Devereaux is here, he hopes to instigate the very anarchy he's railing against."

"Right," Lendra agreed. "And by talking about the president's ineffectiveness, he guarantees she'll send troops out here to keep the peace—probably Elite Ops. He scares the hell out of me. A strong central government? That sounds like a dictatorship."

"With him at the helm," Jeremiah agreed.

"Well," Julianna said, "all we have to worry about at the moment is making certain he doesn't find Devereaux."

Lendra looked from Julianna to Jeremiah and back. She leaned forward, searching the Dr. Mary mask and said, "You're her, aren't you? You're Julianna."

"Did Jeremiah tell you I'm the big bad wolf?" Julianna said. She curled her hands into claws and playfully swiped at Lendra's face. Lendra backed up a step.

Lendra turned to Jeremiah, a wrinkle of distaste in her expression. "She'll betray you again, you know."

Julianna laughed.

"Let me worry about Julianna," Jeremiah said.

"What are you going to do next?" Lendra asked.

"I have to find the Escala who attacked the shelter today. A group like that—eight or maybe ten people—I might be able to pick them up with my scanner. Off to the east somewhere in that forested area."

"That's where they'll be, all right," Julianna said. "Rumors have been flying for months about strange creatures inhabiting the area. I haven't had any backup or I'd have checked them out earlier."

"I'm going out alone," Jeremiah said.

"Oh, no, you don't. You need me."

"What for?"

"If they've got scatterers, you'll need to be able to triangulate their position to have any chance of finding them. You can't do that alone. Besides, you could use a doctor, just in case."

"You're not a doctor."

"I'm the closest thing you've got. And I can cover your back. Who else can you trust?"

"Me," Lendra said. "I'm going with you."

"No, absolutely not," Jeremiah said. "You're no field agent. Remember that little incident with Raddock Boyd?" Jeremiah glanced at Julianna as he spoke, looking for any reaction. She offered none. "Also, I need you to run one of those complicated CINTEP programs through the surveillance vid for the shelter. Compare everybody who's been in or out the past few weeks with prior footage of Devereaux. I'm sure Weiss has done the same but the CINTEP program might be better than his. Despite the fact that Devereaux's obviously changed his appearance and perhaps had genetic surgery, you might be able to identify him. And call Eli, fill him in on what's happened, see if he has any bright ideas about how to proceed."

"I'll meet you out back in thirty minutes," Julianna said. "I need to put Dr. Mary to bed—her cold and lonely bed." She put her palm on Lendra's cheek. "Care to assist me in removing my disguise?"

Lendra backed away. Jeremiah could see her fighting the urge to say something. He admired her restraint. She merely held up her hand in dismissal. But as Julianna smiled and sauntered off, Lendra grabbed Jeremiah's arm and whispered fiercely, "What are you doing?"

"It's getting too complicated," Jeremiah said. "Too many players. I figure a temporary alliance is our best chance to get Devereaux."

"You *trust* her?"

"Absolutely. I trust her to betray me once we've got Devereaux. But until then, she'll use me, just like I'll use her."

"Eli won't approve."

"You tell him that if he comes up with a better solution, I'll be happy to go about it some other way."

Chapter Seventeen

Leaning against her office doorway, her eyes fluttering with fatigue, Sister Ezekiel watched Dr. Mary walk back to her room. Jeremiah and Lendra, with whom the doctor had recently been conversing, disappeared down the hallway toward the guest room Sister Ezekiel had provided. Why did Dr. Mary suddenly seem to have a bounce to her step? Had she decided to ally herself with Jeremiah? Did she know where Devereaux was? Sister Ezekiel found everything so confusing. Yawning, she turned her attention back to Ahmad Rashidi, in the middle of an update on the shelter's legal status.

"You're poor, Sister," Ahmad said. "You can't afford a good attorney. You can't even afford me." A big belly laugh erupted out of him. But he cut it off when she didn't join in. "I don't mind doing a little *pro bono* work for you because it's always interesting and I figure I can use all the help I can get with the big fella upstairs. If Catholicism turns out to be correct, maybe I can get some bonus points for the legal assistance I provide." Ahmad looked at Sister Ezekiel expectantly. She smiled to show she was listening. "But I can't fight the power of the Attorney General. Sooner or later he's gonna get another scanner in here. And the more immediate problem is that with his little confab tonight before the media, we're gonna have a lot of people makin' their way here over the next few days, lookin' for Devereaux. You sure you haven't seen him?"

"If I have, Ahmad, he certainly hasn't made himself known to me."

"Well, Sister, if he does show himself to you, you should let me know immediately—if not sooner.

"Sooner than immediately?"

Ahmad chuckled. "Absolutely."

Sister Ezekiel shook her head. "You're such a clown."

"Yes, Sister. But let me know. We'll have to move very quickly."

"What do you plan to do?"

"Let me worry about that, Sister. Meanwhile, if you don't wanna close up shop, you're gonna hafta borrow from the foundation's endowment to fix this place up. Your operating expenses aren't gonna be sufficient. And I can pretty much guarantee the Army ain't gonna pay for all this damage."

From out in the lobby came a scuffling noise.

"Step back," a soldier ordered loudly. "Now!"

Through the wall-window, Sister Ezekiel saw Rock Man, his hands in the air. He backed slowly away from the soldier, who wielded a stun club. Behind the soldier, Weiss and the colonel stood near two of the reporters. They looked up in surprise.

Sister Ezekiel ran out of her office. "You!" she yelled at the soldier. "Leave him be."

"What's going on?" Weiss demanded.

"He was moving in too close, sir," the soldier said.

"He's a deaf-mute," Sister Ezekiel said as she signed to Rock Man, telling him to stand back from Weiss. "The Good Lord knows he doesn't mean you any harm."

"I'm sorry," Weiss said to Rock Man. He pointed to the soldier. "They can be a little overprotective."

"I think he's just fascinated by the cameras," Sister Ezekiel said. She signed to Rock Man: "Let's get you to bed for the night."

Rock Man allowed himself to be led away, leaning on her heavily as she walked him down the hall. Somehow that dependence gave her strength. She'd never appreciated before just how ancient and frail he was. As they neared the dormitory area, Rock Man stopped. He turned to look at her, raised his eyebrows in a silent question.

"It's okay," Sister Ezekiel signed as she spoke. "Cookie Monster's going to be okay. I'm sure of it."

Rock Man nodded, then stepped to the door of Doug's room. He grabbed the doorknob and let himself in, turning on the light as he did so. He knew he didn't belong here. What was he doing? Sister Ezekiel followed him inside, found him sitting on the bed, old and beaten.

Before she said a word, he straightened his back, his eyes shining with intensity and intelligence, then gestured to the room's sole chair and spoke in a vaguely familiar voice, refined and crisp:

"Please close the door and sit."

Stunned, Sister Ezekiel closed the door, a strange feeling running through her. She sensed something momentous, something beyond the fact that Rock Man could speak. She shivered, though the room was quite warm. Taking a seat, she stared at him, feeling embarrassed and a little angry. How had he fooled her for so long? And why?

Rock Man reached for her hand, wrapping his leathery hands around her rigid fingers. "I'm sorry, Sister," he said. "I never meant for this to happen."

Truth struck her an almost physical blow. She pulled her hands away.

"You're Walt Devereaux!"

He nodded approvingly. "I always knew you were smart, Sister."

"But how…what are you doing here?"

He shrugged. "I almost turned myself in down there. But I'm afraid."

Sister Ezekiel examined Devereaux's face, as if for the first time. Wrinkled and dirty, with a scraggly gray beard, it looked nothing like the face of Walt Devereaux. The cragginess of his leathery skin bespoke years in the sun and his complexion looked unhealthy. His cheekbones were higher than she remembered, his lips thicker, his skin darker. And his nose, now large and bulbous, was covered with the numerous capillaries of a long-time drinker. The hale scientist she recalled from TV had vanished into this fragile frame. But his eyes, which moments before had seemed unfocused and pale—the eyes of a man who had never tasted success—now held the magnetic charisma of the born leader Devereaux had once been, even though they were of the wrong color.

"If you're innocent," Sister Ezekiel said, "you have nothing to fear."

Devereaux smiled. "Oh, I'm not so concerned for myself, though there is that too. I'm more concerned with humanity. You see, my people believe that if I'm captured, the government will forcibly extract from my brain all my knowledge, all my secrets."

"Torture you?"

He shook his head. "There are newer, more effective methods of mining the brain. And I've learned things I don't want humanity to know."

"The bioweapons you designed?"

Devereaux nodded. "I didn't set out to create them. I was researching medical treatments, studying genomic sequences, when the ideas occurred to me. They just hit me one night while I was sleeping. Woke me up. These viruses wouldn't be that difficult to make. And they could wipe out humanity. I never should have told President Davis that I'd conceived of them."

"So why didn't you run?"

"I thought about that. The Escala could smuggle me out despite the roadblocks Weiss has put up. In fact, they were rather insistent that I go. But many of them would be trapped here. It's only a matter of time before the government loses patience and calls in the Elite Ops to wipe them out. I can't leave them."

"Aren't you being a little paranoid?"

"If you knew what I know, Sister, you'd realize that our government is capable of terrible things." He took a deep breath. "I think I have to give myself up and hope that my followers are wrong, that the government won't extract my ideas without my permission. Some of our leaders are honorable."

Devereaux reached into a pocket and removed a plastic cashcard, which he placed in her hand. "Give this to your lawyer. Consider it a thank you for all your kindness. It's prepaid to four million international bank standard and can't be traced back to me."

"Four million? That's far too generous." Sister Ezekiel's hand tightened over the card. "How much is that in dollars?"

"I don't know the latest exchange rate. If it's not enough, I can get more later."

"Thank you. But that's not necessary, Mr. Devereaux."

Devereaux smiled. "You know, I enjoyed being Rock Man for a short time." He got to his feet. "I suppose I'd better go downstairs and give myself up."

Sister Ezekiel put her hand on his arm. "Wait."

He raised an eyebrow.

"I think you should hold off until morning. Sleep on it. You can stay here in Doug's room for the night. I don't think you're evil," she added. "This isn't your fault." She waved her hand to indicate the damage to the shelter.

"I must say, Sister," Devereaux said. "You almost surprise me. You really ought to hate me for everything that's happened."

"I know you never meant to hurt anyone."

"And yet harm has befallen you just the same."

"Can I ask you something? There's something I've been wanting to ask you for a long time."

Devereaux looked at her with arched eyebrows.

"What I want to know is: Why do you think we can be better without God?"

Devereaux smiled. "I was once a man of great faith. *I wanted God.*" Devereaux bowed his head. "But I needed truth," he spoke softly. "As much as I desired reality to be something more than it is, I knew that, ultimately, I had to accept that we must change if we wish to survive. Religion—or rather the tyranny of religion—is the single greatest force for evil the world has ever created."

"You don't believe in Satan?"

Devereaux shook his head. "The evil in this world was all created by us."

"How do you explain the miracles I see every day? The incredible diversity and complexity of life—of human beings."

Devereaux smiled. "Life isn't nearly as diverse as you think, Sister. For example, we share over 98 percent of our DNA with chimpanzees. At least 90 percent of our genes correlate at some level with those found in mice. We're all made up of the same building blocks. And as for complexity…well, we only think life is complex because our brains are so limited. A child thinks a pebble is complex. If we understood more of the universe, we might find life to be incredibly simple. In fact, creating new life isn't that difficult. I've done it."

Sister Ezekiel knew she could not win an argument with this man, but her faith pushed her on, forced her to fight against the darkness he preached. For what sort of world would this be if he were right? What would be the point of living without God?

"No matter how smart you are, no matter how much you evolve, you'll still have a human mind, which makes you inherently imperfect."

"That is the bane of religion, Sister. It allows us to delight in the mysteries of life and accept our imperfections. It inhibits our intellectual growth by promoting spirituality. It embraces fallibility. Without that crutch, imagine what we could become."

"God made us imperfect. And He gave us free will to allow us to create our own destinies. He merely hopes we will work for His will."

"Is Gray Weiss working for God's will? Are all the people who invoke God's name blessed?" Devereaux stopped, closed his eyes for a moment. "I won't argue against faith. Faith has kept me going on many a lonely night. We all need faith…and hope. Christianity was necessary once upon a time. It was a phase humans needed. As were Islam and Judaism, Hinduism and Buddhism."

Sister Ezekiel shook her head and looked up at him. "What you're saying is just another phase too. The world is at war, perhaps directed by Satan. You may even have—unkowningly—played into his hands. I think that some day you'll see that you were wrong, that we need God in our lives."

Devereaux's shoulders slumped. He said, "I almost wish you were right, Sister. But if you are, then humanity is destined to fail. We must become greater than our selfish selves. If we want to be better than the animals we claim dominion over, we have to become creatures of integrity and compassion."

"We already are. God made us that way."

"You are, Sister. I would never dispute that. But there aren't many in this world like you. I wish there were."

"The tragedy of it," Sister Ezekiel said, "is that you mean well. Everyone knows that. Even those men out there hunting you. Strange, that so much evil should result from the actions of one well-intended man."

"If you could see what humanity will be in a thousand years," Devereaux said, "if you could see the changes that will spring from the roots of unflinching truth, you might not be so quick to judge. These dark times, as horrible as they are, are necessary for humanity to survive. Religion cannot coddle us any longer."

"I don't judge you," Sister Ezekiel said. "That is for God to do."

"I thank you for your goodness, Sister, though I fear my judgment will come at the hands of men…and soon."

"Get some sleep," Sister Ezekiel said. "We'll talk in the morning. But I don't know if you should give yourself up."

He sat back on the bed and held her hand to his cheek. His skin felt warm. He looked small and vulnerable, staring at her. His face bespoke a kind of longing, almost as if he wanted to tell her something.

She said, "I'd like to pray for you, if that's okay."

"That's fine, Sister. Thank you. There's nothing wrong with a little prayer."

Sister Ezekiel nodded, not trusting herself to speak.

Devereaux kissed the back of her hand, then let it go and lay back, his head settling against the pillow, his eyes closed. Watching him, Sister Ezekiel no longer felt tired. Devereaux's words had opened some inner wellspring of strength. She sensed the Eternal in him—despite his atheism—a profound goodness shining through, lighting his great soul, blessing all those who came into contact with him. Reaching up to turn out the light, she closed the door softly behind her.

Chapter Eighteen

Jeremiah slid from shadow to shadow, a hunter in his element. The clouds that had begun to move in at sunset now filled the sky with the promise of rain, bringing a deeper quality to the darkness, but with his night vision scope he saw as if it were daytime. His footfalls barely reached his ears. Ahead of him at the edge of the forest, a man stood in that familiar bent posture of the old, a bag over his shoulder. Jeremiah wondered whether he ought to chase the old man away. Then the old man disappeared behind a tree and Jeremiah heard the hoot of an owl.

He relaxed. "Oh," he said, "it's you."

Julianna, in her old man's disguise, peered around the tree trunk at Jeremiah, her head angled sideways, a lopsided grin displaying a crooked set of teeth.

Stepping to the tree, he asked, "How many of those disguises do you have?"

"Only two," she said. Then she slowly peeled off her mask and wig, handed them to Jeremiah and removed her fake teeth. She dropped them into Jeremiah's palm. He shuddered and she laughed softly. "What did you bring to the party?"

"Aside from my Las-pistol and some stun grenades, an electro-magnetic scanner," he said, holding it up while she took off her shirt. "Designed for bio traces."

"I've got a low-level proximity sensor," she said as she slid her thumb down the seam of her torso body suit. She opened the suit and let it slip to the ground. Then she removed her padded pants, bending over to pull them free of her shoes, her white silk panties a beacon in the darkness. Straightening, she stood still for a moment, letting him see her lean, hard body and small, firm breasts. Jeremiah found himself staring at her, memory flooding back, desire haunting him. He looked down at his scanner as she said, "Only problem with these body suits is that you can't move quickly in them."

"I remember that," Jeremiah answered. He glanced at her again, trying not to think about the good years they'd shared.

"You know you want me," Julianna said as she opened her bag and dressed in her camos. Then she put on a belt with a holstered Las-pistol and attached a series of stun grenades and spare charges. Afterwards, Jeremiah helped her fold and stash the old man disguise in her bag, under a pile of fallen brush. "Damn things cost a fortune," she said. "It was so much nicer when Eli was paying for them."

Jeremiah opened his can of face-black and dipped his fingers in it. He began to spread it over her face, working it around her eyes, across her forehead and cheeks.

When he finished, Julianna seated her interface against her temple. She pointed to his night vision scope. "I don't need one of those. I've got vision enhancement that ties into the interface." She took the can he proffered and pulled out a big glop of paint. With quick strokes, she covered his forehead and cheeks. When she finished his face, she held up her blackened fingers and said, "Why are we doing this?"

"So we don't have to wear our face covers. And let's set the camos to half-strength. It'll be easier if we can mostly see each other out there."

Julianna said, "I heard that some Elite Ops troopers are here already."

"It was only a matter of time before they showed. I wonder where they are."

"Don't know," Julianna said. "One more thing. Right now only you and Lendra know I'm here. Weiss and the soldiers think I'm a middle-aged doctor."

"Not for long. Truman saw Boyd's reaction to your code word. Weiss may have too. I'm sure they'll question Boyd. They'll learn you were supposed to be his contact."

Julianna shook her head. "Amateurs. Could you believe that guy? And why the hell did he and his backup attack you, anyway? They were just supposed to follow you, report on your progress."

"How'd you know I was coming?"

"There are a lot of highly placed people in our organization," Julianna said.

"What organization is that?"

"It's not important." She shook her head. "I just knew that idiot was going to say something stupid. After the way he reacted, I had to ignore him or I never would have gotten out of there. Truman's been watching me like a hawk. Good thing I had this extra disguise." She sighed. "I don't suppose Dr. Mary can go back now."

"You liked being her, didn't you?" Jeremiah said. "Here." He handed her his scatterer so she at least would be undetectable by Truman's soldiers.

"All good things must end," Julianna said. "Won't take them long to figure out I've got a price on my head." She gave an exaggerated shrug, raising her eyebrows in mock astonishment. "What are you going to do? Come on, let's play." Laughing, she jumped over a mossy log, ran down a hill and up the other side. She turned at the top, looked back at him and said, "Are you coming? We can't hang around here all day."

He leapt over the log and rushed toward her, exhilarated to be moving so fast. As he came up next to her, she turned away again and darted off. He sprinted after her, admiring the way she glided lightly over the terrain. He could barely hear her footsteps over his. At one point, she disappeared over a hill. Cresting it, he saw a stagnant pond, a cloud of mosquitoes hovering above it. It gave off an odor of rotting plants that made his nose wrinkle. In its center stood a fountain covered with moss and vines, and beyond it, the remains of what had once been a mansion. Julianna wisely stayed well away from the pond, making a wide circle around it and moving off a few hundred yards before stopping. One could never be too careful with the Susquehanna Virus.

When he caught up to her, she put her hand on his chest and said, "Heartbeat's normal. You're an animal."

Perhaps I am, he thought. Perhaps I'm part horse or part wolf or part tiger. His arms and legs tingled, as if yearning for movement, seeking joy in the speed and flowing power of the chase. He caught Julianna staring at him with a frown, so he shook his head and pointed north, saying, "I'm getting an unusual reading over that way."

Julianna leaned over and examined his scanner.

"Let's do it," she said.

They ran along what had once been a road, past mostly demolished houses. The few that remained standing looked oddly frail through his night vision scope. Nature had begun to reclaim her territory; trees and bushes grew through windows and doors. Jeremiah felt a twinge of surprise that their owners hadn't destroyed all the houses upon leaving. Anything associated with the Susquehanna Virus should have been torn down to minimize the virus' spread.

Every few seconds, Jeremiah checked the scanner. He saw several dozen sharp images moving in groups, not individually. Truman's soldiers would be out here conducting their own search for Cookie Monster and the other Escala. What Jeremiah didn't know was whether the colonel had information he didn't about the Escala's possible location. At the top of the scanner was the strange, undefinable energy output. The scatterer Julianna wore masked her bio-signature, while his image came back fuzzy as a result of his nearness to her.

"You see that movement?" Julianna asked.

"Just the soldiers. Why?"

"There's a distortion to my proximity sensor," Julianna answered. "But I can't tell if it's Escala. Straight ahead."

Jeremiah noticed the top of a roof visible above the trees and said, "In there, maybe?"

"Let's check inside," Julianna said.

Together they moved forward, more slowly now, placing their feet carefully to protect against snapping twigs or the rustling of dried leaves. Past a heavy thicket, they came upon a golf clubhouse—its roof and two walls collapsed. As they reached the building, Jeremiah saw crumpled blankets in a corner, glass containers and broken glass littering the floor, empty cans crushed and mangled, graffiti decorating the two standing walls. Piled in the corner were dozens of abandoned power cells still giving off traces of electricity. They must have been what triggered the scanner and proximity sensor.

Jeremiah nevertheless activated the "lamp" setting on his pencil flash. He and Julianna studied the floor. They found no sign of recent activity, no hidden tunnel entrances, only the detritus of the homeless who had occasionally sheltered there.

"One down," Julianna said.

Jeremiah turned off his flash and led the way over the twisted rubble outside. Through the rustling breeze, he could just detect the sound of soldiers approaching. He cursed himself for failing to check his scanner, took a look at it and grabbed Julianna's arm. "You see that?" he asked.

Julianna said, "I've been keeping an eye on them. They're still a hundred and fifty meters away. Follow me."

She moved east, toward the noise. Before he could ask her what the hell she was doing, she began climbing a cottonwood tree. Jeremiah pulled himself up after her. Julianna climbed quickly, almost carelessly, stopping about twenty feet off the ground. He moved up to the branch below her, his head level with her muscular glutes. The branch, several inches in diameter, should have held him easily but he heard a cracking sound as it gave slightly under his feet. "Camos to full power," he whispered, unzipping his camos and adjusting the sensors to maximum. Julianna's legs faded to fuzziness. He wrapped his arms around them, inhaling her earthy aroma.

Below him, he heard the soldiers walking. Although the camos' sensors were working properly, Jeremiah still felt uneasy, like a fish in a barrel. They were trapped up here. He glanced down at the soldiers as they marched through the forest. Two of them, he noticed, wore proximity sensors. The rest wore night-vision goggles. He counted eight total. As they passed below, one of the soldiers with a proximity sensor stopped.

Again the branch cracked, just a tiny sound, but it hit his eardrums like cannon fire. Jeremiah held his breath. Slowly, he edged his fingers toward his Las-pistol. He didn't want to have to hurt anybody. Out of the corner of his eye, he saw the soldier look up, searching the tree. Above him, an owl hooted twice. Julianna.

The soldier raised his weapon, edging around the tree. Would he shoot an owl? Jeremiah's fingers reached the Las-pistol, slipped around its textured grip. Taking care to move slowly so as not to catch the soldier's eye, he eased the weapon out of its holster. Again Julianna hooted, softer this time. What was she thinking?

"Hey," a soldier called out from a few meters away.

Jeremiah nearly startled at the sound of the voice. He pressed himself even tighter against Julianna's legs.

"I think it's an owl," the soldier beneath them said. He took a couple steps forward, continuing to look up. "But I can't see it."

"Genius," the other soldier said. "We're not supposed to be looking for owls. Let's go."

As they moved off to join the rest of their squad, Jeremiah exhaled, realizing that he'd been holding his breath. Even though he was almost certain they were alone, he remained motionless, hesitant to check his scanner, afraid that any small movement might draw a straggler's attention.

Julianna wriggled her rear, bumping his face with her bottom. She giggled softly.

"Cut it out," he whispered.

"Don't worry," she said. "They're gone."

Jeremiah checked his scanner and realized Julianna was right. He re-holstered his Las-pistol, then climbed down and dropped to a crouch. By the time he got to his feet, Julianna had already adjusted her camos to half-strength. He did the same.

"Where to next?" she asked.

His scanner displayed another unusual reading. He showed her the coordinates.

"Okay." Julianna glanced at the scanner, her straight white teeth looking bright in his night vision scope. He suddenly realized he was grinning too. She nodded, then darted off, and Jeremiah sprinted after her, content to follow, watching her slim, muscular body weave through the undergrowth. He felt lighter than he had in years. His feet seemed to barely touch the ground as he trailed Julianna through waist-high grass, across what had been the golf course. When they reached the far end of the course, he moved up next to her. She put her hand out and squeezed his arm, gently pulling him along an old road that they followed past half a dozen houses until they arrived at the second spot with the unusual bio-signatures—a collapsed brick structure that had once been a commercial building. It had undergone some demolition when it was abandoned, but the place had been solidly constructed and three of the outer walls remained largely intact. The roof, however, was gone. Again, Jeremiah and Julianna carefully scanned the area.

"Truman's men were already here," Julianna said. "See the broken branches?" She pointed them out.

Jeremiah nodded. "They might have missed something."

"They probably bugged the place," she warned. "Motion sensor, heat sensor, microphone, camera."

"So?" Jeremiah said.

"So, even with the camos, I don't think we should go inside."

"You're right. You shouldn't. They might detect your presence. But I think they already know I'm out here."

"What do you expect to find?"

"I don't know. But those soldiers might have missed something. I'll be back in a little while."

Julianna sat at the base of a tree to wait while Jeremiah advanced on the building. The door had been removed long ago. Dirt, leaves and twigs cluttered the open doorway. Inside, along the walls that still stood, hung the remnants of conduit and wiring, great electrical boards that had been corroded by time and the weather—an electrical substation. A stairway led downward. Flicking on the flashlight, he descended slowly into a large damp basement. Like the last building, empty food containers littered the floor, as well as a couple crumpled blankets. Jeremiah kicked the blankets aside, but they only covered cracks in the cement. Two hastily mounted cameras covered the stairway and the room. He recognized them as standard military issue. Nothing fancy.

He disabled them, then wondered about their clumsy placement. Surely Weiss and Truman would be more circumspect than that. Were these cameras decoys of some sort? Jeremiah spent a few minutes checking the walls and floors for hidden sensors or cameras. Just as he was about to give up, he found a tiny sensor lodged in a crack on the wall—nearly invisible. He spent another five minutes examining the walls and ceiling before finding another sensor and a tiny camera—so small he almost missed them. That kind of subtlety was more like Weiss. He smiled and waved at the camera. This basement looked something like his stone dungeon. It felt good not to need that device. Was that Julianna's doing? Was he that happy to be with her? He couldn't recall ever being this happy with Catherine—at least since Joshua had been taken. Immediately he felt guilty. Damn it! He refused to feel bad.

"Cameras and sensors," he said to Julianna when he got back outside.

"Anything else?"

"No sign of the Escala."

"Right," Julianna said. "Have you been watching that disturbance off to the southeast?"

"I saw it on my scanner. What do you think it is?"

"I don't know, but it's unusual. We definitely have to check it out."

The terrain as they ran to the southeast grew more hilly, the undergrowth more dense, the abandoned homes less frequent. On his scanner, the strange reading loomed larger. As they neared the spot, Jeremiah detected a lightening of the sky.

"Oh, no," Julianna said, fear in her voice. She sprinted ahead.

Jeremiah smelled burning wood—and something else: bitter and poisonous: vaguely familiar. He couldn't identify it but he knew he'd smelled it before. He took off after Julianna, catching up to her as she slowed. Together they approached a large home set apart from the rest of the development. Flames worked their way up the sides of the house—the fire not yet out of control.

"What is that odor?" Julianna asked.

Jeremiah suddenly remembered. He said, "EOs—Elite Ops."

"That's what they smell like?"

"Not always. But they can emit a neurotoxin that induces panic. It has that terrible smell."

"Like death," Julianna said. "So they're here already. But they wouldn't just burn this place for no reason."

An odd shape caught Jeremiah's eye. Julianna put her hand on his shoulder and pressed him forward. She must have seen it too. And then he recognized it: a pile of bodies, mostly sliced in half.

A strange choking noise came from Julianna's throat.

They ran to the bodies and stared down at them. Some were just kids. Acid built up in Jeremiah's throat. He swallowed it. There had to be thirty people here. Murdered. Julianna knelt by one of the bodies: a little girl with curly hair who hadn't been completely cut in half. She appeared to be seven or eight years old. Julianna touched the child's face briefly.

"You think Devereaux could be here?" Jeremiah said.

The heat from the burning house grew more intense. Julianna ignored him, moving from body to body, turning corpses over so they faced the sky. Jeremiah glanced up at the Moon through a hole in the clouds. It looked almost pink, like a bleached bone wiped with a blood-soaked rag. Then the clouds covered it again. Seeing the bloody Moon reminded Jeremiah of a vid of the EOs, one in which they'd rounded up a group of terrorists. The EOs had sent a pulse of red laser fire through the terrorists, cutting them apart. That must have been what happened here.

A ragged, almost-human cough sounded from the house. Jeremiah glanced toward the front door, where an ancient scatterer stood. The machine coughed again, mingling with the crackling of wood burning. After a few seconds, the scatterer succumbed to the blaze and died. Finally Jeremiah found the will to move. He approached the corpses, examined their faces. How would he even know if Devereaux was among them? "Devereaux might be dead already," he said.

"No, he's not here."

"How can you be so sure?"

Julianna looked up at him and he realized the truth. "You know who he is."

She nodded. Then she gestured to the bodies and in a tired voice said, "Why?"

"They must have tried to fight the EOs. I don't see any weapons, but somebody must have pulled one. The house probably caught fire during the fight." He searched the ground, checking for footprints, and found several heavily indented sets. At least three EOs had been here.

"Such a waste," Julianna said as she straightened up.

"You knew them?"

Julianna nodded. "Doug—one of the men at the shelter—brought me out here to treat a little girl. She had a bad fever. West Nile."

"Who were they?"

"Nobodies. Fugitives and their families, homeless and poor, just trying to survive."

A window in the house exploded. Flames danced through it, flickering at the siding, slowly moving up toward the roof. Jeremiah's face grew painfully hot. He backed away a few steps, but Julianna stayed next to the bodies. How could she endure that inferno?

She shook her head as she stared down at five children. He realized that she was studying the little girl whose face she'd touched earlier. The child looked tiny in death, almost doll-like.

Jeremiah walked over, the heat almost unbearable, his eyes moving past the girls, settling on the boys: two of them, both older than his son—eleven…or twelve. He was surprised to find himself relieved that neither one looked like Joshua. Part of him felt sickened by that. He longed to strike out at an EO. Instead, he blinked three times, sealed himself back in his dungeon. He had to stay focused. Save the pain for later. He grabbed Julianna's arm. When he led her away from the fire to the edge of the wood, she didn't object, just kept her head down. He put his hand under her chin, lifted it and said, "The Army will arrive shortly. With the scatterer out, their scanners will be able to detect this energy output."

Julianna stared right through him, unfocused. Then her eyes narrowed, the muscles of her jaw working angrily, and she finally saw him. Her voice came out throaty and raw: "Think those assholes are still around?"

Jeremiah heard the murderous resolve in her voice, the fanaticism she'd always been able to tap into. She was steeling herself for battle, locking herself in her own little dungeon or whatever trick she used to insulate herself from the distractions of the outside world. He knew she was capable of anything when she got like this.

"I know what you're thinking," he said. "But we can't take EOs on."

"Why not? There's only a few of them."

"All we could do is die. We can't match their firepower." He held her gaze until she closed her eyes and nodded. After a moment, she sighed and looked up at the sky. "It's going to rain soon."

"How can you tell?"

"Can't you smell it?"

"Now I can," he said, catching the moisture beneath the smell of fire and death.

"I need to sit for a second," she said. "I feel like crap." She walked to a fallen tree and lowered herself to its trunk. Staring into the yellow flames, her shoulders hunched over, she looked small in the flickering light. Even from here the fire felt uncomfortably warm. Soon it would completely engulf the house.

Jeremiah wanted to tell her that she couldn't stay here, that the Army would arrive soon, but he decided to give her a moment. His eyes drifted again to the pile of bodies and he realized that despite being inside his dungeon, he didn't have his emotions under control. A slow anger rumbled up from inside. The damned EOs just threw these people in a pile like so much garbage. Were they sending a warning? It was easy to hate the EOs. And then he remembered Jack Marschenko, locked in a basement with nothing but nutri-water to sustain him, driven by hormones and drugs and conditioning until he couldn't tell right from wrong: a big naïve kid who thought he was on the side of the angels. Guilt mixed with Jeremiah's anger, intensifying it.

Julianna interrupted his thoughts. "What are we going to do, Jeremiah?"

He stepped to her side. "Who is Devereaux?"

She shook her head—a long, continuous movement that went well beyond an answer until he knew her mind was elsewhere. Finally she said, "We have to help him get away. Or he's going to end up like this."

"Are you really a Devereauxnian?"

"I'm only about the money, is that it?"

"Well, yeah."

"Not anymore. Screw you."

He felt incredible compassion for her at that moment. He longed to put his arms around her and comfort her. Then he reminded himself that she was very likely playing him and he kept his hands to himself.

Julianna let out a yell, an indecipherable roar of anguish. Then her shoulders slumped, her head sagged and she turned away from him as the first few drops of rain fell. He checked his scanner. The soldiers seemed to have finally spotted the anomaly of the burning house on their scanners, for they had begun to draw closer. When he looked up, he saw a drop of water running down Julianna's face. It couldn't possibly be a tear. It had to be a raindrop.

He took her arm above the elbow and walked her into the forest.

Chapter Nineteen

Doug followed the blond Amazon, Zeriphi, on a tour of the cave. She showed him the kitchen, the bedrooms, the bathrooms—all without doors. As they passed a bathroom, an Escala urinated into a toilet unconcernedly. Zeriphi introduced him as Nulk. He nodded to Doug, showing no embarrassment over his actions. Doug said, "Hello," keeping his eyes focused on Nulk's face. Although privacy had been impossible in prison, since Doug's escape, he'd grown to relish closed doors.

"You all got such unusual names," he remarked. "I don't remember that from the articles I read about the Mars Project."

"We've taken new names," Zeriphi answered. "The old names were burdened with psychological meanings that dragged us down. Our new names have no historical meaning. We chose them only for their sound and beauty."

"Zeriphi," Doug said. "That's a beautiful name—musical."

Of all the rooms he saw, only two had doors: both shut. Zeriphi told him that the first one opened on the monitoring center and was kept closed to keep the noise and dust levels down. The second door led to a tiny room with orange lights in the ceiling. Zeriphi opened the door but stopped Doug from entering. A naked Escala stood inside, basking in the warmth of the lamps.

"Our genetic makeup has been enhanced with an altered kineococcus radiotolerans bacterium," Zeriphi explained, "which allows us to tolerate hundreds of times the radiation you could."

"So you deliberately radiate yourselves?" Doug asked.

Zeriphi nodded. "It's necessary for our survival. It stimulates our immune systems and increases our energy levels." She closed the door. "If you were left in that room for a few hours, you would die."

During the tour, Doug found himself increasingly attracted to

Zeriphi. Her muscular body had initially seemed almost masculine, though there was nothing male about the way she moved. It was just the fact that she was bigger and so obviously stronger than him that made her appear other than feminine. Now, however, she struck him as sensual. The sway of her hips as she walked, the lilt of her soft voice, the almost animal muskiness of her body: everything about her brought him to a state of arousal. He reached down and adjusted himself as he followed her down a curved hallway. Finally they reached a room with beds, chairs and dressers built for normal-sized people.

"The children sleep here," Zeriphi said, pointing inside.

Doug glanced at the small bodies under their covers but found his eyes drawn back to Zeriphi. She tilted her head slightly, leaned forward a little and sighed almost imperceptibly, as if just the sight of the children had brought her great peace. Then he remembered something and said, "I thought I heard that you people are sterile."

"We cannot breed with our own kind," Zeriphi said. "But we have adapted."

Estrus! Doug suddenly remembered what the word meant. They wanted him to sleep with Zeriphi. Why did that make him nervous?

Zeriphi studied his face, as he searched her dark eyes. Then she looked down and saw the bulge in his pants. She said, "You're ready."

She led him to a bedroom much like the others but at the far end of a darkened hallway where they were less likely to be disturbed. Slowly she removed his shirt.

"You don't mind that I undress you?" she asked.

"No," Doug said. "But can't you find no room with a door, or at least turn off the light?"

"Why?" Zeriphi said. "You look fine."

She unzipped his pants while he stood unmoving, aroused. Lowering his pants and underwear to his ankles, Zeriphi gently lifted Doug and placed him on the bed. He remembered his grandfather handling him just as effortlessly when he was a small boy. There'd been something comforting about that—and the sensation he experienced now was markedly similar. He felt safe and warm. As he tried to wriggle out of his pants, his shoes got in the way and he lacked the energy to sit up. He laughed as his legs flailed against the clothing. Zeriphi smiled as she finished undressing him.

Naked, Doug watched Zeriphi unzip her coverall. She seemed embarrassed at having to disrobe before him, hesitating before slipping her arms out. As she did so, she kept her eyes on his, but he dropped his gaze to her breasts. She wore no bra. She had no need of one. Her breasts were firm, not overly large, and her stomach flat.

Zeriphi stepped out of her coverall and Doug whistled softly. Her brown triangle of hair drew his eyes for a second. Then he took in the whole of her body—shoulders, arms, thighs, hips. The hair under her arms was bushy and dark, but light peach fuzz covered her stomach. Desire for her surged through him—something almost inexplicable. No question she was a beautiful woman, strong and healthy. Yet she was also huge—the largest woman he'd ever seen naked.

Zeriphi tentatively climbed onto the bed, blushing as she lay next to him.

"I don't know what it is," she said. "I didn't think it would scare me like this."

"I scare you?" Doug said.

"I've never tried to breed before."

"You're a virgin?"

Zeriphi laughed. "No."

"We don't gotta do this," Doug said.

Zeriphi caressed his face with her fingers. She studied him with her dark brown eyes. "Do you want me to leave?"

Doug shook his head emphatically. "No. I'm an idiot. I guess I'm nervous too."

"Why?"

"I don't know nothin' about you—who you are, what you do, how you came to be here."

"I was a graduate student in chemistry when I applied for the Mars Project," Zeriphi said as she stroked Doug's chest and stomach.

"When I was accepted, I underwent the genetic surgery that enhanced me so I would be able to thrive on Mars. Do you want to know anything else?"

"I want to know everything else," Doug said, "but I can't concentrate right now. I need you."

Zeriphi rolled over and mounted him, cooing and warbling in some ancient song that stirred him. He caught an animal aroma, a muskiness that grew with her rocking—pungent and powerful. Doug wanted to reach up and touch her, caress her, but he could barely move. Even as he lifted one hand, he shuddered in ecstasy and all thought vanished as he surrendered to the pleasure. Afterwards, Zeriphi reached over and grabbed a coverlet at the foot of the bed. She pulled it over them and caressed Doug until he fell asleep.

* * *

When Doug awoke, Zeriphi was gone, though her scent lingered. He could smell her on his body, the odor intoxicating, arousing. Stretching and yawning, feeling refreshed and relaxed, he embraced the warm glow that suffused his core. Although Doug figured that the drugs Zeriphi had given him enhanced or perhaps created his desire, he nevertheless wanted her again. Where had she gone? The room's glow globe, darkened now, floated high above the bed. He had no idea how to turn it on but the light from the hallway provided sufficient illumination for him to see. He needed to relieve himself and he also wanted to look for Zeriphi.

As he sat up, feeling slightly dizzy, the glow globe brightened slowly.

Doug's clothes were neatly folded on a chair. Picking them up, he dressed clumsily, then staggered out into the hallway. Behind him the glow globe dimmed. As he moved along the hall, a hand against the wall to brace himself, the lights brightened at his approach, dimming again behind him. He hadn't noticed that earlier, so focused had he been on Zeriphi.

After finding a toilet and relieving himself, he headed out into the main cave. He wondered what time it was. It felt like night and, indeed, the lights in the main cave had been turned down. The trio of spotlights emitted small, weak beams of orange light. At the main table, under a globe of bright white, sat eight of his hosts, engaged in quiet discussion. Doug saw Quekri and Temala there but not Zeriphi.

When they spotted Doug, their conversation stopped. Temala smiled at him again, an unnerving smile that seemed predatory. The Escala whose back was to Doug turned around. His face was immediately recognizable. It looked like it had been carved out of granite—roughly rectangular, with a slash for a mouth and a block nose. His eyes were black and narrow, his hair short and black; and his broad shoulders were nearly as wide as those of Cookie Monster.

"You're Zhong Wu," Doug said. "You were gonna lead the Mars Project."

The man answered, "I'm called Zod now."

"Zod? That's odd. Odd Zod." Doug laughed nervously. "Sorry," he added as he reached out for a chair, a sudden fit of dizziness overcoming him, "I don't know why I find that so funny."

Zod leapt to his feet. For a second, Doug thought he saw anger smoldering in the big man's eyes, but that quickly vanished. Zod guided Doug to the chair, then stood behind him with his hands on Doug's shoulders.

Quekri, after a glance at Zod, got to her feet and said to Doug, "Your friends are dead."

"What?" Doug stared from Quekri to the other Escala around the table. Though their expressions were largely impassive, he could sense sorrow coming from them, as if they had suffered a great loss. How could they know his friends? And how could his friends be dead? Had the Army found them? He finally managed to say, "How? And how do you know about them?"

Zod said, "We didn't see it—just the aftermath."

Quekri added, "We watched you visit them a while back."

Doug took shallow breaths. He knew he ought to feel sad at their deaths but all he felt at the moment was rising desire. He reached down and adjusted himself inside his pants.

"Were they your prison friends?" Quekri asked.

Doug nodded, his erection throbbing, painful. "I told 'em about the abandoned houses. They had nowhere else to go." He frowned. He tried to think, but his body wanted only one thing. He fought his desire even as he asked, "Where is Zeriphi?"

"She's with the doctor," Quekri said.

Doug tried to stand. Zod pushed him back down. Or perhaps it was just the weight of Zod's large hands. "Is she all right?"

"She'll be fine. The impregnation process is difficult."

"We're sorry for your loss," Zod said. "And I'm grateful for your help."

"My help?"

"Zod and Zeriphi are companions," Quekri said.

Doug twisted around to stare up at Zod's intense face. "She never told me."

"You did not need to know," Quekri said. "I apologize for the way we used you but it was necessary." When Doug did not respond to this, she said, "You feel an emotional attachment to Zeriphi?"

Doug nodded. He opened his mouth to speak, but found no words to describe his feelings.

"That is common. It will slowly fade. If it doesn't, we can give you something to accelerate the process."

"I don't want it to fade," Doug said.

"Of course you don't," Quekri said. "That's natural. Just as it will be natural for you to become angry with us. And when you do, please remember that we only did what we had to do to survive."

"I ain't angry," Doug said, realizing even as he spoke that it was a lie. Anger surged inside him—at the Army, at the Escala, at the world. All he wanted now was to get the hell out of here. "When can I leave?"

"You're not fit," Quekri said. "And we must make certain it's safe."

"I don't care if the Army gets me."

"There arc worse things out there than the Army," Zod said. He grabbed a portable monitor from the table and held it up in front of Doug's face. "Have you ever seen this man?"

On the monitor, a clip of a man in a basement played itself over and over, a few seconds repeating themselves, showing the man in profile and face on. He smiled and waved at the camera, but his face was covered with dark paint and his body looked fuzzy, out of focus. Or was Doug having trouble focusing because of the drugs? He shook his head. "Who is he?"

"We don't know," Quekri said. "We assume he's here looking for Devereaux."

"What about Devereaux?" Doug said. "Where is he? Is he safe? Why ain't he contacted me?"

"All will be explained in time," Quekri said, her voice sounding faint. "You should return to bed." She nodded to Zod. "Get some rest."

Doug's eyelids kept drooping. As Zod effortlessly picked him up, Quekri seated herself at the table and bowed her head, folding her hands in front of her. The other Escala did the same. They almost looked to be in prayer. Doug closed his eyes and let Zod carry him away.

Chapter Twenty

Colonel Truman wondered why he hadn't retired last year when he reached his thirty years. This search for Devereaux, already a mess, had the makings of a true disaster. He studied the monitors by the ruined front doorway, tracking his soldiers as they searched the woods. Then he scanned the black sky, wishing the rain would fall harder, driving the mosquitoes to ground. All his soldiers had been bitten already. So had he. And there was no vaccine against the Susquehanna Virus.

He wondered too about the doctor. Was she involved with Boyd? Or had her use of the word "gander" been a mere coincidence? It wasn't a common a word; he hadn't heard it in years. But Boyd reacted to it. And Truman knew Weiss intended to question Boyd hard. The Attorney General had no bend in him, no softness. There'd even been rumors during his confirmation hearings that he'd tortured people while in the CIA. How far would a man like Weiss go to extract information? Boyd was just a soldier, like Truman—wise enough to have retired, stupid enough to get back in the game—and Truman rather liked him.

Finally Truman worried about the Elite Ops. A full unit was scheduled to arrive in a few hours. Logically, Truman had no reason to fear the Elite Ops. They were on his side. But they brought a brutality that bordered on sadism. Truman found it impossible to trust or even respect them.

"They'll push the timetable," Weiss had told him with a satisfied smile, "force everybody to act more quickly. Devereaux will be anxious to get out of here. Jeremiah will speed up his efforts to find Devereaux. Those pseudos will realize we're going to be hunting them down. And when the Elite Ops get here, they'll go after the pseudos. In the meantime we question Raddock Boyd. Bring him to Sister Ezekiel's office."

When Boyd was brought from the newly repaired porta-cell and secured to a chair, Truman double-checked that the bonds were tight. Boyd was unnaturally strong. Sergeant Corbin, one of the company medics, then took up position inside the door while Weiss darkened the wall-windows and leaned in close to speak to Truman quietly.

"Get a truth kit, Colonel," he said. "We need answers quickly."

Boyd leaned forward and said, "Hey, what's going on?"

Truman ignored the prisoner. "I'm a little concerned about giving him the truth drugs with that chip implanted in his head. Also, he's in a pretty weakened state."

Boyd spoke louder: "I'm not invisible."

Weiss adjusted his tie and looked at the prisoner before turning back to Truman. "It's perfectly safe," he said. "I've conducted a number of these types of interrogations. Never had a problem before. And we need to know what he knows about Devereaux."

Boyd said, "You could at least remove the chip. This one's gotta be defective. My heart's racing."

"Sergeant," Truman said, "set up a medical monitor on this man, then get me a truth kit."

"I'm telling you, there's something wrong with my chip," Boyd said.

"Shut up," Sergeant Corbin commanded as he attached electrodes to Boyd.

"We can't remove the chip," Truman explained to Boyd. "One wrong move and the poison would be activated. I'm sure the doctor could do it safely."

"The doctor!" Weiss scoffed. "Unless I'm very much mistaken, she's involved in all this. Did you see Boyd's reaction when she used the word 'gander'?"

Boyd jerked his head up. "I think I'm having a heart attack."

Sergeant Corbin, studying his monitor, shook his head. "Heartrate, one-forty-six. Blood pressure, two-ten over ninety-four. Just nerves. Nothing to be alarmed about."

"Get the truth kit," Weiss said to the medic.

When Sergeant Corbin left the room, Truman said, "I noticed his reaction, sir. But I watched the doctor very carefully and she did nothing suspicious. I think she may have just been using an archaic term."

"It's possible," Weiss conceded. "But we're going to find out. Aren't we, Raddock?"

Boyd pushed hard against his restraints. "Those drugs'll kill me. If you want information, just ask. I'll talk. I don't know very much, but I'll tell you what I know."

"Very well," Weiss said. "Is the doctor involved in all this?"

Boyd shrugged. "I don't know. She used the code word, but she never said or did anything after that to let me know she's my contact."

"Can you blame her?" Weiss leaned forward. "You practically jumped out of your skin when you heard the word."

"I wasn't expecting it," Boyd said. "I thought..."

Weiss interrupted him: "Why are you here?"

"To protect Devereaux."

"Who sent you?"

"Atheists for a Free America. We're an organization of—"

"I know who you are," Weiss interrupted him again. "Who's your contact?"

"I work through blind drops and web postings," Boyd said. "Safer that way."

"You must know somebody."

Boyd shook his head. "Sorry, no."

"Where is Devereaux?"

"I don't know."

"Is he here?"

"That's the rumor. I don't know."

Weiss looked at Truman and rolled his eyes before turning back to Boyd. "What does Devereaux look like now?"

"I don't know."

"Then how were you going to protect him?"

"Someone was supposed to contact me. The doc used the code word, so I thought it was her. But now I don't know."

Weiss threw up his hands. "This is getting us nowhere."

"I've told you everything I know."

"Which is nothing. Where's that truth serum?"

"Help!" Boyd yelled. "Sister, help!"

"Shut up," Weiss said.

"Somebody," Boyd yelled. "Help me!"

Several soldiers moved toward the office door. Truman waved them away. "Find the doctor," he said as Sister Ezekiel and her lawyer worked themselves into the office.

"What's going on here?" she asked.

"They're gonna give me truth serum," Boyd shouted.

"Truth serum?" Ahmad Rashidi said. He turned to the Attorney General. "Has he consented to that procedure?"

"Need I remind you that I've declared a civil emergency?" Weiss said.

"Those drugs'll kill me," Boyd said to the nun, who put her hand on his shoulder.

"Mr. Weiss," Sister Ezekiel said. "I object to this most strenuously."

"Your objection is noted, Sister. Now I'm going to have to ask you and your attorney to leave."

Sister Ezekiel stood with her hands on her hips as Sergeant Corbin returned to the office and handed the truth kit to Truman. She settled her glare on Truman, who looked from her to the kit to Boyd, wondering how he'd gotten himself into such a mess. He was a simple soldier, not some ruthless National Intelligence interrogator.

"Don't do it," Boyd yelled. "You'll be a murderer. You'll regret it. All of you. Murderers."

"Can't you do anything, Ahmad?" Sister Ezekiel asked.

"I'm afraid not, Sister. They've got the guns on their side. And he does have the power to declare a civil emergency. Whether it's right or not, that's the law. We can call Judge Moline, see if she'll impose a temporary stay but we won't be able to do it in time. Besides, these truth drugs aren't dangerous. He'll be fine."

"I will not be fine," Boyd bellowed. "I'll be dead."

"He's exaggerating," Weiss said to Sister Ezekiel. "Now, please leave."

"What if this procedure is more dangerous than you realize?" Sister Ezekiel asked.

Sergeant Corbin ripped open the two packets—one containing the truth serum cocktail; the other, the brainwave-veracity or BV monitor.

"There are very few risks," Weiss said. "These drugs have been safely tested on numerous subjects. And he hasn't given us any answers."

"That's because I don't know anything," Boyd shouted.

"Calm down, Raddock," Weiss said. "We're going to find out exactly what you know very soon."

He nodded to Truman, who took a step toward Sister Ezekiel and Ahmad Rashidi. Truman said, "I'm sorry, Sister, but you'll have to leave."

The nun glowered at him for what seemed a long time before marching out the door, Rashidi right behind her. After Sergeant Corbin removed Boyd's bandage and tapped a vein, Truman initiated the flow of drugs into the bloodstream. He adjusted the levels of each, adding more narcotic than usual, hoping Weiss wouldn't notice. Truman suspected Boyd's condition was precarious. He watched Boyd's face, seeing for the first time a small, brown mole just below Boyd's left eye. Truman found it odd that he hadn't noticed the mole before. Now it darkened slightly with the increased blood flow to the head.

"Well, Raddock," Weiss said, "No more games. No more lies. You're going to tell the truth now."

"I'm not lying," Boyd said, his voice now into the normal range—an indicator that his anxiety level was already dropping.

"Keep an eye on his vitals," Truman said to Sergeant Corbin.

Truman opened the second packet containing the BV monitor and placed four electrodes on Boyd's head—one at each temple, one behind each ear. Turning on the unit, he watched as Boyd's system absorbed the serum. Across the top of the flat pad, he saw the six drugs being injected. In the middle of the screen, a line appeared on a chart. It slowly traveled up and to the right, indicating the increasing passivity and obedience of the subject. When the level looked right, he began with a few base questions.

"What is your name?" Truman asked.

"Raddock Boyd."

"Have you been genetically enhanced?"

Boyd fidgeted in his chair, his mouth opening and closing several times. Then he said, "Only for strength and endurance."

Truman made a minor adjustment to the flow of drugs and then said, "Why are you here?"

"To protect Walt Devereaux."

After checking the BV monitor, Truman asked, "Where is Devereaux?"

"I don't know."

Boyd's eyes fluttered open and shut, settling at half-closed. The line on the graph remained in the area of maximum passivity and objectivity, showing he was telling the truth. The mole on his face looked black now, the rest of his face suffused with blood.

"Is Devereaux at this shelter?" Truman asked.

"I don't know."

"Has Devereaux been here in the past?"

"I think so," Boyd said.

A small amount of drool emerged from the corner of Boyd's lips. Truman noticed a spike in the pain reading, but Boyd's passivity and objectivity remained high. Truman hoped to God he wasn't killing the man. He glanced at Weiss before slightly increasing the flow of narcotic. Then he continued: "What does Devereaux look like?"

"I don't know."

"Is the doctor your contact?"

"I don't know."

Weiss cut in: "Are you here with the pseudos?"

"Escala," Boyd said. "They call themselves Escala." He slowly shook his head. "I'm not with them."

"Who's your contact?"

"I told you," Boyd said, lifting his head, "We work off web postings and blind drops to protect everyone's identities. The government persecutes atheists, treats us like garbage."

"That's because you are garbage," Weiss said, spittle flying from his lips.

Truman opened his mouth to protest that Weiss had gone too far. But one glance told Truman that Weiss was beyond reasoning. The Attorney General's face pulsed a dark red, his lips quivering, his eyes narrow. So Truman said nothing.

"You're wrong," Boyd said. "We're on the ladder. We've evolved past you." He grimaced as tears rolled down his cheeks. Oddly, the pain reading jumped again. Weiss stepped around to the front of the chair. With his left hand, he grabbed Boyd's short hair and pulled the ex-Marine's head up. Then he slapped Boyd hard, the sound echoing in Truman's ears, which began to burn with shame.

"Who is Devereaux?" Weiss yelled, slapping Boyd again and again.

Boyd screamed, a raw, throaty sound of anguish. When Weiss let go of him, Boyd's head dropped to his chest and his body went limp.

"This is getting us nowhere," Weiss said.

"He's telling the truth," Truman said. "His passivity and objectivity readings show no deception. If I crank up the juice any more I'll kill him. What do his vitals look like?" he asked Sergeant Corbin.

"Two-sixty over one-eighty, sir."

As Weiss lifted his hand to strike Boyd again, Captain Lopez ran into the office, carrying a pile of what looked like human skin. "Sir, we found this in the doctor's room."

Weiss grabbed the material out of Captain Lopez's hands. "Neo-skin. So the doctor *is* involved. Perhaps the good sister is too."

Truman shook his head. "Sister Ezekiel didn't lie."

Weiss turned his back on Truman, threw the neo-skin onto the desk and sighed heavily. "Probably not," he finally said. "Still," he turned back to face Truman with an embarrassed smile. "Wake him up, Colonel. I want to make sure."

Truman hesitated.

"Now, Colonel," Weiss commanded.

Truman altered the mix of drugs slightly, decreasing the anti-resistance drugs but adding more narcotic to lessen the pain. He then increased the stimulant to bring Boyd out of his sleep. Boyd came awake groggily, his face still red, the mole looking bigger now, bulging out from his cheek.

"Is Sister Ezekiel involved in this?" Weiss asked immediately. "Is Sister Ezekiel a Devereauxnian?"

Suddenly, Boyd's whole body twitched in a violent spasm. The chair wobbled as his feet pushed against the floor. On the BV monitor, Truman saw that the pain had spiked again. It was now reading well into the agony level. How could that be? The narcotic should have deadened the nerve endings.

Sergeant Corbin said, "Blood pressure three-hundred over two-ten, sir."

Boyd's jaw worked angrily as blood trickled from his nose. His arms fought against the restraints holding him to the chair. Cords of muscle rippled beneath the skin of his neck. He shouted, "I don't know!"

A beep sounded from Sergeant Corbin's medical monitor, followed by the steady drone of flatlining. Boyd slumped in the chair. His bladder emptied, the acrid odor of urine reaching Truman's nose. He cut the flow of drugs instantly as Sergeant Corbin pounded on Boyd's chest.

"Get him back," Weiss said.

Together, Truman and Sergeant Corbin removed the restraints and lowered Boyd to the floor, where they worked on him for long minutes, Sergeant Corbin administering the heart attack package of drugs. Weiss paced the room, watching anxiously. Finally, the medic stopped trying to revive Boyd. He straightened and shook his head. "He's gone, sir."

"I can't understand how this happened," Truman said. "I was very careful. Plus I doubled the narcotic dosage. He shouldn't have been in that much pain."

Weiss said, "Are you sure you didn't make a mistake, Colonel?"

Truman raised his hands and shook his head as if to say he couldn't be certain, while Sergeant Corbin searched his monitor, looking for anything that might indicate cause of death. Finally, the medic said, “It was the ID chip, sir. The narcotics in the truth serum activated it. Nobody could have saved him.”

Truman looked at Boyd’s face, where the mole no longer stood out on the pale skin. It was barely visible, as if it had contained the man’s life force and was now emptied. A heaviness welled up inside him. In his effort to be kind, he had killed Raddock Boyd.

Chapter Twenty-One

Sister Ezekiel stared at the dead man on her office floor, then looked from Weiss to Colonel Truman. Monsters, the both of them. She was beyond fury, almost in disbelief. How stupid could two men be? And yet, she'd seen too many similar instances over the years to be shocked. The unfortunate truth, the truth she still had trouble accepting, was that for men in power, life was cheap—and the poorer the victim, the cheaper the life. "He warned you," she said. "He told you the truth drugs would kill him."

"It was an accident, Sister," Weiss said. "An act of God. ID chip failure. Colonel Truman did everything in his power to save the man. It wasn't his fault."

Colonel Truman's eyes widened slightly at that.

Was that guilt or fear? Sister Ezekiel silently prayed for the power to calm herself before speaking. "It's up to God to assign blame, Mr. Weiss. I just want the killing to stop."

"I'm trying, Sister. But first I have to find Devereaux. And your Dr. Mary."

"Dr. Mary? What does she have to do with this?"

Weiss pointed to a pile of skin-colored material atop her desk. "You see this neo-skin? We found it in Dr. Mary's room. She was using it to change her appearance. Did you know about that?"

"What?" Sister Ezekiel took a step backward and bumped against the doorframe.

"Here is her mask." Weiss held it up—Dr. Mary's face without the eyes. "I don't yet know who the doctor really is but I'm going to find out. Soon."

She opened her mouth to speak, but found no words.

Weiss said, "We think she was involved with Raddock Boyd. She used the code word his contact at the shelter was supposed to give him. And now she's disappeared. Do you have any idea where she's gone?"

Sister Ezekiel shook her head, swamped by anger, fear, sorrow. How could Dr. Mary have betrayed her? Was it simply to protect Devereaux? She'd never hidden her beliefs. And the fact that she was a Devereauxnian hadn't taken away from her excellent healing arts. But why hadn't she told Sister Ezekiel the truth? As for Devereaux—he must have known of the doctor's false persona. Yet neither had trusted her. Her stomach roiled.

She said, "Excuse me."

Hurrying from the room, she made it to the bathroom before the urge to vomit overwhelmed her. Afterwards, her stomach a little calmer, she rinsed out her mouth and patted her face with cool water. For a moment, she stared at herself in the mirror. The lines around the gray eyes in her thin, gray face announced her exhaustion. All the energy she had drawn from her talk with Devereaux had vaporized at the sight of Raddock Boyd dead on her floor.

When she opened the door, Colonel Truman waited just outside. His eyes darted around before settling on hers. Then he swallowed and said, "You okay, Sister?"

"Are you actually concerned, Colonel, or are you just making sure I don't run?"

"I'm sorry, Sister. I have my orders."

He escorted her back to her office, a hand on her arm. She walked stiffly, quietly—almost incapable of thought.

"Well, Sister," Weiss said after she took a chair, "I think you need to tell us everything you know about Devereaux, Dr. Mary and Raddock Boyd."

"Or you'll give me the truth serum?" She tried to make it sound defiant but she heard only fear. Now that she knew who Devereaux was, she would certainly betray him under the influence of Weiss' truth drugs. She issued a silent prayer to the Virgin Mother, then said, "I already told you I didn't know anything about Devereaux being in the area. I didn't know anything about Dr. Mary's fake identity. And I didn't know Raddock Boyd."

She stared at Weiss, part challenge, part question. Her heart beat in her chest as if she'd just run a mile. Her lungs refused to work properly too, taking in insufficient quantities of air for her needs. At least she was sitting. She doubted her knees would be able to support her if she were standing.

"Shall I get another truth kit?" Colonel Truman asked in an overly loud voice.

Weiss looked from him to Sister Ezekiel and said, "It may be the only way to get the whole truth."

Sister Ezekiel glanced down at Raddock Boyd's body. Had they left it on the floor to scare her? It was working. Her stomach rebelled again. She clamped her jaws together as a bone-shivering chill came over her. She wanted to make a grand sarcastic comment, the kind of thing Dr. Mary was so good at, but she didn't trust her voice.

"Well, Sister?" Weiss said.

She cleared her throat, trying to call forth some moisture. "I can't tell you what I don't know. You can inject me with your drugs. You can torture me if you like, but I can't give you information I don't have."

She closed her eyes as her body began to shake—small tremors, hopefully unnoticeable. A tic started in her left eyelid. Would the drugs kill her, or would she only betray Devereaux? And perhaps she should. After all, he'd been prepared to turn himself in just a short time ago. Yet, she realized as she sat there that if she did turn Devereaux in, he'd be subjected to the same kind of treatment Boyd had received. She had to try to protect him. As she prepared for the worst, miraculously, she heard Ahmad's voice in the doorway. She opened her eyes.

"Mr. Weiss," he said, "are you planning to inject a potentially deadly substance into Sister Ezekiel? You've already killed one man tonight. Do you want to endanger the life of a nun who has devoted herself to helping the poor and disenfranchised? I'll crucify you. I'll contact every media outlet..."

Weiss held out his hands. "Calm down. We simply want Sister Ezekiel to tell us what she knows about all this." He pointed to the dead man and the neo-skin.

"If Sister Ezekiel said she doesn't know anything, then she doesn't know anything. There's not a more honest and honorable person in the world. To imply that she's had anything to do with all this is to impugn her reputation. I could sue you for slander—Attorney General or not—and you would be ruined."

Weiss stepped over to Ahmad and put his finger in the lawyer's chest. He spoke softly, almost in a whisper: "Don't threaten me, Mr. Rashidi, or I'll have you locked away for the rest of your life. Do you understand me?"

Ahmad backed up a step. He said, "You can't—"

"And don't tell me what I can't do. You have no idea what pressures I face every day. I'm going to do what I have to and that includes making tough decisions. Unpopular decisions." Weiss turned back to the desk and picked up Dr. Mary's mask. He looked at Sister Ezekiel. "But in this case I suppose it's possible you were duped—perhaps even likely. And though I'm quite certain the serum is safe, I'm going to assume that you've been telling the truth. I won't force you to undergo the indignity of an injection. Let me make clear that this is not because of anything you said, Mr. Rashidi. And if you ever threaten me again, you *will* be arrested. Immediately. Understand?"

Ahmad stared at him, unblinking.

"I said, do you understand?"

"Yes," Ahmad said.

"Good. Now get out of here."

Sister Ezekiel let Ahmad help her to her feet. She felt unsteady, so she leaned on him as they walked, and after a few steps she was able to move under her own power. As they made their way down the hall, she said, "How did you happen to come by at just the right moment?"

"Coincidence, Sister. I was heading for the kitchen when I heard Colonel Truman say something about another truth kit. Funny, he was looking right at me when he said it—like he wanted to make sure I heard him. I listened for a few seconds, then barged in."

So Colonel Truman wasn't quite the monster Sister Ezekiel had thought he was. Still, intentionally or not, he'd killed Raddock Boyd. That was unforgivable. "Well," she said, "I'm very grateful."

Together, they walked down the long hall past the dorm rooms where her guests prepared for bed. She was surprised at how fragile her emotional state was right now—still afraid and still furious over Boyd's unnecessary death and Weiss' casual acceptance of it. She could barely think straight. Calm down, she thought. The world is unfair and harsh, and you have to work to fix it the way you always have—one small deed at a time.

The first thing she wanted to do was talk to Dr. Mary, find out what her story was. She wanted this to be a simple misunderstanding that could easily be cleared up, even though in her heart she knew it wasn't. This was the end of Dr. Mary's stay at the shelter. That saddened her immeasurably. Dr. Mary was part of some larger political intrigue involving Devereaux; and when Devereaux left, she would too. Sister Ezekiel sighed.

Ahmad interrupted her thoughts. "You worried about Dr. Mary, Sister?"

"Who do you think she is?"

"Someone who wants to protect Devereaux. Perhaps she's his personal doctor. Very sad. I never knew she was a Devereauxnian. I liked her."

"What are you upset about, Ahmad, the fact that she's a Devereauxnian or the fact that she lied to us?"

Ahmad's face colored, his eyes blazed. "A lie is forgivable. Her betrayal of Allah is not."

"But you've promised to help me should Devereaux request my assistance. Wouldn't you also have to betray Allah to do so?"

In the distance, she heard a gunshot, then honking horns, more gunshots and yells coming from the street. They both stopped, listened for a few seconds, and then Ahmad turned to face her, his hands clenched into fists. "I have a legal and ethical duty to assist my client. I will not breach that duty."

Sister Ezekiel nodded as if she understood, but she realized she could no longer trust him. Too many people had lied to her, and Ahmad's contradictory statements demonstrated that he wasn't being fully honest with her, either. As she began walking again, she said,

"This is such a mess. I heard several soldiers talking about the Elite Ops, saying they might be here by morning. They sounded afraid. Do you know who these Elite Ops are?"

"They're a sort of special forces times ten. When they put on their armor, they become ultimate warriers. I'm not sure how it all works but they use the newest technology to enhance their fighting ability—become cyborgs, essentially. They make the Army look like a Boy Scout troop."

"More men with guns."

"I wouldn't worry about it, Sister," Ahmad said, "as long as you don't know where Devereaux is. It would only be a problem if you had that information and tried to keep it from 'em."

He stared at her. Did he suspect that she knew Devereaux's true identity? Was he trying to encourage her to confide in him or was he simply giving her advice? Life was so much more complicated when everyone you knew engaged in lies and secrets and games. Frustrating. At any rate, she couldn't hand Devereaux over—not to save one life, not to save a thousand.

Ahmad grabbed her elbow. Leaning in close, he said, "What's botherin' you, Sister? Can I help?"

Despite her thoughts, almost against her will, Sister Ezekiel blurted out: "What if I knew who Devereaux was?"

Instantly she regretted her words.

Ahmad, backing away from her, a look of shock on his face, said, "You know who he is!"

Sister Ezekiel shook her head. "Forget what I said. I'm tired. I didn't mean it."

"I knew he was here. Who is he?"

She closed her eyes. How could she have done something so stupid? Was it just fatigue or did her subconscious mind want Devereaux caught?

"Sister," Ahmad said, "You gotta look after yourself and your shelter. Besides, the man ain't exactly a saint."

"Have you ever considered the possibility that he might be right?"

"Sister!" Ahmad looked at her in horror. "I never thought you'd have a crisis of faith. You see what he's done? Even you're havin' doubts."

Sister Ezekiel smiled. "I may have doubts," she said. "But I also have faith. My heart says God is using him to test us. I accept my doubts. They're a weakness I haven't completely overcome. I wish they didn't exist, but they do. So I have to rely on my faith. That will have to be enough."

Ahmad swung his arm out. "Look what he's done to your shelter."

"That reminds me," Sister Ezekiel said. "Would you deposit this in our account?" She held out the plastic card Devereaux had given her.

Ahmad reached for it tentatively, as if it were covered in blood.

"He gave you this?" he asked.

"I got it from a friend," Sister Ezekiel said.

Ahmad held the card up in the air. "This don't make up for everything he's done, Sister. Not by a long ways."

"You may sleep in your usual guest room tonight, Ahmad," Sister Ezekiel said.

As she turned to go, Ahmad spoke:

"Sister, I just wanna say that even though I disagree with you, I'll honor your wishes. I'll keep this conversation confidential because you're my client and because I respect you. But I hope to Allah you know what you're doing."

Sister Ezekiel bowed. "Good night, Ahmad."

The lawyer shook his head slowly and turned away.

As she stood alone in the hallway, she felt a grim satisfaction at withholding the truth from him. Devereaux had been right to keep his presence a secret, even from her. When the stakes became this large, no one was trustworthy. What a leap of faith he had taken in exposing himself to her.

A thought crept up on her: a tickling doubt. Why had she admitted to Ahmad the possibility that Devereaux was right? Did she really believe that? Would she have survived all these years without God in her life? Admittedly, she'd been an obstinate nun. She didn't agree with many of the Church's tenets and she'd never been completely comfortable with its male power structure—although she made allowances for the fact that her attitude towards men had been forever changed by that one shattering experience. She had to remind herself every morning that not all men were rapists. Still, some deep and largely hidden part of her flinched whenever she pictured them in positions of power. At times like this when her mind was troubled, she often retreated to the chapel for prayer. The repetition of Hail Marys and Our Fathers clarified her thinking, soothed her cares. But before she allowed herself that indulgence, she had one more thing to do.

Chapter Twenty-Two

Lendra dipped her little finger into the glass bulb of her necklace, coating it with neo-dopamine, then rubbed the drug along her gums. Closing her eyes for a moment, she inhaled, smelling the residue of burned plastic, the remnants of dinner and the musty odor of unwashed men. Metal clanking and snatches of words intruded from outside while rainbow colors drifted across her eyelids. She knew she was right on the edge, straddling the fine line between heightened ability and a dazed overdose.

She re-sealed the glass bulb, then put the necklace back around her neck. She needed to find a way to break into Julianna's interface. No matter how clever the former ghost thought she was, she was no match for Lendra. Refreshing her sat-connection and locating Julianna's signal, Lendra searched for a way inside the programming.

She didn't want to kill Julianna, but she had to ensure that no harm came to Jeremiah. If she could somehow hack into Julianna's interface and sabotage her connectivity, she could render the interface essentially worthless. Then Julianna, dependent on Jeremiah to see her safely back to the shelter, would be in no position to betray him again.

It was delicate work, requiring patience and the silky touch of a butterfly's wing. Carefully, stealthily, Lendra bypassed the field dampener the Elite Ops had set up, then accessed the local sat-connection, examining the flow of data across the link, seeking an opportunity to slip inside Julianna's interface connection. She searched for a pattern she could piggyback on to, essentially becoming a stowaway inside Julianna's interface. Most of the data threads were too tenuous or insubstantial; many flickered out just as she was about to touch them. But several were relatively strong. She spent most of her time with them, experimenting with transcendental poly-algorithmic variables, patiently storming the quantum cryptographic defenses of Julianna's interface.

And then she had it: a foothold through the GPS stream. She established an imperceptible tie-in, the tiniest of connections, a link she could strengthen later, if necessary. For now, she had access and would be able to examine Julianna's incoming and outgoing transmissions. She found nothing suspicious, which was suspicious in itself.

As Lendra surfed the connection to Julianna's interface, she made several further adjustments to the data stream to ensure that Julianna would never detect her presence. Then she watched the link, waiting for the right moment to cut off Julianna's connection to the outside world.

A knock came at the door.

Minimizing the link to Julianna's interface, Lendra got to her feet, opened the door and found Sister Ezekiel standing in the hallway. She said, "Sister, what can I do for you?"

"May I come in?"

"Of course." Lendra gestured to the room's sole chair, closed the door and took a place on the bed. She paused her interface, then said, "Is this a social call?"

Sister Ezekiel looked from Lendra's interface to her eyes. "How are the accommodations?"

"Fine, Sister."

Sister Ezekiel nodded. "Have you seen Dr. Mary?"

Lendra frowned. She detected something different in the way Sister Ezekiel said Dr. Mary's name. Did Sister Ezekiel know Dr. Mary was really Julianna? Did she know what kind of monster worked as the shelter's doctor? "No," she said, "I haven't seen her in a while."

Sister Ezekiel stared at Lendra, her eyes looking larger than normal behind her glasses. She reminded Lendra of her old fourth-grade teacher, Mrs. Lowell, who seemed to be able to read her mind. Lendra tried not to flinch.

"She seemed rather friendly with Jeremiah," Sister Ezekiel said casually. "What about him? Have you seen him?"

"He left, Sister. He had some things to do outside."

"Like looking for Devereaux?" Sister Ezekiel fixed her steel-gray eyes on Lendra's. "Or Cookie Monster?"

"Yes."

"And why aren't you with him?"

"I'm conducting my own search here," Lendra said, pointing to her interface. "Checking surveillance video, looking at your visitors over the last few weeks to see if I can find anything. If Devereaux has been here, I might be able to spot him."

"Do you really believe he's created bioweapons that could wipe out humanity?"

"I don't know, Sister. That's partly why we need to find him."

"What do you think of him personally?"

Lendra sat back and braced herself with her arms behind her on the bed, glad to be talking about something other than Jeremiah and Julianna. "I don't know what to make of him," she said. "He's interesting. I'd like to ask him about his ladder of enlightenment. He had to know it would cause a huge uproar, given how religious our country has become—how religious the world is." Lendra smiled briefly. "I'd also like to ask him about the statue—'Emerging Man.' I think it's partly what inspired him to publish his ladder."

"How so?" Sister Ezekiel said.

"It's more than just the physical look of the statue. There's something else…something I can't quite put my finger on."

With a slightly ironic, devilish grin, and despite her obvious fatigue, Sister Ezekiel looked toward the ceiling and rattled off: "You mean the fact that it was created by two different artists using distinct styles who still somehow managed to blend them together into a cohesive whole?"

Lendra laughed.

Sister Ezekiel said, "I've visited that statue every week for years. I've heard people discuss it at great length. I can cite chapter and verse on it."

"So you know it's important. Do you know why?"

Sister Ezekiel pursed her lips, as if thinking it through. "Ryan Connelly," she finally said, "the one who you said was Devereaux's grandfather, changed the meaning of the statue by sculpting the body in a more abstract style, and also added depth by altering the nature of the struggle depicted in the statue's face. If you study only the face, all you see is a conflict between joy and sorrow. But when you add in the body, you see the eternal struggle to better ourselves."

"Well, you've just put your finger on why I'd like to talk to him about it," Lendra said. "That statue is Devereauxnian fodder. It has an importance Gray Weiss hasn't yet grasped." She paused for a moment, then added, "I also don't like Gray Weiss. He's on a power trip and I don't trust him. Do you?"

"I'm not sure what to think about Mr. Weiss."

"I'm sure he thinks he's doing the right thing. He wants to fundamentally change our government, become our benevolent leader. You see that, don't you?"

"Yes."

"But benevolent or not," Lendra said, "he still wants to be a dictator."

"You speak with great passion. Though it's easy to feel strongly that Weiss is wrong for America."

"And absolute power corrupts absolutely. Always has, always will. Even if by some miracle he manages to stay benevolent, once the democratic process is lost, it will not be regained. Not for a long time." Lendra had a sudden inspiration. "Not until after we've had some terrible leaders—more *men* telling us how to live our lives, as if they haven't ruined the world enough so far. And then there'll be another revolution."

She spotted the flash of anger in Sister Ezekiel's eyes. Lendra felt almost guilty discussing the dominance of men—a subject she knew Sister Ezekiel would feel at least as strongly about as she did.

"You paint a pretty dismal picture, child," Sister Ezekiel said.

"I've studied this, Sister. I've learned how to read society, how to predict the likely consequences of broad influences from trends and polls. You've heard of social prediction?"

"Yes." Sister Ezekiel adjusted her glasses, which had begun to slip down her nose. "But I didn't think it was too well thought of."

Lendra sighed. "If done properly, it can be a wonderful tool.

One has to understand what data to analyze. There are crisis points throughout history, where the world changed as a result. Most were physical in nature. Asteroids hitting the earth. Volcanoes. Plague." She paused for a moment to see if Sister Ezekiel was following her. Sister Ezekiel nodded. "But in recent centuries the crises have become more human-manufactured. Wars. Human-engineered viruses—like the Susquehanna Virus. Terrorism. Societal problems created by disgruntled groups. You know what I mean?"

"Yes."

"And we're close to another crisis point, Sister. Very close. Thousands are dying every day."

Sister Ezekiel held up a hand. "And you think those problems can be solved by removing Devereaux from society?"

Lendra shook her head. "Certainly not. But his bioweapons are a threat that must be contained."

"Is Jeremiah with Dr. Mary?"

Lendra's head jerked back, surprised by the sudden change of subject. This nun was sharp. Lendra would have to be careful around her. She said, "Why would you think that, Sister?"

"Did you know that Dr. Mary isn't who she appears to be?"

Lendra shrugged and said, "Who is she?"

"I don't know. But I can tell you that she's a Devereauxnian and that Mr. Weiss and Colonel Truman think she was working with Raddock Boyd before his death."

A tic developed behind Lendra's right eye, a sign that she'd taken too much neo-dopamine. "Boyd is dead?"

"Mr. Weiss' truth drugs killed him."

"Now you know why I oppose him."

Sister Ezekiel nodded, then said, "I think Dr. Mary—the woman who's been masquerading as Dr. Mary—is with Jeremiah. I think you knew that. What I don't know is what they're up to. If Dr. Mary really is a Devereauxnian, why would she be helping Jeremiah unless he's a Devereauxnian too?"

Lendra shook her head slowly, her eyes on the floor. She too wondered about Jeremiah. Was he planning to double-cross Eli and run a rogue operation? If so, how could she benefit from that? Lifting her eyes, she met Sister Ezekiel's stare, then sat forward, crossed her arms over her chest and said, "I thought you wanted to help Devereaux."

"I want the truth."

"All right, Sister. Here it is. I don't know what Dr. Mary has in mind. But I don't trust her. And you shouldn't, either. She's dangerous. She's out there with Jeremiah right now and I wouldn't be surprised if she got him killed."

"That's not all the truth, is it? What more do you know that you're not saying?"

"I've told you everything I can, Sister."

"I expected an answer like that," Sister Ezekiel said. "Another half-truth from another person with a hidden agenda." She got to her feet and opened the door. Without looking back, without saying good-night, she left.

Lendra closed the door behind her. She told herself she had no reason to feel guilty. She hadn't just been exploiting Sister Ezekiel's past. Men *were* the cause of all the world's major problems. Witness Devereaux and Weiss and even Eli. When Lendra's turn came to run CINTEP, things would change.

Chapter Twenty-Three

Rain fell steadily. Dry in their Camos, Jeremiah and Julianna sat quietly. They had moved about a half-mile downwind, stopping to make certain that Truman's soldiers found the burning house, the dead bodies. Jeremiah stared into the darkness at nothing, his emotions threatening to overwhelm him. He had to overcome the anger, the insane urge to lash out at the EOs regardless of the consequences. That kind of thinking would only get him killed. And he had to stay alive for Joshua.

Julianna's thigh touched his, making him tense. He blinked three times, relaxing his muscles and holding himself in a state of hyper-awareness, prepared to defend himself against Julianna should she suddenly decide to strike out at him.

After a few minutes, he checked his scanner. Apart from the soldiers, he found nothing resembling a human. And since the Escala would register as humans, Cookie Monster and his friends likely had scatterers. For Mars Project scientists, building a scatterer would be simplicity itself. They would be difficult to track down.

More disturbing was the fact that the Elite Ops didn't appear on the scanner. They should have appeared on the screen, if not as human bio-signs, then at least as distortions of bioelectrical patterns. But the scanner showed nothing. Had the EOs moved out so quickly that they were no longer in range, or were they now using scatterers? That wasn't their style but, if they were, Jeremiah could be in real trouble. The only saving grace was that EOs couldn't move silently. With their nuclear power packs and heavy body armor, they made so much noise that they'd have no chance of sneaking up on him.

Julianna leaned heavily against him. He felt a tremor running through her and noticed her eyes glistening as she looked at the dying fire through the trees. Mixed in with the smell of the earth, the pines and the ozone, Jeremiah caught faint odors of burning wood and melting plastic. This whole mission was becoming more impossible every hour. A part of him longed to run away, leave all this madness behind for Eli or Weiss to clean up, and return to the search for his son. He wondered if Devereaux had really designed bioweapons that could destroy humanity. In the end it didn't matter. Jeremiah had a larger duty to the world. He had to find Devereaux, get him to the President and let her figure out how to deal with the threat.

Julianna hadn't spoken for ten minutes. Twice Jeremiah started to say something. Both times he stopped. What could he say to make her feel better? What had anyone been able to say to console him after Joshua disappeared? Words simply didn't matter. Still, he ought to say something. He put his arm around her and she put her head on his shoulder. Whatever her thoughts were, they were as dark as his.

He tried a third time, "I'm sorry, Julianna."

"I made a terrible mistake, Jeremiah."

"What are you talking about?"

"When I betrayed you. You were the only man who ever treated me as an equal."

"What about Eli?"

Julianna laughed. Jeremiah wondered if she was getting hysterical. She said, "The leech? I was nothing but a tool to him. So are you."

"I don't think so."

"You think Elias is your friend?"

"I trust him," Jeremiah said, wondering if Julianna would detect the lie.

"He doesn't trust you," Julianna lifted her head and turned to look at him. His arm dropped away. She touched his leg tentatively, then pulled her fingers back. In the darkness she was little more than shadow. "He didn't want you in on this job, Jeremiah. You were his second choice."

"What are you talking about?"

"He called me first and asked me to do the job for him."

"That's a lie."

"He knew I was here."

Jeremiah's stomach contracted as he sensed the truth of her statement. "You've been in contact with him?"

"Of course."

"Unbelievable! God, you two are a pair." He spread his arms and pushed his belly forward. "Why don't you just stab me now and be done with it?"

"Calm down, Jeremiah."

"This is bullshit. You're both insane."

"He asked me to kidnap Devereaux. I refused."

Jeremiah dropped his hands. "But…why would he keep in contact with you?"

"Why not? There was nothing personal in what I did before."

"Nothing personal? How about a quick knife to the gut? How about a betrayal that still burns like…" Jeremiah's voice trailed off. She'd already apologized. He said, "Have you done other jobs for him since…"

"Since I stabbed you? Yes, darling, I have. Nasty, difficult jobs that no one else wanted. Jobs he knew you wouldn't take. And some that he wanted kept secret from you or the agency."

"I can't believe this," Jeremiah said. Yet a part of him did believe. He'd always known that was the way Eli worked—compartmentalizing everything, keeping information back, hiding his true goals from his minions.

"Anyway," Julianna said. "I just wanted to say I'm sorry. If I'd known then what I know now, I wouldn't have done it." She sighed. "I think, even as I was betraying you, I knew I was making the biggest mistake of my life."

"Are you asking me to forgive you?"

"I would never ask that. But I want you to know I regret what I did. If I could turn the clock back, if I knew then what I know now, I wouldn't make that mistake again." Julianna looked down.

"What's gotten into you?" Jeremiah asked. "Every time I brought up anything serious like that you used to laugh at me."

"Devereaux lets us change. And I have. I'm not the same person I was. Funny," she said with a harsh laugh, "I've often thought back to my training with the leech, back to the tests he made me take, the psychological assessments and the bizarre scenarios he cooked up in the simulator. Remember that damn simulator?"

Jeremiah nodded. "I haven't thought about it in a long time. I stopped using it. That virtual reality crap gives me migraines, just like the interface."

"I don't know what the scenarios were like when he ran them on you, but with me, they almost always involved diversions, counter-attacks, unseen enemies or friends who betrayed me. Games within games. He kept twisting the scenarios, programming changes into the system to keep me from trusting anyone who didn't have a completely selfish motive. It was like he was programming me to betray you."

"Why doesn't that surprise me?"

Julianna raised her head. "He needed an agent on the outside, someone who would answer only to the lure of money, someone who would not be bound by the dictates of principle, someone he could turn to for that occasional delicate mission where no one could learn of his involvement."

"You still could be playing me," Jeremiah said, "trying to confuse me."

"I'm telling you the truth," Julianna said. She shifted position, swinging her lower leg over his, pulling him in tighter. Jeremiah wanted to hold her. He wanted the warm embrace of another human being, the comfort of physical closeness, to compensate for the separation he felt in his mind. At the same time his stomach clenched. He wondered if Julianna had her knife with her. "If you think about it," she added, "you'll see I'm right. Elias is always playing a different game than the one he lets you in on. He can't be trusted. That's one of the few things in this world I'm absolutely certain of."

A mosquito buzzed near Jeremiah's ear. It struggled for purchase against the hairs of his neck. He flicked it away and in the instant he did so, felt like he was about to be flicked away too, by something much greater than him.

"Why are you telling me this?"

"Because, Jeremiah, I've reached the end. Win or lose, this is my last job. I can't go on doing what I'm doing. Not if I want to live with myself."

"You've got me all screwed up. I don't know what to believe anymore."

Julianna took out a small flashlight and turned it to the lamp setting, illuminating only a small circle around them. She placed it on the trunk between them.

"You shouldn't do that," Jeremiah said.

"Look in my eyes, Jeremiah." Julianna reached up and touched his cheek with her cool fingers, her brown eyes looking black in the rain. "I want you to know I will never betray you again." She paused for a moment, then said, "I may have to kill you but I won't betray you."

Jeremiah burst into laughter and after a few seconds Julianna joined in.

"Seriously," she finally managed to say, "it's all due to Devereaux. I feel like an apostle. It started with the Mubarno mission. Remember those long discussions I had with Mubarno about Devereauxnianism?"

Jeremiah nodded.

"At first, it seemed like so much crap. But after I stabbed you I began to look into it—because of you, Jeremiah; because of your principles and your honor—and I realized it was just Mubarno who was full of crap. He'd distorted Devereaux's words until he'd gotten the meaning completely wrong. But Devereaux is right. We *can* change. You can too. You helped make me what I am even though you're still as lost as I was."

Jeremiah sighed. "I don't know whether to believe you or not. You might be telling the truth. But you're the greatest liar I've ever known. And I mean that as a compliment. I can't read you at all. So I hope you won't be offended if I don't accept what you say at face value."

Julianna's head dropped. "That's exactly what I expected." She paused for a moment, grimaced, then lifted her head. "I won't say I'm not disappointed. But I'm not sorry I said it. Let's get on with the mission. What now?"

"I wish I knew why the EOs are here already."

"I think it's because the President didn't trust you to do the job."

"You think she wants Devereaux dead?"

"No," Julianna answered. "But she wants to make certain he doesn't get away."

"Well, we've got a little time. The main body won't be here for a while yet, but when they arrive, they'll come in strong. No subtlety with them. What we need to do now is find that Cookie Monster fellow."

"Done. He's standing behind you."

Jeremiah sensed the man's presence even as he turned to look. Some smell or sound that came to him too late. But he knew Cookie Monster was there. The big man stood silently less than ten feet away. Jumping to his feet, Jeremiah reached for his Las-pistol, but Julianna grabbed his arm.

"He's wearing a shield," Julianna said.

Jeremiah looked closely and spotted the faint shimmering of the energy barrier. Even though he couldn't see the man very well in the darkness, he knew it was Cookie Monster. He picked up the small light Julianna had placed on the trunk and shone it on the man's face. Cookie Monster accepted this without moving. He just stared at Jeremiah.

Jeremiah glanced down at his scanner and saw nothing. So the big man had a scatterer as well as a shield. Jeremiah's scatterers had never worked very effectively when combined with a shield. And he'd thought he'd gotten the best. But this Cookie Monster's technology was better than his.

Moving the light down Cookie Monster's sides, Jeremiah checked for weapons and found none. Nevertheless, he kept the light focused on the center of the big man's body.

"Okay, Cookie Monster," he said, "it's your party. What do you want?"

"His name is actually Quark," Julianna said. "This is Jeremiah."

"You're working for them," Jeremiah said to her.

"No," Julianna replied.

"Then who?"

Julianna didn't answer.

The big man called Quark turned to Julianna and lifted an eyebrow.

"I don't know," Julianna said.

"You don't know what?" Jeremiah asked.

"I don't know what you're going to do."

"That makes two of us." Jeremiah shook his head, disgusted with himself. "You just got done telling me you were never going to betray me again. And I nearly believed you."

"How have I betrayed you?"

"You two obviously know each other. You appear to be working together despite your denial. And by keeping me here talking, you allowed him to sneak up on me."

Quark smiled and said, "That was easy."

"You're such an idiot," Julianna said. "You're so blinded by the past. It was your idea to stop here, not mine. And don't blame me for letting him sneak up on you. That's your fault. Maybe you're getting too old for this kind of work. Did you ever think of that?"

Quark laughed.

Jeremiah opened his mouth to make a vicious comment, then realized she was right. The only reason he was angry was because he'd lost focus and let Quark approach unnoticed. And he couldn't blame anyone else for that. He turned to Quark and said, "Well, what do you want?"

"We have a common problem," Quark said.

"Weiss," Jeremiah said.

"You got any ideas?"

"You want me to trust you?" Jeremiah looked from Quark to Julianna. "Either of you? A full unit of Elite Ops will be here soon. And we can't beat them."

"Elite Ops?" Quark asked.

"That's right," Julianna said. "An advance force killed that group of fugitives living off that way." She tossed her head to indicate the direction. Her eyes became more liquid. "I don't know how long we've got before the main body arrives."

"This complicates things immensely," Quark said.

Jeremiah pointed at Quark, his frustration rising rapidly. "Are you two working together or not? What's really going on? Tell me the truth."

"I don't trust you, either, little man," Quark said. He reached into one of his pockets and removed a small device. Jeremiah grabbed his Las-pistol, even though he knew it would be useless against Quark's shield. Quark looked at Julianna, "I suppose you won't leave him."

Julianna shook her head, stood up straighter and said, slowly but firmly, "Not this time."

Jeremiah's eyes welled up. He blinked. Three little words: his whole being seemed to expand with uncontainable joy.

Quark nodded. "That's what I thought." Then he pressed a button on the device and tossed it at them.

Jeremiah heard an ear-shattering noise, then everything went black.

Chapter Twenty-Four

Doug sat up slowly, his head throbbing. As the glow globe brightened, he noticed the picture of "Emerging Man" on the wall. His mind kept drifting back to Zeriphi; his body longed for another touch of her soft skin. He knew he ought to feel worse about the deaths of his friends but every sensation except desire seemed muted. Was that the drugs, or had prison left him incapable of experiencing true grief?

While at the Redwing Correctional Facility, Doug had formed a Devereauxnian group, discussing concepts like the ladder of enlightenment. He'd been shocked when Devereaux contacted him and told him the ladder was for everyone. Devereaux had encouraged Doug to use his time for bettering himself. He'd offered support and a belief in Doug's abilities that had left Doug in awe of the great man. And when Devereaux sent him the disk bearing the image of Emerging Man, and told Doug he was going to be in Crescent Township, Doug had escaped. He hadn't been able to help himself. He simply had to meet Devereaux. After arriving in town, Doug had talked Sister Ezekiel into giving him a job at the shelter.

Doug had contacted his friends shortly after arriving at the shelter, notifying them of the abandoned houses. And since they'd had nowhere else to go, they'd come running. Mostly they'd stayed hidden in the woods. But a few weeks ago they'd asked for help when a little redhead named Madeline had fallen gravely ill with what turned out to be West Nile Fever. Dr. Mary's treatment had saved Madeline's life—until now.

A surge of anger flashed through Doug. He pictured Madeline's pale face in his mind—her curly orange hair. A cute girl, very quiet. But even as sorrow washed over Doug, his thoughts drifted back to Zeriphi. He desperately wanted to take her in his arms one more time. Hopefully it would take weeks or months for her to become pregnant. Boy or girl: Doug didn't care.

He got to his feet, the pounding in his head gradually diminishing, then adjusted his pants to ease his discomfort and took a closer look at the picture of the statue. He wondered at its significance—for variations on the picture seemed to be in every room he'd visited. Some were drawings or paintings. This one was a moving photograph that had been taken through several exposures at night, offering multiple images of the statue. As he leaned in close to study the picture, an alarm sounded. Low-pitched, it wailed insistently, impossible to ignore. Doug jumped back, then ran into the hallway. Two Escala came up behind him and pushed him along toward the main cave.

"What's goin' on?" Doug asked.

They didn't answer, just rushed ahead.

When they reached the common room, Doug saw about fifty people—mostly adults but a few teenagers—standing by the table looking grim. Doug had never seen the teenagers before. Where had they been hiding? They looked gawky and uncoordinated. Behind them stood Temala, her ugly face furrowed in concentration or anger. Quekri stood at the head of the table with Zod, who wore a fierce expression, as if daring anyone to challenge him. No one spoke. Doug nearly asked what was happening, but when he spotted Zeriphi standing off to the side with an older female, he stopped abruptly and turned toward her. She shook her head and held up her hand. Within seconds, another dozen adults made their way to the table from the two hallways. The alarm stopped.

"I just talked to Quark," Quekri said. "A few Elite Ops are in the area." She looked at Doug. "They're the ones who killed your friends. Their main force will be here soon. And they'll be coming after us." She looked around the table at the others, who nodded in agreement. "But," she continued, "their secondary mission will almost certainly be to find and capture Devereaux. We are expendable. Devereaux is not."

Everyone nodded again.

"Quark will let us know when the main force arrives. In the meantime, we must prepare for action. Probably no more than nine of us should go. Quark has asked Zod to put together the team."

"Why only nine?" Doug asked.

"We have only nine Las-rifles."

"We can use other weapons. Knives, rocks, whatever."

Zod said, "Have you ever seen the Elite Ops in action?"

"No," Doug said.

"You would be killed immediately," Zod said, a hint of satisfaction behind the words. Doug supposed if he were in Zod's shoes, letting someone else sleep with his wife, he'd feel hostile too.

"Devereaux has asked that you be kept safe," Quekri said. "You've shown tremendous potential, overcoming your past. You're on the ladder. You can help others. So you cannot go."

"Who is Devereaux?"

"It's best if you don't know that yet."

"But…" Doug looked at Quekri's face, at Zod's, at Zeriphi's: at the pain and determination on each. He wanted so badly to fight for Devereaux in glorious combat—to finally have a cause worth dying for. Not drugs or turf, but ideas and the future of humanity. Didn't they know he was a warrior? Yet apparently Devereaux had made other plans for him. How could he refuse that great man? He sighed. "Okay."

Quekri smiled briefly—the first time Doug had seen her do so—and she looked almost beautiful in that moment. She said, "I will remain behind too, as will Zeriphi, Probst, Wellon and Keelar." Quekri indicated an older male and two females. "Zod will choose from those who remain."

"We've seen the Elite Ops before," Zod said. "We know what they're capable of. Volunteers?"

Sixty hands went up. Sixty people crowded around the table. How Doug longed to be one of them.

"Come," Quekri said to Doug. "Let's give them space to make their plans." She grabbed Doug's arm and directed him away from the table. Zeriphi, Keelar and Probst detached themselves from the group and followed Doug and Quekri away. Wellon stayed at the table.

"Zeriphi," Doug said, reaching for her hand. She let him take it. "I woke up and you were gone. Then when I checked on you later, they said you were with the doctor. Are you all right?"

"I'm fine," Zeriphi said.

"You sure?"

Zeriphi smiled. "I'm pregnant."

"Pregnant?" Doug said. "You know already?" He blinked several times in rapid succession while he processed that information. "That means I'm gonna be a father."

"Yes."

"That's wonderful!" Doug lifted Zeriphi's hand to his face and kissed it.

"Please, don't," Zeriphi said, pulling her hand free, her smile vanishing.

"Why not?"

Zeriphi shook her head. "I'm with Zod."

"But I'm the father. It's my child."

"The child belongs to all of us and we to it."

Keelar nodded and put her hand on Zeriphi's shoulder.

"What's the matter with you, Zeriphi?" Doug said. "You've changed. You're so…cold."

"You seem nice, Doug. But I don't know you. I'm not with you and I'm not going to be with you. That will never happen again."

"I'm not askin' you to marry me. I just thought we could be together for awhile."

"No," Zeriphi said. "It's best if we make a clean break, before things get emotional."

"It's too late for that. I care about you, Zeriphi. I wanna help you and the baby. Even if you're with Zod, I deserve a place here too. I got nowhere else to go."

"You care about me because of the drugs in your system. They will soon wear off. Then you'll be angry."

"I'm already angry. But not at you."

"Why not me?"

"You were just doin' what you had to do. I understand that."

Zeriphi gestured to encompass the others. "We all did what we had to."

"I know. And I ain't blamin' anyone. I'm just angry that you people didn't trust me. If you had just asked me to help you, I woulda. You didn't hafta do it the way you did."

Probst said, "Yes, we did. There were certain hormones and chemicals that…"

Doug glared at him. He hated these people's concept of privacy. "Look," he said to Zeriphi, "even if you don't wanna be with me, it's my child too. I got certain rights. And I wanna be involved."

"We can discuss this later," Quekri said. "Zeriphi, you should return to the infirmary. These early stages are critical."

Zeriphi turned and walked away, Keelar following her.

"I can make you feel better," Probst said, "if you like."

"She got no right," Doug said. "It's like I don't exist."

Probst grabbed Doug's hand and squeezed firmly. When Doug looked down, Probst released his grip, pulling away a small pad. Almost immediately, Doug experienced a tingling in his arm that spread to his shoulder, then his chest.

Doug shook his arm and said, "What the hell was that?"

"Just a small dosage to accelerate the removal of drugs from your body. Your emotional state should recede quickly."

Doug stabbed a finger at the large Escala's chest. "I didn't give you permission to do that. And those recovery drugs don't work on me."

"These will. They're for your own good."

Doug's heart thumped heavily. Blood rushed to his face. His erection drooped. Rage and guilt overwhelmed him. "How the hell you know what's good for me?"

With an expression of surprise, Probst held up a small plastic monitor. "That's strange," he said. "The dosage is working, but you still seem quite angry."

"Damn right I'm angry."

"I don't understand. This should have—"

Quekri held up her hand. "Enough, Probst." Probst bowed slightly and moved off in the direction Zeriphi had headed with Keelar.

"I think it's about damn time you told me what's goin' on," Doug said to Quekri. "You said everything would be explained later. Well, it's later. Where the hell is Devereaux?"

"He's safe for the moment. And we must protect ourselves. There are many people who wish to harm us. The Elite Ops will try to kill us. Others seek to lock us away. They say we aren't human and have no constitutional rights. They say we're a threat to society."

"Maybe you are. Druggin' me, seducin' me, then druggin' me again."

"I told you. We do what we must to survive. Our children do not appear to have the sterility problem we do, so we may no longer need to use people like you once they mature."

Across the room, a consensus appeared to have been reached. Eight Escala left for one of the back storage areas. Zod made his way toward Quekri and Doug, while those who would be staying behind stood around the table looking dejected.

"We leave soon," Zod said.

"Nine of you?" Quekri asked.

"Quark was right."

"You're goin'?" Doug said to Zod.

The big man turned to him and nodded.

"I should go in your place," Doug said. "You got a child comin', with Zcriphi. And if these Elite Ops are as dangerous as you say, you shouldn't be out there."

Zod's eyebrows rose and a trace of a smile touched his lips. He spoke quietly, almost outside the range of Doug's hearing: "Devereaux was right."

Quekri turned to Doug and asked, "Do you want to die like your friends?"

"No," Doug answered. "What makes you think I will? I survived the streets. Drugs. Prison. I think I can help fight for Devereaux's freedom."

Quekri slowly shook her head. "No normal human can beat the Elite Ops. Those Army folks out there," Quekri waved her hand to indicate them, "are nothing compared to the Elite Ops. We're the only ones who stand a chance."

Zod looked at Quekri with a frown, as if something she'd said puzzled him greatly. For a moment, he and Quekri stared at each other, communicating silently. Then Zod turned to Doug and extended his hand. When Doug took it, the big man carefully increased the pressure until Doug winced in pain. "Doug," he said, "I remember you."

What an odd thing to say, Doug thought. "Me too," he replied.

Then Zod loosened his grip, all the while looking Doug in the eye, as if saying goodbye to a fellow inmate just released, knowing he would never see that man again.

Doug stood with Quekri while the team prepared to leave. The fifty who would remain behind waited by the table. Temala, Doug noted, would be staying behind as well. She'd already been out on a mission, so he would have thought she'd be picked to go, and he'd seen her hand shoot up just like the others, but Zod had obviously decided against taking her. Perhaps she wasn't very bright. Her dark face seemed more animalistic than ever. Yet she appeared calm enough. They all did: calm and somber. No one spoke, no one moved—not even the teenagers. It was amazing how quiet fifty people could be. It felt like a funeral.

When Zod and his team entered the room, dressed in camouflage suits, wearing weapons and smiles, a cry went up—fifty people roaring their approval. Zeriphi, Probst and Keelar emerged from the infirmary and joined them. People hugged one another. A few small items changed hands. A woman Doug hadn't met—one of those who would be leaving—gave a ring to Dunadan, the big red-haired Escala who had seemed so close to Temala. Glancing over at Temala, Doug decided she hadn't noticed, for she was talking with another Escala. Dunadan pocketed the ring, then stood with Shull and Warrow.

As those Escala nearest the stairs began to ascend, voices rang out:

"Garrad. I remember you."

"Nall. I remember you."

"Vona. I remember you."

So this was how the Escala said goodbye.

The goodbyes went on for minutes, each person promising to remember one or more companions, until all the team members but

Zod were on the stairs. No one looked sad. Yet if what they'd told Doug of the Elite Ops was true, this had to be mere bravado.

Zod stopped before Zeriphi, caressed her cheek with his massive hand. Then he leaned into her and they touched foreheads for a long moment. He said, "Zeriphi. I remember you." She replied, "Zod. I remember you." When he pulled away, straightening up, he nodded once and took the steps two at a time, disappearing into the darkness. Gradually the noise in the room died away until all that could be heard was the faint echo of footsteps.

"They ain't coming back," Doug said, "are they?"

Quekri looked at him, her face fallen with sad acceptance, then looked away.

Chapter Twenty-Five

Outside the shelter, Colonel Truman listened for the sound of approaching jet-copters. The overhead cloudbank, while still dark, had lightened with the promise of dawn. He wondered if Emily was awake yet. Probably not, even though it was an hour later on the East Coast: she wasn't a morning person. Why had he suddenly thought of her? He had no intention of calling, though it would be nice if they still talked like they had in the old days. How he missed those quiet conversations. He couldn't remember the last time he'd felt so tired.

Three of his soldiers had begun to manifest symptoms of the Susquehanna Virus during the night—severe headache, weakness and excruciating pain in the joints. They were now confined under armed guard, frightened and confused. If they'd actually contracted the virus, they might be dead within the hour. The medics claimed that their illness had to be psychosomatic, that the virus' incubation period was too long for them to be infected already. Nevertheless, Truman felt compelled to order the quarantine.

His mind flashed to the thirty-two corpses piled up in the woods—five of them children—all dead at the hands of the four Elite Ops who'd been sent here earlier. Weiss insisted on keeping the discovery of the bodies from the media, at least for the present.

And now more Elite Ops were on the way.

All this bullshit about them being the greatest advance in military history—as far as Truman was concerned, they were mutants: worse than the pseudos. Sadistic killers. Dead inside. These...*things*...were the future?

Truman contemplated calling General Horowitz—the Chairman of the Joint Chiefs—who had instructed him to follow the Attorney General's orders. Doing that had already gotten a lot of people killed, including Raddock Boyd, whose death, to be honest, bothered Truman more than the others. Truman had killed before in service to his country but never that way—never a helpless man strapped to a chair. And it irked Truman that Weiss seemed to feel little remorse over any of the deaths. Was that due to his background with the CIA? Had the man seen so much death and waste that he was inured to human suffering?

The two jet-copters approached from the south. Their landing lights shone downward with such intensity that Truman had to look away for a moment. Although the machines were capable of traveling in silent mode, the roar of their engines sounded loud through the quiet morning. He wondered how many soldiers each copter carried. It took only a couple dozen Elite Ops troopers to equal the firepower of five hundred Army regulars.

At the edge of the parking lot, close to the encroaching forest, as if they were considering using the trees for cover, his soldiers watched the jet-copters land. When the engines powered down, six Elite Ops troopers jumped from each copter. They hit the ground heavily—all machinery and weaponry—and moved outward in a precise pattern, at the same speed, with identical spacing, aligning themselves in an oval around the jet-copters, weapons at the ready, examining their surroundings. Out of the woods, four Elite Ops troopers now emerged. They strode past Truman's startled soldiers and joined their companions in the oval. So those four were the killers, not that they were distinguishable from their fellow troopers. Sixteen total, Truman saw. More than enough to handle every soldier under Truman's command if it came to that.

The reporters on the scene began taking video of the Elite Ops. Surprisingly, no one stopped the cameras. Truman thought that odd: the Elite Ops were technically still a secret force.

From the lead copter, a man opened the passenger door and stepped down. He bent low, balancing himself against the rush of air from the great engines, and ran toward the shelter. Tall and lean, he wore a dark suit and, despite the pre-dawn hour, sunglasses. When he spotted Truman, he changed course and jogged over. The jet-copters powered up, their engines roaring louder. In unison, the machines lifted off the ground. At a hundred feet, their engines tilted and they shot away in a cacophony of thunder. After they were gone, the man removed his glasses and spoke.

"Colonel Truman, I presume?"

"Yes?"

"Richard Carlton." The man offered his hand.

Truman hesitated a second before shaking it. "What are you doing here, sir?"

"Where's the Attorney General?"

"Inside the shelter, sir."

"Very good, Colonel. I'll see him now."

Truman gestured toward the hole in the wall. As Carlton preceded him, Truman glanced back. The Elite Ops closed ranks, maintaining perfect spacing as they formed a smaller, tighter oval at the end of the parking lot where they could keep an eye on the road. Their gray armor absorbed light, making it difficult to get a good grasp of the scope of their firepower, but Truman knew that in addition to their Las-rifles, the troopers carried particle beam cannons and a variety of grenades. They looked menacing in the dim light—huge and robotic.

Weiss waited in the lobby. He stepped forward, hand extended, and said, "RC, it's good to see you again."

"Looks like you took one in the shoulder, Gray Velvet." Carlton poked the bloodstain still visible on Weiss' suit. "You're getting too old for this sort of game."

"It's nothing," Weiss answered as he reached up to massage his shoulder. "I've already had it treated. It'll be good as new in no time."

Colonel Truman found himself immediately disliking Carlton. He looked around, saw no reporters and said, "Excuse me, but there are a lot of dead people here. Killed by your Elite Ops." Truman pointed to Carlton, "What is your role, sir?"

Carlton smiled as if pleased by the death count, then replied: "As the designer of the Elite Ops system and the owner of the hardware, I'm here as an observer. The software has minor glitches, and we're still exploring the limits of the systems' capabilities. Until we have them perfected, we need to continue running field tests."

"And was that a field test last night?" Truman asked. "When your troopers murdered thirty-two people?"

"Those people fired the first shots," Carlton said. "My men responded with appropriate force."

"Appropriate force? My God! None of their weapons could have hurt your men."

Weiss said, "That's enough, Colonel. RC, what's the plan?"

Carlton said, "This was supposed to be a low-profile operation. But as usual," he looked at Truman, "the situation is getting out of hand. Gun battles in the streets. Psuedos running free."

Truman flushed with anger. "Are you saying that's our fault?"

"No one's blaming you, Colonel," Carlton said, his lip twitching in a sneer. "But your soldiers aren't capable of restoring order. My troopers can. The President has declared martial law for this area. We're here to enforce that."

He lifted his head and stared down his nose at Truman, whose anger rose, threatening to explode. The condescending prick!

"My priority," Weiss said, "remains finding Devereaux. I assume your Elite Ops will be combing the woods looking for any sign of pseudos?" When Carlton nodded, Weiss continued, "Jones is still out there somewhere. And a woman posing as Dr. Mary McCaffery seems to have disappeared as well."

Carlton lifted an eyebrow. "My men will keep a special eye out for them. We'll make sure to take Jones alive."

"The *Escala*," Truman emphasized the word, "have sophisticated weapons, not just old fashioned guns like those fugitives your men slaughtered."

"Escala?" Carlton's face wrinkled in distaste. "They're pseudos, Colonel. Sub-human."

"Mr. Carlton," Truman raised his voice, his body quivering with rage. "You are a civilian under—"

"Colonel," Weiss said. "Control yourself."

Truman leaned forward, jabbed his finger at Carlton. "And there won't be any children among the *Escala*, either. They'll actually put up some resistance."

"Colonel!" Weiss spoke harshly. "Don't make me relieve you of command. Those fugitives sealed their fate when they attacked his troopers."

And the children? Truman thought. Did they deserve to die as well? Truman's fists shook. Through the rush of blood in his ears, he heard Emily say, "Temper, dear. Remember, that's why you didn't make general." He opened his hands, bile rising in his throat, and said: "I apologize. I was merely pointing out that the Escala will not fall as easily as the fugitives did last night."

Carlton scoffed. "You can't possibly think the *pseudos* are a match for the Elite Ops?"

"What about the Battle of Rochester?"

Carlton's eyes narrowed. "How did you hear about that?"

Truman couldn't stop his lips from forming the beginnings of a smile.

Carlton waved his hand dismissively and said, "We had them beaten. And if it hadn't been for a disruption to the communications software, we would have eliminated them completely. We've rebuilt the entire communications system from the ground up. No one can penetrate it anymore. It's completely secure."

"And wasn't there some flaw in the Elite Ops' shielding?" Truman attacked again, careful to keep his tone neutral. "I recall hearing something about troopers blowing up because of defective shields?"

"Yes," Weiss agreed, "I remember thinking it was ironic that the only weakness the Elite Ops had was their shielding."

Carlton frowned. "We've strengthened those too. They no longer overload in close proximity to the power packs. They're only susceptible to particle beam cannons now and…" Carlton pressed a button on his wrist-com, examined the screen, then looked back up, "apart from the sixteen cannons the Elite Ops have, I see none in the region."

Truman glanced over at Sergeant Mecklenberg, who stood by

the side of the ruined doorway, Jeremiah Jones' particle beam cannon strapped to his back. Apparently, without the converter, it didn't register on Carlton's scanner.

A member of the Elite Ops appeared in the ruined doorway next to Mecklenberg, one of the few invitees ever to have turned down the opportunity to train for the Elite Ops. Truman had never asked him why. The kid was deeply religious and, like most of Truman's soldiers, rather poorly educated. Perhaps he felt some spiritual taboo over the mechanical crust he would have had to wear. Mecklenberg backed up a step, eyes widening in fear.

The Elite Ops trooper stood nearly seven feet tall in his armor. For a moment he remained motionless, then his huge gray helmet swiveled, his sun visor hiding his eyes. In each hand he carried a weapon—particle beam cannon in the left, Las-rifle in the right. Around his waist dangled several concussion and sonic grenades. Attached to his chest was a box that contained his shielding mechanism; on his back, he wore a nuclear power module that emitted a high whine. As he stood in the doorway, a stench emanated from him—a miasma of rotting flesh. Truman suddenly felt terrified. Instinctively he shrank back, noticing his soldiers and Weiss doing likewise: everyone in the room but Carlton. The Elite Ops trooper holstered his weapons, then pressed two buttons on his left wrist. Gradually the odor diminished, the fear melting away with it. Truman knew the horrible smell came from a neurotoxin each trooper could release to dull the responses of his enemy, giving him an edge in battle. The gas had no lasting effect, so it did not technically violate the global ban on chemical weapons, but it hampered thought processes so effectively that opponents who inhaled it often became powerless. The trooper must have disseminated a counteractive gas.

As his mind began to clear, Truman focused on the trooper's helmet, which was the key to every system in the Elite Ops' arsenal. It covered the entire head, including the mouth, giving no glimpse of the trooper beneath it. The dark visor reflected the room before it, the mirror image swiveling as the man inside the helmet surveyed the lobby.

Truman had seen an Elite Ops helmet a year ago, so he knew its large size was necessitated by the protective padding, the heating/cooling system, and the circuitry and sensors that connected the brain to the computers that ran everything else—computers that also linked each trooper to his comrades and to ComSat (the satellite command center). Truman remembered picking up the helmet and being surprised at its lightness. He'd seen no visible connective points in the helmet, no wires or metal discs that affixed to the skull. Everything was internalized, of course. Still, he wondered what the troopers' heads looked like under those helmets. Did they still appear human? When he'd been a student of military history, he'd been fascinated by the potential applications such technology offered. Now he fought down revulsion and fear at the sight of this creature. He hated that they were in the same military.

A faint aura surrounded the Elite Ops trooper: his shield. He stepped forward and saluted the colonel. His nametag read: "Payne" but his rank was not immediately identifiable. Truman stared at him, Weiss and Carlton by his side, looking on silently.

"Colonel Truman?" the man said.

"Yes?"

"Major Payne, Elite Ops."

"Major Payne?"

"Yes, sir. I've heard all the jokes about my name, sir."

"What can I do for you, Major?"

"My men are deploying now, sir. We're keeping four men in town, two near the shelter. I just wanted to give you a warning to keep your soldiers out of our way."

Truman clenched his teeth, biting back a response he might later regret. "Fine, Major. Anything else?"

"The pseudos. Do you have any idea where we might find them?"

"No. We searched all night and found no sign of them."

"We'll draw them out."

"How do you intend to do that, Major?"

"The bio-signs of pseudos have a slightly different signature than humans. Actually, so do the bio-signs of enhanced humans. Our scanners are more sophisticated than yours. If we can get close enough, we can detect almost any modification beyond surgical repair or correction of a genetic flaw. They don't work well in crowds, but out there—" Major Payne swung his arm in the direction of the woods— "we'll get close enough. We'll find them."

"And what do you intend to do when you find them?"

"We're here to protect the civilian populace from the threat of the pseudos."

Truman said, "In other words, you plan to hunt them down and kill them like you did those fugitives in the forest." When Major Payne did not respond, Truman spoke in his command voice, "There will be no killing here, Major. I want the pseudos taken alive."

Major Payne spoke with contempt: "I don't take orders from you, sir."

Weiss held up a hand. "Oh, Major."

Payne swiveled his head toward the Attorney General. "Yes, sir?"

"I want Colonel Truman to accompany you."

"I'm sorry, sir. But that won't be possible. I don't take orders from you, either."

Weiss looked at Truman for a second, his brow wrinkled in concern. He said, "Who do you take orders from?"

Major Payne looked at Carlton, who said, "I can take that one, Gray. The Elite Ops get their mission orders from the President, through General Horowitz. But while in the field, they act as a team, with coordination from the commanding officer—in this case, Major Payne."

"And where do you come into it, Richard?"

"As I said, Gray, I'm merely an observer. Just protecting my investment, not to mention doing my part for America." Turning to Major Payne, Carlton said, "Are the surveillance drones over the area?"

"Yes, sir."

"Good. I'd like to do a final systems check before you go into the field. Okay?"

Major Payne disengaged his shield, then reached down and turned off the power module. Finally, he unclipped four connectors on his neck and took the helmet in both hands. As he lifted it, Truman found himself leaning forward, straining to get a glimpse of the man. He hadn't known what to expect but he was surprised when the helmet came free. The man stared straight ahead, his jaw square, his cheekbones high, his nose Roman, his eyes a clear gray. Close-cropped dark hair covered his flawless, tanned skin. By all appearances, he was normal, if a bit too perfect. Arrogant. Artificially handsome. One of the rewards, no doubt, for agreeing to become a member of the Elite Ops.

Chapter Twenty-Six

Sister Ezekiel spent the night in the chapel, the soft buttery candlelight and the scent of melting wax, as always, soothing her. Good old Flyer: the inveterate alcoholic took great pains to prepare the chapel for her prayers each evening. He also played the organ during services. Sitting in her usual chair in the front of the small room, Sister Ezekiel grasped her rosary and prayed. But her mind drifted to Dr. Mary. Even though Sister Ezekiel knew very little about the doctor—not even her real name—she knew a good person when she met one. Whoever Dr. Mary was, whatever secrets she harbored, Sister Ezekiel trusted her. Her work the past two months had been exemplary. She liked the men and they liked her. Dr. Mary was a gift from God.

So she was a Devereauxnian. That lumped her in with many Minnesotans these days. More importantly, she was a first-rate doctor with a generous heart. Sister Ezekiel could never doubt that. Despite their religious differences, they had become friends. Or at least as friendly as two people could become when one lived a lie. Why did everything have to be so complicated?

In the flickering light, Sister Ezekiel prayed for the soul of Raddock Boyd, the safety of Dr. Mary and the wisdom to do the right thing with respect to Walt Devereaux. If Dr. Mary were here, she would offer wise counsel—that stranger, that liar, who hid her past just as Sister Ezekiel hid hers behind service toward men who could no longer care for themselves.

She felt a twinge in her back and shifted position on the folding chair. Was that a shuffling sound?

"Flyer?" she said. "Is that you?"

She looked around and saw nothing, heard no other sound, so she returned to her rosary. Fingering the beads, wrestling with her conscience, she wondered if she was doing the right thing. If the betrayal of Devereaux would save the shelter, didn't she have an obligation to hand him over? Wasn't he, for all his gentle speech, still the enemy of Catholicism?

And perhaps Devereaux wanted her to be his Judas, putting himself in her hands so she would betray him. Uncertainty, that bitter poison, seeped into her soul.

Always before, she had treated Devereaux's existence as an abstract challenge to her faith—a person who didn't directly affect her. But now she knew him. And he wasn't distant or abstract anymore; he was immediate and concrete.

How she longed for Dr. Mary's counsel.

"Where are you, Mary, when I need you most? I still trust you."

Moving through Our Fathers and Hail Marys, Sister Ezekiel occasionally drifted off, her head jerking up as she tried to remember her place on the rosary. The sensible thing to do was go to bed. But she wanted to finish her prayers.

Unbidden, a nightmare memory returned—her body slammed to the ground, the men on top of her, violating her—the unbearable agony to both body and spirit. Some nights, the memories nearly dragged her into despair. Prayer and, more recently, her conversations with Dr. Mary kept her sane. But her exhaustion tonight was beyond anything she'd endured in a long, long time. It was not so much physical as mental. It sucked her into fitful dreams and wild imaginings.

Although she knew the chapel was empty, she felt eyes upon her. A presence hovered, something more than human. It stalked her silently, staying its attack, delighting in her discomfort. Every few minutes, her eyes drifted into darkened corners.

As she tried to relax, the previous day's occurrences ran through her head. Dead bodies paraded across her dreams, led by Raddock Boyd. In one, God laughed at her. When she turned to face him, Rock Man stared back at her, his hands holding a stone shaped like Dr. Mary.

For a moment she snapped awake. Another image overwhelmed her—the rapists atop her, grunting and sweating, pinning her arms to the ground and stealing her virginity, then turning her over and taking her from behind. She cried out to God for help. None came. She closed her eyes, damming the tears, as she struggled to imagine herself in some other place. After a time her fatigue crept past the adrenaline barrier that kept her alert.

She awoke to the sound of falling pebbles, realized that her straining muscles had broken the rosary. Beads exploded outward, skittering across the floor, disappearing into the shadows like cockroaches.

Shortly after the assault Sister Ezekiel had been offered therapeutic forgetting treatment, but she had rejected it because she wanted to preserve the horror intact. It made up a part of who she was. Blunting that memory seemed wrong. But at times like this, when she recalled the assault so vividly, she often tasted bitter regret at her decision. Forcing the memory back into her subconscious with a litany of Our Fathers and Hail Marys, she vanquished the demons of old and turned again to the same unanswered questions. Why God? Why must so many suffer?

She really ought to drag herself to bed. Her back ached, and shifting position on the folding chair offered little relief. Just a few more minutes, she told herself, and then she'd go. She closed her eyes, fighting the utter exhaustion.

When she opened her eyes, she found herself standing in a cathedral, looking up not at God but at Devereaux. Intuitively, she knew it to be the presence that had been watching her.

You cannot turn me away from God, she protested.

That is not the intent.

I want to talk to God.

Then talk. I'm listening.

You are not God.

God is in me, Sister. Surely you do not contest that. Is not God in all of us?

You said there is no God.

God is always with us, Sister. He lives in each of us.

But that's not *the God*. The one and only true God. That's just your idea of man as God. What you say is contradictory.

That's what it is to be alive, to be human.

If you're really God, then why are you telling us not to believe in you?

Because I need you to believe in yourselves.

You've seen the mess we've made of the world.

The world will survive, Sister. It's only humanity at risk.

How do we save ourselves?

You must stop relying on me. Not everything that happens in this world is my will. And I refuse to protect you from each other.

So you're a cruel God.

Yes. A cruel and loving God.

A twinge of pain grabbed Sister Ezekiel's left ankle and she knew she was now awake. Had that been a dream, or a vision? She thought she heard footsteps retreating. When she looked toward the door, she detected what might have been a slight movement, as if it had just closed. No, she decided. That wasn't real.

She got to her feet, knees cracking, mind confused—but her heart burned with the pure flame of God's love—or Devereaux's. She knew from her stiffness that she'd spent the entire night in the chapel. Outside, somewhere off in the distance, she heard the sound of gunfire. Oh, no, here we go again.

* * *

When she reached the lobby, she saw Weiss and Colonel Truman huddled with a third man. Lendra hurried from the hallway.

"Good morning, Sister," Weiss said. "You look tired. I hope you got some sleep. This is Richard Carlton. He's here with the Elite Ops. They'll be maintaining order and assisting us in the search for Devereaux."

Sister Ezekiel sensed that Weiss was trying to keep her calm. She said, "I don't need soothing. What's going on out there?"

"Nothing for you to be concerned about, Sister," Weiss said. "Just a small disturbance."

"Minnesota separatists are attacking the Army, Sister," Lendra said. She pointed to her interface. "I've been monitoring communications traffic. They're not after Devereaux. They're hoping to drive the Army out of the area. Unfortunately for them, the Elite Ops are here."

Sister Ezekiel walked to the opening and glanced out. Two huge men, as large as Cookie Monster, dressed all in gray, patrolled the area in front of the shelter. They looked robotic in their armor, dark against the pink and yellow sky. Obviously, they were Elite Ops troopers. At the sides of the building, many of Colonel Truman's soldiers stood, alternating between watching them and eyeing the road or the woods, their weapons moving in a jittery fashion. The reporters had gathered together behind the smoldering hulks that had once been the Army's transport vehicles. Standing alone, acting as if he wasn't one of them, a young man with an orange Afro and scruffy beard looked around innocently. Sister Ezekiel knew he must be a reporter, for he didn't have the bearing of a homeless man. He was too confident.

To the north, in the direction of the famous statue, Sister Ezekiel heard yelling, followed by an explosion. The two Elite Ops troopers out front seemed oblivious to it. Walking past each other, they swept their great pumpkin heads from side to side. Colonel Truman's soldiers at the side of the building weren't as casual. A few trained their weapons on the woods. Others swung their Las-rifles toward the street, their faces looking pinched. Lendra joined Sister Ezekiel at the door.

"More trouble," Sister Ezekiel said. "More soldiers, more fighting and more dead. It looks like something's happening by the statue—some sort of attack. When will this madness end?"

Lendra stared at the large troopers out front. She shook her head. "When Devereaux is away from here, Sister."

Sister Ezekiel nodded wearily. All she had to do was say, "Devereaux is Rock Man," and these soldiers would take him and leave. The shelter would once again become a quiet haven for the lost and troubled. Still, wasn't Devereaux lost and troubled too? How she longed to have the decision made for her. She'd never asked for this kind of responsibility.

She heard a noise off to the left, turned to see a familiar old pickup drive slowly into the parking lot. It stopped as it cleared the road, its engine running roughly, then two men in the back jumped up, raising guns to their shoulders. Almost instantaneously, the Elite Ops troopers fired at them. A loud explosion made the ground tremble. An immense black cloud mushroomed out. As it rose, the chassis of the pickup became visible: just a twisted mass of metal. Three bodies lay scattered around it.

Sister Ezekiel suddenly found it difficult to swallow. As she started toward the fallen men, Carlton grabbed her sleeve. "You can't go out there," he said. "We need to make sure the area is clear."

Sister Ezekiel glared at him until he pulled his hand away. Then she marched out toward the burning truck.

"They're dead, Sister," Weiss called after her. "You can't help them."

Nearing the men, Sister Ezekiel saw that Weiss was right. The bodies had that curious rag-doll look of the dead. She recognized two of them: Ruberg and Hanson: Minnesota Guardsmen who had recently lost their civilian jobs. The third man she didn't know.

Feeling a hand on her shoulder, she turned and saw that Lendra had followed her outside. "It could be dangerous, Sister," Lendra said. "We should go back until we're sure it's safe."

Sister Ezekiel inhaled sharply. Ruberg and Hanson and the stranger: poor souls. Why had they done it? She knew the community had begun to rip itself apart. There simply were no good jobs anymore. Everyone was angry. These men must have reached a point where all they could do was lash out. A hollowness hit Sister Ezekiel's chest, an emptiness very like nausea. Such a waste.

She glanced north along the road and saw more vehicles approaching. Just then one of Colonel Truman's soldiers grabbed her from behind, lifted her off her feet and ran with her back to the shelter. Lendra followed them. Ignoring Sister Ezekiel's protests, the soldier set her on her feet inside the ruined door. Weiss had his eyes on the monitors along the wall, while Carlton, his sunglasses on, seemed to be staring at nothing.

Gunfire erupted now from the north.

"Come on, Sister," Lendra said as she grabbed Sister Ezekiel's arm and led her deeper inside the building. Henry, Ahmad and a dozen homeless men stood at the edge of the lobby looking at them. Devereaux—she had to think of him as Rock Man—was not among them.

Sister Ezekiel spoke above the noise: "It's all right, everyone. Stay calm. It will be over soon. Henry, get everybody into the basement."

Henry nodded and began directing men through the dining area to the kitchen, where the basement entrance lay.

Lendra said, "I've got expensive equipment in my room. Can't leave it behind." She fought her way against the tide, moving toward her room. Sister Ezekiel followed, determined to make sure no one was left in the dormitory area, particularly not Rock Man. "Don't panic," she said to the men as she passed them. "Stay calm."

The building shuddered with a large explosion. Dust drifted down from the ceiling.

"Are you all right, Sister?" Lendra asked. "You look pale."

"I'm fine," Sister Ezekiel answered. She touched a hand to her face, as if her fingers might be able to detect any change. "I guess I'm just not very good under fire."

"You're doing fine, Sister."

When Lendra reached her room and slipped inside, Sister Ezekiel walked toward Doug's room, where she had left Rock Man. She found the door ajar, Rock Man gone. Had he left during the night? Had he been in the chapel with her? Sister Ezekiel plopped onto the bed, listening to the battle outside.

She picked up the pillow he'd slept on, held it to her nose, breathed in the earthy but subtle aroma of Devereaux's scent. A warmth seeped through her chest. Then she thought of the dead men outside and a guilty chill went through her.

Ahmad poked his head into the room. "Sister, you all right?"

"Ahmad, what are you doing here?"

"I followed you. You looked kinda funny. I wanted to make sure you were safe. Can't have you blowin' up, Sister. Where would I do all my charity work?"

Sister Ezekiel put down the pillow, got to her feet, then turned and straightened the bed sheets. "Well, as long as you're here, you might as well help me. I want to check every room, make sure nobody's left in the dormitory. I want everyone together in the basement. I'll check this side of the hall. You take that side."

Another explosion, louder, jolted her. More dust settled over her. Sister Ezekiel knew the shelter must have been hit. She steadied herself against the wall, ran her hand along it as she worked her way down the hall, opening doors to bedrooms, glancing briefly into each. Behind the second-to-last door stood Rock Man, supporting an old man who had been forgotten in the chaos—Flyer—her organist and cleaner of the chapel. Fear, relief, annoyance and gratitude swept over her. She blushed as she made eye contact with Rock Man, who looked back at her with an inquisitive stare.

"No," she said as she looked around to make sure Ahmad wasn't in view. "You can't surrender to these men."

Rock Man closed his eyes briefly, then nodded and shuffled off with Flyer while Sister Ezekiel checked the last room. Empty. Across the hall, Ahmad backed out of Lendra's room.

"Hurry," Ahmad spoke through the doorway. "Sister Ezekiel wants everyone in the basement."

Another loud blast hammered the building. The window at the end of the hall shattered. Sister Ezekiel balanced herself against a doorjamb while Ahmad checked the last room on his side of the hallway. A few seconds later, Lendra appeared at her door with her pack. She caught sight of Sister Ezekiel and said, "Okay, let's go."

Ahmad emerged from the last room, shook his head at Sister Ezekiel, and together the three of them headed for the basement.

Chapter Twenty-Seven

Jeremiah came awake instantly, whatever dream he'd been having now lost, and saw Julianna's disembodied face only inches away. For a moment, he was confused about where he was.

"About time you woke up," Julianna said. She lay beside him on the ground, her body barely visible in her camos, but her face had been wiped clean of the paint he'd applied earlier.

Jeremiah noticed that his camos were no longer functioning properly. Occasionally they would flicker on but they mostly stayed off. His arms and legs tingling, Jeremiah began to sit up. Julianna put a hand on his chest.

"Stay down," she said. "Let the effects of that sonic grenade wear off. I don't know about you but my legs aren't working yet. And the perimeter's clear."

He checked his scanner, saw that she was right. "What the hell was going on between you and Quark?"

"He has trust issues," Julianna said. "But he's a good man."

Jeremiah cocked his head for a moment, listening. Over the familiar call of a redwing blackbird, he heard the sound of jet-copters in the distance. He checked his scanner: still clear. "That'll be the Elite Ops. We don't have much time. We've got to get you out of here. If they capture us, they'll find out you're wanted for treason."

"My mission is here," Julianna said. "I won't leave Devereaux." She caressed his cheek as she stared into his eyes. "And I can't leave you."

A warmth stole through Jeremiah's body. He suppressed an almost uncontrollable urge to laugh. How could he still have feelings for this woman?

Julianna smiled. "That's right, I care for you. So what? It doesn't change anything. I'm still here to protect Devereaux. If anything happens to you, I won't grieve for you. And if I don't make it out alive, I don't want you to grieve for me, either. Okay?"

"I never heard you talk like this before," Jeremiah said.

"I never thought I was vincible before." Julianna paused for a moment. "I understand now that I am. So what do we do next?"

"I don't know," Jeremiah said. He climbed to his feet, his legs feeling shaky and a little numb. "First I have to find Devereaux. Then I'll decide."

Julianna raised herself up on one elbow and stared up at him. "He's right, you know."

"I'm more concerned with the bioweapons he designed."

Julianna snorted. "You think anyone should have those? You trust our government with those designs? Better that Devereaux should take them to his grave than that people like Weiss and Elias should have them. Those men are the real problem."

"So you want me to kill Devereaux?"

"I want you to listen to him," Julianna said. "I want you to put yourself on the ladder of enlightenment. You and I have the power to improve the world. More than that, we have a duty to act for the betterment of humanity."

"Because we're enhanced? Because we're like the Escala?"

Julianna's eyes widened. "How did you know?"

"I didn't," Jeremiah said. "I suspected. My enhancements are too good."

She nodded. "I told Eli you'd discover the truth. Yes, you're like the Escala, but while they were adapted for Mars, you've been designed for Earth." Julianna shook her head. "I'm not Escala. I'm just enhanced. My genetic profile didn't allow for me to have the same modifications you had."

He held out his hands, lifted Julianna to her feet. As she began to walk in a shaky circle, he said, "Why didn't you tell me?"

"I didn't want you to know. I was getting ready to betray you, remember? But now I'm giving you all the facts, everything I know to help you turn your life around. We need you, Jeremiah. You have tremendous potential. More than anyone I know."

He glanced down at his scanner, noted movement off to the west:

single blips moving along the road toward the town; multiple blips closing in on the shelter. The sounds of fighting erupted: explosions mingled with the occasional whistle of a rocket or mortar.

"So I'm not even human," he finally said.

"Of course you're human—like the Escala. A little animal DNA doesn't make you less a person. If anything, it makes you more. As Devereaux would say, it connects you better to the world, to the elemental core that makes up all of us."

"All life is just life," Jeremiah recited. "Distinctions are egocentric."

"Exactly," Julianna said. "Did Devereaux say that?"

"I don't remember. I probably read it somewhere. Can you run?"

"I can jog," she replied.

They started walking east, limbering up muscles shocked by the stun grenade. Jeremiah looked into Julianna's face, searching for some sign that things were different between them now that he was part animal.

She seemed to sense his anxiety, for she grabbed his arm and said, "I never saw you hurt anyone who didn't deserve it. You're too good for this profession."

Jeremiah pulled his arm free. "I don't know what I am anymore."

"You're the best hope for saving Devereaux," Julianna replied. "I'll save you. You save him."

Jeremiah snorted. "Who is he?"

Julianna glanced at him as she began a slow jog, then said. "The man you know as Rock Man is Devereaux."

"Rock Man?" Jeremiah stopped Julianna and peered into her eyes, which showed no trace of humor or deceit, though Jeremiah had to remind himself that he'd never been able to read her eyes. "So you really are a Devereauxnian."

"I really am," Julianna said. "I think I can run now. How are you doing?"

"I'm fine," he answered, stretching his arms and back. "What now?"

"Remember that electrical substation you searched?"

"The one with cameras and sensors?"

"Some of them were put there by us."

"Of course. I should have known. Those smaller devices were too sophisticated for the Army."

Jeremiah checked his scanner, noted the approaching troops. He rubbed his face, his hands coming away clean. Julianna must have wiped off his face paint as well. He wondered if he shouldn't just give up—walk back to his van and drive away, return to his search for his son. Everything was too complicated. And he no longer possessed the energy to sort it all out, to make any decisions at all. On the scanner, the dots moved with a rapidity that defied logic. The EOs had arrived and they'd be hunting the Escala.

Which meant, he realized, that they'd be hunting him.

"Well," he finally said, "we can't outfight them. We can't outrun them. Can we get to that substation?"

Julianna shook her head. "Too dangerous for them. But there's a cave not far from here. If we can get to that, there's a tunnel leading out under the cemetery. I think I can hold the Elite Ops off from the cave entrance long enough for you to get away."

And then it hit him: a sudden understanding that she was no longer the Julianna of old, that she really did care for him, more than she cared about herself. As his emotions welled up, he blinked three times, centering himself in his dungeon. He looked to the west, where the sound of movement through the forest increased.

EOs didn't worry about stealth. They wanted people to know they were coming.

"Okay," Jeremiah said. He adjusted his camos to full strength, but the control mechanism must have been damaged by the sonic grenade. He cursed himself for not wearing the new set. "Turn up your camos," he said. "And if they get too close, leave me behind. With that scatterer, they won't find you."

Julianna pulled her face cover over her head, then blurred into the background as her camos came up to full power. When she took off, Jeremiah followed her mostly by sound, moving in a steady pace behind her, conserving his energy. Every few steps, he checked his scanner.

Closing fast, he realized. He wasn't going to make it. He wondered how close they'd have to get before their scanners identified him as part animal.

He looked for a good spot to break away from Julianna. Now that she had turned her life around, he couldn't risk her safety. And the EOs, once they discovered what he was, might not give him a chance to surrender.

Relax. Stay calm. Plenty of time.

Yet he knew the EOs would catch him. Their advantages far outweighed his. Ahead, he could barely make out Julianna's movements, just blurs. Behind them, the EOs closed the gap, crashing through the woods, muscling their way past branches and undergrowth. Jeremiah sensed that Julianna was looking back.

"Keep going," he called.

He glanced at his scanner. Eighty meters. He wondered how far the cave was.

Have to leave Julianna soon, for her own sake. She'll be safe. The EOs will come after me. They'll know I'm a pseudo now.

But he found it difficult to actually break away.

Seventy meters.

Above the din of his pursuers, he heard the high whine of a nuclear power unit. Confirmation that the hunters were indeed EOs.

Sixty meters.

He spotted an old intersection and took it, sprinting away as fast as he could. His only goal was to put as much distance as possible between himself and Julianna. He heard Julianna call his name.

He tore past demolished houses, down a long-neglected street. Mingled with the rush of air past his ears and the padding of his feet, came the whine of multiple power units. When the hair on the back of his neck rose, he dodged left. A laser pulse flashed by. He dove behind a pile of rubble as three EOs loosed a stream of laser pulses at him, tiny blue arrows. Clearly they wanted him alive.

He kept his head down. With his peripheral vision, he saw two EOs leap through the air. Soaring fifteen feet above the ground, they flew over his head, landing in front of him, obviously trying to force him back the way he'd come. He caught a strong whiff of rotting flesh.

Ignoring the poisonous odor, Jeremiah sprinted away, retracing his steps. He fired continuously at the last trooper, forcing the man to keep his shield up. Buying time. As Jeremiah ran around another pile of rubble, more blue laser pulses flashed past.

He jumped, twisted, dodged—left, right, right again, left—always moving toward objects that offered at least minimal cover, slipping behind trees and bushes and ruined houses. Never before had he run so quickly. Somewhere deep inside him, he found a wellspring of energy: some animal instinct. It hit him almost like joy. A release. The freedom to be what he was. Laser pulses flashed all around him, warming the air, but so far—miraculously—he hadn't been hit. Why were they toying with him?

Coming through a stretch of trees, Jeremiah reached a relatively open area. Though it offered little cover, he had nowhere else to go. Even without looking back, he somehow knew the three pursuers had been joined by at least two more. Weaving and dodging, he made his way across the space. Twice he turned and fired his Las-pistol, hoping to slow the EOs down, make them think before moving. It almost worked.

As he reached the thicket on the far side of the opening, the burning sting of a laser pulse hit him in the back. He fell into the growth, his body on fire, and leveled his Las-pistol at a group of EOs on the far side of the clearing. Firing at each in turn, he emptied the power cartridge, causing no damage but slowing their advance. He then removed a stun grenade from his belt and flung it. He nearly fainted with pain as he released the grenade. His whole back, from his neck to his hips, protested with an agonizing stab that took his breath away. At least the wound had been instantly cauterized by the laser pulse.

The EOs' shields absorbed most of the grenade's concussive force. Still, the troopers held their line at the far side of the clearing, firing at preprogrammed intervals designed to seem random. They would approach cautiously, he knew, wary of a suicide bomb.

Jeremiah checked his belt. He had seven more stun grenades and three spare cartridges for the Las-pistol. He inserted a charged cartridge in the Las-pistol, though he would only be wasting his ammunition. Without his particle beam cannon he might as well be throwing rocks.

A twig snapped behind him. He twisted around, wincing at the movement, his Las-pistol lining up on the approaching target. It was Julianna. Her face pale under the smudged paint, her camos disengaged, she held her interface in her shaking hand.

He said, "What the hell are you doing here?"

Julianna gave him a fierce look. "I'm not leaving you."

Jeremiah pointed at her shaking hand. "What happened to your interface?"

"I tried to communicate with Quark and suddenly got this terrible feedback pulse. Damn near knocked me out. The EOs must have somchow tapped into it."

Jeremiah fired another long burst at the EOs, who began to edge around the clearing. He said, "I don't need your help."

"Why did you run?" Julianna fired a long red burst at the EOs.

"I was saving you," Jeremiah said.

"Good job." Julianna dropped her interface and threw two stun grenades, one after the other, into the woods across the clearing. The sound of EOs crashing through the undergrowth came from all sides, mingling with the miasma of fear.

"There's no escape." Jeremiah fired off the rest of his laser charge, then threw two more stun grenades. "They're already behind us. We have to surrender."

He dropped his Las-pistol and held up his hands.

A quick glance to the side showed him Julianna dropping her weapon and raising her hands too. But in that same instant the EOs fired, blue and purple pulses. Agonizing bolts of heat knocked him to the ground as Julianna cried out. Jeremiah felt three distinct hits—on his right arm, right leg and stomach. He turned onto his side and saw Julianna lying motionless.

"We *surrender*," he shouted.

Slowly, hoping not to draw the EOs' fire, he reached for Julianna. Her face looked pale. She had a smudge of dirt on her forehead. Her eyelids fluttered and she moaned quietly. Brushing the dirt off her forehead, his stomach sank. He couldn't bear to look at her back, at the bloody mess he knew he'd see. Even in a hospital, he wouldn't bet on her survival. Out here, she had no chance at all. He glanced up at the EOs, six of them now surrounding him, their weapons pointed at his chest.

"Hands behind your head," an EO said.

"Julianna," he said as he locked his fingers behind his head and bent over her. "Wake up. Come on. Wake up."

Julianna opened her eyes and found his. "Hurts," she said. "Feels good…to be alive." Then she saw the EOs. "So these are them."

"EOs," Jeremiah agreed.

Julianna lifted her hand to his face, her fingers tracing the outline of his lips. "Dear Jeremiah," she said. "What a ride we had."

His eyes filled with water until her features became blurred. He blinked until his vision cleared and when it did, he saw that she was already gone.

A heavy numbness filled him. He struggled to breathe as the EOs lifted him to his feet. Just when he'd found Julianna again, she'd been ripped away from him.

"Back to the homeless shelter," the EO behind him said. "If you run, you die."

Jeremiah blinked three times, centering himself in his dungeon as he walked away. He refused to grieve for her.

Chapter Twenty-Eight

Inside the monitoring room, three Escala technicians stood at a computer bank facing the far wall, manipulating holographic projections emanating from dozens of nozzles.

Quekri said, "We have hundreds of cameras and sensors outside, all feeding us data from around the forest."

Doug shifted his attention to the far wall. Every few seconds, the projections on the wall vanished, replaced by views from another angle. Even though all the images came from above, Doug found the constant flux disconcerting.

"Why do the scenes keep changing?"

"We shift cameras every few seconds to ensure the Elite Ops will not be able to intercept their signal."

Doug pointed to one of the projections. "What's goin' on there?"

Two huge creatures with monstrous heads crashed through the woods, sweeping their obscene heads from side to side, metallic appendages protruding from where the hands ought to be. On another projection, more creatures moved in the same fashion, continually swinging their heads back and forth as they jogged forward.

Doug said, "Are they…?"

"Yes," Quekri said. "Elite Ops."

"What are they doin'?"

"Hunting. Watch."

She pointed to one of the projections and Doug suddenly saw a fuzzy image of a man running—possibly the same man who had been upstairs earlier. He wore camouflage clothing that didn't seem to work properly, and weaved back and forth as the Elite Ops fired at him. Although he moved faster than Doug had ever seen a human run before, the Elite Ops closed on him. He dodged, leaping and ducking, darting back and forth more like an animal than a human.

"He's Escala," Doug said.

"Apparently," Quekri agreed. "But he's not like us. He's not with the Mars Project."

"Will they catch him?"

"Probably." For the first time, Doug sensed emotion in Quekri's voice—just an edge of fear and fatigue—and he wondered when she had last slept. As he watched the man run, he found himself becoming increasingly nervous.

"Where are your people?" Doug asked.

"They're preparing to attack."

"What about him?"

Quekri sighed. "We can't save him. Besides, they're only toying with him…and he's buying us time."

The man raced across a relatively open space. He turned to fire a Laspistol twice, then dove into a thicket as a pulse of light hit him. Almost immediately, a furious volley came from the undergrowth where he'd fallen. More Elite Ops closed in. This was it, Doug could see. There would be no escape now. The Elite Ops carefully surrounded the area, taking their time. Patient. Relentless. In one blinding moment, a fusillade of pulses flashed. The Elite Ops rushed forward; the thicket went quiet.

Quekri said, "They've taken him."

Doug shook his head. "All that effort for one man?"

"They see him as a threat—as they do us."

"But why?"

Quekri signaled for Doug to move to the side of the room. She spoke in a low voice. "How much do you know about the Mars Project?"

"Just that you were gonna establish a colony on Mars. And that because of the hostile conditions, you were gonna undergo genetic modification."

"That was necessary for survival, due to the higher cosmic radiation on Mars. If we wanted to go—and we all did—we had to alter our DNA. Most of us have no regrets. But the genetic surgeons did not understand the full scope of the changes. And none of us understood the risk of sterility. Or about the rage."

When Doug wrinkled his brow in confusion, Quekri added, "Side effects of the transgenic process. The rage developed slowly and didn't hit all of us equally. At the time, we were confined to the Mayo Clinic. And when funding for the Mars Project dried up, problems started. Fourteen of our people became delusional, uncontrollably angry. They attacked various officials they perceived had wronged us."

"I never heard about that."

"It never made the news," Quekri said. Doug followed her glance to a projection, which showed the Elite Ops moving again, carrying a body with them through the forest. In their midst, the man they'd been chasing walked with a limp. How did the extra person get there?

"Can you get a better view of that body?" Quekri asked.

"In a few seconds," one of the technicians said.

Quekri turned back to Doug. "We, the less affected, lost the ability to reason with the fourteen. We couldn't prevent their attacks."

"And that's when the Elite Ops came into the picture?"

Quekri nodded. "At first, they only went after the fourteen. The rest of us were tested and cleared but we remained at the Mayo Clinic. The Elite Ops were stationed outside...to provide security. They began to harass us. When we protested, the security measures against us tightened."

"There," the technician said, manipulating a projection until two faces appeared. Doug recognized neither but Quekri clearly knew one of them.

"Julianna," Quekri said. She looked at Doug. "You know her as Dr. Mary."

"That's Dr. Mary?"

"Yes. She's been helping us protect Devereaux."

"Is she dead?"

Quekri shrugged. "I think so. The man must be the one she told us about—the one she said would come for Devereaux, the one she was hoping would help."

"Is Dr. Mary...Julianna one of the Escala too?"

Quekri said, "No, she's just a Devereauxnian. A reformed killer. A trusted friend. They're beyond our help now. Julianna," she said as she stared at the holo-projection, "I remember you."

Quekri and the three technicians bowed their heads. Doug did the same. When he looked up, he saw that the two faces had vanished; the technicians manipulated the projections again to continue tracking the Elite Ops' progress. Doug waited a few moments before asking: "What about the Mayo Clinic? The Elite Ops?"

Quekri looked at him. "Oh, yes. Well, it didn't take long before certain high-ranking officials decided we constituted a threat. Even though we'd been tested and retested, they were convinced we would continue to regress, as they called it. They believed we would grow more violent. We knew they would only tolerate us for so long. The final confrontation was inevitable." Quekri sighed. "The Elite Ops tracked down the fourteen violent ones and killed thirteen of them. But they took heavy losses. And one of the fourteen managed to escape."

"Cookie Monster," Doug said.

"Quark," Quekri confirmed with something like pride. "How did you guess?"

"He's got a darkness about him," Doug said. "An edge of anger or brutality just beneath the surface. I saw it in prison a lot—tough guys tryin' not to give in to the rage."

"I don't know how he defeated the anger. We thought he was gone forever. His self-control, his will, must be phenomenal. But now he blames himself for the deaths of the others. I think that's why he stays at the shelter, away from us. I doubt he can be truly happy anymore."

Doug shook his head. "He seemed kinda happy around Rock Man—at least some of the time."

"Rock Man?"

"Just an old mute back at the shelter. Gives people rocks. Gave me this polished agate." Doug pulled a small stone out of his pocket—almost perfectly round, with banded layers of red and brown.

"That's nice," Quekri said.

"Yeah," Doug rubbed the agate for a few seconds, then put it back in his pocket. "So what happened next?"

"The Elite Ops came after us. We anticipated such a move, of course. But we didn't think they would be homicidal. We believed they just wanted to isolate us from each other. Lock us away where we couldn't harm anyone. And I still think that was all they intended. But whether due to some miscommunication or malfunction or just some prejudiced idiot, a few shots were fired. Two of our people died immediately.

"We fought back then. We didn't have the weaponry they had, or the training. But the Elite Ops were new too. They'd only recently been wired into their armor. They were still getting used to being part machine. Even so, they would have destroyed us if not for Devereaux."

"Devereaux?"

"He was one of the pioneers of transgenic modification. He empathized with us and approved our aspirations. In fact, he was the first to warn us that we would eventually be perceived as a threat."

"But how did he help you?"

"At the time of the attack, he was monitoring us heavily. He predicted when the assault would begin. Shortly after the attack started, he hacked into the Elite Ops' communications network and sent out signals that disrupted many of their non-combat functions. Because of the safeguards built into their systems, he couldn't shut down their shields or weapons, but he could give them double or triple vision, and he targeted their inner ears so they lost their balance. He attacked their motor coordination skills and bodily functions. Then he directed us to this forgotten underground facility, where he knew we could hide—at least temporarily."

"Unbelievable," Doug said. He felt something like a thrill at this revelation, for it fit precisely with the image he had of Devereaux.

Quekri said, "We think Devereaux's involvement in our escape is one of the reasons the government hates him so much."

The technician who had spoken gestured to Quekri and pointed to another projection. He said, "More bad news."

"What is it?" Quekri asked.

"Watch," the technician said. "I'll replay it."

The projection showed the statue, "Emerging Man," and several homeless men standing near it. Doug knew they often panhandled there. As they cowered away from something outside the camera's view, two Elite Ops troopers entered the projection. They stopped in front of the statue and fired their weapons at it. In a thunderous blast, the top of the statue blew apart. Shards of rock flew everywhere. All that remained was the abstract part that emerged from the earth, barely recognizable as the statue's legs.

Chapter Twenty-Nine

Colonel Truman had to admit that the Elite Ops were effective. In two separate attacks, the two troopers out front had defended the shelter, the soldiers and the journalists outside—who recorded every second of the battles. Yet, despite the amazing coordination of their assaults, the speed and power with which they moved, Truman saw cracks. They were a little too reliant on input from their fellow troopers. They had to analyze too much data at any given moment. A few good men with particle beam cannons could inflict a lot of damage by acting separately.

Even against the reservists they hadn't been completely successful. The shelter, though still standing, had sustained several direct hits, mainly to the front of the building, collapsing part of the roof, sending debris flying in all directions and turning the lobby into an obstacle course of concrete and steel that his soldiers were now clearing. Thanks to the efforts of Sister Ezekiel, all the civilians made it to the basement before the rocket-propelled grenades struck.

Through the smoke, Truman saw a group of homeless men running toward the shelter. When they saw the Elite Ops, they yelled and shrieked, then made a wide circle around the troopers. Eventually, they reached the ruined door, where they began babbling about explosions and the statue.

Sister Ezekiel, Lendra by her side, emerged from the kitchen and said, "Calm down, men. Now what's all this about the statue?"

One of the homeless men stepped forward, bleeding from a cut under his eye. He said, "These two giant robots, Sister—like the ones out front—they come up the street and they stop in front a the statue and they fire some sorta weapons at it and the whole top a the goddam—sorry, Sister—the whole top a the statue blows apart in a gazillion pieces and a piece a the statue hits me in the face and I start bleedin'. And then they looks at me and I runs away as fast as I can and I grabs Freddy and some a these other guys here and we runs as fast as we can here."

Sister Ezekiel turned nearly as white as her habit. Truman strode forward and grabbed her arm. "Are you okay, Sister?"

Lendra took the nun's other arm. Together, they managed to steer her to a chair. Truman unscrewed his flask and handed it to her. She drank without protest, a bit of color returning to her cheeks.

"Stupid, senseless violence," she said. "Ignorant fools."

Truman said nothing but privately agreed with her. Such a waste. These Elite Ops had so far murdered thirty-two relatively harmless fugitives and blown up a reknowned work of art. A proud day. And the pseudos weren't much better—attacking the shelter yesterday, putting all those children at risk.

Lendra said, "I've been researching the statue, Sister, and I've discovered that the Escala revere it. They believe it points to the future of humanity. They see in it what Devereaux saw all those years ago—promise and possibility."

"The future of humanity," Truman snorted. "As far as I'm concerned, these *Escala* and Elite Ops can both go to hell."

At that moment, Major Payne walked through the ruined doorway, Jones behind him, limping slightly. Only a trace of the rotting flesh odor flowed in with them. Following Jones were two more Elite Ops troopers, Las-rifles in their hands. One wore a gold cross affixed to his left breast, an oddity that seemed ironic given the circumstances. Congealed blood showed on Jones' clothing but his face betrayed no sign of pain—no emotion at all.

Bringing up the rear, another Elite Ops trooper carried a body. Even though the lobby was crowded, men moved out of the way for the Elite Ops. The men lined the walls, trying to get as far away as possible. The last trooper dropped the body to the floor. It landed with a thud, making Truman wince. It was a woman—clearly dead. An odor of burnt flesh and torched electronics emanated from her.

Sister Ezekiel swayed slightly in her chair and Truman reached out a hand to steady her. Looking at Jeremiah, Lendra stepped forward, stopping only after Jones shook his head.

Carlton the observer, wearing his sunglasses again, stepped out of Sister Ezekiel's office, Gray Weiss trailing him. He stared at Jones, who ignored him. Instead Jones stared at the dead woman, pain evident on his face, his eyes glistening. Carlton asked, "How did it go out there, Major?"

"No problems, sir. But all we found were these two. This one," the major indicated Jones, "may be a pseudo. The woman was enhanced."

"Jeremiah, a pseudo?" Weiss said.

"He's at least been enhanced. Speed, strength, endurance. Very dangerous."

Sister Ezekiel used Truman's hand to pull herself to her feet and marched over to Carlton. She said, "Why did your men blow up the statue?"

"Icons of false ideologies promote blasphemous thoughts," Carlton said.

Weiss said, "Who's the woman?"

Major Payne looked at Carlton before replying. "No ID on her," he said. "She's wearing a scatterer, so we didn't pick up her enhancements until we turned it off. She's no innocent."

Truman saw Lendra glance at Jones, who didn't notice her. He kept his eyes on the dead woman, his body quivering ever so slightly. He seemed to be fighting the urge to go to her. Lendra said, "Her name is Julianna Wentworth. She was masquerading as Dr. Mary."

"Dr. Mary?" Sister Ezekiel grabbed Truman's arm. When the homeless men began to grumble, shifting their feet and glancing at the Elite Ops troopers, Sister Ezekiel let go of Truman and took a step toward Major Payne. "You killed my doctor?"

Now the homeless men moved forward en masse, closing in on Major Payne. He and the other Elite Ops troopers touched buttons on their arms and once again that poisonous, noxious odor filled the room. The homeless men shrank back. Truman fought the revulsion in his stomach. He knew it was just a chemical reaction in his brain. But when he looked down he realized he was crouching. Slowly, almost against his will, he forced himself to stand erect. Weiss too fought off the effects of the gas. Jones seemed untroubled by it. He simply continued to stare at the dead woman as if nothing else in the world existed, as if his sadness had no room to spare for fear.

After a few minutes, the Elite Ops pressed more buttons and the odor began to dissipate. Once again, the unreasoning fear melted away. The homeless men seemed to have been cowed, however, for they stayed by the walls, as far away from the Elite Ops as they could get.

Weiss shook his head, shrugged his shoulders and stepped forward. He looked down at the body and said, "So that's Julianna Wentworth. Interesting. I want a verification scan run on her, Colonel."

"Who is Julianna Wentworth?" Truman asked.

Weiss ignored him. "As for you, Miss Riley, you seem to know a lot more about what's going on than I would have suspected. Perhaps we should have a talk. Come with me. You too, Colonel."

Truman signaled for Captain Baynes to scan the woman's body, then followed Weiss and Lendra to Sister Ezekiel's office, which Weiss had commandeered. Behind him, Carlton and Major Payne moved forward. They stepped into the office too, Major Payne blocking the doorway with his bulk, his large helmet presenting a blank screen.

Weiss held up his hand. "I don't think we'll need you or the Major here, RC."

Neither man spoke; neither showed any inclination to leave. Truman looked at Weiss, wondering what he should do. The Attorney General just shrugged and straightened his tie. "Very well," he said, "we all have our responsibilities." He turned to Lendra. "What are yours, Miss Riley?"

Lendra spoke in a soft voice that trembled slightly. "I'm here with Jeremiah on behalf of President Hope."

"Who is working through CINTEP and Elias Leach," Weiss said. "I wonder why."

Lendra stared back at him, her jaw rippling slightly, her back stiff.

"I know Jeremiah is his best ghost. But who are you, a field agent in training?"

"No," Lendra's voice gained power but the tremor remained. "I'm here to assist Jeremiah, relay messages to CINTEP and provide information as needed."

"How did you know Julianna Wentworth?"

"She used to work for CINTEP. I met her for the first time yesterday. Jeremiah introduced us."

"She was Jeremiah's ex-partner, wasn't she?"

"Yes."

Weiss rubbed his chin. "Did you know they were enhanced?"

"All CINTEP's field operatives have been enhanced," Lendra said.

"Approval must be granted for all non-medical enhancements. And they must be registered in the national database. I don't remember seeing Jeremiah's name in the database."

"If you have any questions about it, you can call Eli."

"No doubt he told you Jeremiah was legal, but we'll have to verify that. All requests for genetic alteration must go through the Genetics Enforcement Agency, which is part of the Justice Department. Not even the President can authorize such a procedure without clearing it through my office."

Carlton said, "How many enhancements does he have? His readings put him at the upper limit of the human spectrum."

"What about you, Mr. Carlton?" Lendra said. Truman noticed that the tremor was now gone from her voice. She spoke clearly, her voice carrying beyond the confines of the room. "You've got the same implants as your Elite Ops troopers."

Carlton turned his head toward her, a bead of sweat trickling down the side of his face. Major Payne stayed motionless, like some robot waiting to be called into action.

"Is that true?" Weiss asked.

As Carlton continued to stare at Lendra, she said, "You shouldn't have kept records of the procedures. Records can be compromised."

Carlton said, "That is top secret. Ordered by the President. The only way to monitor the Elite Ops is to be connected to them. With their instantaneous communicative abilities, it's the only way to insure that oversight can be brought to the project."

Weiss narrowed his eyes. "What does that mean?"

"It means, there could be problems discovering the truth of what happened after a particular incident if I were not linked. For example, I was able to see everything that happened during Jones' capture through these." He removed his sunglasses and showed them to Weiss, then put them back on.

"Just as I'm linked to them, they're linked to me. Everything they see or hear, I have the ability to see and hear. And vice versa. However, I have the option of terminating the link at my end so they can't observe me. They don't have that luxury."

"So you're one of them?"

"No, Gray. I could have been. But I'm a simple businessman. And I'm far too busy to get caught up in all this. Plus," Carlton patted Major Payne on the shoulder, the master bragging about his dog, "these men are all huge. They work out constantly. Even though their power packs assist with their movements, they carry a lot of weight around with them. Like you, I'm too old for that."

"I don't understand why you need to be linked to them," Weiss said. "Couldn't a machine monitor them just as well?"

"As we discovered in Rochester," Carlton said, "machines can be deceived. To this day, we don't know who breached our defenses, allowing the pseudos to escape. We suspect it was Devereaux, though we can't be sure. But now that I'm linked to every member of the Elite Ops, I'll be in position to observe and repel any attempt to infiltrate the system."

"It sounds to me," Weiss said, "like that's another serious weakness of the Elite Ops."

Carlton shook his head. "Not really, Gray. Major Payne's men could function equally well without me. It's just that with me linked to the network, they can concentrate all their efforts on the task at hand, without having to devote any effort to monitoring the system."

"All right," Weiss said. "You may leave, Miss Riley. But please stay within the confines of the shelter."

"Hold it," Major Payne said. He stepped to the side, positioning himself in front of Lendra. "Where are the pseudos?"

Lendra looked up at his helmet and said, "I don't know."

When she tried to walk around him, Major Payne grabbed her arm. She struggled against his grip.

"Stop that," Truman ordered.

"The more you struggle," Major Payne said, "the more it will hurt."

Truman took a step forward but Major Payne pushed him back. Truman fell over a chair and experienced an adrenaline rush of anger. But before he could get to his feet, Weiss was standing over him, hands outstretched, signaling caution. As Weiss helped him to his feet, Truman glared at Major Payne, who seemed not to notice. Truman longed to plant a fist squarely in that arrogant face, again heard Emily's voice saying, "Don't be a fool. Do you want to get yourself killed?" For some reason he flashed on an image of his older brother Ned, who disappeared in South America years ago on an assignment for the CIA. Why had he suddenly thought of Ned? Maybe because Ned also would have counseled caution. He straightened his uniform, wondered how tough the major would be without all his equipment. Probably still damn tough.

Major Payne pressed a button on his right glove and took Lendra's hand in his. She stared at his opaque visor, eyes wide, a slight tremble running down her frame, while he asked her name, address and occupation, waiting a few seconds after each response. Truman had heard the Elite Ops could detect lies. He realized Major Payne was establishing a baseline.

"Do you know where the pseudos are?"

"No," Lendra said.

Major Payne held Lendra's hand for several more seconds, then released her. "Go," he said as he stepped aside.

Weiss pointed to Carlton and Major Payne. "You two may leave now as well. I have some things to discuss with Colonel Truman."

"I think I'll stay," Carlton said.

Weiss said, "Sorry, RC, Justice Department business."

Carlton stared at Weiss through his sunglasses, his jaw clamped shut. Truman edged forward, his fists clenched at his side, almost hoping Carlton would make an aggressive move. He noticed that Major Payne had turned slightly, facing him. The four of them stared at each other for several seconds, nobody moving. Then Carlton said to Weiss: "I don't like your lackey."

Truman said, "I don't like yours, either."

Weiss held up his hands. "Please, Richard, this is a sensitive matter. And as you yourself pointed out, you're a civilian."

Carlton's eyes were invisible behind his sunglasses but the anger in his face was easy to read. After another few seconds, he pivoted and headed out the door, Major Payne following him.

"We have a problem," Weiss said when they were gone.

"Sir?"

"They're arrogant bastards, aren't they? I thought bringing the Elite Ops in would simplify things—force Jeremiah's hand, make the pseudos move before they were ready, possibly even drive Devereaux out into the open. But I also thought I had a handle on them. I thought Carlton would be on my side. I was wrong."

"You think Carlton's planning something?"

"I'm certain of it. I used to think he was in this to help me make a positive change for our country. We talked about replacing a broken system with a new kind of leadership. I thought he just wanted to use his influence to increase his wealth but I see now that he's been playing both sides—working with the President as well as me. Not to mention becoming one of those things."

Truman looked out to the lobby and said, "Perhaps I should call General Horowitz, see if he'll recall the Elite Ops."

Weiss shook his head. "He won't. Carlton has the President convinced he's on her side. I'm sure he's also explained the necessity of using the Elite Ops. Any request to remove them would only reinforce the President's determination to keep them here." He picked up a pen and began tapping on the desk. "We need to find Devereaux and get out of here. After this is over, we'll conduct a complete re-evaluation of the Elite Ops program. Until we leave, I want your men ready for anything."

"Sir," Truman said, "my soldiers are willing to fight. But they're no match for the Elite Ops. Maybe if we had a working particle beam cannon."

"Hopefully, it won't come to that. If I'm not mistaken, the pseudos and the Elite Ops will soon be at each other's throats. When that happens, Devereaux will reveal himself."

"How can you be so sure?"

"Because Devereaux was the one who helped the pseudos in Rochester."

"How do you—"

"We can't prove it. But we know Devereaux helped them. He was the only one with the expertise to breach the system and cause the kind of havoc that occurred. Plus, he's the only one who had a motive for doing so. After all, he created them. They're his children."

"His children?"

"Didn't you know, Colonel? It was Devereaux's research into transgenic modification that led to the creation of the pseudos."

"I knew he was involved in work on brain-muscle-computer connectivity, which sped up the development of the Elite Ops."

Weiss nodded. "Yes, that's true. But he left that work relatively early, claiming that the future was in evolution of the species. He said man-machine technology was not ultimately self-sustainable."

"So he'll show up to save the pseudos?"

"Exactly."

Chapter Thirty

Sister Ezekiel knelt before the body of Julianna Wentworth and gave her a blessing, noting the perfectly aligned white teeth of Dr. Mary, which removed any doubt about her identity. This young woman would have made a great doctor. Sister Ezekiel's eyes drifted across the room to Rock Man, who looked at her with piercing intensity. She shook her head, indicating that he should not yet give himself up.

Rock Man stood beside Flyer, flanked on either side by Elite Ops troopers. Half a dozen of the big soldiers dominated the lobby. Huge, faceless: they inspired fear by their very presence, and killed without remorse. She thought of Ruberg and Hanson, corpse-piled out there with a number of other separatists, and shivered.

Forcing her eyes away from the giant soldiers, she glanced at Jeremiah, who stood motionless, staring at Julianna's face with a sadness that caused a pain in her chest. He looked as if his whole world had collapsed. Finally he turned and stared at Rock Man, and Sister Ezekiel knew that Jeremiah had somehow figured out Devereaux's identity.

At that moment Lendra emerged from the office and moved toward Jeremiah. The Elite Ops trooper guarding him prevented her approach, stepping between them, his weapon barring the way.

"You can't deny him medical attention," Lendra said loudly.

Sister Ezekiel pushed herself to her feet. She walked toward Jeremiah, noticed the gold cross on the Elite Ops trooper's chest, and nodded to him. He let her pass. When Jeremiah looked at her, Sister Ezekiel asked, "How are you feeling?"

He smiled briefly and said, "I'm fine, Sister."

She grabbed his shoulder and turned him slightly away from her, gasping as she saw his burned and bloody back. "You need medical assistance. Medic."

Jeremiah looked over her shoulder. She turned and saw Carlton and Major Payne striding over, focusing on Jeremiah.

"This man needs medical attention immediately," Sister Ezekiel said.

Carlton ignored her. Major Payne put a hand on her shoulder and moved her aside as Carlton grabbed Jeremiah by the shirt and said, "Where are the pseudos?"

"And where is Jack Marschenko?" Major Payne asked.

Jeremiah stared straight ahead, his back held stiffly.

Sister Ezekiel said, "Can't you at least put a QuikHeal bandage on him?"

"No," Major Payne said. "I want him just like that."

Sister Ezekiel shivered at the callousness. She wondered how much pain Jeremiah felt. With his enhancements, he might have a much greater tolerance than most people.

"We'll get answers from you very soon," Carlton said to Jeremiah. "Though we may have to damage your brain to get them."

"And you'll pay for what happened to Julianna," Jeremiah answered, glancing down at Carlton's hand on his shirt. Then he looked back up into Carlton's eyes. "And for taking my son." Jeremiah stood quietly, making no threatening move forward. But for all his inertness, he looked dangerous, like he might suddenly erupt in violent action. Major Payne saw something in his eyes too, for he pulled Carlton away.

"You'd better hope nothing happens to me," Carlton said, poking a finger in Jeremiah's direction, "or the wrath of the Elite Ops will rain down on you all."

Weiss and Truman emerged from Sister Ezekiel's office and made their way over. "What's going on here?" Weiss asked.

"We're taking custody of this man," Carlton said.

"No," Weiss and Lendra said at the same time.

"And we're going to find the pseudos," Major Payne added.

"Jeremiah is here on the President's orders," Lendra said.

"Enough," Rock Man said, his voice forceful and controlled. He stepped forward.

Sister Ezekiel held up her hands to stop him, knowing the gesture was futile even as she made it. The mere act of speaking had given him away.

Rock Man reached up and slid his fingers under the skin—the false skin—at his neck. Slowly he lifted the mask up, removing the face of Rock Man and becoming again the great and charismatic figure who somehow managed to be larger than life. Sister Ezekiel heard gasps and murmurs as people finally accepted what they were seeing—Walt Devereaux was here! His face looked painfully thin. He held the mask out to Weiss and said, "I'm surrendering to you. Now please take your troops with you and go."

Weiss took the mask from Devereaux, studied it for a moment, then nodded slowly and lifted his eyes back to Devereaux. "Colonel," Weiss said, "I want you to place Mr. Devereaux under arrest for treason."

As Truman grabbed Devereaux's arm, Devereaux said, "Please call off the Elite Ops. They'll massacre the Escala."

"That's rather the point," Carlton said.

Major Payne turned to Devereaux and said, "Where are the pseudos?" But even as he asked the question, his body stiffened. Carlton's head jerked to the left. Both men stood still for a second or two. At almost the same time, Sister Ezekiel heard a loud but distant explosion.

"The pseudos," Carlton said.

"What's happening, Richard?" Weiss asked.

"The pseudos have just launched an attack on the Elite Ops in the woods."

Major Payne and five of the Elite Ops troopers bolted out the door, leaving Carlton and a single guard behind—the one with the gold cross. He kept his weapon trained on Jeremiah, ignoring everyone else.

Carlton smiled as he pointed to the screens that Colonel Truman's soldiers had placed along the wall by the ruined front door. "The pseudos," he said, "are about to be destroyed. I'll put it up so you can watch."

* * *

The Escala filled the monitoring room. Although they showed little strain outwardly, they had to be anxious over the fate of their friends and relatives. Doug looked for Zeriphi, but she was either resting or receiving medical attention. Temala was there, however, staring at him as usual. Perhaps she didn't trust him, or maybe she just didn't like him. Whatever the reason, he quickly looked away. She made him uneasy.

Along the far wall, the battle with the Elite Ops played out on the projections. An Elite Ops had his shield blasted away, then fell heavily after an Escala fired once more. Several Escala nodded grimly. The teenagers whooped, while Doug jumped in the air, pumping his fist and yelling, "Yes!" This brought bigger smiles. On another projection, two Elite Ops found themselves facing four Escala and quickly turned tail. The Escala let them go with a few parting shots.

"We're kickin' some serious ass, here," Doug said.

"Patience," Quekri reminded him. "We have a long ways to go."

"We got them on the ropes. If we had a few more people out there, we could finish them off."

Quekri, silent, kept her eyes on the projections.

"You can't hide forever," Doug said.

"True," Quekri answered. "But we hope to buy ourselves time. They don't know how many of us are here. If we can make them believe there are only a few, we might be able to escape detection long enough for our plan to work."

"What plan is that?"

"To get the Mars Project reinstated."

"This is a big underground complex. I can't believe you ain't been found already."

"It used to be smaller. We expanded it." Quekri said. "Years ago this was an electrical substation for a power company. Devereaux went into the archives and erased all records of the place. This cave will be located soon. But it's served us well so far."

"Here they come," one of the technicians said.

The Elite Ops spread out in groups of twos and threes, moving more slowly now, more carefully. Three who had converged on their fallen comrade now moved off in the direction the Escala had gone. They took great running leaps, jumping out of camera view on one occasion. Doug followed their progress as they shrank on one camera and grew on another. Being unused to the projections, he found them disorienting—almost as if he were there, watching it all happen from a great height.

On one of the projections, two Escala moved quickly. Even so, the three Elite Ops caught up with them in less than a minute. As they spotted the Escala, the Elite Ops began firing. They drove the two Escala down an overgrown road. When the Escala reached an intersection, two more Elite Ops stepped out from behind trees and fired their weapons. The Escala exploded.

"Nall," the technician who had spoken earlier said, "and Jork."

That was it. That was all anyone said about the loss of two of their number. Doug shivered. These were astronauts and scientists, not warriors. The Elite Ops began moving faster, more confidently. And Doug could see now that the Escala were fighting a lost cause. His companions must have known it from the start. Even the teenagers seemed to have grasped the inevitability of defeat. They stared at the projections blankly. Yet no one showed fear or anger. Neither Quekri nor anyone else issued orders to retreat. Maybe they'd already resigned themselves to these deaths.

On another projection, a female Escala ran down a road, pursued by Elite Ops. Doug put his hands to his eyes. He didn't want to see this. And yet he opened his fingers enough to peek through—as if his brain demanded that he record the moment. Every time the woman attempted to leave the road, laser fire kept her moving toward another intersection. When she reached it, two Elite Ops stepped out and fired at her, blew her apart in a thousand pieces. Doug shut his eyes.

"Tellera," the technician said, the reaction the same as for the two males who had been killed.

Doug thought he might retch. He clenched his teeth tightly,

removed his hands and opened his eyes, forcing himself to follow the action, to witness the Escala fighting the impossible fight. On the third projection, an Escala jumped from a pile of rubble to a tree, pulling herself up as laser blasts surrounded her. Soon, the tree was enveloped in flames. Three Elite Ops stood below the pyre, waiting for the body to drop. After a few seconds, it did. They fired a series of laser blasts into it.

"Vona," the observer said.

The stillness in the room ate at Doug. He smacked a fist into a palm and said, "How can you be so calm? You just lost four people. Don't that bother you?"

Quekri smiled, not without sadness. "They are doing what any of us would do—sacrificing themselves for the greater good. We honor them by accepting their gift."

"So their job is to die?"

"We've led the Elite Ops to a place of our choosing." Quekri pointed to the first projection, where a group of three Escala sprinted along, pursued by four Elite Ops. Occasionally, one of the Escala would turn and fire a laser pulse but they mostly just ran, their shields absorbing laser fire as they moved toward a huge pile of rubble. Behind it, another Escala crouched. Zod. Doug could barely make out his face.

Just before the Escala reached the shelter of the rubble, the Elite Ops fired their weapons. As the Escala blew up, Zod stepped from cover and threw a large object high in the air. From off to the side, a single laser pulse pierced the object and a tremendous explosion followed. Even underground, Doug felt it—a small quake that rumbled throughout the cavern. Something fell to the floor. On the projection he saw nothing but blackness, the cameras gone dark.

The technicians rapidly pressed buttons and moved joysticks, manipulating cameras until the projections showed the same scene from a greater distance. Through black smoke, a large crater appeared in the ground, two Elite Ops bodies sprawled out in the base of it. Two others lay at the periphery, moving feebly.

"Garrad," said the technician who called out the names of the dead, followed by, "Felko" and "Jode."

"What the hell was that?" Doug asked.

"Old fashioned," Quekri replied. "An RDX-HMX derivative that requires superheating to explode. We didn't have time to make anything more advanced. Zod threw the charge and Quark set it off with a laser pulse." She turned to the technician who had spoken. "Zod? Alive?"

"Yes," the technician replied. "His readings are weak, though."

"Will he make it to the hideout?" Quekri asked.

"I don't know."

"Is Quark alive?" Doug asked.

"We have no readings on him," Quekri said. "He's operating on his own. I'm sure he's fine." But her face was lined with worry and she kept her eyes on the projection, searching for any sign of him.

The technicians switched between two cameras monitoring the crater. One image slowly drew closer, focusing on the bodies of the two Elite Ops in the center. As they grew larger on the projection, an arm moved.

"Oh my God!" Doug said. "Did you see that? He survived!"

The Escala in the room exchanged looks with each other, betraying their astonishment. Now the other Elite Ops trooper moved an arm and a leg.

"They're tough," Quekri said, "We thought an explosion of that magnitude would penetrate their shields. Still, they'll be stunned. Take their time regrouping. Then they'll come after Zod."

The technicians began directing cameras in an effort to locate Zod.

Quekri turned to the observers and asked, "Is he moving?"

"Not yet."

"We may have to call Quark." Quekri rubbed her cheek for a few seconds before re-focusing her attention on Doug. "We built an underground hideout, much smaller than this place. A few beds, not much else. We need to direct the Elite Ops there. If they find it, they may conclude only a few of us remain in the area. If they don't find it, they might assume we're all here. And if Zod can't get them to the hideout, we'll have to call Quark, risk exposing ourselves, to get him to lead the Elite Ops to the area. I'd rather—"

"He's moving," the technician said.

Doug stared at the projection, saw nothing but black swirling smoke. Then he caught an image of two men—one holding up the other—moving slowly through the woods. Quark and Zod.

Zod clearly couldn't walk without help. He leaned on Quark, who held him up as the two men half-walked, half-trotted along an overgrown road. On another projection, Elite Ops raced and bounded toward the explosion. Eventually, half a dozen reached the spot. The two who had been at the periphery of the blast had already managed to regain their feet. The other two lay stunned, no longer moving. As quickly as they arrived, the Elite Ops took off again, trailing Zod and Quark. The two Elite Ops who had been at the periphery remained behind to assist their unconscious companions.

Doug found himself staring from projection to projection, trying to gauge how soon the Elite Ops would catch up to the fleeing duo. Eventually he realized that he could use the different houses as a guide. When Quark and Zod passed a large home with a brick façade and four pillars, one of which had toppled sideways, Doug turned to the projection following the Elite Ops. He began counting seconds, looking for the fallen pillar. After nine seconds, the Elite Ops bounded past. And they were moving much faster than their prey.

Doug switched back to the projection following Quark and Zod. They now turned off the road and headed toward a collapsed house. As they reached it, Zod seemed to regain energy. He got his feet under himself and pushed Quark, waving his arm, shooing Quark away. Then he lifted a branch and dropped through a hole in the ground next to what was left of the building's foundation. Quark vanished into the shrubbery.

The Elite Ops pounded into view seconds later. Spotting the hole in the ground, they surrounded it. One of them dropped into the hole behind Zod. Another explosion rocked the ground—this one farther away, less intense. Doug barely heard it, possibly only imagining the resulting tremor at his feet. The Elite Ops outside the hole fell to the ground. Then two sprang to their feet and lowered themselves into the hole.

Almost immediately, Doug heard the technician speak again: the single word, "Zod."

So Zod was dead. Doug looked around the room, wondering if there would be greater reaction to the news that their leader was gone. Nothing. A few murmurs, the same as before.

Doug threw his arms up. "How can you watch this without any emotion? Those people are dead. They ain't never comin' back. Don't that mean nothin' to you? I barely knew them, yet even I'm sad at their loss."

"We grieve," Quekri said. "We just don't show it like you do."

"And that makes you evolved?"

"Emotion clouds judgment," Quekri said. "And if we don't control our emotions, we don't survive. Besides, you're having a conversation in the middle of a battle."

Doug clenched his fists together. "Gimme a weapon and let me go after 'em."

Quekri shook her head.

"What are you gonna do?" Doug asked.

"The Elite Ops will either believe only a few of us lived here or not," she said.

"Why didn't they go after Quark?"

"He's wearing a scatterer—newly modified. He hoped it would prevent their scanners from detecting him. It must be working."

Doug said, "Can we modify enough scatterers to get you away?"

Quekri shook her head. "No time," she said. "If the Elite Ops aren't fooled, they'll come for us quickly. Quark will try to protect us. He's the one they want most. He's the one who organized and led the resistance against them. He caused most of the casualties they took in Rochester. In their minds, he's the most dangerous Escala of all."

Doug turned to look at the projections, wondering if he might spot Quark there, but all he saw were Elite Ops. They removed two bodies from the hole in the ground and began heading toward a camera. One body was Zod; the other, the Elite Ops trooper. On another projection, the two Elite Ops troopers who had been unconscious earlier slowly walked away from the camera, supported by their comrades.

The battle appeared to be over, the Elite Ops no longer rushing around searching for prey. Doug felt a wave of relief. The Escala were safe. Zod and Quark, along with their heroic volunteers, had fooled the Elite Ops.

Yet no one dared leave. They stood quietly, watching the projections, their faces tense with anticipation. Didn't they know their plan had succeeded?

"We won," Doug said. "They're leavin'." Even as he spoke, he knew he was expressing a wish more than a reality, but he nevertheless believed he was right.

However, as the Elite Ops neared the camera, they began to spread out—one here, two there—moving through 360 degrees. Only two carried on with the recovered bodies. The others all resumed their search pattern, more methodically now. Something inside Doug sank as he realized their efforts had been in vain.

* * *

When the battle on the monitors ended, Sister Ezekiel removed her glasses and wiped her eyes. A hollow feeling worked its way to the core of her being, an emptiness that stained her soul. Replacing her glasses, she whispered a prayer for the dead, and for the lost souls of these Elite Ops troopers. Glancing around the quiet room at the shocked faces, the sickened expressions, she noticed the deathly pallor of Devereaux's face. He'd been right to be concerned about the Escala. Had he also been right to be concerned about the future of humanity? She had no trouble believing the government would invade his brain to learn the secrets of his bioweapons. But when they forcibly extracted those designs from his brain, would they use them? Someone would, she knew—someone who cared more about power than his fellow man.

"We need to call the President," Weiss said. "Colonel, bring Mr. Devereaux along." He started for Sister Ezekiel's office. Colonel Truman, holding Devereaux by the arm, followed.

"I think not," Carlton said. In his right hand he held a small weapon, which he aimed at Weiss. "Sorry, Gray. You're no longer in charge here."

Through the open doorway, Major Payne and two Elite Ops troopers appeared. The troopers grabbed Jeremiah by the arms, while Major Payne took Devereaux from Colonel Truman's grasp.

Seconds later, two more Elite Ops troopers filled the doorway. The two who had Jeremiah in their hands hustled him out of the room, down the hall toward Dr. Mary's bedroom.

Chapter Thirty-One

The plastic handcuffs bit into Jeremiah's wrists, painfully restricting the blood flow to his hands, causing his fingers to tingle and itch. They were attached to a bracket on the wall by a five-foot plastic leash he tested only once—a quick tug that tightened the cuffs and left him with a growing numbness in his hands. He sat on the bed where Julianna had tended his wound yesterday, his back throbbing, an agony that radiated outward, making his head ache and his gut roil. He deserved the pain.

Why had he let the EOs dictate his course? They'd played him like virtuosos. He was too old, too tired to survive in the field any longer. He should have diverted the Elite Ops away from Julianna, away from the other Escala, away from Devereaux. But he'd stayed close by and now Julianna was dead.

And it wasn't just Julianna. The Escala were in trouble too. He felt like he owed them something. He and they were alike—all mutants. Some small fraction of him was what: lion or tiger or panther? He felt catlike. As if whatever changes had been made were feline. Leopard, maybe. No doubt some combination of animal genomes.

Also, Carlton now had Devereaux and would certainly figure out a way to extract the bioweapon designs from Devereaux's head.

Jeremiah longed to put Carlton in a cold, damp basement where he could discover what Carlton knew about his son's disappearance. He wondered if he would ever learn the truth about Joshua, or if he'd have his mind taken apart like Devereaux's—Jack Marschenko's location extracted from it before he was killed or locked away in some dark cell to stew in the failure that was his legacy. And he'd never see his son again.

What Jeremiah needed was action, any sort of physical movement that would allow him not to think about what Eli had done to him, or the fact that Lendra must have known he was a mutant. Or the fact that now, too late, he saw that Julianna had truly managed to turn her life around. She'd found her way back from the depths of the horror to which Eli had consigned her.

He glanced around the room, hoping to find something that might help him escape. It looked different now, more like a doctor's room, with a sterile quality about it, a clinical coldness that sprang from emptiness, or perhaps from the fact that Julianna was never coming back. It seemed tiny now. He'd never before been claustrophobic, but he now experienced a sudden, almost overwhelming urge to break free.

An EO trooper opened the door, looked the room over, then let Carlton and Lendra enter. Carlton said, "Where is Jack Marschenko?"

"Is he missing?" Jeremiah said.

Carlton's head went still, and though Jeremiah couldn't see his eyes behind the sunglasses, he figured the man was staring at him, trying to intimidate him. After a few seconds, Carlton said, "You have twenty minutes, Miss Riley." Nodding to the EO guard, Carlton departed. The EO shut the door, remaining outside.

Lendra sat next to Jeremiah on the bed, the faint flowery aroma of her perfume surprising him for some reason. It was such a civilized smell, so out of place here.

"I'm sorry I didn't tell you—"

Jeremiah held up his hands to stop her. He leaned over and whispered in her ear, "Push that button next to the door three times in rapid succession."

"What?" Lendra said aloud.

Jeremiah shook his head and pointed to the button.

Lendra stood, walked to the door and pressed the button three times. The light went on and off and on, then the room hummed almost imperceptibly.

"Privacy field," Jeremiah said. "We can only leave it on for a few seconds before they get suspicious at the lack of sound."

Lendra nodded. She clasped her hands together and said, "I'm sorry I didn't tell you you're like the Escala. Eli felt your best protection was not to know."

"Why do they have doubts about whether I am one?"

"Because you're the next generation. Your DNA was a perfect match."

"Turn it off," Jeremiah said, indicating the button. "And remember, they're monitoring what we say."

Lendra pushed the button again and the humming stopped. When she returned to the bed, she lowered herself slowly.

Jeremiah sat quietly. Out of the corner of his eye, he saw Lendra reach out tentatively toward his hands, which rested on his thigh. He shifted slightly, moving his hands a couple inches away, and she retreated.

"I'm sure Eli's talking with the President right now," Lendra said. "They'll be figuring out their next move. Before we left, the President granted you amnesty, making your…modifications…legal. So you don't have to worry about that."

Jeremiah snorted. "So I won't have to worry about being prosecuted for Eli's decision to alter my DNA without my knowledge or consent? What about the Elite Ops?"

"The President will contact Mr. Carlton soon. She'll order your release. Now that Devereaux's in custody, the President will take care of this mess. I don't think Devereaux actually produced his bioweapons or the Escala would have used them on us already."

Jeremiah shook his head. "He never intended to use them. The President wants them. Eli and Carlton want them. Maybe even Weiss. But Devereaux never intended to destroy humanity. This was all for nothing—worse than nothing. Now dozens are dead, including Julianna."

Lendra reached out hesitantly and, when he did not pull his head away, touched his face, her fingers cool and delicate. She turned his head until he was looking at her. "I'm so sorry, Jeremiah. I know you cared for her."

"She saved my life. She had a chance for freedom but she chose to come back for me…*for me*."

Her eyes began to water. Dabbing at the tears, she said, "You're worth saving."

"No, I'm not."

"You don't see it, do you? You're so much better than you think you are."

Jeremiah shook his head. He stared at her dully, not wanting to hear compliments when he'd failed so miserably. Why couldn't she just leave him alone?

She grabbed him again, pinching his jaw between her fingers and shaking his head. "Don't you quit! Not on me and not on yourself, either. Understand? Otherwise, Julianna's death will have been for nothing. You hear me?"

"What do you care about her?"

She dropped her hands to his, began massaging his fingers as a frown ridged her forehead. "I don't care about her. I care about you. Maybe you don't want to hear that. Maybe you're still too wrapped up in the pain. But I understand you. You blame yourself for her death. You feel this stupid need to accept responsibility for every bad thing that happens. You're so gifted, so intelligent, so caring, you think you ought to be able to save everyone. And when you can't—because after all you're just one man—you figure it's your fault. Well, I'm sorry but that's wrong."

He shook his head, wanting to deny what she said. But he did blame himself and for good reason. He should have done more.

"You're not perfect," Lendra added, as if reading his mind. "Everyone makes mistakes. But by dwelling on them, you compound your errors."

She sounded like Julianna and even a little like Catherine: all of them strong women in their own ways. But Catherine had broken and Julianna had died and it was his job to go on even though he wasn't sure he wanted to any longer. If it weren't for Joshua, he could surrender to the pain. But he refused to give up.

Before he could reply, Carlton opened the door. "That's enough for now, Miss Riley."

Lendra pulled her hands away from Jeremiah's and said, "Has the President called yet?"

"Yes, she has."

"Then Jeremiah is free to go."

"I'm afraid there are still some things to clear up. Until that's done, he will have to remain in custody."

"You can't treat him like a prisoner."

"I can do as I please, Miss Riley. And right now it pleases me to keep Mr. Jones under guard."

"This will not go unreported, Mr. Carlton."

Carlton smiled—the smile of a predator.

Lendra turned to face Jeremiah and said, "I'm sorry."

As Jeremiah nodded, he kept his attention on Carlton.

"Now," Carlton said, "where is Jack Marschenko?"

Jeremiah shook his head. "Where is my son?"

"Dead, most likely," Carlton said. "You'll be joining him soon enough—as soon as we get Jack's location from you."

"Mr. Carlton," Lendra said. "The President has granted Jeremiah amnesty. She's also sent us here as her representatives. And she expects us to be returned to Washington safely. Need I remind you—"

"A lot of things can happen between now and Washington," Carlton said. "For example, Mr. Jones could try to escape. He could be seriously injured in the attempt—even killed."

Carlton stepped forward and punched Jeremiah in the face. Lendra screamed. Anticipating the attack, Jeremiah managed to avoid the bulk of the blow, snapping his head backward at the moment of impact and falling to the bed. Carlton advanced on him, his fists in position to strike again.

"Get up," Carlton said.

"Stop it," Lendra yelled.

Carlton reached down with his left hand and grabbed Jeremiah's camo-fatigues, pulling him off the bed. Holding Jeremiah with his left hand, he let fly with his right. Again, Jeremiah timed the blow, moving his head to the side so that the force of the punch was minimized. Carlton shifted position in front of the bed, his legs slightly apart, making him vulnerable. But Jeremiah, held up by Carlton, could gain no purchase. With his hands locked together and tethered to the wall, he couldn't even take a swing.

Carlton punched him twice more. Twice more, Jeremiah managed to lessen the impact of the blows. But Carlton began to adapt, driving his punches deeper, hitting Jeremiah again and again. Each blow landed with brutal power.

Fighting to stay conscious, his head feeling like a punching bag, Jeremiah swung his legs up and kicked out, pushing Carlton away. When Carlton let go of him, Jeremiah fell to the bed. His back sent jolts of pain through his body, but a rush of adrenaline surged through him as Carlton closed again. This time, Carlton avoided Jeremiah's face. His fists pummeled Jeremiah's stomach, each heavy blow sapping Jeremiah's energy. Jeremiah focused on Carlton's movements and positioning, looking for an edge.

He took punch after punch, twisting his body to avoid the worst of them. Then he sagged suddenly, letting Carlton hit him without resistance. As Carlton shifted his legs for an uppercut to the jaw, Jeremiah brought his right leg up with all the force he could muster. His foot landed squarely between Carlton's legs, dropping Carlton in a shriek of agony, his hands clutching himself and his head banging against the floor, breaking his sunglasses and cutting him beside his left eye.

The EO guard watched without interfering, but never took his Las-rifle off Jeremiah.

Gasping for breath, Carlton finally managed to croak, "Kill him."

"No!" Lendra threw herself on Jeremiah, covering him as best she could with her body. She wrapped her arms and legs around him, her face pressed against his, her eyes scrunched shut in anticipation of pain. Jeremiah could see almost nothing but her head, though the EO guard appeared to be moving to his left for a better shot. Instinctively, Jeremiah moved, swinging Lendra to his right to keep her body as a shield.

Finally, the guard reached out with his left hand and pulled Lendra free, as if she weighed no more than a child. Dropping her on the floor, he aimed his Las-rifle at Jeremiah's head. Jeremiah stared into the helmet. This was it. He felt no sorrow at the prospect. Many regrets, but no sorrow. He wondered if Devereaux was right and this was all the world there was. Or was there an afterlife? Would he see Joshua there with Catherine?

Would Sister Ezekiel say a prayer for him? Would Eli even care that he was gone? Or would he just find someone else to do his dirty work, someone else he could modify into a stronger, faster killing machine? And what about Lendra? Would she miss him? Was her effort to protect him anything more than a simple compassionate reflex?

The soldier should have fired by now. But he never pulled the trigger. Instead, Major Payne strode through the door and helped Carlton to his feet. He must have been monitoring the soldier and countermanded the order to fire.

"I want him dead," Carlton's voice came out as a hoarse whisper.

"Not yet," Major Payne said. "Not until we find Jack." He grabbed Lendra's arm, pulling her to her feet.

Carlton's breathing came in ragged gasps. He glared at Major Payne before shifting his gaze to Jeremiah. "You'd better be careful, Jones. Anything happens to me and you'll see a holocaust like never before."

Then Major Payne hustled Lendra and Carlton out the door.

Chapter Thirty-Two

Colonel Truman approached Gray Weiss, who now sat in a chair by the side of the lobby, face pinched in pain, shoulders hunched, skin pallid gray, with dark marks of exhaustion under his eyes.

"What's happening out there?" Weiss said, motioning him to sit. "Are your people prisoners too?"

"I don't quite know, sir." Truman took the chair next to Weiss. "They're not letting my soldiers leave the parking lot. They're claiming it's not safe beyond that point. They're also restricting the media and the homeless men to the immediate area. But we can move freely about the shelter and they haven't taken away our weapons."

"I've made a royal mess of things," Weiss said. He looked across the lobby at the two Elite Ops troopers guarding the entrance. One faced out, the other in. "I just wanted to stop terrorism, rescue America, and all I required was for Carlton to act honorably."

Truman bent forward, speaking in a low voice. "He can't think he'll succeed. Even if he controls every Elite Ops trooper, there are less than two hundred nationwide. The combined strength of the Armed Forces will—"

"Defeat them? I wouldn't count on that, Colonel. The way Carlton and I had it figured, most of the military would sit out this uprising, wait to commit their units until they understood the potential consequences. By the time they decided to throw their support behind one side or the other, it would be too late. I would be firmly entrenched in office and my policies would have brought back a strong central government, restoration of civil order, a revitalized military."

"Why would you partner with a man like him?" Truman asked.

"We were effective together once, Colonel, when we were in the CIA. He was a good operative. Now, with the Elite Ops to back him, he might succeed in overthrowing the government."

"Carlton's just the head of a security company. How can he take over the country?"

"There's an old saying, Colonel. 'All it takes for evil to triumph is for good men to do nothing.' That's what Carlton is counting on."

"And what you were counting on too, sir. Don't forget that."

"I'm not likely to forget it. But my intentions were always honorable. I simply wanted to replace a dysfunctional democracy with an oligarchy that could ensure our survival. Our existing government clearly doesn't work anymore."

"And this is better?"

"I didn't anticipate it would turn out like this, Colonel. I didn't realize that Carlton is nothing but a power seeker—a megalomaniac."

"Is that supposed to make me feel better, sir?"

"Why did you stick by me?"

Truman shrugged. "I hadn't decided to, actually. After we killed Raddock Boyd..."

"That was an accident, Colonel."

"I contemplated calling General Horowitz but I waited too long. Now the Elite Ops' communications blackout prevents that. I'm surprised they're letting the media record stories for later."

"Those stories will never be filed."

Truman looked at Weiss, realized immediately what the Attorney General was saying, and shivered as a chill traveled down his spine. "You think the Elite Ops will murder them?"

"You saw what they did out there. This coup has to be quick and relatively bloodless. Carlton has to take control before the President discovers she's lost power. He'll want to buy as much time as he can. And the best way to do that is to make sure there are no leaks—no witnesses."

"What about my soldiers? Are they at risk?"

"I may be wrong," Weiss said. "I hope I am. But I know the way he thinks. And I wouldn't be surprised if he ordered the Elite Ops to kill everyone. At a minimum, he'll detain everybody until he's safely back in Washington."

"Surely the Elite Ops won't all back Carlton? Some of them must be rational."

"They'll do as they're ordered. Carlton told me he knew how to control…"

The sound of a body being slammed against the wall came from the hallway, followed by a cry of pain. Truman looked up and saw a homeless man skidding across the floor. Behind him Carlton emerged from the hall, limping heavily, Major Payne at his side. Carlton's sunglasses sat slightly askew on his nose and a fresh cut at the side of his eye bled a little. As he neared, he reached up and touched it with his finger. After a quick glance, he wiped the finger on his trousers. Despite his wan pallor, he wore a determined look. Had Jeremiah done that to Carlton? Truman wished he'd seen it.

"Two hours, Major," Carlton said. "I want to be out of here in two hours."

"We need more time to locate the other pseudos."

"Most of your men can stay. But I require your presence in Washington with me. Once the situation has stabilized, you can return to finish the mop-up duties."

"If there are any pseudos left alive." Major Payne sounded disappointed.

"There may be a stray pseudo for you to track down. You can even order your men to take a few of them alive. I'm sure they're wonderful sport." Carlton paused, looked down at Weiss. "Now, then, Gray Velvet. What to do about you?"

"You planning to kill me, RC?"

Carlton's smile stopped almost before it began. "I could get away with it, but no. You and Devereaux are far too valuable to waste."

"And how do you plan to use us? As admirers of your coup?"

"That's not too far off, actually. You see, Gray, in our experimentation with the Elite Ops, we've discovered a lot about the human brain. We can manipulate electrical signals to get a person to do what we want him to."

Weiss laughed bitterly. "You're going to brainwash us?"

Carlton displayed his fleeting smile again. "Such an old-fashioned term for such an advanced science. We alter your neural pathways, stimulate certain regions of the brain while repressing others. When I'm finished with you, you will truly believe that what I've done is in the best interests of the country. And you will say so for the world to hear." Carlton held up a hand to preempt any response. "Don't worry. Forewarned is not forearmed. You won't be able to resist. We've had a perfect success rate. You'll still be you. Nothing will have really changed except that when I trot you out to the cameras, you'll say what I want you to say—that for national security reasons we must suspend the protections of the Constitution. Temporarily. The President will agree with you. She will regretfully conclude that, in these troubled times, we need the Elite Ops to run the country until the terrorists have been stamped out."

Truman jumped to his feet. "You're insane!"

Major Payne put out an armored hand and easily pushed him back to his seat.

Carlton spoke softly, contemptuously, "You, Colonel, I don't need at all. I would suggest you rein in that temper."

"I'm afraid you underestimate the public," Weiss said.

"Oh, but I don't. After I empty Devereaux's brain of all its secrets, I'll turn him loose on the intellectuals. You'll convince the conservatives that this necessary suspension is only temporary, and the President will do the same for the liberals. And if the public doesn't buy it, what can they do about it? Die before the power of the Elite Ops? Or one of the bioweapons Devereaux designed?" Carlton smiled. "Yeah, we're going to build those weapons if he hasn't done so already. We'll be able to hold the world hostage. Once order has been re-established, elections will return—for most offices. It's largely your plan, Gray. I've merely refined it. Don't go anywhere now."

Chuckling to himself, Carlton limped away, Major Payne at his heels.

Truman wanted not to believe it. It sounded ludicrous. "We have to do something, sir," he said to Weiss. "We can't just let him fly out of here with you and Devereaux."

"I'd like to stop him, Colonel. But I don't know how."

"Perhaps we could use Jones."

Weiss looked around, noticed that no one was paying much attention to them. "What did you have in mind?"

Truman hunched forward, lowered his voice still further. "We both know my men are no match for the Elite Ops. But perhaps, together with Jones, if we could somehow spring him and return his particle beam cannon, we could defeat them."

"Jeremiah?" Weiss shook his head. "Even if he'd be willing to help us, how do you propose we do that?"

"I don't know yet, sir. Obviously, we need a distraction large enough to draw the attention of the Elite Ops. But short of attacking them, which would almost certainly be suicide, I can't think of a way to get the job done."

Weiss pursed his lips. "I know a little about how Carlton conditioned the Elite Ops. And provided he hasn't given any kill orders yet, so long as your soldiers don't use their weapons—strictly hand-to-hand combat—the Elite Ops shouldn't respond with lethal force. At the very least, they won't be expecting a diversion like that. You might also check with Lendra—see if she'll aid us in recovering the converter to Jeremiah's weapon."

Truman nodded. "Assuming she knows where it is. I'll speak to her...and Sister Ezekiel too. She may be able to help as well."

Weiss slapped his closed fist into his palm. "If we can get Carlton out of the picture, I'm sure the Elite Ops would be controllable. But we've got to move quickly. You heard Carlton. We've got less than two hours."

* * *

Truman located Sister Ezekiel with the albino, Henry, and a couple dozen ailing homeless men in the chapel. Everyone was avoiding the infirmary because of the soldiers quarantined there. The medics had confirmed that the three soldiers had in fact contracted the Susquehanna Virus.

Sister Ezekiel said, "How are your infected soldiers doing?"

"Private Xiong could go at any moment. Corporal Douphmaly and Specialist Hanaka are hanging on."

"And how are you holding up, Colonel?"

"My nerves are on edge, my patience gone. Of course, the Elite Ops have that effect. They emit a sonic wave—that high whine you hear coming from their nuclear power packs. It jangles the brain. Grating."

Sister Ezekiel actually smiled. "So it's not just me? That's a relief. I thought I was falling apart under the stress."

"No. Add in their nerve gas and it's a wonder any of us can think straight."

"What can I do for you, Colonel?"

"I need a private word."

Sister Ezekiel turned to Henry and said, "I'll be back in a moment." Truman led her out to the hall, where two homeless men sat with their backs against one wall, blankets up to their chins despite the heat, staring at nothing, blank expressions on their dirty, gaunt faces. Truman passed them by, continuing on to the kitchen, where he found Lendra standing by one of the large sinks, rubbing her arms as if to keep warm. It must be the fear that makes everyone cold, Truman thought.

He beckoned Lendra over and immediately got to the point. "We have to somehow free Devereaux," he whispered, "before Carlton leaves. We can't let Carlton have him. He'll unleash Devereaux's bioweapons on the world."

Sister Ezekiel put up her hand. "How? How can your soldiers fight those Elite Ops? They're like machines."

"It's going to be difficult, Sister. We may all die in the attempt. But better to go down fighting than sit around waiting for death."

"You believe our lives are in danger?"

"Yes, Sister. I do. Carlton is a dangerous man—much more so than Weiss. I think he'll have us killed when he leaves, to ensure secrecy in his attempt to overthrow the government. His troopers murdered thirty-two fugitives last night."

Sister Ezekiel's jaw dropped and her face, already pale, lightened further.

Lendra said, "It's true, Sister. I've been able to monitor local communications traffic with my interface. And I agree with Colonel Truman that Carlton is a threat." She looked at him. "What do you want us to do?"

Truman said, "To have any chance at all, we need to get the converter to Jeremiah's particle beam cannon. Do you know where it is?"

Lendra said, "I can get it. But you need Jeremiah too. He's the only one who can handle the weapon. Your men would never be able to get off more than a single shot. And they probably wouldn't hit what they were aiming at."

"What do you know about particle beam cannons?"

"Their heavy recoil requires tremendous strength, a steady hand and superb reflexes."

Truman stared at her. He knew enough about particle beam cannons to know she was telling the truth, but he wondered how she knew so much about a classified weapon. Perhaps Jones had told her. Or perhaps she was a field agent after all. "Don't worry," he said, "Jeremiah's an integral part of the plan. We obviously need his help. I just have to figure out a way to free him."

Lendra grabbed the glass bulb of her necklace between thumb and forefinger. Rubbing it, she nodded deliberately. "Sister Ezekiel and I will take care of that. You just keep the Elite Ops busy until Jeremiah gets loose."

Chapter Thirty-Three

Accompanied by Ahmad Rashidi, Sister Ezekiel approached her office. Major Payne blocked the doorway, an imposing presence, his shield glowing faintly. Behind him, Devereaux sat on a chair in front of the desk. Carlton reclined on the sofa, his legs spread apart, feet on the coffee table. The quartz paperweight Rock Man—no, Devereaux—had given her lay on the corner of the desk, shining in the light.

She prayed. Courage, Lord—give me courage. "Excuse me," she said.

Major Payne didn't move. Carlton looked up but said nothing.

"Look," Sister Ezekiel said, "I've got a shelter to run. I know your jobs are important, but people are relying on me. This is my office. Between you two and Mr. Weiss, I've had barely five minutes in here the past couple of days. Now, come on, you big lug. Out of my way."

She put her hands through Major Payne's shield, feeling an electric tingle as she did so, and pushed against his armor. The major backed up a step, allowing her to pass. Ahmad squeezed in behind her.

Carlton looked at Major Payne, smiled and shook his head. "I'm sorry, Sister. But we need a temporary office. We'll have this man out of your hair in less than two hours."

"So this is the famous Walt Devereaux," she said.

Carlton nodded. "He hasn't spoken to us yet, but he will."

Ignoring Carlton, Devereaux looked at Sister Ezekiel, no sign of fear or panic in his eyes, and said calmly: "I'm afraid your shelter is going to have to be rebuilt, Sister."

"It speaks," Carlton said.

"Are you okay?" Sister Ezekiel asked Devereaux.

"I sense that you're troubled, Sister. Let me assure you that what you're doing is right. It's good. It serves an important purpose. You give these lost men—" Devereaux paused, smiled— "you give *us* dignity, respect, a reason not to give up on the world, even though it may have given up on us."

"All right, Devereaux," Carlton interrupted. "Now that you're in the mood to talk, I've got some questions for you."

Devereaux glanced at Carlton, said nothing, then turned back to Sister Ezekiel. "I will see to it, Sister, that you get whatever funds you need to rebuild. You must keep this place going."

Carlton said, "I don't think you're in a position to promise anything, *Walt*."

Sister Ezekiel addressed Carlton. "Why is everyone being kept under guard? Several people have told me that your soldiers won't let them out."

"It's dangerous out there, Sister," Carlton said. "We know there are still some pseudos running around. We're close to finding them. They may be like Jones, not registering as pseudos on our scanners. Not to mention the separatists who attacked earlier. Some of them might still be on the loose. I've already lost two men today. I don't want to lose any more."

"There have been a great many lives lost lately. But that's no reason to keep us locked up. We ought to be able to decide for ourselves whether we want to risk leaving."

"Do you wish to leave, Sister?"

"We're running short of supplies," Sister Ezekiel said. "We need to make a trip to the market. We weren't expecting to have to feed so many people."

"My men can take care of that for you."

"That's all right," Sister Ezekiel said. "We'll go. I just need to get my purse."

Carlton nodded. "Very well, Sister. But I can't guarantee your safety."

"And I would like Ahmad here to talk with Mr. Devereaux for a few minutes. Do you have any objection to that?"

Carlton turned to Ahmad, said, "You think he'll talk to you?"

"I'll talk with him," Devereaux said to Carlton. "He's worth talking to."

"And why is that?"

"Because Ahmad is a believer in the great god, Allah, whereas all you believe in is power and killing."

Ahmad shook his head. "I don't understand you, Mr. Devereaux. But I would certainly like to speak with you." He looked at Carlton with a raised eyebrow.

"We stay in the room," Carlton said.

"Excellent," Sister Ezekiel said. "Ahmad, please see if there is anything we can do for Mr. Devereaux."

"I'm surprised at you, Sister," Carlton said. "I would have thought you would hate a man like Devereaux."

"You should talk to Mr. Weiss," Sister Ezekiel said. "He and I have already had this conversation."

Ahmad said, "Mr. Devereaux, if you wish, I will serve as your attorney while you are here in custody of the Elite Ops."

"He has no right to an attorney," Carlton said.

Sister Ezekiel said, "Mr. Weiss told me he did."

"Mr. Weiss is no longer in charge here."

She grabbed her purse. "We'll be back in about twenty minutes. I'd like to speak to Mr. Jones when I return, if that's all right?"

"Why do you want to speak to him?"

"I merely wish to assure myself that he is not being mistreated on shelter property. I have a Christian duty to ensure his well-being. Surely you can appreciate that?"

Carlton stared at her. "Very well, Sister. Come see me and I'll take you to him."

* * *

Sister Ezekiel left for the market with Lendra, Henry, Jackson and Tremaine, and five of her guests who were looking for something to do. Sister Ezekiel knew two of them—Santos and Melville—rather well. The other three she recognized even though she couldn't recall their nicknames. Since the road was impassable, they had to walk. Two Elite Ops troopers guarded the parking lot in front of the shelter, where the reporters and Colonel Truman's soldiers were confined. Another two were stationed at the entryway. The one with the gold cross on his chest nodded to her as she passed. The reporters shouted a jumble of questions, out of which the only word she could understand was "Devereaux." She ignored them. Through the lingering smoke of the morning battles, the sun bathed the wrecked vehicles and twisted armor that littered the ruined street in a golden glow, making them look like part of a sculpture—as if Armageddon had occurred along this one block. The surreptitious reporter with the orange hair was talking to one of the homeless men—it looked like Flyer—and his hair shone in the light.

Her heart lifted slightly as she moved away from the shelter, as if the increasing distance diminished the effect the Elite Ops had on her. She still felt exhausted; she still worried about Devereaux. But all she could do now was act, and hope her actions didn't get anyone else killed, even as the facts told her more people would die. Yet more were going to die whether she helped or not. So she chose to help.

The walk to the market seemed like a walk through a ghost town, all its residents hidden behind locked doors. The market was closed.

Sister Ezekiel pulled out her PlusPhone and called Ernie Olsen, the store's manager, who lived across the street. When he finally answered, she asked if he could open for a few minutes so she could restock some supplies. She spotted him peeking out through his curtains, his thin, nervous face looking both ways before settling on her and her entourage. He told her he'd be right over.

After he unlocked the door and let them in, Sister Ezekiel gave the grocery list to Henry and said, "I should be back in five minutes. Remember, only what's on the list."

"Where are you going?" Henry asked.

"I'm walking Lendra to her vehicle," Sister Ezekiel said. "Now do as I say."

Lendra headed out the door, Sister Ezekiel following. "I still think we can trust Henry," she said to Lendra as they walked down the street.

"He would do whatever I asked of him."

"No doubt, Sister," Lendra replied, "but the fewer people who know what we're up to, the better. Not to mention, safer for them."

Up ahead, Sister Ezekiel saw the shattered base of the statue and experienced anew the disgust and fear from the night before. A part of her felt worse about the statue's destruction than about the loss of life. Had she loved the statue that much? How could she place the value of a piece of rock above the lives of human beings? She chided herself for her unholy thoughts, promising to do penance when she got an opportunity, and asked, "Did the Elite Ops really murder thirty-two fugitives last night?"

"I assume the fugitives fired first," Lendra replied. "But there were women and children in the group as well. Everyone was killed."

"And you think they might kill us?"

"People who could blow up something as beautiful as that," Lendra pointed to the jagged granite sticking out of the ground and shivered, "well, I wouldn't put anything past them."

Sister Ezekiel said, "What about this invisible cloak idea? Will it work against those *creatures*?"

"Normally, I would say no. The way scanner technology is today, camo-fatigues don't have the same effectiveness they used to. But we're counting on the Elite Ops not being able to use their scanners effectively with all the people around. Too much interference."

Lendra reached Jeremiah's van and punched in a code next to the door handle. When the light went from red to yellow, she opened the door and climbed inside. Rummaging through Jeremiah's bag, she found the converter Jeremiah had placed there and handed it to Sister Ezekiel.

"Hold this for a minute," she said as she pulled out the camo-fatigue coveralls. She stepped into the coveralls, pulling them up over her shoulders and slipping her hands into the coverall's gloves. Then she tucked her hair into the hood. Before zipping it up, she showed Sister Ezekiel the control pad inside the left breast. "It's activated here. Millions of tiny sensors read the background in every direction, adjusting how light is reflected and absorbed, making the wearer invisible to the human eye. Plus, Jeremiah modified this unit with a scatterer, which diffuses the wearer's bio-readings. That should make it almost impossible for a scanner to lock onto my bio-signature."

"But didn't the colonel say these Elite Ops have enhanced vision? Infrared, radiation—I don't remember what else."

"We have to take a chance, Sister. The scatterer should take care of that. Besides, we have no other choice."

"You're putting yourself in awful danger. I don't like to think what those soldiers will do if they spot you."

"Colonel Truman said he would try to create a distraction as we enter the building. Hopefully, that will be enough to get me inside. Hand me the converter."

Sister Ezekiel handed the device to Lendra, who placed it in an inside pocket. She then reached inside the van and grabbed a knife, which she slid into a sheath. Moving her fingers over the control pad, she activated the scatterer and sensors. Finally she finished zipping up the coveralls. Within seconds all but her face vanished. Even though Sister Ezekiel had known it was coming, it startled her. Suddenly encountering a disembodied face left her with a feeling of unreality.

"Impressive," Lendra said, "isn't it?"

"Amazing. Like you're no longer there. But what about your face? I can still see that."

"There's a separate piece that pulls down from the hood. Let me just find it."

Lendra's face cocked at an angle, her face scrunching up with effort. Then it too vanished.

"All right, Sister," Lendra said. "How does it look? Can you see me at all?"

"No," Sister Ezekiel said. "I can't see anything."

"Good."

As Sister Ezekiel continued to stare, she imagined that she could see something where Lendra stood. At first, it appeared to be a slightly greater brightness to the space Lendra occupied. But it slowly grew into a distinct emanation of light.

"Wait," Sister Ezekiel said. "There's something wrong. I can see a glow of energy or something. It's green."

"I see it," Lendra said. "It must be the converter reacting with the sensors. You're going to have to carry it, Sister."

Sister Ezekiel heard the sound of a zipper being undone, saw a flash of Lendra's shirt, then the converter appeared before her. It had no glow about it now. She grabbed it out of the air and placed it in her right pocket. Lendra zipped the coveralls up.

"How about now?" she asked.

Sister Ezekiel looked again. The glow had vanished. "You're completely invisible," she said.

"Good. Let's get back to the market. Just forget about me as best you can. I'll follow you to the shelter. Now that you've got the converter, everything depends on you getting in to see Jeremiah."

"How will I know if you made it inside the shelter?"

"If I don't, there'll be a ruckus."

* * *

Ernie Olsen hurried through the transaction, helping them bag their groceries for the first time ever. While they packed the bags, Sister Ezekiel looked up and saw one of the Elite Ops at the window. He stared at her or at least seemed to—his visored head motionless. Was this it? Did he know Lendra was missing? Could he see her despite her camo-fatigues? Sister Ezekiel watched him until he turned away. Then she realized that she'd been holding her breath and inhaled.

In less than a minute they were out the door, Ernie Olsen locking it behind them and hurrying back across the street to his house. The Elite Ops trooper was nowhere to be seen. As Sister Ezekiel led the group to the shelter, she tried to be nonchalant, but each noise portended betrayal for Lendra: the scuffing of shoes on pavement, the rustle of one pant leg against the other, the crinkle of the grocery bags.

Agitation swept through her, despite the silent prayers she uttered, until a picture formed inside her mind: a gentle soul who wished harm upon no one; a man who preached peace and spirituality even in the absence of the Eternal. As she felt his warmth, she relaxed slightly. Everything was going to be all right. Then her foot caught on a crack in the sidewalk and she tripped. One of her bags spilled its contents to the sidewalk: oranges and apples. She managed to break her fall but her glasses flew off, and she scraped her knee and the palm of her hand.

Henry grabbed her arm and said, "Are you all right, Sister?"

"Stupid," she answered. "I should have watched where I was going." She looked toward the shelter, noticed the fuzzy images of the Elite Ops. A point on one of the troopers reflected the sun—a glittering diamond that dazzled with its brightness—and she knew it had to be the one with the gold cross on his chest. Henry helped her to her feet as the men rushed to repack her bag.

"Your glasses, Sister." Henry handed them to her. One of the lenses had cracked and the frame was twisted. Sighing, Sister Ezekiel put the glasses in her left pocket.

"Let me carry your bags, Sister," Henry said.

"No," she replied. "Your arms are full. I can make it." Something touched her elbow—Lendra. She shrugged it off as she trudged forward. Up ahead, the Elite Ops searched one of the homeless men before allowing him to re-enter the shelter. She was going to be searched! Colonel Truman had said he'd create a diversion, have one of his men challenge an Elite Ops trooper to a fight, but she didn't see how that would get her inside. She had to do this on her own. She could think of only one thing to do—something completely unexpected—but she was afraid. The hair on the back of her neck stood up, goose flesh pimpling her forearms. There was no other way.

It's only pain.

For an instant she thought she heard a scream; she realized almost too late that one had been forming in her brain, working its way to her throat. She noticed Henry watching her. Had she made a sound after all? She smiled to show him she was fine.

The two Elite Ops troopers patrolling the parking lot followed their progress. Sister Ezekiel imagined that they could see right through her—human x-ray machines. Her palms and face were sweating, her heart pounding. A single rivulet worked down from her forehead, over the bridge of her nose to her lips. She licked the salty droplet.

Henry said, "Are you sure you're okay, Sister?"

"Of course," she answered. "Why?"

"You look whiter than me. If you like, we can leave your shopping bags here and come back for them. You really don't have to go along on these trips, you know. I'm sure you have more important things to do."

"I enjoy the walk," Sister Ezekiel croaked, her knees shaking, her sweaty back clinging to her habit, her mouth dry, the overwhelming fear she remembered so well returning once again. How she hated that fear. It shut her mind down, flooded her with painful memories. She forced herself to breathe deeply and walk at a normal pace. Up ahead, she heard a commotion. Now, she thought. Don't be afraid. God will protect you.

* * *

Truman walked past the monitors by the side of the jagged doorway and saw that Sister Ezekiel must have fallen, for she was picking herself up and retrieving her bags before starting once again for the shelter. He hoped she was okay. Where was Lendra? Did the nun have the converter, or was Lendra still looking for it? He glanced over at Lieutenant Adams, who sat outside the infirmary with Jones' particle beam cannon under a blanket. Truman had grabbed it from Sergeant Mecklenberg and given it to her to hold temporarily. He'd get it back from her once he knew Jones had the converter. Stepping outside, he tried to make eye contact with the nun. Although she wasn't wearing her glasses, she seemed to be eyeing the Elite Ops trooper guarding the door— the one with the gold cross on his body armor. Truman took a deep breath. He'd always hated the waiting, the dread and anticipation leading up to battle. The nun and her party made slow progress, but eventually neared Weiss' ruined command center—Sister Ezekiel looking frail and uncertain. Should he go through with the plan? He decided he had no choice. He had to assume that Sister Ezekiel and Lendra had been successful.

Truman nodded to Sergeant Mecklenberg, who stepped toward the Elite Ops. "Hey," Mecklenberg said as he pushed a trooper. "I heard you guys are tough. Why don't you take off that armor and we'll see?"

The Elite Ops trooper took a step backward, but his partner hit Mecklenberg from behind, knocking the big man to the ground. Mecklenberg skidded along the asphalt. Some diversion! These Elite Ops troopers were just too strong. Mecklenberg roared in pain as he got to his feet. He drew back his fist but, before he could deliver the blow, was knocked to his knees by one swing from the trooper. Truman glanced at Sister Ezekiel, who suddenly fell, her knees buckling and her face crashing into the ground.

Truman's stomach dropped. He rushed forward, but the Elite Ops trooper with the gold cross beat him to the spot, turning Sister Ezekiel over. Blood gushed from the nun's nose, splashing onto her habit. Her eyes focused on nothing; obviously she was unconscious.

Effortlessly, the Elite Ops trooper picked up Sister Ezekiel. Off to the side of the building, several soldiers snickered. Truman would punish them later. He glanced over at Mecklenberg. Somehow the big sergeant had gotten his arms wrapped around the waist of the Elite Ops trooper he'd targeted. But the trooper's arms were free. He brought his Las-rifle around and fired a purple pulse. Mecklenberg dropped.

Damn!

The trooper carried Sister Ezekiel inside the shelter. Henry called out and tried to push past the other guard, who stopped him with a hand and began searching his bags. Truman rushed past them, following the trooper and Sister Ezekiel inside, where he called for a medic. The trooper lowered Sister Ezekiel to the lobby's sofa as Corporal Snow rushed over. She went to work on the nun, whose nose was clearly broken. The areas around Sister Ezekiel's eyes had begun to darken.

Major Payne appeared next to him and said, "What happened?"

"She fainted," Truman said.

"Why did your man attack Red—Sergeant Combs?"

"Sergeant Mecklenberg thinks he's a tough guy," Colonel Truman said. "I told him to stay away. He must not have listened."

"Well, he won't be hearing anything anymore."

Truman shivered with regret and fear. Would Payne search Sister Ezekiel? And would he find the converter on her? Meanwhile, Major Payne stared at Truman. Was he receiving information from his troopers, replaying images from the past few minutes? Truman hoped there would be nothing incriminating there.

Corporal Snow, reaching out with a thumb, reset Sister Ezekiel's nose before the nun awoke. Even so, the unconscious woman moaned softly.

Henry knelt next to the sofa and said, "Is she going to be all right?"

"I think so," Truman replied.

Sister Ezekiel began to move her arms and head. Blinking rapidly, she opened her eyes and slowly focused on Truman—fear and confusion plain to see on her face.

"It's okay, Sister," he said, trying to smile reassuringly. "You're in the shelter. Looks like you fainted. Probably just stress. Right, Corporal?"

Corporal Snow nodded. She gave Sister Ezekiel an Icy-Pak for her nose.

Major Payne turned his visor to Sister Ezekiel. Was he scanning her for the converter? If she had it with her, would it emit an energy signature in this state? Finally Major Payne said, "Where is Ms. Riley?"

Henry answered: "She went to her vehicle."

"Why?"

Henry shrugged. "She didn't say."

Major Payne stared at him as if contemplating the veracity of his response. Slowly he turned his head, scanning the lobby. Then he marched into Sister Ezekiel's office. The trooper wearing the gold cross returned to his position outside the door.

As Sister Ezekiel struggled to sit up, Truman reached out to assist her. She put the Icy-Pak on her nose, winced, then turned to Henry and said, "I'm okay—just a headache. Please don't make a fuss. Would you help Jackson and Tremaine put the groceries away? Colonel, if you'll give me a hand, I would like to see Mr. Jones."

He pulled her to her feet. His voice filled with admiration, he said, "You are a formidable woman."

She whispered, "I have the converter. Lendra's inside."

"How…never mind. Get it to Jones. I'll get the particle beam cannon."

A hand grabbed his arm. Lendra! Ultimate Camos! He concentrated on looking out of the corner of his eye, imagined he saw a blurred shape that vanished immediately when he stared at it. A warm body pressed against him. She whispered in his ear, "Have it by the infirmary in twenty minutes."

As Sister Ezekiel walked unsteadily to her office, Truman quietly told Corporal Snow to pass the word that as soon as Jones broke free, every soldier was to attack the Elite Ops. "No weapons, though. Strictly hand-to-hand combat. Got it?"

"Yes, sir," Corporal Snow said. She moved off to tell Sergeant Corbin. Between the two of them, Truman knew they'd get the message across.

* * *

Lendra followed Sister Ezekiel to her office, where Major Payne stood just inside the door conversing in low tones with Carlton. Ahmad Rashidi sat beside Devereaux, gesticulating wildly, invoking Allah's name. When he and Devereaux looked up and saw the nun, their eyes widened. Carlton said, "Whoa, Sister. You look like you ran into a truck. You okay?"

Lendra, in her Ultimate Camos, tried to stand still. She felt completely exposed, convinced that the Elite Ops would spot her any second.

Devereaux and Ahmad leapt to their feet and reached out to Sister Ezekiel but she waved them off. "Sit. I'm sure it looks worse than it is. Just fainted. Haven't had much sleep lately. I'd like to see Mr. Jones now."

"Certainly," Carlton said calmly. "By the way, did Ms. Riley say whether she would be coming back?"

"No, she didn't," Sister Ezekiel said.

"Find her," Carlton said to Major Payne—a harsh command.

Lendra shrank against the outside of the doorframe, pressing herself into the wall.

Major Payne said, “I’ll notify my men to look for her. Also, I think we’ve found the pseudos’ hiding place. We’re checking it out now.”

“Excellent,” Carlton smiled. He glanced at his watch. “The copters are on their way. We’ll be out of here in half an hour. Stay sharp.”

Sister Ezekiel said, “May I see Mr. Jones now, please?”

Carlton looked her over before answering. “What you really need is a doctor. But if that’s what you want, I’ll take you to him.”

Major Payne stepped aside and Sister Ezekiel followed Carlton down the hall to Dr. Mary’s room. Lendra stayed a step behind her. She hoped the nun, after taking that terrible fall, wouldn’t forget about the converter. And she wondered how Sister Ezekiel intended to pass it along to her. Why hadn’t they discussed that?

“There,” Carlton said when they reached the open door. “You can see he’s fine.”

“May I speak with him, please?”

At Carlton’s signal, the guard moved, allowing Sister Ezekiel to pass. She hesitated just a second before entering the room, causing Lendra to run into her. As Sister Ezekiel stumbled, Lendra reached out and grabbed her arm. The nun managed to keep her feet, but dropped her Icy-Pak. The movement of her body looked very strange. Carlton stared at her, his dark glasses impenetrable, his jaw tense.

Jeremiah reached down for the Icy-Pak but his hands jerked against his bindings, stopping him short. He leaned back on the bed, looked at Lendra for an instant as if he could see her, then turned his attention to the nun. “Nice save, Sister,” he said. “I thought you were going to fall. What happened?”

“I fainted,” she answered as she bent down to pick up the pack. She pressed it against her nose. “Simple exhaustion. How are you, Mr. Jones?”

Carlton stepped forward and grabbed Jeremiah’s wrists. “Looks painful,” he said. “You keep struggling against those bindings and you’re liable to lose your hands.”

"Doesn't hurt anymore," Jeremiah said.

Carlton forced a smile. "We'll get you out of those once we're in the air."

Lendra could tell from his tone that he was saying what he thought Sister Ezekiel wanted to hear—still trying to manipulate her. Did he realize how transparent he sounded? Sister Ezekiel said, "Is there anything I can do for you?"

Jeremiah shifted his eyes to Carlton, raising one brow.

"You can ask," Carlton answered the unspoken question. "I may not allow it."

For a few seconds, Jeremiah said nothing. He reminded Lendra of a caged animal left in too small a space for too long. Cowed. Then he said, "I feel like I'm on display. Everybody who walks down the hall stares at me like I'm some sort of freakshow attraction. Could you just close the door when you leave? Give me a few last minutes of privacy?"

"Mr. Carlton?" Sister Ezekiel asked. "It seems like a harmless request."

"That's what bothers me," Carlton said.

"Aren't you leaving soon, anyway?"

Do it, Lendra thought. Stay on Sister Ezekiel's good side.

"Very well," Carlton said. "I can be magnanimous." He turned to the guard. "Keep your ears open. The copters will be here in twenty-five minutes."

The guard nodded.

"Sister?" Carlton said, gesturing toward the door. "I have a few things to take care of before we leave."

As Carlton turned to precede her out the door, stepping between her and the guard, blocking the guard's view for just a second, Sister Ezekiel reached into her pocket and pulled out the converter. Almost before her hand cleared her pocket Lendra snatched the device away.

Chapter Thirty-Four

As the door closed behind Sister Ezekiel, Jeremiah tried to relax his hands. Had he seen a faint swirling motion out of the corner of his eye when she entered the room, a slight imbalance in the distance between him and the wall that had then vanished? Was it a visual trick or was someone in the room with him?

Jeremiah heard three soft clicks as the light went on and off and on; then the faint hum of the privacy field engaged. He said, "Lendra?"

When her face appeared before him, he barely controlled the urge to laugh with relief.

"I brought a knife," she said as she turned off the camo-fatigues, "and this." She held the converter up with a tentative smile. Then she removed her hood, her dark hair framing her face, the smell of her sweat earthy, yet mixed with a hint of the flowery perfume he remembered she wore. He'd smelled it briefly when Sister Ezekiel was in the room but hadn't made the connection then. Careless. Jeremiah took in her scent, gazed upon her face and felt his heart reaching out to her. She unzipped the coveralls, and pulled out a knife.

Jeremiah shook his head. "Nice idea. But it won't cut through this stuff."

Lendra's shoulders slumped. "That's all I brought."

He pointed toward the chair behind the desk. "Take a seat."

"What? We don't have time for…"

"Sit down," Jeremiah said. "Unless I'm mistaken, Julianna would have hidden a weapon away in easy reach."

"Wouldn't they have already found it?" Lendra asked as she moved to comply. She placed the knife and converter on the desk, then sat in Julianna's chair.

"I doubt it," Jeremiah said. "Julianna would have found a way to give herself an edge. I never saw her go anywhere without a weapon, so she would have kept one here in case of emergency. Probably in the desk."

Lendra opened the top drawer and bent down to search through it.

"It won't be in any drawer," Jeremiah said. "It will be hidden, probably on the right side—she was right-handed—probably behind a false panel, just about where your hand would normally come to rest if you pushed the chair in."

The chair scraped against the floor as Lendra ducked behind the desk. She cursed softly. Then she began tapping on the wood.

"There," Jeremiah said when her tapping produced a hollow sound.

"I heard it," Lendra said. She reached up for the knife. A popping sound preceded a cry of triumph. Lendra emerged from behind the desk, a tiny Las-pistol in her hand.

"A disposable," Jeremiah said. "Limited use. Very nice. Bring it over."

She brought the gun to him, held it up for him to take a close look at it. He didn't try to grab it with his numbed fingers.

"Okay," he said. "Activate it, then set the power level to low. I want you to shoot right here, where my wrists are bound together."

Lendra's face scrunched up as she frowned. "That'll hurt you!"

"Don't worry. The pain won't kill me." The gun shook in her hand. He said, "Calm down. Take a deep breath."

Yet, even as he instructed her to relax, he felt a growing intensity inside, an animalistic frenzy coursing through his body, as if his blood were actually boiling—a rage fueled by hope.

Lendra adjusted the power setting. As she lowered the weapon, bringing the barrel right down to the bindings at his wrists, she closed her eyes. Jeremiah tugged at his hands as hard as he could but the polymer bindings kept them locked tightly together. A flash of blue light exploded out of the Las-pistol and a searing stab hit his wrists. His hands flew apart.

Jumping to his feet, he grabbed Lendra, hugged her tightly and said, "Thank you. You're fantastic."

When he pulled his arms away she kept hers wrapped around him for a second longer. Then she too released her grip. Stepping back, he picked at the plastic remnants, disentangling himself from their grip. At the same time, Lendra wriggled out of the camo-fatigues. He watched her shimmying free as he massaged his hands, waiting for the familiar, painful tingle of blood flow being restored.

"How are they?" Lendra asked, pointing at his hands.

"They'll be fine." Jeremiah continued rubbing, grimacing with the pain. The insides of his wrists burned. His hands throbbed. He said, "Where's my particle beam cannon?"

"Colonel Truman has it waiting for you. He intends to create a diversion with the Elite Ops—keep them occupied with hand-to-hand combat. He can probably only delay them a few minutes, but that might be enough time for you to get Devereaux away safely. If you can get to your van…"

"And leave the rest of you here?"

"Nobody else has a chance to break Devereaux out. You might be able to get him away before the Elite Ops can regroup."

Jeremiah shook his head as he began to don the coveralls. "The EOs are close to finding the Escala. They may have even found them already. And when they do, they'll kill them all. Somehow, we have to stop Carlton and draw the EOs away from the Escala. If I simply take out Carlton, his death may unleash the EOs on all of us."

"How could he do that? Some sort of programming designed to kick in upon his death?"

"Exactly. A deadman switch in the brain that shuts off when he dies, initiating an order to kill."

"What makes you think that?"

"Remember his saying we'd better hope nothing happens to him?"

Lendra nodded. "Or the wrath of the Elite Ops will rain down on us all. He also said we'd see a holocaust like never before."

"Right. I think he installed a deadman switch as an insurance policy."

"So can't you just sneak out of here and grab Carlton?"

"Too risky. The EOs might try for me and kill Carlton in the process. They won't know about the deadman switch. No, I've got to take out as many of them as I can—spread confusion—get them to come after me and give Truman a chance to capture Carlton. I wish I had some way to warn him that Carlton must be kept alive." Jeremiah flexed his fingers and wiggled his hands until the tingling was almost gone. "How many EOs are out there?"

"You can't get them all, Jeremiah," Lendra said, her voice catching in her throat."Aside from the guard outside and Major Payne," Jeremiah said, "how many others are close by?"

"Two at the door. Two outside the shelter. The rest are in the woods."

"Six," Jeremiah said, keeping the fear out of his voice. "You're right. I can't take them all down. But I might be able to draw their fire. If I can get them to attack me, they might leave Carlton unprotected. If we can somehow isolate him, Colonel Truman and his soldiers can capture him."

"What about Devereaux?"

Jeremiah said, "He can't be my top priority anymore. Besides, he never built those bioweapons. And even if he did, the Escala won't use them, or they would have done so already."

Grabbing the Las-pistol, Jeremiah adjusted the setting to medium. Then he handed the weapon to Lendra. "When I open that door, you fire at the guard's chest. Keep firing until it runs dry. Understand?"

"Jeremiah," Lendra said, her voice cracking slightly. "You can't..."

Fear could be a good thing, Jeremiah knew, if it didn't overwhelm you. He blinked three times, centered himself in his stone dungeon and said, "I'll be ducking underneath, so keep the weapon up."

Lendra bit her lower lip and wiped her eyes with the back of her hand. Finally, she said, "Shouldn't it be set at the highest power level?"

"If we do that, its charge will only last a few seconds. We need more time. Besides, you're not trying to kill him. You're just trying to keep him busy. If he has to leave his shield on, he can't fire at you. That just might buy me enough time to load the particle beam cannon and take him out."

"Okay," Lendra said, her hand shaking. "I'm ready."

Jeremiah grabbed the converter off the desk and pressed the control pad, activating the sensors and scatterer, then zipped up the suit, pulled the hood over his head and arranged the flap that covered his face. "Remember," he said, "keep the weapon aimed at his chest. If he starts to move away, stay with him. Don't let him get away from you or he'll be able to shut down the shield and take you out. Okay?"

Jeremiah moved toward the doorway while Lendra continued to look where he'd been standing.

"I'm terrified," Lendra said.

"You'll be fine," Jeremiah said from the door. "You just keep firing that weapon, okay?"

She turned in his general direction and nodded, her face pinched and pale.

"I'm switching off the privacy field now," Jeremiah said. He took a deep breath, then pushed the button, grabbed the handle and opened the door, immediately dropping into a crouch to avoid her line of fire.

Lendra caught the guard in the chest as he turned to face the door, and Jeremiah, who had waited an instant to make sure she did as instructed, dove under the laser pulse and sprinted down the hallway. He heard yelling ahead of him. Truman leaned against the wall to the infirmary, the particle beam cannon half hidden under a blanket. Jeremiah ripped it out of his hands, opened the stock and slapped the converter inside. As he powered up the cannon, he spun toward the hall, aiming for the guard.

The guard had dodged to the side of the doorway, evading Lendra's faltering laser. Jeremiah fired once, the particle beam cannon bucking in his hands with the recoil, but even as he did, he saw a purple light fly from the guard's weapon through the open doorway at Lendra. She screamed as Jeremiah's blast knocked the EO off his feet, his shield destroyed.

Fighting the urge to run to her, Jeremiah swung around, his weapon lining up on Major Payne, his invisible camos now essentially useless. The energy signature of the particle beam cannon, not to mention the sight of it floating in the air, gave his position away. And he wore no shield. If he took a hit, his body would be shredded.

Major Payne already had his weapons lined up on Jeremiah when Weiss and Truman dove into his legs. As the major fired, his right knee buckled slightly. The blast from his particle beam cannon went into the ceiling, showering the lobby with debris. But his Las-rifle fired a blue pulse that struck Jeremiah in the left shoulder. Several soldiers threw themselves at the EOs guarding the door. A powerful smell of rot flooded the room—the nerve gas. Rage filled Jeremiah, displacing the fear. He aimed the cannon at Payne, who kicked backward, freeing himself from Weiss and Truman as he brought his particle beam cannon up.

More soldiers flung themselves at Payne. Jeremiah had to hold his fire. Payne was less concerned. He fired at the soldiers indiscriminately. Brave fools! One was hit by a particle beam pulse and exploded, bits of skin and bloody bone flying across the lobby. Another began screaming and ran toward the door, where he was cut in half by red laser fire from one of the EOs. The homeless men fell to the floor, moaning in terror. A few soldiers collapsed. Jeremiah ducked, but he still couldn't risk firing at Payne. Two soldiers clung to Payne desperately. The major tossed one off, shooting him with a red laser pulse. The other hung from the arm holding the particle beam cannon, his jaw working angrily. Screams and the intensifying whine of the EOs' power packs assaulted Jeremiah's ears.

The EOs guarding the door also hurled soldiers aside. To the soldiers' credit, some of them managed to keep clear heads and continue the fight; others screamed, trying to escape the poisonous gas. One flailed his arms in a berserk motion, barking like a wounded seal until a laser pulse in the head silenced him. A female soldier clinging to one of the EOs snarled in fury just before she was thrown off. She crashed into the monitors along the wall and slumped to the floor. Jeremiah peered through the smoke, his heart racing, his eyes darting from the monitors to Payne and the EOs, waiting for an opening. When an EO with a gold cross on his chest managed to free himself from the last of the soldiers, Jeremiah fired the cannon. He hit the shield squarely, knocking the EO off his feet, the concussive force rendering the man unconscious.

Carlton leapt into the fray, throwing himself at Weiss as Truman again tackled Payne. Jeremiah, holding his position, waited for an opening. Payne tossed another soldier aside before firing the cannon at Jeremiah, narrowly missing only because Truman had grabbed his arm. The cannon's pulse slammed into two homeless men at the far side of the room, splashing blood and flesh across the walls. More soldiers piled on, driving Payne to the floor. The air in the room grew fouler, the smoke heavy.

The EO at the door twisted his body, separated himself from the last of the soldiers, turned his cannon and Las-rifle on Jeremiah and fired at the same instant Jeremiah pressed the trigger. Jeremiah's body tensed in expectation of the explosion that would tear him to pieces. But miraculously, his round impacted with the round fired by the EO. The resulting detonation hammered him to the floor as another laser pulse hit him in the thigh. He landed with a grunt, the pain stoking his fury. His muscles contracted. Adrenaline surged. With a bellow that chafed his throat, he struggled to his feet and limped toward the EO, wanting only to kill. He fired again, blasting the man through the ruined doorway. The soldiers outside were being tossed about by two more EOs, who sliced them in half with long red laser pulses. Slowly, the EOs converged on the shelter. On the monitors, Jeremiah saw EOs entering the power substation that led to the Escala.

He spun back to face the center of the room as Payne jumped to his feet, his Las-rifle coming up, aiming at Jeremiah. But even as he fired, Quark, in a blur of motion, shoved Jeremiah aside and launched himself through the air. Payne backed up, trying to evade the big man as Payne's laser pulse sliced through Jeremiah's stomach. Fighting the nausea, he rolled to his feet and brought his particle beam cannon up, but Quark had Payne in his grasp now, his massive hands locked around the major's neck. And as Payne fought to turn the particle beam cannon and Las-rifle on Quark, Quark pried the major's helmet off. Then one hand grabbed the particle beam cannon while the other twisted the Las-rifle from Payne's hands. The weapons crashed to the floor as Quark drove Payne against the wall.

Jeremiah left them struggling with each other and half-ran, half-hopped outside. One of the two EOs had just thrown off a soldier, who flew through the air. The EO fired his particle beam cannon, blowing the soldier apart. Less than a second later Jeremiah fired. His cannon's blast demolished the shield. The EO fell backward, unconscious. Three soldiers immediately jumped him.

The last EO fired everything he had at Jeremiah—the Las-rifle and the particle beam cannon. Jeremiah's legs gave way and he fell forward, firing the cannon as he hit the ground, his aim slightly off, the recoil pulling the shot wide despite his efforts to hold the cannon steady. Still, he managed to nick the EO's shield, which must have been defective because the EO exploded, arms and legs flying apart.

Jeremiah tasted blood. His body ached—his arms numb after the heavy recoils of the particle beam cannon. Needle-sharp stabs from the laser strikes shot up his legs, but his blood still sang with rage. He got his hands under his chest and raised himself to his feet, where he wobbled unsteadily. Although he saw no EOs approaching, he knew more would arrive soon. He had minutes at most. Clenching his teeth together against the pain, he ran back inside the shelter. On the monitors, the EOs were inside the power substation, descending into its basement. Jeremiah knew they would find the hidden entrance very quickly. He had to find a way to stop them.

In the center of the lobby two men were locked together, their hands at each other's throats: Weiss and Carlton. Rolling across the floor, Quark and Major Payne continued to grapple. Payne, with his exoskeleton and armor plating, had fewer exposed areas and tremendous strength but even so, he couldn't match the power of Quark. The big Escala fought with an intensity Jeremiah had never seen before in a human being: punching, kicking, twisting. Writhing like some cornered animal. It was all Payne could do to protect his head. Finally Quark managed to get his hands around the major's wrists. Then he smashed his head into Payne's nose—once, twice, three times—until Payne went limp.

Down the hallway that led to Lendra, the EO he'd shot earlier began to stir. "Don't kill Carlton," Jeremiah yelled to Weiss as he jumped over them, shoving men aside. For an instant, he considered firing the particle beam cannon again, blowing the EO into a thousand bits now that his shield was down. Instead he took half a dozen steps and heel-kicked the EO in the helmet, sending a shooting pain up his leg.

He found Lendra where he'd left her, just inside the doctor's office. Fortunately, the EO had fired a purple laser pulse at her instead of his particle beam cannon. She was still alive. She lay on her back, barely conscious, clutching her stomach and moaning. Jeremiah flung himself at drawers until he came across the QuikHeal bandages. He ripped one out of its package, knelt before Lendra, pulled her arms apart, tore her shirt and thrust the bandage onto her stomach.

For the first time he noticed that his camos were ruined—torn and blood-covered, the sensors no longer working. A laser pulse must have hit the control panel. He pulled off the hood and face covering. Lendra, the pain in her eyes slowly receding behind the mask of anesthesia, looked at him dully, and he knew the bandage wouldn't save her.

She cringed, moaned as a fresh wave of pain hit her, then reached out a hand and clutched his shirt. Her eyes clamped shut. She pulled him toward her, mewling quietly.

"You're going to be okay," Jeremiah lied.

She opened her eyes, brought them into focus on his and said, "Don't leave me."

Jeremiah took her hand in his. She held on ferociously.

He wanted to stay by her side, but too many lives were at stake. As he pulled away from her, he got an idea. He grabbed the knife she'd brought and sliced open the back of his hand. Then he shoved his fist under the QuikHeal bandage, letting his blood mingle with hers.

She writhed in agony, screaming as he held her down. He had to sit on top of her to control her. "Keep still," he said. "I'm trying to help you. Giving you some of my blood. It might keep you alive. Okay?" She grimaced, squeezed her eyes together tightly and stopped struggling.

"I've only got seconds," Jeremiah said as he pulled his hand free. Slick with blood and gore, his hand throbbed, but it had almost stopped bleeding. "If I'm going to save you, I've got to go." Eyes still closed, Lendra nodded briefly. Jeremiah wiped his hand on her shirt, then re-positioned the QuikHeal bandage, adjusting the anasthetic setting to maximum. As the pain lines in Lendra's face succumbed to the narcotic of the QuikHeal bandage, Jeremiah slipped out the door and ran to the lobby.

Chapter Thiry-Five

On one of the projections, Doug watched three Elite Ops enter a building. As they crossed the threshold, an alarm sounded.

"Shut that off," Quekri said.

When the noise died away, Doug said, "They're here, ain't they?"

Quekri nodded. The Escala wore blank expressions, as if their imminent discovery were unimportant. Doug's stomach fluttered. Maybe he could still get out. The Elite Ops weren't after him. If he could run away, give up the Escala, he'd be free. Hell, he'd even go back to jail—happily. Then he caught sight of Zeriphi across the room. She looked at him and he thought of his child, yet to be born.

"We gotta fight," Doug said. "Or run."

"There's nowhere to go," Quekri said. "And we're scientists, not soldiers."

"You're gonna be dead scientists if you don't do something. They're gonna find us any minute."

"Yes," Quekri said.

The others in the room nodded their agreement, as if some scientific theory had just been proven. Their calm exterior drove Doug into a near-frenzy.

"Where you keep the weapons?" Doug asked.

"Zod's team took them all."

Doug threw up his hands. "But you must have a few, right?" As Quekri shook her head, Doug said, "What about Quark? Can he help?"

"He's going to the shelter to try to rescue Devereaux," Quekri said. "We're on our own."

"You got a air vent we can climb out of?"

Again Quekri shook her head. "We use air recyclers."

"Then we gotta fight," Doug said. He glared at Quekri. Slowly, the others turned to face him. Were they smiling? Did they think this was funny? He said, "You people may be smart. You may be evolved. You may be where humanity's gonna be in a hundred years but, unless you fight, you're gonna die right here. My child too. Don't you wanna stop that happening? Don't you wanna continue your species?"

"I'll fight," Temala said as she glared at Doug. For an instant, he thought she meant to attack him. But when she smiled uncertainly, he smiled back.

"Okay," he said.

"We can't defeat the Elite Ops," Quekri said. "Even if we had their weaponry, they would win. All we can do is drag out the inevitable."

"Then that's exactly what we're gonna do," Doug said. "You're human, ain't you?" At their nods, he said, "Well, humans've always been fighters. So prove you're human and fight. Find anything that can be used as a weapon. Bring it to the table in the main room ASAP. Okay?"

Temala immediately bounded away. The others stared at him, then looked at each other, eyebrows arching, shoulders shrugging. Doug wanted to scream. He was barely holding himself together and they acted like this was some kind of game. Finally they began to depart, glancing at him as they did so. One patted Doug on the shoulder as he went by. Only the technicians remained behind. The one who had called out the names of the dead looked at Doug and said, "We'll fight," before turning back to his projections.

Doug stepped out into the main cavern, where he waited for the Escala. They drifted in, carrying odd items, which they either placed on the table or leaned against it: four laser torches, two RDX-HMX explosives, several dozen small-charge detonators, three shields and an ancient handgun. There were also about a dozen shovels and other tools that could be used as clubs. Temala held one of the shovels—almost a child's toy in her massive hands. She, at least, looked ready to fight. Standing around the table, the Escala looked at Doug, hands at their sides. Calm. Maddening. Doug's throat tightened up.

"That's it?" he said. "That all you got?"

"I told you we're not fighters," Quekri answered.

The technicians emerged from the monitoring room and walked over to the table. The one who had spoken before said, "They're coming." He stared at Doug, waiting for his orders. The Escala all turned to Doug. They were depending on him! What was he supposed to do? He'd assumed that because of their genetic transformations, they would be better than him at everything; and no doubt they were smarter, stronger and faster. But they were scientists too, with no experience in battle. And who was he to lead them? A recovering addict who'd been in a few street brawls.

Doug picked up a las-knife and flipped it on. It put out a purple laser pulse that projected out a few inches. This was the device they'd used to cut away the cell bars. Doug said, "What are we supposed to do with this junk?" They stared at him, as if he could magically transform these few items into successful defense mechanisms. Doug put the las-knife back on the table. "I'm just a stupid black man." He winked at Temala. "You guys be the geniuses. Ain't there some kinda weapon you can make from this? Anybody?"

"Perhaps," Probst said, "we could use the las-knives to detonate the explosives, bring the cave down on top of us once the Elite Ops reach us."

"Interesting," the technician replied. "The calculations would be tricky but…"

"Okay," Doug said. "Good. Better than nothing. What about surrender? That an option? Any chance they'd let you live?"

"Doubtful," Quekri said.

They inclined their heads in unison, craning their necks. And then Doug heard it too. The Elite Ops were shooting at something.

"Okay," Doug said, "everybody grab a weapon. Anybody fire a gun before?"

When they all shook their heads, he picked up the revolver.

"Strobe the lights," Quekri said. "And let's put smoke in the corners. Heat sources might confuse the Elite Ops' infrared sensors."

"Good thinking," Doug said. "What else?"

Shull, Dunadan and Warrow—the three young astrophysicists—

reached for the shields. Dunadan looked at Doug and said, "We'll set off the small-charge detonators—try to take out their shields. If you see them flicker, that's when you fire. Okay?"

"Got it," Doug said.

Probst and the technician each grabbed an explosive. Probst said, "We've got to draw as many Elite Ops into the cave as we can. We'll try to blow the RDX-HMX using the las-knives. The small charge detonators won't provide enough energy to do the job. If we time it right, the explosion might bring the cave down on top of the Elite Ops." And us, Doug thought. "Of course," Probst continued, "if we wait too long..."

"Eight or maybe ten seconds," the technician said. "That ought to be enough time to blow the RDX-HMX."

Doug nodded. He tried to swallow, found that he had no saliva in his mouth.

"Most of us can move to the tunnels," another technician said as he grabbed a pickaxe. "We'll have a better chance in close quarters. And if the cave comes down..." He looked up at the ceiling. Doug followed his eyes into the blackness. He shivered.

Quekri put a hand on Doug's shoulder and said, "They're going to emit a nerve gas that smells like rotting flesh. It will paralyze you with fear. Indecision. Panic. We've found that the best way to fight through that is with anger. Understand?"

Doug tried to smile. "So I'm gonna be more scared than this?"

Quekri nodded. "Lots." She clapped him on the back and grabbed a shovel, then made for one of the hallways.

Zeriphi stepped out from behind a group of Escala and grabbed a metal pole with a claw on the end. Doug so wanted to comfort her, be comforted by her. She held the pole up in front of her and stopped in front of him—so beautiful, her eyes black and somehow bright in the dim light. He reached out, grabbed her arms, looked up into those dark eyes and said, "I'm sorry about Zod."

"Thank you."

"Zeriphi, after this is all over, perhaps you and I can make a new start, just the two of us, until the baby comes along. I want to try. I—"

She shook her head with a sad smile and said, "We're not going to survive this." Then she walked away.

My child is going to die here.

Doug watched Zeriphi until she vanished in the darkness, then crouched behind the massive sofa in the main cave. Though it offered only the illusion of a hiding place, he felt better not completely exposed to the Elite Ops. He could still maybe work an angle once they came in—if they were as bad as Quekri said they were, if everything went to hell, he could put up his hands and say, "Thank God you're here. They were holding me captive. I think they were gonna eat me!"

No.

He'd fight, hoping his death would miraculously save Zeriphi and their child. Probably, this was going to be the way it ended for all of them. The void of death was coming. He thought of Devereaux—the man's courage and dignity—and drew strength from that. The lights now flickered on and off, and the smell of smoke grew thick. Doug's eyes watered. He'd never before been in a fight where death seemed a certainty. He'd never even thought about death back then. Plus, he'd usually been high on something. He wished he'd gone to the bathroom while he had the chance.

Doug looked over at the technician working with Probst, whispering together under the stairs. He'd been the one who had called out the names of the dead. Doug realized he didn't know the man's name. That suddenly became very important to him.

"Hey," he called out softly, "what's your name?"

Probst looked at him and said, "Probst."

"Not you, Probst," Doug said. "I know you. I mean the guy next to you."

The technician looked over at him, bowed solemnly and said, "Paddon."

"Paddon," Doug repeated. "I'll remember you." He felt happy knowing Paddon's name. He was finally contributing to something bigger than himself. Transferring the gun to his left hand, he wiped his palm on his pants, then slipped the gun back into his right, his finger on the trigger. He heard a scratching noise, then a loud metallic groan.

Doug cocked the hammer of the pistol as the Elite Ops broke through the hidden door above. He looked up as a giant robot jumped down to the cave floor, bypassing the stairs completely. Because of the strobe lighting, the robot towered over him faster than seemed possible. The foul stench of death overpowered Doug. He fell to the ground, his body curling into the fetal position. Come on, you can do this. Remember what Quekri said. Anger can help you get past the fear. Get mad!

Another Elite Ops trooper jumped down next to the first, then a third. They began to fire laser pulses, purple and red colors that flew past too quickly to identify—just tinting the air. Shull, Dunadan and Warrow ran across the cave, ducking and weaving, their shields faintly glowing as the Elite Ops lined them up. When they neared the Elite Ops, they threw their small-charge detonators.

Doug couldn't breathe. He reached for his throat and began to massage it as the room closed in on him. He cringed, waiting for the cave to collapse, all the while clawing at his mouth and throat. Finally he managed to take in great gulps of air.

Get up and fight, you coward!

The small-charge detonators exploded, echoing off the rock walls. Doug's ears hurt. He wet himself. Escala emerged from the hallways, raising shovels and other clubs. An Elite Ops aimed a weapon at Doug, and Temala ran out of a hallway, leaping high in the air, her shovel swinging down at the big trooper. He turned, fired a long red pulse at her. She screamed—a horrific, spine-tingling shriek of agony and fear—as her arm fell off, its hand still clutching the shovel. Doug winced as the shovel hit the ground. Another red pulse hit her face, turning it even blacker, silencing her.

She died for you, coward. Stand up! Don't just lie there.

He realized suddenly that these people had known all along they were going to die. And they let him browbeat them into fighting because they sensed how afraid he was. They knew he needed the distraction. That's why they're fighting—to help me.

Shull screamed and fell, his torso nearly separated from his legs.

And Dunadan flew against the wall with a sickening thud. A severed arm hit Doug in the face.

Well, they're not going to fight alone.

Doug raised the gun, aimed at the center of the nearest Elite Ops trooper. The man was huge. Doug screamed as he pulled the trigger; the shield deflected his shots. As he fired, he saw two small purple flames behind his target. Probst and Paddon, trying to blow the RDX-HMX explosives. Warrow ran toward the Elite Ops from the far side of the cave and went down in a hail of red laser fire. Doug kept his eyes on the purple flames and counted seconds—two, three, four. An Elite Ops turned and fired in that direction. Probst and Paddon fell. Doug pulled the trigger again. The hammer clicked as it dropped on a spent shell: the revolver empty.

Dropping the gun, Doug stood, his hands out to the side as he stepped from behind the sofa. There's still a chance. You can claim you were brainwashed, forced to fight against your will.

Chapter Thirty-Six

Breathing heavily, fighting against gas-induced panic, Colonel Truman pushed himself to his feet. His knee nearly gave way. Looking down, he noticed blood trickling from it. He didn't remember getting hit. The two Elite Ops troopers who had been guarding the door were either unconscious or dead. So was the one who'd been guarding Jones. But more would be coming soon. Half a dozen of his soldiers lay on the ground moving their limbs weakly; one of them, he was happy to see, was Captain Lopez. All the other troops inside the shelter were either dead or unconscious. He hoped the soldiers outside had fared better, but with the field dampener the Elite Ops had activated to impose their communications blackout, he had no way to find out. We're going to die today, Emily, Truman thought. He wondered if he still loved her or if he just wished he did.

Across the room, Weiss struggled with Carlton. As Truman took a step toward them, reaching for his Las-pistol, he discovered that it was no longer in its holster. It must have been jarred loose during the battle. Spotting a Las-rifle on the floor near where Cookie Monster continued to wrestle with Major Payne, Truman maneuvered around them and picked up the weapon. The ringing in his ears began to diminish, and he heard moans and cries coming from the wounded.

Carlton had Weiss pressed up against the wall, his hands around Weiss' throat. Weiss' hands struck at Carlton feebly. Cookie Monster, meanwhile, lay atop Payne, his muscular arms pinning the major's arms to his torso, his massive legs squeezing Payne's legs together. Payne struggled against the big pseudo ineffectually. Truman aimed the Las-rifle at Carlton.

"Let him go!" he yelled.

Carlton stared at him.

"I mean it," Truman said. "Let him go or I'll fire."

Carlton kept his hands on Weiss' throat for another few seconds, then released Weiss with his right hand. But as he started to back away, a small Las-pistol jumped out from under the sleeve of his suit and Carlton jammed the weapon under Weiss' chin. He pulled Weiss away from the wall and wrapped his left arm around Weiss' shoulders. "I don't think so."

Weiss' eyes bulged. He stood on his toes, lifting his head in an attempt to free himself, but Carlton held on tightly.

"You wouldn't dare," Weiss hissed through clenched teeth.

Carlton grinned. "I'm tired of your rules, Gray Velvet." He looked at Truman and barked, "I want all the weapons on the floor. Now."

As Truman began to lower his weapon, Weiss shouted, "Disregard that order!" Truman re-centered the Las-rifle on Carlton's face.

"He dies if you don't," Carlton said, his Las-pistol digging into Weiss' throat.

"And then you die," Weiss answered, his voice a fierce whisper.

"I think not—unless you want all these people to die too."

Truman hesitated. Could he get off a shot, take Carlton out before Carlton pulled the trigger? Or would Carlton's hand tighten, firing his Las-pistol into Weiss' head? As he aimed at the brachial nerve near Carlton's collarbone, which would paralyze Carlton's arm, he spotted a red figure in his peripheral vision. He realized that the bloody creature moving toward him was Jeremiah Jones.

"Hold your fire," Jones said to him, his particle beam cannon aimed at both Carlton and Weiss. "We need Carlton alive. I think he's implanted a deadman switch in his brain, something that will trigger a 'kill' response in the EOs upon his death."

"Very astute," Carlton said. "But it's not just a deadman switch. I can also give a 'kill' order at any time."

Devereaux now emerged from Sister Ezekiel's office, followed by Sister Ezekiel and Ahmad Rashidi. The lawyer's eyes practically bugged out of his face. His hands shook as he wobbled across the floor. He bent over a fallen body and retched. Behind him, Captain Lopez staggered to his feet, his Las-pistol in his hand. He pointed it in the general direction of Carlton.

"You have to call off the Elite Ops," Devereaux begged Payne. "They'll slaughter the Escala."

"No," Payne grunted.

"We're going to have EOs here any minute," Jones said.

"You can't win," Weiss said to Carlton.

"Oh, but I can," Carlton said. "I've still got all communications blacked out. No one knows what's happening here. And Jones is right. My men will be back very soon." He tilted his head toward the monitors. Truman glanced that way, caught glimpses of Elite Ops troopers and Escala fighting in an underground cavern. It was difficult to be certain how things were progressing given the strobe lighting and the moving cameras mounted on the Elite Ops' helmets. "A few are on their way. The rest will be here as soon as they eradicate the pseudos," Carlton added.

"Please," Devereaux said. "The Escala are peaceful."

Sister Ezekiel took a step forward, holding up her hands. "This killing is completely unnecessary."

"You!" Ahmad Rashidi yelled, his face purple with rage. "This is your fault!" Rashidi screamed as he launched himself at Devereaux, a knife blade flashing in his hand. He must have picked it up from among the discarded weapons on the floor.

"No!" Sister Ezekiel, Weiss and Carlton all shouted at the same moment.

Devereaux's arms came up as Rashidi plunged the knife deep into Devereaux's stomach, yelling: "There is no God but Allah! No God but Allah!"

Jones, moving faster than humanly possible, covered the space between he and Devereaux in an instant, and threw Rashidi off Devereaux so violently that Rashidi flew a dozen feet. But the damage was done, the knife blade now pulled out of Devereaux's stomach, blood seeping between his fingers as he held his stomach.

"Medic!" Truman yelled as Captain Lopez fired a blue stun pulse at Rashidi.

Cookie Monster let out an animalistic roar, squeezing Payne in a fierce grip until the major cried out. Jones lowered Devereaux to the floor as Payne howled. Carlton pulled Weiss in tightly, while Sister Ezekiel rushed to Devereaux's side, followed closely by Corporal Snow. Payne's cries trailed off until he went silent, at which point Cookie Monster released him and hurried to Devereaux's side, his jaw quivering, his eyes glistening with moisture. Devereaux lay on his back, still conscious. Yet even though he had to know how much blood he was losing, he showed no fear, just calm acceptance.

At that moment Carlton whispered something inaudible and Weiss stiffened.

"You can't do that," Weiss said.

"Let's find out," Carlton said.

"Don't even think about it," Truman said, his Las-rifle aimed at Carlton's collarbone.

Carlton looked at Truman and smiled. Then he winked and pulled the trigger.

Weiss dropped. No pain, no suffering: he was dead before he hit the floor. Again Jones moved so quickly Truman's eye could barely follow him. Jones jammed the particle beam cannon into Carlton's stomach with one hand, grabbing Carlton's wrist with the other. The crack of breaking bone sounded above Carlton's cry as the Las-pistol clattered to the floor.

"You have no idea how much pain I can inflict," Jones said, his knuckles white as he squeezed Carlton's broken wrist. "Rescind that order now!"

Carlton howled in agony until Jones eased up the pressure. "Okay, okay," Carlton managed to say. Then he mumbled softly, using a sub-vocal command.

"Get those EOs out of there," Jones said, nodding toward the monitors. Carlton squealed as Jones applied more pressure to the broken wrist, but again he mumbled softly, issuing another sub-vocal command.

On the screens, the Elite Ops surrounded Doug as the lights flicked on and off, their weapons pointed at him. But they held their fire. Around them, Escala lay on the ground. Some of them looked like they were in pieces, though the smoky air made it difficult to be sure—

Truman didn't think he wanted to know. A few bodies seemed to be giving off smoke as well. Truman's gaze went from the monitors to the carnage around him in the lobby. The two scenes were eerily similar.

"Bring them back," Jones said. "All of them." Turning to Truman, he asked, "How many are there?"

"Sixteen," Truman said.

"Okay," Jones said. "I want sixteen EOs out front in ten minutes." He indicated the fallen Elite Ops troopers. "Dead or alive."

"This one's alive," Captain Lopez said, bending over Major Payne.

Jones turned to Carlton. "And bring those copters in on schedule. We'll let you bring out your dead and wounded, and we leave just like you planned." Finally he turned to Truman and added, "Lendra's in the doctor's room back there. She's been hit. Bad. Have a couple of your men bring her out here. She's coming with me."

Truman said, "Have you seen yourself lately?"

"I'll be fine," Jones said. He turned to Corporal Snow. "What about Devereaux? Is he going to make it?"

Corporal Snow, who had ripped Devereaux's shirt open and put a QuikHeal bandage on his stomach, shrugged.

Cookie Monster and Sister Ezekiel knelt beside Devereaux, Cookie Monster gently cradling Devereaux's head, Sister Ezekiel clinging to Devereaux's bloody hands. Devereaux looked up at Jones and tried to sit up, then lay back down with a grimace.

Jones nodded to Devereaux and Cookie Monster, then said, "I want you two to come with me. We're going to see Elias Leach and we'll be bringing Carlton along. Right now we've got a stalemate situation. We need to figure out what to do next."

Devereaux looked at Cookie Monster and nodded.

"Okay," Cookie Monster said as he got to his feet. "We'll go with you provided we can be assured of my people's safety."

Jones pushed Carlton toward Cookie Monster. "All we have to do is keep him under our absolute control."

Grabbing Carlton by the front of his suit, Cookie Monster lifted the smaller man off the ground. He spoke in a deep, gravelly voice as he glared at Carlton, "If the Elite Ops kill the Escala, you die. Painfully. Understood?"

Carlton, his face pale, nodded.

Jones asked for a knife. When Truman handed his over, Jeremiah sat on his particle beam cannon, cut the back of his own hand, then lifted the corner of the QuikHeal bandage and stuck his fist against the wound, letting his blood drip inside. Devereaux squirmed, gritting his teeth against the pain, but the whole time he stared at Jones and said nothing. Sister Ezekiel, however, touched Jones on the shoulder and said, "What are you doing?"

After a moment, Jones removed his hand and replaced the bandage. "It's all I can think to do," he said. Then he picked up the particle beam cannon, planted it in Carlton's gut and clamped down again on Carlton's wrist. Jones nodded to Cookie Monster, who released Carlton. Then Jones turned to Truman and said, "When the EOs get here, they're going to want to kill us all. Carlton's got them so pumped full of hormones and drugs that they don't always act rationally. They could do anything."

"They're going to kill you all," Carlton said.

"You'll be the first to die," Jones replied, squeezing Carlton's wrist until Carlton cried out.

The sound of jet-copters reached Truman's ears as the first of the Elite Ops troopers crashed into the lobby. The trooper aimed his weapons at Jeremiah and Truman. Behind him, three more troopers came to a halt, their weapons angled out to encompass the rest of the lobby. They stood fiercely rigid, their faces hidden behind their visors. Like everyone else in the room, Truman froze, waiting for the Elite Ops to fire.

After a few seconds, he realized that wasn't going to happen. When the first trooper stepped forward, Truman's soldiers—eight of them on their feet now—held their ground. Ignoring them, the trooper stood over the still-unconscious Payne. He looked down, holstered his weapons, then knelt and gently, effortlessly, lifted the major. As he turned to the doorway, another trooper holstered his weapons, made his way down the hall and returned with the one who had been guarding Jones.

He was also unconscious. The trooper with the gold cross and the other trooper who had been stationed at the ruined front door groggily got to their feet and stumbled outside under their own power. After they departed, the two troopers still inside the shelter slowly backed out, their weapons leveled at Truman's soldiers.

Truman waited only a few seconds before following them. Behind him, Jones led Carlton outside, the particle beam cannon pressed firmly into Carlton's stomach. They halted next to him as two jet-copters landed, both piloted by Air Force officers. Half a dozen Elite Ops troopers formed a perimeter around the jet-copters.

Jones said, "I'll be taking Devereaux, Cookie Monster, Carlton, Lendra, and the bodies of Weiss and Julianna in one copter. The EOs go out on the other."

"Just the dead and wounded," Carlton said. "The others stay behind. Anything happens to me and they take out the shelter, the pseudos, the Army. And it's not just this unit, either. It's all of them—one hundred ninety-two troopers." He slowly reached into his pocket with his free hand and retrieved his PlusPhone. "Take a look for yourselves."

Although the communications blackout remained in place, Carlton's PlusPhone was able to receive transmissions. On the 24-Hour Real News Network Truman saw images of Elite Ops troopers surrounding National monuments, the White House, the Capitol and the Supreme Court. A newswoman explained that the Chairman of the Joint Chiefs had ordered all branches of the Armed Services to a state of readiness. Jet-copters had taken to the air; submarines were moving to defensive positions on both coasts. Carlton turned off the PlusPhone and put it back in his pocket. He said, "You'd better make damn sure I stay in perfect health. And ease up on that wrist."

Jones moved his hand an inch up Carlton's forearm as two of Truman's troops carried Weiss' body outside. While he respected the man Weiss had been, Truman also couldn't forget the preventable tragedy of Raddock Boyd's death and the cavalier manner in which Weiss had dismissed it.

After the Attorney General's body was loaded into the jet-copter, Cookie Monster carried Devereaux outside, Sister Ezekiel following to "say her goodbyes." Truman watched the Elite Ops gather up the bits and pieces of the blown-up trooper. They modified their scanners to locate even the smallest parts, placed them in a body bag and sealed it up. Carrying it to the other copter, they laid it on the floor. Then they brought the other dead troopers out, laid them alongside the body bag. A few at a time, the surviving Elite Ops troopers walked over, the one with the gold cross on his chest wobbling unsteadily. Each of them touched the body bag, then placed a hand on each dead man's chest. When they finished, the one with the gold cross removed his helmet and held it against his side. The troopers flanking him did likewise. Together, they turned to face Jones—three handsome men with hate in their eyes.

They held their pose for a moment, then said goodbye to each other. All but seven climbed inside the copter. One of those leaving was the trooper with the gold cross. He stepped over to Sister Ezekiel before boarding and said something Truman couldn't hear. Sister Ezekiel reached up and put a hand on his chest. She spoke to him briefly. When she finished, he bowed his head and returned to his copter. He was the last to board. The seven who would be staying behind maintained position in a circle around the copter, facing outward, their weapons leveled.

As Sister Ezekiel came over to Truman and Jones, Jeremiah said, "I'm concerned about you, Sister. And your men too, Colonel."

Carlton bristled. "They'll be fine as long as you keep me healthy. We don't wage war on innocents. They stay calm, they stay alive. You have my word of honor."

Truman nearly choked at the man's audacity, but he said, "We'll be meek as lambs, though I'd appreciate it if you'd resolve things quickly."

Carlton said, "We all want this resolved quickly and peacefully."

Jones stared at Carlton for a moment, as if ascertaining the veracity of Carlton's statement, then turned to Truman, who could only shrug. "He seems sincere," Truman said.

"Because I am," Carlton replied. "Now that my advantage is gone, negotiations are the only sane option."

After Lendra was put aboard, Jones walked Carlton to the jet-copter. Jeremiah kept his left hand wrapped around Carlton's broken arm, his right holding the particle beam cannon pressed against Carlton's stomach. The seven Elite Ops troopers turned as one to watch Jeremiah's progress. One swung his particle beam cannon to follow Jones as he passed. The trooper next to him barked a command and he lowered the cannon, swinging it back around to face the soldiers as Jones nodded grimly to Truman and stepped into the copter, pulling Carlton in behind him.

When the jet-copters lifted off, Truman's eyes wandered back to the seven.

Chapter Thirty-Seven

Arms outstretched, Doug stared at the Elite Ops troopers' weapons, gritting his teeth. His body shook. But the Elite Ops didn't fire. Doug looked from one to another—flashes of nightmare robots winking in and out of the darkness brought by the strobe lighting—fighting the panic of the gas. Yet he stood his ground. The Elite Ops remained motionless for a few seconds, then retreated, stomping up the stairs.

"That's right, I'm bad!" he shouted at their disappearing feet. "Don't you be comin' back now, neither!"

As the lights returned to normal, Doug bent over Dunadan. The big Escala's chest was a pulpy red mass; his arm had been severed just below the shoulder. Doug touched Dunadan's neck, but found no pulse. Before he could move on to the others, Quekri, Zeriphi and the remaining Escala emerged from the tunnels.

Quekri knelt before Warrow, Zeriphi examined Shull, and Keelar lifted Paddon to a sitting position; Paddon's eyes opened briefly.

But the Escala tending to Probst dropped his head and became still.

Doug moved over to Temala, who had rescued him from the cage, who had bought him time to gain his courage by attacking an Elite Ops trooper with a shovel, sacrificing herself for him. He couldn't think of her as ugly anymore.

"Temala," he said. "I remember you." He got to his feet and looked up the stairway. "What the hell happened there?"

Quekri said, "I don't know. Perhaps Devereaux or Quark bought us some time. We have to get packing—be ready to go ASAP." Three Escala moved forward to help Keelar with Paddon. They lifted him up and carried him down the hallway that led to the rooms. The rest of the Escala followed. The dead were left where they lay. Quekri saw Doug looking at them and said, "We'll take care of them later. But we have to be ready to move quickly. The Elite Ops will be back."

"Where we goin'?" Doug asked.

"I don't know. You, at least, must return to your people."

"What are you talkin' about?" Doug said. "I'm one a you now."

"I'm sorry." Quekri put a hand on his shoulder.

"But the Elite Ops are still out there. They'll get me."

"We can't protect you," Quekri said, smiling sadly. "We can't even protect ourselves. If they want to kill us, we're dead. And if you stay with us, you'll be killed too. Your odds are better away from us. Besides, they already had their chance to kill you and they didn't."

"But I…we…"

Quekri squeezed his shoulder. "That fight was just survival. It's not who we are." She looked at the massive bodies sprawled on the ground and sighed. "You have your duty and we have ours."

* * *

Doug found Zeriphi in her room, packing two duffel bags. He stopped at the open door, waited for her to notice him. When she looked up, he said, "If I coulda taken his place, I woulda."

Zeriphi's eyes glistened brightly. She rubbed them with the backs of her hands and said, "You're a good man."

Doug stepped inside and took her hands in his. He began caressing them—slowly, softly—feeling her tears. "We survived, Zeriphi. Now let me help you. Together we can raise the baby. And in time, perhaps you'll come to care for me the way I care for you."

Zeriphi shook her head but didn't pull her hands away. "I belong to Zod."

"But he's…" Doug squeezed her hands, pulled them to him. "We had a connection. I still feel it. Don't you?"

Zeriphi's hands were non-responsive lumps of flesh. She said, "I can't take you where I'm going."

Doug gripped down harder as if hoping to press his will upon her through his fingers. "Isn't that my decision?"

Her hands remained lifeless. "You would not…have a pleasant life."

Doug leaned forward, stared deep into her eyes. "I want to come with you."

"You belong here. We don't."

"I belong with you," Doug said.

He squeezed her hands again, but this time Zeriphi squeezed back, clamping his fingers in a vise grip until he heard the joints popping. He grimaced. Then she relaxed the pressure slightly and said, "You belong to Earth. Your duty is here. Remember the ladder of enlightenment and your obligation to fulfill your greatest potential." She released his hands and turned her head away. "Now let me finish."

As she returned to her packing, Doug watched her for a moment, trying to memorize her profile. Out in the hallway, Quekri hurried by with a bag from another room. When Doug caught up with her, she said, "Temala liked you."

"Temala?" Doug recalled that dark, homely face staring at him. He'd never forget it now.

"But you only saw Zeriphi. And Zeriphi only sees Zod."

He nodded. Together they walked back to the main room—the cavern he would probably never see again. Looking around at the walls, the furniture, he said, "What are you gonna do? You still think they're gonna let you go to Mars?"

"I don't know. But we can't stay here. Devereaux believes he can get the Mars Project reinstated. He and Quark are on their way to Washington now. Quark thinks Devereaux will get an audience with the President. And Devereaux can be very persuasive. Who knows? In a few days, we might be on a lunar transit vehicle, stopping off at one of the Moon bases and spending the next several months preparing for the trip."

"And then what, you go to Mars and don't never return?"

"Yes," Quekri said. "It's where we're meant to be."

"I could live there too," Doug said. "People have lived on Mars before."

"For short periods. And they all had health problems, even after they returned to Earth. As for you, your genetic profile won't allow for the modifications necessary to be successful there."

"How do you know that? You already check me out?"

"Of course. But don't worry. Your daughter will be fine."

"My daughter? I'm gonna have a daughter?" Doug felt like laughing, like picking Quekri up in his arms and twirling her around. He probably couldn't even lift her.

Quekri smiled. "Your daughter will always link us to you. But if we stay here, we'll die. Our bodies aren't meant for Earth anymore. We've evolved. We're still evolving. And the Elite Ops want us dead. Sooner or later, they would kill us. You must return to the shelter. Tell your people why we've gone—spread Devereaux's message to as many people as will listen."

"What about Devereaux? Can't he spread the message?"

"I think he'll be coming with us."

"But Devereaux's no different than me. He's not Escala, is he?"

"No," Quekri said. "And his genetic profile won't allow for the modifications necessary to become one of us. So he won't live a long life."

Doug shook his head. "I never got to meet him."

"Yes, you did," Quekri said. "People called him Rock Man."

"Rock Man," Doug said. "I shoulda known. He was always hangin' 'round with Cookie Monster." Pulling the small, polished agate from his pocket, Doug held it up. "He gave me this." Doug rubbed the rock between his fingers. It felt warm to the touch. Comforting. He said, "Cookie Monster and Rock Man—Quark and Devereaux. It makes perfect sense. But he looked so different. And he never said a word."

"Surely you saw people who had changed their appearance in prison."

"Yeah, it ain't that uncommon. Height, weight, eye color, skin pigmentation, voice. I just didn't put it together. Clueless. As usual." Doug flipped the small rock up in the air and caught it. "We hung out together—the three of us. But he never spoke to me."

"He was protecting us. You might have done or said something that would have given us away." Quekri put a hand on Doug's shoulder. "It's time."

Doug nodded. "I still don't wanna leave."

"I know," Quekri said. "But it's best. You can carry the message. Through us, you've seen what humans can become in a short time. Imagine the possibilities for the next generation."

* * *

Doug stood in the main cave, Quekri's arm over his shoulder, as the Escala emerged from the hallways. They approached him, one at a time. And each of them said only four words: "Doug. I remember you." As he absorbed their goodbyes, hoping somehow to delay the leaving process, he soaked in the musky smell of the cavern and its people. He had trouble swallowing and his nose suddenly ran. It all went by so quickly.

Lastly, Zeriphi stepped forward.

Doug's voice quavered as he said, "A daughter. We're having a daughter."

Zeriphi grabbed his shoulders, leaned down and kissed him on the cheek. When she straightened, she said, "Doug. I remember you."

Doug croaked, "Zeriphi. I remember you."

When Zeriphi turned away, she said, "Take care of yourself." Doug wiped his eyes but said nothing. He let Quekri lead him up the stairway and through the broken trapdoor. They climbed out together, into the electrical substation's basement, then up another stairway to the ruins in the forest, where the evening sun looked orange. They walked west through the woods that had so recently been a battleground.

Quekri wore a small device on her belt. When she saw him looking at it, she said, "An old scatterer. Not very effective but I won't be out long."

As the thinning forest gave way to the road, Doug spotted what remained of the giant statue—Emerging Man—off to the right. It stood only a few feet above the ground in a jagged stump. Shards of stone littered the area. To the left, the road led to the shelter, to Sister Ezekiel and the life he thought he'd left behind.

Quekri stopped before they cleared the trees and put out her hand. He'd noticed that the Escala didn't shake hands but, as he took her warm hand in his, he was grateful for the contact. He said, "I didn't realize how empty my life used to be until I met you people. Sister Ezekiel and Henry—they're kind—but their life revolves around religion. And there's nothin' wrong with that. But that's not who I am. I'm like you. How can I just let you go?"

Quekri shrugged, then looked upon the shattered statue. "It's a shame," she said. "It was such a beautiful piece." Doug turned to follow her gaze. As he did, he heard the rustle of leaves behind him and knew she was gone. He thought about Devereaux, about his daughter, about the life they would have on Mars—a life he wouldn't share—then he blinked his eyes until his vision cleared. Without looking back, he stepped out onto the debris-cluttered sidewalk and turned left toward home.

He'd gone no more than a hundred yards before encountering one of the Elite Ops. "Stop," the creature said. It was the first time Doug had heard one of them speak. The voice sounded normal, only a little muffled by the helmet. Doug stopped and instinctively put up his hands. "Doug Robinson," the Elite Ops said.

Doug shivered. He asked, "How did you know my name?"

"Drug addict. Gang member. Escaped prisoner. You were in the pseudos' cave. Back to the shelter now."

"You gonna kill me?"

"Move."

* * *

The Elite Ops had brought in a tank-like vehicle to move the wrecked vehicles in the shelter's parking lot into a sort of corral. They were now herding bewildered townsfolk into it. Wearing her spare pair of glasses, Sister Ezekiel stood at the center of the enclosure next to Henry, Chief McKinney and a shackled Ahmad. Her homeless men clustered at the west side of the makeshift corral, nearest the shelter. They frequently peered up at two of the Elite Ops who wore some sort of jet packs, flying in slow circles around the enclosure. Sister

Ezekiel found her eyes drifting up to the two massive creatures every few seconds also.

Colonel Truman and his soldiers gathered along the south side of the corral. The colonel had sent a few of his soldiers into the woods immediately after the jet-copters left, but one of the Elite Ops had gone after them and ordered them back to the shelter. So despite Carlton's assurances, Sister Ezekiel believed that the Elite Ops might actually kill them. For a second, she considered escape. They might let her go. After all, she was just a harmless nun. She might be able to talk her way free. But almost before the thought reached fruition, she buried it. Her place was here. Her calling was to save these men—even from their own dark impulses. She turned to Ahmad and said, "Why?"

Ahmad lifted his hands, stared at them for a long moment, then shook his head. "I don't know, Sister. It's complicated. I couldn't think straight."

"Do you know what you've done? Not to Devereaux but to yourself?"

Ahmad shrugged. "He ruined you, Sister. He poisoned your mind. I didn't want to hurt him, but…"

"I thought you understood tolerance," Sister Ezekiel said. "How can you face God with this stain on your soul?"

Ahmad opened his mouth to reply. Then he caught her eye and looked away.

Sister Ezekiel said, "By the way, Devereaux asked me to tell you… how did he put it? Oh, yes. 'The path to enlightenment is long and torturous, wending its way past the confines of religion.'"

"See, that's what I'm talkin' about, Sister. He's convinced you that there's no God. That's the evil we have to destroy."

"No, Ahmad." Sister Ezekiel shook her head. "I still believe in God. I always will. But I think perhaps our concept of religion needs to be reexamined. The old books—the Bible and the Koran, the Torah and all the others—limit our thinking. We need new stories and myths to celebrate the continuing evolution of our species. As Devereaux said, 'We are not the final product. We're just passing through this phase of humanity.'"

Henry and Ahmad stared at her, open-mouthed. Ahmad said, "Sister. That is blasphemy."

Henry added: "God made us in His image."

Sister Ezekiel said, "The Koran states that 'God changes not what is in a people, until they change what is in themselves.' Doesn't that allow for the evolution of humanity?"

Ahmad's head jerked back, his eyes blazing with intensity. "It also says: 'Do not veil the truth with falsehood, nor conceal the truth knowingly.' Allah will punish unbelievers, Sister. Even Devereaux. Even you."

"What if Earth was not God's only project? What if it was just one design, one experiment? Isn't it possible we're just one of the species God created in his image…"

A rapid movement drew Sister Ezekiel's eye. She turned as Ernie Olsen stopped in front of Chief McKinney. "A couple of those big soldiers are movin' through town," Ernie said, "orderin' people outside. They're knockin' down doors, pushin' us here. They wouldn't tell us anything other than to move to the shelter. I saw two teenagers try to run away and they shot 'em, left 'em lyin' in the street. Don't know if they're dead or alive. What's goin' on, Chief?"

Chief McKinney looked at Sister Ezekiel. His eyes narrowed; his jaw clenched. He turned back to Ernie Olsen, his voice trembling only a little: "I don't know. But it's not good."

Colonel Truman separated himself from his men and, followed by Lieutenant Adams, moved up beside Sister Ezekiel. He said, "My soldiers are prepared to fight the Elite Ops. But I already lost forty-three people. If it comes down to a battle—their weapons against ours—they'll kill us all."

Lieutenant Adams said, "We contained them last time. I say we take 'em on again."

"I'll fight," Chief McKinney said. He bent down stiffly and pulled a small Las-pistol from a holster strapped to his ankle. When he straightened up, his back cracked and he grimaced, but he looked Colonel Truman in the eye. "I like to hold a little something back, keep the natives thinking I'm harmless."

Colonel Truman shook his head. "Against their shields, Chief? I don't think so."

"If they're going to kill us anyway," Chief McKinney said, "I'd rather go down fighting."

Colonel Truman rubbed his forehead. "Disarming might be our best chance of survival. If we're unarmed and we don't provoke them, we just might make it through this. I think the Elite Ops need some justification to start firing. On the other hand, they're different now—angry. They may be looking for an excuse to wipe us out. What do you think, Sister?"

Sister Ezekiel struggled to keep her focus. After a moment she said, "What can we do but pray?"

"That certainly wouldn't hurt," Truman agreed.

Townspeople trickled down the street in twos and threes, moving hesitantly, looking up at the flying Elite Ops every few steps. For the most part, they huddled together along the north side of the corral, avoiding Truman's soldiers, the police and especially Sister Ezekiel and the homeless men. The reporters moved freely among them, filming everything.

Sister Ezekiel looked for the young man with the orange Afro. He stood next to several homeless men, hands in his pockets, his head following the movement of the flying Elite Ops.

"I can't just stand here doing nothing," Sister Ezekiel said. She began moving from group to group, providing encouragement—and prayer where it was wanted—but accepting that some people just wanted to air their frustrations and worries. As she talked with each of them, calming their fears, taking their burdens upon herself—not willingly but of necessity—she found herself gaining strength. They would live or die by God's grace. Nothing she said or did would alter that fact. She let people vent, barely concentrating on the words they spoke, nodding her head and absorbing their panic until they thanked her, letting her know they could go on for a little while longer. She felt her soul shining brightly, repelling all the blackness in the world. And she knew that no matter what Devereaux said, religion was necessary for times like these.

"Sister," Ahmad said.

She looked into his eyes, realized that she'd come back to where he stood. "Yes?"

"How can you be so calm? You realize they're gonna kill us, don't you? They're gonna wipe us out, and it's all Devereaux's fault. Why did you save him?"

"I was acting for the greater good, Ahmad. Devereaux, whatever he did, deserves to live. He's a good man. And we need him. If for no other reason than to strengthen our faith."

One of the Elite Ops stepped forward and spoke in a loud voice amplified by something in his helmet: "Close up ranks. Move together." The Elite Ops stepped inside the corral and began shoving townspeople toward the center of the enclosure. "Hurry," the Elite Ops blared. "One big group. All weapons in a pile over there." The Elite Ops pointed toward the driveway, which formed the entryway to the enclosure.

Looking that way, Sister Ezekiel saw Doug approaching along the sidewalk, followed by an Elite Ops trooper. Doug walked with his head up, no longer slouching, eyes ahead, as if unaware of the huge menace following him. When he saw Sister Ezekiel look his way, he waved. Sister Ezekiel couldn't help but smile, buoyed by Doug's unquenchable spirit. He seemed different somehow—stronger, more confident—as if his time away had enabled him to realize he possessed value after all. Sister Ezekiel had been trying to instill that sense of self-worth in him for months. Now he seemed to have finally achieved it. She felt a tremendous sense of pride in his accomplishment.

As Doug came closer, his smile vanished, his face betraying his concern, and when he entered the enclosure and stopped in front of her, he said, "What happened to you, Sister?"

Sister Ezekiel reached out and hugged him with her trembling body, the embrace calming her. She told him it was nothing, explained that she'd fainted. Colonel Truman's soldiers moved toward the spot designated by the Elite Ops and began dropping their weapons in a pile. "You too, Sheriff," the Elite Ops organizer said.

"Why?" Chief McKinney said. "So you can kill us more easily?"

"Drop the weapon now," the Elite Ops ordered.

"I'm the law in these parts," Chief McKinney said. "And I don't answer to you."

Two red laser pulses struck Chief McKinney from the two flying Elite Ops. A few of Colonel Truman's soldiers began firing at the Elite Ops. People screamed. Lasers sizzled. Doug pulled Sister Ezekiel to the ground. Others dropped too. The smell of burnt chemicals mingled with the smell of rotting flesh the Elite Ops gave off.

"Stand down," Colonel Truman yelled over the noise. He stood with his arms in the air. "Stand down your weapons now."

The firing stopped but the screaming continued.

"Quiet!" the Elite Ops organizer commanded. "If you do as you're told, you will not be harmed."

Colonel Truman unclipped his Las-pistol and tossed it on the pile. "Weapons over here now," he said to his soldiers. "That's an order, people."

As his soldiers moved to comply, Lieutenant Adams walked over to those half-dozen soldiers who had fired at the Elite Ops and paid with their lives. She collected their weapons and brought them to the pile. Colonel Truman, bending over the old police chief's body, picked up the chief's weapon and tossed it on the pile, shaking his head. As Doug helped Sister Ezekiel to her feet, she said a silent prayer for Chief McKinney's soul.

When the last of the weapons had been placed on the pile, the Elite Ops organizer herded people away from it and toward the shelter. Colonel Truman found Sister Ezekiel's hand, gave it a reassuring squeeze. She took comfort from that and did the same for Doug. Four steps away, the young man with the orange Afro stood sideways to the Elite Ops, facing her. She knew he was filming her.

As the Elite Ops got the last few people gathered up, Sister Ezekiel began to pray out loud, "Our Father, who art in Heaven…"

Was she praying because that's what people would expect of her in this moment? No, she was reaching out to God. She could feel a channel open, a direct link between her and the Sweet Lord.

Other voices joined in, even Ahmad's. They echoed behind her and she felt a smile coming as they spoke the words Christ gave them. Was she about to die? Would she find out now if there was a God? And what if Devereaux was right? Then she'd never know it. But she was happy she had God in her life. She wouldn't have it any other way. She was part of a community, leading her people into the dark land, and her voice grew in power as she prayed to the one true God.

While she prayed, a breeze sprang up, carrying away the smoky stench of the ruined vehicles, the burnt chemicals, the poisonous rot of the Elite Ops, and replaced it with an indefinable odor of autumnal vegetation—grass, mixed with the woody aroma of oak trees. She looked up at the tree line, where it joined the rich blue sky, just now beginning to change color with the lowering sun.

Sister Ezekiel projected her voice even louder despite the soreness in her jaw: "…But deliver us from evil. For thine is the kingdom…" The breeze dropped as the crowd behind her finished the prayer. She could smell her own sweat now, mingling with the sour stench of her fellow victims. A droplet trickled down her side and another weaved its way along the underside of her arm.

The Elite Ops flying around the enclosure were joined by two others. All four aimed their weapons at the people below. The Elite Ops organizer moved to the pile of weapons. Two other troopers stood at the entrance to the enclosure. Their weapons—aimed belly-high—emitted a red glow and a sizzling, crackling sound. Many voices faltered but Sister Ezekiel launched into her favorite prayer, slowing down the words to savor every one of them: "Hail Mary, full of grace. Our Lord is with thee…"

Now the Elite Ops organizer joined the other two Elite Ops at the exit and leveled his Las-rifle at the group. The reporters, bunched in with everyone else, struggled to film the scene, while the young man with the orange Afro continued to stare at Sister Ezekiel. She closed her eyes, hoping that if they were all killed, others would view and remember this terrible moment. Immediately she felt shame that such a thought should occur to her. That wasn't why she continued praying.

The rotting odor of the Elite Ops intensified, overpowering all other smells. The high-pitched whine of their power packs grew in volume. Sister Ezekiel's mind faltered, as if suddenly drained of the ability to think. She stumbled over the words, fought the chalky dryness of her mouth, managed to keep praying. She would die on her terms. She would fight back in the only way she knew, with a prayer to the Lord—for these killers as well as their victims.

Unbidden, an image of the men who assaulted and raped her flashed into her head—two men laughing as they left her sobbing in the dirt. Another image, in court, the young men no longer looking malevolent, facing her as she asked the judge for lenience—one of them crying softly, the other looking blankly past her, as if indifferent to the sentence he would soon receive. Or perhaps his forced withdrawal from the drugs left him emotionless. If she could forgive those misguided wretches, she could forgive these troopers too.

There was peace in the Blessed Lord and if she prayed well enough, He would help her overcome her fear. She opened her eyes, her voice clear and strong, looked past the weapons to the visors of the young men before her and prayed: "...Holy Mary, Mother of God, pray for us sinners, now and at the hour of our death."

Chapter Thirty-Eight

Jeremiah spent the flight in his dungeon, trying to keep the fear at bay. It took all his effort to focus on the stones surrounding him, the torchlight flickering on the unsteady walls. He was grateful for his wounds; the pain helped take his mind off the nauseating smell of jet fuel and the vibration of the jet-copter. Quark sat grim-faced, one massive hand encircling Carlton's arm just above the broken wrist, while the other gripped the particle beam cannon. Devereaux and Lendra slept. When they finally landed, Jeremiah shivered with relief. He noticed that his body itched where he'd been wounded, while his stomach felt like it was home to a swarming nest of ants.

Devereaux awoke and smiled hesitantly.

Soldiers—Army soldiers—opened the doors and two medics reached for Lendra. They pulled her stretcher from the helicopter and carried her inside.

Two more medics reached for Devereaux. He allowed them to assist him in stepping down from the copter, then said, "I have to see the President right away."

"You need medical help," one of the medics said.

"That can wait."

The medic then turned his head to look Jeremiah over. He pointed to the blood on Jeremiah's shirt and said, "You need help?"

Jeremiah shook his head and got to his feet. As he jumped out of the copter, the soldiers directed him to a stairway. Several surrounded Devereaux, supporting him as he made his way down the stairs. Another took the particle beam cannon from Quark. Jeremiah looked out over the familiar buildings of Washington, DC, and realized that they'd landed on the roof of the CINTEP building. Eli would be waiting inside. The other jet-copter carrying the dead and wounded Elite Ops hovered over the landing pad for a moment, its pilot saluting before it flew off.

Quark kept a firm grip on Carlton as they stepped through a doorway. Descending the ramp, Jeremiah remembered that Eli had a miniature hospital in the building—two operating rooms and half a dozen beds—for sensitive medical procedures. Jeremiah's genetic modification had occurred here. He stopped at the end of the ramp, where an older woman with gray hair stood next to a female Army captain. Less than a minute later, a body was wheeled inside. Jeremiah recognized it as Weiss. The captain halted the gurney and opened the body pouch, turning to the gray-haired woman with a small nod. The gray-haired woman stepped forward, tears running down her cheeks, and touched Gray Weiss' face. After a moment she withdrew her hand and the captain gestured to the soldiers, who wheeled the gurney down the hall, the gray-haired woman following at a slower pace, clutching the captain's arm. Jeremiah nodded at her as she passed.

Julianna's body came next. Stopping the gurney, Jeremiah opened the body pouch and stared at her face. Julianna—energetic, irresistable—gone forever. Her bright teeth shone through her partially open mouth. Jeremiah touched her cold forehead. He refused to feel sorrow over her loss. Blinking three times, he centered himself in his dungeon and caressed her cheek softly. She'd talked once about retiring to the Virgin Islands, where she'd spent a few years in her childhood. Jeremiah would have to see that her remains were sent there.

"We'll take care of her, sir," one of the soldiers behind the gurney said.

Jeremiah stepped back, his breath catching in his throat as he watched her gliding away. Could his blood have kept her alive? Why hadn't he thought of that before, when it still might have been possible to save her? He felt rage building up inside, tamped it down, then made his way to the conference room.

Eli sat at the head of a large table, his PlusPhone next to his right hand. Across the room at the other end of the table, President Angelica Hope waited. Halfway through the long table, a wall of light shimmered—a shield. Jeremiah smelled a hint of the President's perfume drifting through the barrier. At the President's side sat General

Horowitz, Chairman of the Joint Chiefs, and standing in a semi-circle around them were half a dozen Secret Service agents dressed in black, their weapons held discreetly by their sides. They kept their eyes on Carlton, Jeremiah and Quark.

In one of the corners, a projection played. Eli's technology expert, Jay-Edgar, manipulated the footage, shifting from scene to scene, images of EOs surrounding national monuments and government buildings, their weapons aimed outward in rock-steady hands.

Quark sat beside Carlton at the table, a firm grip on Carlton's forearm, just above the broken wrist. A major and two sergeants had taken up position behind them. On the other side of the table, two captains flanked Devereaux while a team of doctors wearing surgical scrubs ran diagnostic scans on him. Jay-Edgar sat at Eli's right hand. He slid a computer over to Devereaux.

Eli got to his feet and walked over to Jeremiah. "Lendra?" he asked.

Jeremiah shrugged. "She took a laser pulse to the stomach. They just brought her inside."

Eli glared at Carlton. "You'd better hope she pulls through," he said before turning back to Jeremiah. "How are you?"

"You know I'll be fine. And you know why."

Eli reached up and patted Jeremiah on the shoulder. "We'll talk about that later. Elite Ops troopers surround dozens of government buildings. Panic is spreading across the country. We couldn't keep this situation a secret. There's rioting in Philadelphia, New York, Los Angeles—dozens of cities." He returned to his chair opposite President Hope and gestured for Jeremiah to sit at his left hand.

President Hope cleared her throat and said, "Gentlemen, we're at a standoff. The Elite Ops are not responding to General Horowitz's orders. And Mr. Carlton's demands are unacceptable. We need another way out of this mess."

Devereaux sat hunched over the computer Jay-Edgar had passed him, occasionally glancing at Jay-Edgar, who nodded back, smiling broadly as his fingers raced over his keyboard. Carlton smirked at Devereaux from across the table and said, "You'll never breach my system. I use a quantum key distribution security code. Unbreakable." When Devereaux ignored him, Carlton added, "You think we didn't find your backdoor passwords? We took the system apart after what happened in Rochester two years ago. Rebuilt it from the ground up. There's no way you can access it."

Devereaux continued working on the keyboard, while a doctor crouched down beside him and adjusted the setting on his QuikHeal bandage.

"Perhaps," Carlton said, "you require a demonstration of my total control over the Elite Ops."

President Hope said, "I hardly think that will be necessary, Mr. Carlton."

Carlton said, "Bring up the footage of the Tessamae Shelter."

Eli nodded to Jay-Edgar, who held up a hand and said, "Coming up now."

On the projection, four EOs flew in jet packs around Colonel Truman's soldiers, Sister Ezekiel and the homeless men. The other three EOs stood at the entrance to an enclosure formed by the twisted debris of ruined vehicles, their weapons leveled at the crowd.

"I can have all those people killed," Carlton said, "without blinking an eye. I can destroy all your monuments." He caught Jeremiah's eye, as if flaunting his promise not to hurt anyone. Jeremiah got a sick hollowness in his gut as he realized just how badly he'd misjudged Carlton. Yet there was still hope that Carlton wouldn't do anything drastic.

"Do you want a civil war?" President Hope asked.

Carlton looked at Quark, then back to the President and said, "Given my choices, I think I might."

* * *

Doug's feet ached from standing in the shelter's parking lot. The sun was halfway down the horizon and the sky looked pink and orange. But the smell of rotting flesh made him queasy. For the past hour, Sister Ezekiel had kept everyone's spirits up by alternately leading prayers and hymns. Now, one of the Elite Ops troopers strode forward and placed his Las-rifle under Sister Ezekiel's chin. Everyone else stopped talking but Sister Ezekiel immediately launched into another Hail Mary.

"Please, Sister," Doug said. "Don't make them angry. Please be quiet. They're gonna kill you." He squeezed her hand hard but she kept right on praying. Doug flinched. He could almost feel the rifle pressing into his own skin. He said to the trooper, "She's never harmed anyone."

The trooper turned his helmet toward Doug, who shivered as he saw his image reflected in the visor. These men were cold. Sister Ezekiel continued to pray, her head tilted up away from the Las-rifle. Beside him, Henry gripped his hand tightly and Doug suddenly felt ill. Somehow he knew that when the trooper turned back to Sister Ezekiel he was going to fire. When Doug saw the helmet move, he yelled, "No!"

Sister Ezekiel's head jerked sideways. Her glasses and wimple flew off, exposing her stiff gray hair, and she crumpled as the laser buzzed. Her hand dragged Doug's down.

A loud metallic voice spoke: "Stay where you are or more will die."

A chill ran through Doug. He gaped at Sister Ezekiel's lifeless face, at the sightless eyes, blackened from the fall she took earlier. Henry bent over and retched, his vomit landing on the boot of the trooper. Before Henry could straighten up, the trooper kicked him in the face—a sickening crunch. Doug almost didn't notice the screaming voices around him. All he could focus on was Sister Ezekiel lying motionless on the ground. A young man with an orange Afro leaned forward to peer at Sister Ezekiel, small lenses peeking out from behind the hair.

The bastard's filming her!

The young man's face was nearly white as he bent to look at the fallen nun. Doug wanted to punch him. Colonel Truman stepped forward, his hands clenched into fists, a strangled sound coming from his throat.

Dropping to his knees, Doug grabbed Sister Ezekiel's wrist. He felt no pulse. Straightening her legs, he crossed her arms over her chest, then closed her eyes.

Screaming people began pushing into him. Doug fought to his

feet and held them back, so no one would step on Sister Ezekiel's body. He recognized Colonel Truman and Ahmad next to him, pushing back against the crowd. Staring off to the northeast, where the Escala hid, Doug avoided looking at Sister Ezekiel's ruined face as he tried to block out the noise and the smell.

* * *

As Sister Ezekiel dropped to the ground, her limbs sprawled awkwardly, Jeremiah pushed himself out of his chair, fists clenched at his sides, fighting a sudden bout of nausea. But before he could reach Carlton, Quark assaulted the man. Growling, Quark pummeled Carlton, punching him over and over. Carlton screamed—a high, piercing wail interrupted by the sickening sound of ribs cracking.

"Get him off! Get him off!" Carlton yelled. "He's killing me. Get him off or everybody dies."

He curled up in a defensive posture as the sergeants and the major moved forward to protect him, but Quark threw them off like children. Jeremiah dove between Quark and Carlton, absorbing body blows from the big Escala. He struggled to separate them, pushing and kicking at Carlton while his arms tried to pinion Quark. It was like trying to wrestle a bear. But finally he freed Carlton from Quark's grip. As the sergeants pulled Carlton free, Jeremiah grabbed Quark by the ears, his face just inches away, and yelled, "We can't kill him. We can't kill him."

Finally Quark stopped thrashing and Jeremiah loosened his grip. At that moment, Jay-Edgar said, "Got it. That's amazing!"

Jeremiah looked across the table. Devereaux—oblivious to the scuffle in front of him, the captains and doctors at his back—continued to work at his computer.

"What have you got?" President Hope asked from the other side of the shield, where she stood behind her Secret Service agents, protected from a possible attack.

General Horowitz pointed to the projection, which continued to show EOs surrounding government buildings and the fallen nun at the Tessamae Shelter. "Looks the same to me," he said.

"We've temporarily sabotaged all local satellite connections in the frequency range used by the Elite Ops," Devereaux said. "But we can only disrupt them for about ten minutes."

"Knock him out," Eli said.

The major pressed a pad into Carlton's neck and Carlton's head immediately dropped.

"Quickly," Eli said. "We need that deadman switch out of his head."

The two sergeants dragged Carlton from the room at a run, the major following them. Two of the doctors behind Devereaux also jogged out.

"Sister Ezekiel!" Devereaux said. He raised himself up, then bent over in pain, and Jeremiah realized he'd only now seen what had happened to the nun. The two captains flanking Devereaux helped him back to his seat. The doctor beside him examined her scanner and shook her head.

Parting her Secret Service agents with her hands, President Hope stepped close to the edge of the shield. Her hair sparkled in the light. She said, "Are you sure about this?"

"They're not attacking," Eli replied.

Jay-Edgar said, "The satellites are trying to reconfigure themselves. We've got about eight minutes before they find an alternate pathway."

"Would the Elite Ops attack without an order to do so?" President Hope asked.

No one had an answer.

Jeremiah stared at the screens as Jay-Edgar manipulated them—the Capitol, the White House, the Lincoln Memorial and Sister Ezekiel's body with a cluster of people around it. Other bodies lay off to the side. For the moment, the EOs simply held their positions.

Devereaux, his face pale, sat down heavily and began to weep. The tall doctor bent over him for a second before backing away as Quark, his massive body shaking, worked his way around the table past Eli and put his hands on Devereaux's shoulders, then turned to glare at the room's occupants as if daring them to twitch a muscle or say a word. Jeremiah met his eyes briefly before returning to his seat.

President Hope slumped into her chair while General Horowitz picked up the pitcher of water, poured a glass and passed it to her. Taking a sip, her hand trembling, she stared at Eli. Jeremiah sensed some meaning behind the look but he couldn't say whether it was accusation or question.

General Horowitz looked down at his PlusPhone, touched the President's hand and said, "The Elite Ops still aren't responding to my orders. But at least they're not attacking."

"Six minutes," Jay-Edgar said.

President Hope put her face in her hands. After a few seconds, she rubbed her eyes and said, "We still have a hell of a problem. We need those Elite Ops under control. How long to find and take out the chip in Carlton's head?"

"Can't be more than ten minutes," Eli said. "We don't have to be too careful. We just have to make sure he doesn't die during surgery."

"We don't have ten minutes," President Hope said.

"Excuse me," Devereaux said, his voice quavering slightly. "But there's a more important problem here."

Eli frowned in confusion.

"Sister Ezekiel," Devereaux said, his face flushing, "was just murdered by that madman. An innocent, gentle creature: the best person I've ever met. And you're dismissing it as insignificant, as if you had no responsibility for it at all."

President Hope said, "Eli didn't kill Sister Ezekiel."

"Yes, he did." Devereaux's voice crackled with anger. "He's part of it. You're all part of it."

Eli said, "You're to blame too."

"Let's all calm down," President Hope said. "Sister Ezekiel's death is most regrettable. But it's Richard Carlton's fault—no one else's. Once this crisis is over, we'll re-examine the Elite Ops program."

Jay-Edgar said, "Four minutes."

The holo-projections in the corner showed the EOs holding their positions outside the government landmarks. Jay-Edgar switched channels briefly to show continuing riots in a dozen major cities, where National Guard troops now began arriving.

"Mr. Devereaux," the President said. "You may have saved a great many lives today. But you're dangerous. The weapons you've designed…"

"I never should have told President Davis about them," Devereaux said. "I never meant to build them. I only wanted to make him aware that such weapons were possible, that humanity could be destroyed. I wanted to encourage him to work toward establishing a colony on Mars."

"Still," President Hope said, "What am I going to do with you?"

"You could have me killed," Devereaux said, his face showing no sign he was joking. "You could dig into my brain to pull out the secrets of the bioweapons I conceived. But that way leads to oblivion. Whether you use the weapons or someone else does, eventually they will be used, so I'll never give them to you voluntarily."

"I don't want them."

"Others in your government do." He glanced at Eli, then at General Horowitz. "I won't surrender that knowledge. You could eliminate the problem, the temptation, by reinstating the Mars Project, sending me to Mars with the Escala."

The President lifted her hands. "We don't have the money."

"Find it," Devereaux said. "I can't stay here any longer. Too many people want too much of me. And as for the money, the cost of keeping me here might ultimately be greater than the cost of sending me away."

"Two minutes," Jay-Edgar intoned.

Jeremiah felt like his insides had just been run through a shredder. He found it difficult to focus on the conversation. How could these people discuss the Mars Project so calmly while the EOs prepared to burn the city to the ground? Jeremiah kept his eyes on the monitors, checking for any sign of aggressive movement by the EOs, as if he could prevent an attack by his vigilance.

President Hope addressed Devereaux again: "You want me to send you to Mars when I have all these other more urgent problems to address? Terrorism, the Susquehanna Virus, the condemnation of religious governments around the world for allowing you to remain free. Not to mention the fear people have of what the Escala might do on their own, unsupervised, with a whole planet's resources at their disposal."

"We're scientists," Quark protested. Then, as if realizing his outburst had been inappropriate, he lowered his head, angling it to the side, and stared up at the President.

"The Escala," Devereaux said, "have no desire to dominate humans. They simply wish to fulfill their destiny—to learn and grow, to achieve their full potential. Keeping them here will kill them. Surely you know that."

"And letting them go may kill us," Eli said. He looked at Quark. "With your intelligence and physical abilities, it wouldn't take much for you to overcome humanity. Not tomorrow, certainly, but in a few generations." He pointed at Devereaux. "You've made no secret about wanting to *improve* humanity."

"This is better?" Devereaux replied, his eyes shifting between Eli and President Hope. "Rioting? Chaos? The murder of innocents in the name of patriotism or religion or some archaic notion of what it means to be human? You will be well rid of us, believe me. Out of sight, out of mind."

"Zero," Jay-Edgar said. "Satellite connection now restored."

Everyone stared at the monitors. The EOs in front of the White House and the Washington Monument brought their particle beam cannons to bear on their targets. But they held their fire. Jeremiah stared at the projection of the Tessamae Shelter, where the camera still showed a picture of Sister Ezekiel on her back. After a few seconds, the camera shifted to show the four EOs circling the enclosure with jet packs. They slowly descended, joining the three at the entrance. When all seven were together, they headed for the tank parked in the street, the trailing EO walking backwards, his weapon aimed at the crowd. As they reached the vehicle, the trailing EO fired a long blue burst at a pile of weapons, and everybody in the enclosure dropped to the ground. Jeremiah cringed, expecting an explosion. None came. When the EOs climbed into the vehicle and drove away to the south, Colonel Truman and another tall black man knelt before Sister Ezekiel. Together they lifted her and, surrounded by the crowd, each of whom reached in a hand to touch her habit, carried her to the shelter.

The major ran into the conference room and came to attention. "Sir," he said to General Horowitz, "the doctor's got the chip from Carlton."

"Put it on screen," Eli said to Jay-Edgar.

The holo-projection scene changed, showing an operating room. The doctor held a small chip up to the camera, which then zoomed in on Carlton's head. His face had gone slack and his eyes were open wide, staring blankly ahead, not blinking.

"Afraid we did some damage to his cerebral cortex," the doctor said.

"Well done," President Hope said. She reached out an unsteady hand and took a sip of water. "I don't mind telling you I was a little nervous just then." She leaned back in her chair and turned to Devereaux. "I can't guarantee anything. But I'll do everything in my power to get you to Mars. I owe you that much."

"Thank you," Devereaux said.

"What about the Moon?" Quark asked. "Couldn't we temporarily relocate there? The increase in radiation would be beneficial."

"Good idea," Devereaux said.

President Hope nodded. "That can be arranged."

"One other thing," Devereaux said.

"Yes?"

"I'd like to record a broadcast to the people of the world—a goodbye message. Although my ideas haven't been accepted as well as I'd hoped, I would still like a chance to address my brothers and sisters—explain why I've done what I've done, hopefully help them through these difficult times."

Jeremiah immediately caught the reconciliatory nature of that gesture, realizing that if Devereaux wanted to, he could send the message without the President's approval.

But President Hope seemed to take the request seriously. She pursed her lips and said, "We'll let you tape something. And if it's not a threat to our national security, we'll broadcast it. Elias can set that up for you." She glanced at the projection showing the ruined Tessamae Shelter. "Again, I'm sorry for your loss." Then she looked at Eli. "Anything else I need to be aware of?" When Eli shook his head, she nodded. "Very well. Good work, gentlemen."

She got to her feet and strode out the door without a backward glance, her Secret Service agents surrounding her, General Horowitz bringing up the rear. As her side of the room went dark, the shield fading to nothing, Eli pursed his lips and said, "Well, I guess that's over."

Jeremiah stared at him. "What about Carlton?"

"Carlton?"

"If Marschenko kidnapped my son on Carlton's orders, how am I supposed to find out where Joshua is with Carlton like that?"

"We're close to finding Joshua. Come with me." Eli rose to his feet, started for the door. "If you two gentlemen will excuse us," he said to Quark and Devereaux. "You too, Jay-Edgar. I won't need you for this."

Before he reached the door, Quark strode over and blocked the exit. He said, "When do we leave?"

"The sooner, the better," Eli answered, his neck arched way back to look up at the big man. "We can start putting people on Lunar Base 2 in a week or two. As for Mars, well, there's a chance you can be on your way inside a year."

Eli, stepping around Quark, waited at the door as Jeremiah got to his feet and walked around the table to where Devereaux sat. The two captains flanking Devereaux moved back a step. "I'm sorry," Jeremiah said, touching Devereaux's shoulder, "for the way everything turned out. I should have listened to Julianna."

"You're a good man," Devereaux said. He reached up and put his hand over Jeremiah's. "Julianna was right about that. If there's anything I can do for you, please let me know."

"I was going to make the same offer," Jeremiah said. "Are you sure you should be going to Mars? You're not genetically altered."

Devereaux smiled, patted Jeremiah's hand. "Ever since I was a little boy, I used to look up at the stars and planets. I always wanted to go to Mars. Just to stand on its surface for a moment would be enough for me."

One of the doctors behind the chair cleared her throat. "Mr. Devereaux, we need you in surgery now."

Jeremiah squeezed Devereaux's shoulder gently, then made his way to the door. Quark nodded to him as he passed and Jeremiah nodded back. Then he followed Eli down the hall to Eli's office, his gut churning. "What do you know about Joshua?" he asked as he entered the office, only then noticing Mrs. Harris at work cleaning the top of Eli's desk.

Eli gestured for Mrs. Harris to leave, then closed the door behind her and activated the sunset rainbow lighting he seemed to prefer. "We've begun accessing Carlton's computer files. We found references to a program of genetic modification. Many of the records were destroyed by an anti-tampering virus. It may take some time to recover them. The files we could access contain a code name—Lucas. It looks like a classic cutout. None of the participants knew all the others. They each just knew one other person. We don't know yet who Lucas is or how he's connected to Carlton."

"How does that tie up with Joshua?"

"The name Joshua Jones appeared in the Lucas file. We'll get what we can from Carlton. But that may not be much. Still, we're closer than we were."

Jeremiah sensed Eli knew more than he was saying—a slight quaver in the old man's voice. He focused on Eli's face and said, "Why did he take Joshua?"

"My guess?" Eli rubbed his chin. "Carlton was trying to develop even better Elite Ops troopers—genetically augmented as well as mechanically enhanced."

Jeremiah said, "And Joshua became part of this program?"

Eli nodded. "It seems he has nearly perfect DNA for transgenic alteration."

Jeremiah took a step forward. "So he's like me?"

Eli shrugged. "Not quite. Your DNA is incompatible with nano-implants."

Jeremiah struggled to calm himself. He wanted to lash out, achieve the temporary peace that came with overwhelming violence. He blinked three times, centering himself in his dungeon.

"I'll do everything I can for you," Eli continued. "But they've probably altered him substantially. He may not even know you anymore."

Jeremiah walked to the sofa and sat heavily. He found it hard to breathe. Wiping his eyes, he stared out the window at the lights of the city. Washington, DC: the center of power: where men like Eli, with enough motivation, could arrange anything. At least Joshua was alive. Somehow, Jeremiah would bring his son home. "Why?" he asked.

Eli shrugged. "You should know by now that everything comes back to power. The world is an increasingly dangerous place, Jeremiah. Our national security is a paramount issue. You think we're the only country with Elite Ops soldiers? Or even transgenic people? All the major powers are developing programs of super-fighters."

"When will you know about my son?"

"Soon," Eli said. "Get cleaned up and go home, Jeremiah. I'll find him. Trust me. We'll leave no stone unturned."

Jeremiah got to his feet. He couldn't remember the last time he'd felt so exhausted, so emotionally drained. He nodded to Eli as he made his way out of the office.

Chapter Thirty-Nine

Jeremiah sat beside Lendra's bed, rubbing the back of her hand with his thumb until he felt movement in her fingers. When she opened her eyes, it took her a few seconds to focus on his face.

"Jeremiah?" Lendra said.

"How do you feel?"

"Not much pain." She closed her eyes for a moment, then stared into his and said, "Thank you for saving my life. They told me that without your blood I wouldn't have survived."

"I'll let you get some rest," Jeremiah said. "I just wanted to make sure you're okay." He got to his feet and tried to pull his hand away but Lendra gripped it firmly and said, "Please don't go yet."

Jeremiah lowered himself back to his chair. "I suppose I can stay for a few more minutes."

"You're a strange man...and yet...I think I'm falling in love with you."

Jeremiah closed his eyes and took a deep breath. Shaking his head, he replied, "You barely know me."

"I know you. You've killed for your country. And you think that makes you bad. But you're not. You're kind and gentle and smart." Lendra pulled Jeremiah's hand to her lips and kissed it. "Tell me you feel nothing for me and I'll let you walk away."

"It's not as simple as that," Jeremiah said. "If I let you in, they'll kill you."

"I'm not Julianna," Lendra said, "and I'm not Catherine."

"You don't know what these people are capable of."

"I'm not afraid of them. As long as you're with me."

"We'll talk about this later," Jeremiah said.

Lendra stared at him intently, as if deciding whether to let go of the topic. After a few seconds, she said, "Will you stay here until I fall asleep?"

Jeremiah settled back in the chair with a sigh.

* * *

Elias watched Devereaux approach the cameras. The great man had shaved, showered and had his hair cut. He looked like the Devereaux of old, only thinner; he still had that great presence, that ability to take over a camera, or a room. His abdominal surgery had been a complete success, his recovery accelerated by Jeremiah's blood. Elias worried about that, wondered if it was too late now to take corrective action. Perhaps he'd talk to President Hope about it.

Even though Devereaux wouldn't be leaving for a few days, he wore a flight suit. Next to him, Quark stood in similar costume, looking like some giant ape: still unshaven, black hair sticking out in all directions. Behind them, Lunar Transit Vehicle C reached as tall as a two-story building and nearly as long as a football field. Elias knew it was a holographic trick, that Devereaux really stood before a green screen, but it looked real enough. Elias wanted to impress upon the public that Devereaux would be leaving as soon as possible and the image of the LTV-C conveyed that idea perfectly. It looked ungainly on the ground, like some giant medicine capsule—long and cylindrical. Its wings were nowhere near big enough to provide the lift it would need to fly if it were a traditional airplane. But they were attached merely to offer stability and steerage. Four Toninato-Huxley fusion engines generated the power required for liftoff.

Devereaux looked into the camera and said, "Friends, I know a lot of you are angry with me. I've said and done things that don't fit with your views of the world. How can I deny the existence of God? Or work for the evolution of humanity beyond what you know it to be?" He paused for a few seconds.

"I'm sorry if I hurt you. Believe me, that was never my intention. I only want what's best for this world. I want us to become better than we are. I see in each of us the potential for greatness—the possibility of perfect altruism. I see a future where we can accomplish things we never imagined, if only we trust each other and work together. Can you see us reaching out to the stars? I can. Can you see us making a heaven right here on Earth? I can see that too. But we're not heading in either direction at the moment. We're destroying our habitat and each other—and we all know it."

Devereaux paused again, lending emphasis to his previous words, before continuing: "We always seem to have good intentions, but those intentions are usually tempered by our self-interest. Almost never do we honestly ask ourselves, 'What can I do to help others, even if it means I must sacrifice a little?' But until we learn to do that, until we accept that we are all responsible for the whole of our world, not just our little sector of it, we will never move beyond the narrow thinking that has brought us to this dangerous point.

"Brothers and sisters, I'm leaving this lovely planet—traveling to a cold, harsh world where I don't expect to live a long or comfortable life. But we won't be fighting wars on Mars, or committing acts of terrorism. We won't be plundering our planet of its riches to satisfy our appetites at the expense of our children's future. We won't be seeking bigger and more dangerous weapons to destroy our enemies. We'll be working together, cooperating to build a better world than the one we found. If there were a beautiful statue up there that combined artistic excellence with the idea that we must evolve to survive, we would not destroy it. Hopefully, in the end, you will come to realize that we as humans must do better. We must move beyond the limitations of our emotions. If we are to overcome the challenges ahead, we must become more intelligent, more rational, more peaceful. We must achieve an understanding that, united, we can accomplish great things. Yet we must never subsume our individuality to the groupthink that has often led us down the wrong path."

The camera moved in as Devereaux paused for a third time. When he began again, he spoke slowly: "My friends, if we try, if we really focus on developing our mental abilities, if we work every hour of every day to be better creatures, we can evolve beyond the small, short-term, warrior thinkers history proves we have been, and grow into vast instruments of peace, vessels of enlightenment, beacons of hope for a future that nurtures us all." He raised his right hand slowly. "I hope that you fare well."

Elias turned off the screen. He knew the networks would immediately begin seeking reactions to the speech, undoubtedly finding a mix of people, pro and con, to discuss its impact. Pollsters would have their results out by tomorrow. Some would be outraged simply at the fact of Devereaux's continued existence, much less that he would presume to speak for all humanity. A few pundits would call him the Devil, evil incarnate or a misguided misanthrope. They'd call for demonstrations, hoping to speed the "God haters" offworld. Others would praise Devereaux's ideals and integrity while wondering if his admirable goals could actually reach fruition in a world where narrow-minded religious fanatics ruled, blissful in their ignorance, happily reshaping science and history to fit their scriptural teachings. But for most it would be just a minor diversion from the day-to-day work of living. In a few months, certainly in a few self-absorbed years, Devereaux would be forgotten.

* * *

President Angelica Hope strode out to the Rose Garden where Elias awaited her. She wore a dress of shimmer cloth that reflected a rainbow of colors and made her appear slimmer than she was. As she approached, he renewed his awe of her figure: nearly six feet tall, with muscular legs and broad shoulders. Of course she'd been a world-class tennis player, but he wondered also if she'd secretly undergone genetic enhancement surgery. Her face looked little different than it had in the days of her second career: as an action movie star. She looked him in the eye, shook his hand with a firm grip and said, "Thanks for meeting me. Better to keep this conversation completely private."

As she began to stroll through the garden, taking small steps so he wouldn't have to work hard to keep up, he fell in beside her. "What about the Elite Ops?" he said, trying to keep the fear out of his voice.

"General Horowitz is putting together a proposal on whether to keep them."

"And Devereaux?" he said. "You think we should let him go to the Moon?"

"Don't you?"

"He could tell us so much. The weapons he's designed—"

"—are planet killers," the President finished for him. "They're lose-lose propositions."

"We might be able to modify them to suit our purposes—target select groups."

"And they might run amok, decimate the planet's population. We're not ready for that kind of power. And he told us he wouldn't cooperate. If we wanted the information, we'd have to take it by force."

"Do you have a problem with that?"

"Yes," the President said, "when it comes to him, I do. You saw his speech?"

"I found it interesting," Elias said. "But he's wrong about the chance for a peaceful future."

"Is that why President Davis authorized the taking of Jeremiah's son?"

"He believed that the only way to save the people of Earth was to bring them together against a common enemy."

"As do you."

Elias shrugged. "Only the iron hand can enforce lasting peace."

President Hope glared at him. "I want it clear that your plan will not be put into play on my watch."

"Yes, Ma'am."

"It's madness, you know," she said.

"Do you want me to return the son to Jeremiah?"

"You're the long-term planner. Even if I'm re-elected, I'll only be here for a little over six more years. You can take your plan up with my successor. I don't want to hear anything about it ever again. It's between you and President Davis and whoever replaces me. I need plausible deniability."

"Of course," Elias said. "We never discussed it. But in a more general sense, I would note that man is ultimately a fighter. That is the only constant throughout known history. We are a violent, aggressive species and without an outside target upon which to focus our energies, we soon turn on each other."

President Hope stopped in front of a multi-colored rosebush, pointed at its sprouting blue, pink and gold blossoms: a perfectly symmetrical hybrid. She said, "You don't think we can change? Become enlightened and logical?"

"We're not roses," Elias answered. "We're ruled by our emotions—always have been, always will be. We like to believe we can change, that we can grow into better, more intellectual beings, but our true nature is immutable. We do what we do because we're driven by anger or fear or lust or envy or some other emotion—each of them stronger than rational thought. Emotion-driven action is why there have been so many wars in our past. Did you know that there has never been a decade in all our known history without a war somewhere in the world? Probably not a single year. Ever. The only way to make us peaceful is to make us something other than human."

"Perhaps," President Hope said. She stared at the bush for a few seconds, as if distracted by its beauty, then continued along the path so that Elias had to walk quickly to catch up. He said:

"People are getting more dangerous all the time. And we're getting closer to Armageddon every year. By sending Devereaux to the Moon, and eventually Mars, we're only putting off the development of a super-weapon. I don't suppose we need it anyway. We already have weapons that can wipe out an entire planet—the orbiting Las-cannons, for example. And others will come along… until that day—I'm not sure when it will be, but I'm certain it will come—when one of those weapons gets used. Humanity as we know it will perish. We can only prolong the inevitable."

"That's a depressing thought, and too distant for me to worry about. I'm concerned with the here and now."

"Which brings me back to Devereaux," Elias said. "As long as he's alive, he's a threat."

President Hope shook her head. "I don't want any accidents on the journey to Mars. If I thought Devereaux intended to build any of the weapons he's designed, I would argue differently, but I truly believe he'll take his secrets to the grave."

"I happen to agree that he has no intention of building a weapon. But anyone who has the knowledge he has must be taken seriously. And if he refuses to provide us with the information, perhaps we should ensure that no one else can possess it, either."

The President sighed. "I have no desire to harm him, Elias. President Davis contemplated killing him. Gray Weiss did too…yet another reason to keep him alive." When Elias nodded, the President smiled. "Good meeting," she said.

Elias lifted his arms and spread his hands. "You're the President."

Angelica Hope laughed. Then she turned away and resumed her walk. Elias followed again, watching the prismatic effect of her dress as they made a circuit through the garden. He found shimmer cloth almost disorienting the way it shifted colors so quickly. The President did not stop again. Nor did she speak.

* * *

Carrying a peace offering of a hamburger, fries and a Coke, Jeremiah descended the stairs to the basement, dreading the battle he was bound to have with the big EO. He doubted the food would be enough to quell Marschenko's rage. And Jeremiah no longer wanted to fight at all. Devereaux had made him see the senselessness of violence. Yet if Marschenko forced his hand, Jeremiah would do what was necessary to survive. However, when he reached the bottom of the stairs, he saw the heavily bearded Marschenko sitting on the toilet looking lethargic and shrunken, his muscles no longer showing that sharp bodybuilding definition. "What happened?" Jeremiah asked.

"Water," Marschenko rasped.

Jeremiah reached for the nutri-water tube and immediately saw that it had been chewed on and kinked. Jeremiah opened the Coke, which he handed to Marschenko, staying clear of the big man's reach.

Marschenko gulped greedily.

"Easy," Jeremiah said.

Marschenko nodded, drank more slowly.

"If you feel up to it," Jeremiah said, "I've brought you some lunch."

"Thanks." Marschenko took the proffered bag and began eating the fries, one at a time.

On the television, the newscasters continued their reporting on Devereaux's speech, the imminent departure of the Escala and the Elite Ops' recent deployment around the Capitol. Jeremiah glanced at the screen, where talking heads discussed rumors that the Elite Ops had nearly taken over the country. A government official maintained that the whole thing had been a secret military exercise.

Then footage of Sister Ezekiel's death played yet again as commentators discussed her saintly life and the tragedy of her murder. Marschenko dropped the bag and turned his head away, his eyes welling up. Jeremiah focused on the screen, letting Marschenko have his privacy.

The footage shifted to the destroyed statue, and a commentator opined that a new statue should be erected in the spot—one honoring Sister Ezekiel rather than the nameless man promoting evolution that had been there previously. "We don't need another tribute to Godlessness from the atheistic left. They're the reason our society has the problems it does. They're why we've created creatures who aren't even human anymore. Good riddance to them. And good riddance to Devereaux. Any fool can see that it was Devereaux's teachings that accelerated the moral decline of our nation. If it had not—"

"That's just more of the same," another commentator interrupted. "Religious zealotry. And it's an obvious misunderstanding of the importance of 'Emerging Man' as a metaphor for the human condition. Further, Devereaux teaches that humanity can become better than we are. That's what the Escala are—enlightened humans who are better for encompassing more of nature. How does that worsen our moral condition?"

"By ignoring the essential truth that God intended us to be pure and wholly human—"

"All Devereaux did was try to lift us up. And the sad thing is that now he's abandoning us."

"Good. I want him to give up on us."

"Don't you see? We need to work for a world with more unity, not less."

"Unity's fine. But not without God."

"Gentlemen," the moderator said, "let's get back to our discussion about the Elite Ops and whether that program should be dismantled."

Jeremiah muted the sound, then pointed to the nutri-water tube and said, "What happened?"

Marschenko clenched his fists as he looked up at the television. "I jerked on it when I saw that nun being murdered. I didn't realize how out-of-control we'd become." His voice quavered. "I didn't realize a lot of things till I was forced to sit here and think. I never would have done that if you hadn't…" Marschenko's eyes welled up again. He blinked back the tears. "I can see now that we're monsters. We deserve to die."

Jeremiah shook his head. How could he blame the EOs when they didn't know what they were doing? They'd killed innocents never understanding the wrongness of their actions.

Marschenko looked Jeremiah in the eye and said, "I'm sorry I took your son. I didn't know what I…" He looked away. "That's no excuse. It was just all so fuzzy. How could I have done such a thing? How could Donny have killed that nun?"

"You know him?"

"He's a good guy. I've worked with him before. He would never do such a thing…except I saw him do it."

"It was Carlton's fault—he ordered the killing. Somehow he learned to shut off the morality response in the EOs—creating the perfect killing machines. But I don't blame you or Donny. I blame Carlton."

"Did you ever find out what happened to your son?"

Jeremiah nodded. "Carlton wanted him for some secret project to turn him into an advanced fighter—genetic as well as mechanical enhancements. Like you and me, Jack. They want to turn my boy into a killer."

"We heard rumors about that program. Believe me, the Elite Ops don't want that to happen, either."

Jeremiah studied Marschenko, noted the new humbleness, the rational thought process.

"You have to kill me, Jones," Marschenko said. "I understand that."

"No. Actually, I'm setting you free."

Jeremiah grabbed a Las-knife from a shelf, then stepped over and cut away Marschenko's bonds. Tossing Marschenko his clothes, Jeremiah set Marschenko's Las-pistol on the floor next to the helmet, then turned off the television and backed toward the stairs. He blinked three times, centering himself in his stone dungeon, just in case.

After dressing, Marschenko massaged his wrists, then picked up his Las-pistol and helmet. He stood in the center of the room, ten feet away, not aiming the gun but pointing it in Jeremiah's general direction.

The bottom stair pressed against Jeremiah's heel, a possible source of leverage if he had to dive out of the way. A vein in Marschenko's forehead throbbed rapidly, and Jeremiah knew that the big man was also primed for action. He said, "You want to kill me, Jack?"

Marschenko watched him warily, massaged his throat with his free hand and took a step to his left. He shrugged. "Kind of, yeah."

"Now you know how I feel."

Marschenko raised his Las-pistol six inches. All he had to do was swing it a foot to the right and it would be centered on Jeremiah's chest. "What are we going to do about that?"

Jeremiah inhaled deeply through his nostrils, his jaw clenched, his eyes never leaving Marschenko's. He said, "I'll leave that up to you, Jack. I've got no reason to keep you here."

"You know they'll try to stop you from getting your son back?"

"Yes."

For long seconds neither moved. Neither spoke. They simply stared at each other, giving no quarter. Jeremiah heard the hum of the air conditioner, smelled the burger and fries above the musty odor of a body confined too long to an enclosed space. Finally Marschenko said, "Let me access the files, see what I can find. But you'll have to..." Marschenko lifted the helmet to indicate the dampening field.

"I already shut down the field," Jeremiah said.

Marschenko nodded. Then, keeping his eyes on Jeremiah, he lowered his weapon and carefully tucked it into his belt. Relief swept across Jeremiah. He hadn't realized how tense he was. As Marschenko donned his helmet, Jeremiah brought his heart rate and breathing under control.

Marschenko stayed motionless for only a few seconds. When he took off the helmet, he said, "I can't access anything. My helmet's been deactivated." He pointed to Jeremiah's computer in the corner. "Can I use your system?"

Jeremiah entered the necessary codes, then stood aside as Marschenko's thick fingers flew across the keyboard. It looked odd, that big man hunched over, so adept with the computer. After a moment, Marschenko gestured to the screen. "Nothing stands out. You see anything?"

Jeremiah glanced at the screen, spotted a familiar name. "What about this file? Lucas."

"No idea what that is," Marschenko said. He typed in a series of passwords to access the file. "Here it is. Four years ago, Carlton Security contracted to acquire dozens of subjects for a gen-mod program."

"Genetic modification," Jeremiah said.

"I'll download the file to your system," Marschenko said. "One other thing. Someone tampered with this file recently."

"How do you know?"

"There's a misspelling in the first sentence." Marschenko pointed it out. "Carlton built that into the software. Unless the proper codes are used to secure the data, a single word always comes up wrong the next time the file is opened."

"Eli," Jeremiah said, a sinking feeling settling in his gut—more a confirmation of a nagging suspicion than a surprise.

"So let's go after him."

"He's too powerful. Even if I could get to him, I couldn't save my son. And Joshua's life is more important than revenge."

Jeremiah shifted to the side and gestured toward the stairs but Marschenko didn't move. Instead, the big man blushed and said, "I can't believe you captured me so easily. You're a hell of a soldier. I'd like to help you get your son back. I'd like to make that right."

"You might regret that offer," Jeremiah said.

"Honor is important to me," Marschenko said. He looked Jeremiah in the eye, nodding once, almost imperceptibly. Jeremiah nodded back and Marschenko stepped past him, climbing out of the basement, his footsteps echoing off the stairs.

Book Club Questions

- Sister Ezekiel represents the believers, Walt Devereaux represents the nonbelievers, and Jeremiah Jones falls somewhere in the middle. Does the outcome of the book imply that one way of life is better than the others? Is one character more sympathetic than the others?

- Jeremiah is genetically enhanced, while the Elite Ops troopers are mechanically enhanced, and Doug Robinson isn't enhanced at all. What does this say about where humanity is going or should be going? Should we be trying to enhance ourselves, or is that a recipe for disaster?

- A virus has killed hundreds in the city of Rochester, MN, and caused most of the population to flee. Do you think a scenario like the one presented here, with Susquehanna Sally claiming to have unleashed it upon the world, is likely or even possible?

- Jeremiah is extremely cynical about the government and its willingness to tell lies to the population. Yet he continues to work for an entity that furthers the agenda of those in power. And he's also killed in pursuit of that agenda. Does that make him an anti-hero? Many of the characters in the book see him as good. Do you agree?

- Jack Marschenko and his fellow Elite Ops troopers do some bad things under a compulsion they're unable to fight. How much responsibility should they bear for their actions?

- Lendra Riley seems to be falling in love with Jeremiah. Yet she also recognizes that she needs him to further her career. How much of her affection do you believe is genuine, and how much is contrived to advance her ambitions?

- What role does the statue of Emerging Man play in the story?